Nick Holland

The Girl On The Bus

The Girl On The Bus

By Nick Holland

First Published 2007

ISBN 978-1-84799-012-9

Acknowledgements

To my Mum and Dad, family and friends without whom nothing would be possible. To all of the people on Myspace who gave me such great feedback, including Spidercloud and their music. Special thanks go to Katie Clegg for having the patience, fortitude and deciphering ability to type up my play 'Kolbe' for me (watch this space) and to Lea Harrington who was a great motivator with her weekly reviews and kind words.

Dedicated to the constant and loving memory of my wonderful Grandmother, Ivy Tollerfield.

Gloria in excelsis Deo, et in Terra pax hominibus.

Chapter One

Looking back now, to that bleak mist bedraggled January morning of five years ago, it seemed at the time to be a most inauspicious start to a year. One year into a new Millennium and two years after the event that had cast a drear shadow over each subsequent moment, it seemed as if every day would continue like the one before – as if life was just a long road leading to some unknown and unreachable horizon. And yet I was about to start a short ten minute journey that would herald a most remarkable change in my existence, that would lead me to discover a talent hitherto undreamt of and reveal a new world that I had not known existed.

My mobile phone buzzed eagerly intruding on my, as always, fitful sleep. It was eleven minutes past seven and the date was January 2nd 2001. One year and one day ago people had celebrated across the globe, revelling in a new thousand year cycle and all the hopes and dreams that it promised. People had danced in fountains, made furtive love under the first rising weak-rayed sun of this new age, made promises never to be broken: for me it had felt like everyone was revelling in a wild bacchanal, a party to which I hadn't been invited. To put it more accurately I suppose it was a party to which I would have, as everyone else, been welcomed but I had returned the invite unopened and unwanted. I hadn't been in a party mood that day, or for the year and six days preceding it, and had stayed at home lonely, cold and desperate drinking cheap own brand whisky diluted with bitter sweetened lemonade doing as much as I could to block out the noise from the streets all around my rented house in this normally sleepy suburb of Barnsley.

Time had moved on a year from that momentously disappointing Millennium day. During the progression of the year 2000 there seemed to be an ennui sweeping the world as people realised that the dreams that had been harboured for so long wouldn't come true just because of the turn of a page on a calendar. Ambitions that had seemed within reach now seemed as distant as ever and an unmistakable apathy gripped the nation, a mood that I had felt much more at home with, little comfort though I found this to be. In the year that had passed my hidden rages and frustrations continued as in the previous year and, if anything, my grief intensified and the more it was hidden away and pushed deep within my souls recesses the more I felt my secret revulsions grow. And so as the alarm on my phone continued to beep with insistent cheeriness my half opened eyes gave it a look of contempt and my cold blue tinged hands pushed it to the floor in the same robotic movement that swept the blue and green striped duvet sluggishly from my bed.

It was a day like any other, the New Year was over and more importantly the bank holiday that had come with it, and so it was time to return to work. Another year with little or nothing to look forward to until the summer holidays came and with them the opportunity to be bored and restless in a completely new location.

Work, as for many people then and now, was a necessary evil. It provided the money to keep some sort of life together but took away the time to enjoy it. If a stranger had told me on that most unpromising of mornings that people could tolerate or enjoy, yes even love, their work I would not have believed them. I was not as lucky then as I am now.

I was working in what was ostensibly a customer services bureau – providing what were laughably referred to as customer focussed solutions for a range of companies within the automotive industry. In reality this was a call centre smaller but no less brutal and profit oriented than any other. The bottom line was that every last penny had to be squeezed out of a companies profit potential and customer satisfaction was an inconvenience that was barely given lip service.

I enjoyed the company of the people that I worked with: or at least some of them. Enough of them to mean that it was still bearable to drag myself from my bed day after relentless day and head into the office. I got through the hours by playing petty practical jokes on the people that I worked with: I would put coffee in their tea, or exchange letters on their computer keyboard so that they would type nad instead of and or pis instead of sip, or I might start the wildest rumours to see how many people harboured a secret malice enough to believe them. Nobody seemed to begrudge me these little idiocies, seeming to think of me as a harmless and diverting eccentric. In truth I did not do these acts out of any spite or innate mean-spiritedness but rather out of a need to make time pass and to stop myself thinking too deeply: specifically I needed to stop myself thinking of what I was doing with my life, or indeed what I wasn't doing with my life.

The office seemed to have an air of shabbiness enshrouding it, a washed out glamour like a seaside resort whose erstwhile beauty now faded along with the peeling gold plate on a disused pier. I suppose that this building had once been a high technology piece of modern industrial workspace but its best days, even at the dawn of 2001, were well behind it just like the best days were behind most of the workforce cocooned within its walls.

Sixty to seventy souls were contained in the relatively small building and signs on the wall shouted slogans such as: 'Smile While You Dial' or 'Do Something At Work Today That Makes You Feel Proud.' These were obviously designed as a motivational tool but had become a constant irritant, a mockery, to all but the freshest of incumbents. When I thought of what I could do today at work to make me feel proud it invariably involved planting a right hander on the jaw of some director or other but this was just another of those dreams that helped the monotonous sequence of eight hours pass by.

Behind these over large signs were walls of a gaudy colour – half yellow, half green and guaranteed to induce headaches within a few hours. The air conditioning overhead coughed and spluttered asthmatically. In summer the building was always stiflingly hot and portable fans became de rigueur yet at least one unfortunate per week would pass out in a sweat soaked moment of hazy confusion. In winter the temperature dropped dismally low: workers wore scarves, gloves and two or three pairs of socks as routine and the smokers among us looked forward eagerly to their hourly cigarette breaks to bask in the relative warmth that was to be found outside of the building. Engineers, with a permanently vacant look and a mumbled vocabulary, inspected the air conditioning system annually but whatever they did, consisting as it did mainly of shaking their heads while drinking sickly sweet instant coffee, made no difference to the complete inefficacy of the air conditioning when it came to either increasing or decreasing the temperature.

What the air conditioning was successful in doing however, although in fairness I must say that this was purely in my opinion and based on the evidence of my own eyes throughout the too numerous years that I wasted at the company, was spreading any kind of sickness with alarming rapidity throughout the length and breadth of the building. When one person coughed the next day two people would be coughing and by the end of the week fifty people would be coughing: sickness was an occupational hazard of life within this most sick of sick buildings.

All of the equipment available to the average worker was old and semi-obsolete. Computers took ten minutes to warm up and five minutes to save the most meagre amount of information; mice became cumbersome, unwieldy and eventually unusable; the fax machine ate more paper than it ever produced and the print cartridges were so inadequate that after a handful of pages it would become necessary to remove the toner cartridge and shake it rapidly before attempting each and every print run. We used recycled cartridges in an apparently laudable effort to help the environment but I always wondered who really benefited from the few pence that were saved on each purchase.

Workers, poorly paid as they were, had to bring in their own milk to drink if they wanted reviving cups of tea or coffee throughout the day and every second spent away from the desk had to be accounted for as if we were all part of some diabolic time and motion study. I often thought that it was as if we had all had prison sentences passed upon us, eight hours every day with no time off for good behaviour, but for some strange reason none of us remembered the trial or what our initial offence had been?

And yet, unlike the prisoner to which in my day dreams I compared myself to in mostly unfavourable terms, at least we got paid. And what pay! The wages were kept ridiculously low and for every two people that left, escape seemed tantalisingly possible, only one new employee was brought in at a lower starting rate than either of the two people that they had replaced: the net result being that while our average wage shortened our average workload increased. In April we received our annual wage review which was not looked forward to with the eagerness that one would expect. In theory it was possible to receive a five percent pay rise but then I suppose in theory it is possible to run a marathon in two hours yet it didn't seem likely that any of us, the desk bound and desperate, would achieve it. Any slight excuse was found to knock off a percent here or half a percent there so, for example, if a person had been caught in traffic jams and arrived two minutes late on two occasions they would automatically lose one percent from their pay award: no account was taken that they were compelled to work it back nor that they had worked over seventy hours of unpaid overtime throughout the year. The only reward that such dedication to duty ever received was a reassurance that it had been 'noted' by the senior management: how nice it was to know that one had been noted whilst surviving on toast for lunch every day for a week before pay day. And so invariably the actual pay increase worked out at two or, if astonishingly lucky, three percent. Transport costs, meanwhile, had risen twenty or thirty percent, the price of a pint by five percent, the cost of childcare by ten percent and so we all grew gradually and imperceptibly poorer and poorer year upon year.

Not all in the company suffered this fate: the directors earned amounts that we were never told and that we could never begin to estimate. All that we knew was that the cars in the directors' parking spaces changed frequently and became more and more ostentatious: Volvos were replaced by BMWs which were replaced by Porsches which were replaced by Bentleys and Ferraris. We ordinary workers saw them seldom and cared to see them less in case we hit upon the sudden realisation of where the profits that our hard work was earning were actually going to. And this was the work that awaited me on that cold and dark morning of the second of January 2001 as I swung my cold and unresponsive leg out of the bed and put my foot down clumsily upon the still chirruping mobile phone that I had knocked earlier to the floor. This produced a sharp intake of breath and the first curse words of that day which, now I look back this handful of years later and seemingly a world away, was to become of such momentous importance to me.

I raised my foot and rubbed it sharply to dispel the momentary pain that had shot through it. Picking my phone up from the floor I switched the unit on to see if anybody had tried to contact me through the night? Nobody had tried to call me and I was glad because it had been a while since anybody had tried to contact me during the night other than in the dreams that sometimes disturbed my sleep so.

Walking across to the guest bedroom I turned the dial on the central heating and warmth began to flow slowly but steadily into the radiators. With the heat beginning to rise throughout my house I could feel life returning to my body and walked with increasing energy to the bathroom. Flicking the light switch I stared into the large oval mirror that was facing me as if I was a stranger seeing this creature for the first time. Another year had come and gone, another lonely twelve months crossed off, and yet the reflection that I studied seemed to have changed little. Perhaps there were a few lines beginning to emerge at the corners of my eyes, a hint of grey in the hair – but no, I conceded that there was little external sign of the changes that I had been living through since that Boxing Day of 1999. Even now, five years on, I retain a relatively youthful air for a man in his mid thirties and would recognise the face that greeted John Halle early on that morning five years ago.

My hair was jet black and cropped short to save on the time and expense that would be required to give it any type of recognisable style. Hazel eyes, surprisingly inexpressive, lurked dolefully below a pronounced forehead and above a nose that had all too obviously been broken in a childhood incident that lay semi forgotten. My skin was pale as if a stranger to the sun and thin lips remained tightly shut. It was a face that stood out in a crowd, not unattractive but simply different. It was also a face that could hide emotion well, a skill that I utilised at every possible opportunity in an effort to maintain the aloof and disinterested stance that I tried to project. When I did smile, normally after the discovery of one of my regular little practical jokes, it was a warm smile that gave a rare clue to the genuine warmth that still dwelt somewhere within me hidden away in case the years should bring some kind of happiness back into my life.

My face was thinner than it should be and heading inexorably towards a gaunt and drawn appearance: I ate poorly and infrequently, picking at my food with suspicion. My body was thin but toned; I worked out every day more out of habit than any desire to keep fit. I did this now and reached for the dumbbells that were stacked in the corner of my bathroom, five kilo weights on either side of a short plastic coated bar. I pulled off 100 curls in quick succession and then followed this with 50 crunches, feet suspended in the air whilst I struggled through them. Satisfied with the familiar burning sensation from my stomach and my hands I headed back to my bedroom and took long gulps from the pint glass full of water that sat atop the bedside table. The water tasted good, it had been a night of excess the day before and dehydration had taken hold.

Whilst I was eating little I was drinking a lot: it was another device, like the mindless practical jokes and the unthinking exercises, to keep my mind from dwelling on the pain that lurked within me not far below the surface. Most of my days seemed to be dedicated to forgetting the thing, the woman, which had pained me the most. Although I had said that I would always remember her, and though I had promised her own mother as much, I did all that I possibly could to forget everything about her and to forget that she had ever existed.

The previous 48 hours had been spent in a variety of public houses drinking large quantities of cider sometimes accompanied by whiskey chasers in deference to the time of the year. The celebrations of New Years Eve had ended at around three in the morning and after stumbling back home I had slept, allowing for the usual fits and starts, until around midday on the first day of the year. I was back in the pubs by One in the afternoon and had made the usual rounds during that afternoon and the evening: The Bunch of Keys to The Fox and Hound and from there to The Kings Arms to The Star of Bethlehem and then on to the working men's club where I kept up my annual subscription. This round of hostelries was repeated more than once during the course of the day. I, like all of my friends that drank with me, knew which pubs were best to visit at which times and which barmaids could be relied upon to perform such little services as providing free packets of crisps or pouring a pint and charging for a half: there were benefits to being a regular.

The New Year celebrations were not something that I particularly enjoyed then or now. The bars were packed to bursting point with once a year drinkers blocking the path to the pumps and voices were raised along with fists as old scores from the previous twelve months were brought up before being officially forgotten as the midnight chimes rang out. Far worse than this, though, was the false bonhomie that people wore like a tiger's smile, flashing teeth kept in a semi permanent grin and sticky hands always ready to grasp yours in an attempt to force you to sing some old Scottish poem that they didn't know the words to and whose sentiments they didn't really share. Nevertheless it is a ritual which I always put myself through as the opportunity to get drunk and be encouraged to do so is not one to be dismissed lightly. To the greeting of 'Happy New Year' I would, and still do, inevitably say 'Happy New Day' as if to emphasise that this wasn't really an unexpected or joyful event, but my general air of sullenness was accepted with the temporary tolerance that seems to evaporate every year with the rising of the sun.

I had been drinking with Steven, Ed, Gail, Bethany, Bernadette and Mick: old school friends who, like me, had been unable to escape their roots and now looked destined to spend the rest of their days in Barnsley. We all encouraged each other to drink, and the girls kept pace with the boys with well practised ease. The only difference between myself and the old friends that shared the drinks with me on New Years Eve and New Years Day was that I was the only one who was unlucky enough to have to work on January 2nd. And so as I thought back to the excesses of the day before I emptied my bedside glass and refilled it from the bathroom sink: I was going to need a lot more water to prepare me for my return to the job that held so little attraction for me.

I straightened up the framed photograph that I always opened my eyes to and a radio played quietly in the background as I dressed for work but I wasn't listening, I was struggling inwardly against the feeling of impending doom that always seemed to strike before returning to work after any period of time off.

My shoes needed a polish and trousers needed ironing but, as always, I was in a hurry and so they would have to suffice until tomorrow. I had mastered the art of split second timing when it came to getting to work. At seven eleven the alarm went off, by seven twenty I had to finish my ablutions which gave me five minutes to work out with the dumbbells, this was followed by five minutes to shower meaning I returned to my bedroom from the bathroom at precisely half past the hour. I then had eight minutes to dress and two minutes to collect my belongings in a carrier bag and exit the house at twenty minutes to eight. My bus was due at seven forty three but unfortunately the bus company seemed to run to a less reliable schedule then myself and so it could arrive at any time between twenty to eight and ten to eight. This initial bus would take me to the train station at nearby Elsecar and from there I would catch a train to the transport interchange at Meadowhall, this being a suburb of Sheffield noted for its sprawling and soulless shopping centre and the place where I would decamp every workday morning to catch my final bus to my place of work.

Two buses and one train had to operate in unison with each other in order for me to get to work on time: if one came late then my chances of making my subsequent connections were reliant upon them being delayed as well. I was frequently late for work, sometimes by a minute and sometimes by an hour and whilst I had to work the time back it was these instances beyond my control that contributed to the deductions in my annual pay review.

As a child I had found public transport to be relaxing: I could read a book or just stare out of the windows, grime encrusted though they were, and watch the familiar world pass by. Now I would often sit there fuming as the driver seemed to make no effort to make up lost time, or shake my head mournfully as yet another passenger would get on and spend four interminable minutes in conversation with the driver before realising that, sorry, this bus didn't go where they wanted to be after all, goodbye. My silent seething frustrations grew as I thought of my wage packet shrinking as each wasteful second slipped by.

At moments like these I often thought of climbing behind a wheel and driving again. When I was 17 I had, like most of my contemporaries, applied for a provisional driving license and taken my lessons. The lessons started surprisingly well, and I found the vagaries of controlling a motorcar as natural as riding a bike but soon the novelty began to wear off: I stalled at traffic lights time and time again and would panic as the queue of traffic behind me grew ever larger and increasingly impatient. Old women at pedestrian crossings would attract my wrath by pressing the button and forcing me to make emergency stops before they commenced their treacherously slow journey across the black and white stripes.

I would forget what road signs meant from one moment to the next and my instructor would have to leap in with his dual control brake pedal as I began to turn the wrong way down a one way street. I would mix up my left and my right, a trait I still have to this day but now with less significant consequences, and would write 'R' and 'L' on my hands before each lesson as a reminder of what should have come so naturally. My spatial awareness was poor and so I had no idea of whether I was one foot or four feet from the curb and narrow streets would fill me with dread as I negotiated my way painstakingly through gaps with little idea of whether my wing mirrors would escape unscathed or pay the penalty as they had so many times previously.

I would often miss the gear change when moving up from second to third gear and would bring the car juddering and protesting to an unexpected halt by attempting to move into fifth. My instructor, I remember clearly, was a man in his late forties who seemed aggrieved by the passage of time and longed to be back in his youth. He had long blonde hair and a receding hairline and would wear a leather jacket and blue jeans as a matter of course however hot it was outside of and inside the car, a red Renault Five whose paintwork betrayed the faint signs of scrapes and resprays – legacies of previous lessons from drivers of even less promise than myself.

On one occasion, a rain sodden early Summer day like so many experienced in the North of England, he said to me:

"When I bang my fist on the dashboard I want you to veer sharply, and for a split second, to the left before straightening up again."

His timing was impeccable and I followed his instructions to the letter. As he banged his fist upon the grey plastic dashboard I turned the steering wheel and directed the car into the huge puddle of rainwater that had accumulated in a recess of the road: subsidence was a legacy from the town's mining past and the roads were in dreadful, pot hole riddled, decay throughout the district. As I quickly straightened the car up I noticed that the mission had been successful and the pair of hikers, in previously white t-shirts and flannel like shorts, who had been passing at the time were now soaked to the skin and their faces incredulous and mud splattered.

"Drive on, drive on" my instructor managed to gasp out between high pitched giggles that lasted for at least another five minutes. Not every lesson was as pleasurable as that one.

After twenty lessons, that seemed more like two hundred, my instructor decided that either I was ready for my test or that he couldn't risk sharing his car with me any longer and so I was entered for the driving examination. I knew in my mind that I wasn't ready for it yet but I had quickly grown tired of my instructor making me slow down as we passed any slightly attractive young woman and embarrassed by his wolf whistles to them through the half opened window: I was longing to drive on my own.

It is generally believed, although officially denied, that driving test centres have a target to meet and so they have to pass so many drivers per month and not a driver more. By a stroke of good fortune my test had been scheduled for the last day of September 1988, a Friday of surprisingly calm weather where all seemed to be calm after the winds that had whipped across the Pennines in the previous weeks. I can only assume that the test centre had been some way short of fulfilling its quota and would have passed anybody who could proceed through the test without causing a major incident or bumping into too many pedestrians. I was incredulous when my examiner told me that I had passed at my first attempt but it didn't take long for my swelling pride to take over and I imagined that maybe I had found my great talent in life: it wasn't until the events over thirteen years later that I am about to relate that I found out where my true skills lay.

My father was as surprised as I had initially been at the result and added me to the insurance of his car with seeming reluctance. He was a proud and meticulous man who had served on the town's council for many years and always liked to keep his vehicle in pristine condition as if it was a symbol of his status within the community. Nevertheless I was determined to drive solo and so began to take the car out whenever I could: journeys of a few yards to the newsagents that used to take me two minutes to walk now took three times as long to drive as I struggled to squeeze my father's car into parking spots that seemed impossibly tight. I began to enjoy driving less and less as I imagined I could hear the voice of parental disapproval coming from the empty backseats: sometimes it almost seemed as if I could actually hear the voices telling me to slow down, or speed up, or check the mirrors. Long journeys tired me greatly and I would return home to find that my shirt had become sweat soaked from the sheer concentration that I had put in. I frequently fell victim to what is now known as road rage, being both the aggressor and receiver due to my erratic driving. Eventually the time came for me to leave home for the lure of University life and so my driving days were put on hold for an initial period of three years. That period came and went and I realised that the simple truth was that I didn't enjoy driving; I wasn't very good at it and so why not take the environmental option and use public transport? Many frustrating bus and train journeys since then have supplied me with a perfectly good answer to that question but yet I still found myself, on that bitingly cold January morning of 2001, at the old familiar request stop waiting for bus number 325.

On some mornings I was joined at the stop by five or six other regular commuters: students, teachers and office workers. I was on nodding acquaintance with all of them and speaking terms with none of them. Today, however, was different. I was the only one called out of bed at this ungodly hour, so soon into the new year. As I stood in unthinking solitude by the side of the road I didn't expect the bus to be full as it sometimes was and therefore expected it to run on time to the schedule that it found so hard to keep when it had to stop every thirty seconds en route to let passengers on or off.

My assumption was proved correct as the bus came into sight at seven forty three precisely and came to a halt before my outstretched hand. Service number 325 ran from Barnsley town centre to Elsecar, a short journey and one that had thus far escaped the stringent cut backs that had emasculated much of the public transport system throughout the county. Single decked buses in white and blue livery ran every fifteen minutes: they were largely dilapidated and it was not unusual for the buses to break down during their short journeys or to run late because it had taken some half hearted mechanic at the depot twenty minutes to start up its reluctant engine. Because of these problems it was usual practise for the four buses per hour, which you will remember should have run at convenient fifteen minute intervals from one another, to congregate together during the day and all arrive within five minutes of each other followed by nearly an hour of nothingness. Guessing correctly which five minute slot the buses would turn up in was one of those fun little games that daytime passengers were privileged to play. For us morning commuters however the service was relatively reliable.

The normal driver on the seven forty three to Elsecar was a jovial Scottish man named Bob. He was a man of small stature but loud voice and he would greet each passenger warmly, and often by name, and the passengers retuned his smile with interest. Admittedly, it was hard to understand what Bob was saying as his Glasgow accent had not melted during his long years in Yorkshire but his effort at friendliness was always appreciated by those of us on our way to cold and unwelcoming offices, shops and factories.

We were out of luck today and Bob was not sat behind the wheel, presumably he had taken a week's holiday to visit his family in the far North and celebrate Hogmanay in style. I had noticed before that three or so weeks after the new year celebration he would again take a couple of days off and although I never imagined him as the bookish type I had little doubt that he was remembering Rab Burns somewhere and toasting the haggis with a vintage glass or two.

In Bob's usual place sat a large heavy eyed man who had squeezed himself into the chair and sat hunched over the wheel like a gigantic vulture surveying the road ahead for a meal. He was a taciturn and singularly unhelpful man. If people asked him a question, any question, he would grunt and let his passenger guess if that was supposed to indicate either a yes or no. I accordingly said nothing as I climbed aboard but merely held my weekly bus pass up in front of his eyes.

With an unblinking nod of his oversized head he gave a small grunt and pressed a button on his machine. He removed the brake and set the bus in motion and jolted me forward as I set off to find a seat. I was glad, as always, that the driver had not looked too closely at my pass. The weekly pass that I had presented was in the form of a scratch card on which one would rub off seven consecutive dates before folding sticky plastic over the top of it and sealing the result. Whilst considering myself a generally honest man I was not averse to making economies whenever I could and I always scratched off eight days instead of seven, thus giving myself one week's free travel for every seven that I had paid for. In my own defence I felt that the transport company was charging extortionate amounts for an increasingly underperforming service and my mediocre salary made me seek ways to save money in every way that I could: looking back now I do not feel any guilt over my conduct and would do it again if I was ever in the same situation. I relied upon the bus drivers not looking at the pass, or at least not being able to differentiate with a cursory glance the difference between seven figures and eight, and this premise had never failed me. Conductors that had once prowled the buses with menace ensuring that all tickets were valid and that passengers were not terrorising each other or vandalising seats, had long since been pensioned off as the rival transport companies made cut backs after cut backs. I was safe with my doctored pass on that day as I was on every day.

I raised my head and looked down the length of the aisle looking for a premium seat. In a few days time, when the country in general had shaken off its turn of year torpor and returned to the classroom or the workroom, I would be lucky to find a double seat available and had to decide either who I felt likely to be getting off in a few stops, thus affording me at least a handful of minutes in relative luxury, or who looked the most attractive proposition as seat mate. Today, however, I was spoilt for choice as to my location and so I had the rare opportunity to take into allowance the design of the bus or more accurately the positioning of the seats.

It might seem obvious that the seats should be spaced out evenly but this wouldn't do for the fiendish minds that had obviously designed the layout. Some seats had large gaps between them and some, especially the ones seated directly behind the wheels, had very small gaps between them. The seats with large gaps were on busy days invariably taken up by the smallest of passengers who got on the bus at early points during its journey. This left people who were either tall, like me, or excessively overweight, as many of the passengers were, to manoeuvre embarrassingly into the cramped spaces that would leave us facing uncomfortable journeys with knees tucked under our chins and shins pressed against the groaning seat in front of us jarred by every bump in the road that we jolted across.

I found a double seat around two thirds of the way towards the back and settled down to partake in my favourite pastime. Some people like to collect stamps, some people like to renovate furniture, and others collect hundreds of miniature bottles of spirits and yet are never tempted to take a drink from one. Some people spend their winters tracking down and buying this year's must-have toy and then throw a fit ten years later if somebody opens the box. Some people like to walk down by the reservoirs with binoculars and cameras and go twitching in the bushes – I believe that it's commonly referred to as dogging? I saw my favourite hobby as more wholesome, and certainly less expensive, than these ways that other people found to fill up their days – I was an inveterate people watcher.

I didn't like to look around too much whilst I was on the way down the aisle of a bus or a train or a tram: it seemed too obvious, too intrusive, and I often found that if ones eyes met the eyes of a fellow passenger theirs would stare back at you with a ferocious burn as if you had attempted to snatch their handbag or had been reading the newspaper over their shoulder. I preferred to wait until I was safely seated to look surreptitiously around me with more or less impunity: yes, I suppose some would say that I had a voyeuristic tendency, but I preferred to call it a curiosity, an anthropological interest, rather than any desire to hang around peoples bedroom windows.

At first I thought that this particular morning's journey would provide me with very slim pickings. Not many more than a dozen people were on the bus, myself and the ape like driver included. On busier days the bus could be full and people were stood cramped unnaturally together like a scene from a Hieronymus Bosch painting.

I knew only two of my fellow travellers. Three seats forward of my position and across the aisle to the right was my old school friend Richard Clay, Little Dicky as he had been known at the comprehensive school where his life had been reduced to misery. After he left school and found a job his character had changed along with his appearance and his luck. He became more confident, talkative even, and soon money and girls had been drawn to him in a way that eluded us few who had gone on to Universities. I lost touch with him after my student days were over and now I only saw him, and seldom at that, if we were sharing a bus ride together or if we bumped into one another in a bar. He seemed to have changed again now, but this time for the worse: the wheel of fortune had spun again and his clothes were beginning to look shabby and his appearance veered towards the unkempt. His face had grown thin, even when compared to mine, and his cheekbones were the prominent feature on his tight grey skinned face. He was obviously ill but as I had no idea what particular ailment it was I decided to sit some way away from him just in case it was catching. I said 'hi' as I passed and he returned the greeting with a half smile, I then venture to wish him a happy new year but this wasn't returned and as I seemed to have exhausted his conversation for the day I headed down the bus: seeing him looking so old and ill had made me strangely melancholic as we were of course the same age.

Looking around to the very back of the bus I saw, seated in his usual position, Paul. Paul had also been at school with me and later at the same University as well but we were never particularly close. He always sat on the back seat as he too liked to watch people, or a certain kind of person, but I never felt that his intentions were as well meaning as mine. Paul was a fair haired man of stocky build with a goatee beard that he should have removed in his mid twenties. He always dressed immaculately, with silk tie and woollen overcoat and occasionally a purple or gold waistcoat visible. His shoes shone brilliantly and he once told me that he put boot polish on them using a knife that had been heated in front of the fire so that the polish was actually burned into the leather: it certainly seemed to work. Because of his carefully cultivated appearance, and his tendency to carry large books under the crook of his arm, people always assumed that he was a lawyer but I knew that he was simply a middle manager for a catalogue chain who was living beyond his means. He couldn't afford a car that would go with his high roller image and as he refused to ever compromise he caught buses instead.

Despite his extravagant dress Paul could never have been described as good looking, his face seemed to be out of alignment with itself as if one eye was higher than the other or as if his right side was attractive but his left half ugly. Unsuccessful with women he lived alone and spent his bus journeys lusting over the barely legal college girls who got on and off it. He sat on the back seat so that he could see every single one in front of him and on days that he especially enjoyed he might have some seated at the side of him blissfully unaware of the bad intentions that lurked within his heart. He hated weeks that were, as of now, outside of college time but at the height of term time when the bus would be full of girls in bright raiment, chunky jewellery, short skirts and tall hair he would take me in confidence and refer to the bus as his 'fox mobile': I always found this reference to be quite distasteful but while his intentions were lustful I knew that he would never carry any of them out so I let it pass. Today he sat morosely on the back seat, engrossed within a book that he carried, and didn't even notice me as I sat down in the rows in front of him.

I looked around me to see who else was sharing the journey with me: I liked to try to work out who a person was, what made them tick, by the way that they dressed or acted. Today, however, there seemed to be a general listlessness from everyone that I saw. People were seated separately, not even one couple, and there was a distinct lack of conversation. It seemed that the post new year malaise that I myself had been suffering from was all pervasive.

The majority of my fellow travellers seemed to be obvious alcohol victims who had entered the party atmosphere with too much abandon and were now paying the price for their overindulgence. Their eyes that had surely seemed so glassily merry were now heavy and pink, the rims red with tiredness. The women had hastily applied make up in a seemingly haphazard fashion in a futile effort to disguise the temporary ravages, the blotches and blemishes, that dehydration had made on their skin. It was as if I could smell the alcohol fumes on them from twenty paces and they all carried packets of mints or chewing gum in their pockets and handbags.

An aging man was seated towards the front of the bus. His hair was thinning and in many places absent. He wore a cream coloured gabardine style raincoat and a silk scarf, which a loved one must have presented him with for Christmas and which he therefore felt compelled to wear, was wrapped around his neck with a paisley pattern on general display. On the seat next to him lay a tightly rolled miniature umbrella that would blow inside out at the first gust of wind and a black leather-effect briefcase.

On my normal 'people watching' duty I would have considered whether this briefcase held important, top secret, documents which would reveal his true identity as an honoured and trusted member of Her Majesty's more secret services and maybe a small loaded pistol alongside them. Alternatively, if I found myself in one of my more irreverent or fanciful moods, I might have wondered if he would open it to a supply of top shelf magazines and women's underwear conveniently in his size or maybe a supply of Rizzla papers and a pouch of exotic tobacco. No, I guess in all likelihood it contained nothing more interesting than a salad sandwich, an apple, three pens of various colours and a copy of the Daily Telegraph from the last year - crossword as yet unfinished. The briefcase was there for show, as if looking important was of more concern than actually being important. He fell asleep from time to time and his eyes would open and head jerk forward at every speed bump. Did he know, or care, whether he would make his retirement date or not?

Today, however, I was too tired and melancholic to consider this for long and my gaze strayed to another passenger: a young woman in her twenties with an i-pod in her pocket and the already familiar white bud earphones plugged in as an anaesthetic against the world outside. I could hear, as could all of the bus, the tinny treble and irritating bass grumble of some r'n'b track or other: the noise must have been deafening through her earphones but she seemed past caring. Her long, pony tailed, hair was a strange mixture whereby the top half was blonde and the bottom half was black, it produced the effect of making her look like a badger and I wondered if that was the look that she had been aiming for or whether it would seem better in any way when she unleashed the tightly screwed ponytail and let her hair fall down?

And then all at once I saw someone completely different and wondered how I hadn't noticed her before. She was seated in front of me and had turned her face to the left so that I could see her face in a profile that suddenly and strangely captured my attention. She was a girl of around twenty years of age with long brown hair that fell past her slender shoulders. She was thin and with pale almost washed out features. She accentuated her paleness with a light blue eye shadow and a fine toned blusher that made her green eyes even more striking. Her full lips seemed made for pouting and were framed by a dark and almost purple lipstick. She wore a golden chain around her neck and on it was suspended a small and delicate crucifix.

She was wearing a shirt of pastel blue and white stripes and the top buttons were undone to show her all too pale skin below and the sharp beginnings of her shoulder blades. Above this shirt she wore a sand coloured jacket made of suede that seemed as if it may have been passed down in the family since the Sixties. Her dress looked somehow different to that of anyone else on the bus, or indeed anyone else that I knew, as if she had transcended, or ignored, the fashion of the day. She was staring with some determination out of the window with unblinking eyes and for some reason I found it hard not to stare at her, this beautiful girl not yet a woman, who seemed an anachronism on our bus. Was it for this reason that my heart and mind jolted when I first spotted her as if a sudden electric shock had awoken me from a dream?

I forced myself to look away but although I gave a hard stare at the filthy back of the seat in front of me I didn't see the obscenities that people with names like Gaz had scratched into the plastic; all I saw was that face, that neck, that person who had remained unknown and unseen to me until a few seconds previously. I wondered why I hadn't noticed her earlier and had instead wasted my time on looking at the old man with the sleeping sickness or the brusque looking woman with the badger hair? I glanced back at Paul still seated impassively on the back seat – he didn't seem to have noticed her or else his book would have sat closed by his side rather than open in his hands.

I spent the next few minutes in a vain attempt to blot her out of my consciousness. I gazed out of the window and counted the cigarette packets that lay thrown everywhere instead of in the empty refuse bins and pretended to be interested in calculating which was the towns' brand of choice. I looked at cloud formations and thought I saw images of people and things long since gone. I dared not look back along the length of the bus.

Eventually, and as the bus grew ever nearer to the railway station, my destination, I passed by my old school. A building that had seemed vibrant and huge when I was a child now seemed a mediocre and ugly building which was surrounded on every side by large and impenetrable corrugated fencing – whether to keep people out or people in was a matter for speculation. I had spent many formative years here, consisting of the usual mixture of happy and sad times, but the school had always seemed to have a threatening mystique about it throughout my childhood: a grandeur that had vanished many years ago. Now whenever

I passed it, and especially when I passed the poppy laden cenotaph that stood to the side of it, I felt sadness at the people who had passed through it never to be seen again. A memory of times past which was out of step in a society that seemed happy to exist only in the present tense. Time had passed and I felt it safe to risk another look up, a surreptitious glimpse at the girl who had produced such an unexpected and inexplicable feeling within me. As I did so she ceased to look sideways out of the window, as if she had seen what she needed to see, and turned to look straight into my eyes. I was lost within them; they seemed to draw me in to depths and places hidden inside them that as yet remained unknown to me. Her face betrayed no sign of emotion, her lips did not smile, and her eyes did not blink or grow as they looked into mine but yet I could feel something burning within me, signalling me as if talking without words and across a vastness that belied the few rows of seating between us.

Her right hand, thin and milk white with a large green stoned ring on one finger, reached up to press the bell on the pole beside her seat. She pressed it but no sound came and the familiar 'bus stopping' sign remained unilluminated. I imagined that, as often happens on these old outdated buses still in use, the bell had simply stopped working and wondered why she didn't rise up and walk down to the driver or at least motion or shout to him to stop until he grunted acknowledgment of her request.

Again she seemed to turn to me, only for a second, and I saw, or thought that I imagined, her dark lips open momentarily and mouth the word 'here'. No sound could be heard.

I looked away, confused – this wasn't the way that I wanted to start my year: I wanted everything to continue in the same unchallenging and lonely rut that the previous year had followed. I knew then, although as yet I didn't appreciate how, that this was out of the question: that something had changed with a significance that would somehow and some day become apparent.

I noticed nothing now, I was within myself and the external world seemed to melt away. People must have got onto the bus, for when I looked up the coach was unexpectedly busier, but I had not seen or noticed them get on. With surprise I realised that I had reached my stop. I pressed the bell out of instinct and the clear signal rang out and the sign showed 'bus stopping'. The driver pulled into the stop in jarring and sudden fashion and I headed down the aisle. I wanted to speak to her, I had to speak to her, but I had no idea what I wanted to say or why I wanted to say it? When I reached her she looked away again out of the window and over her shoulder this time. My heart was beating with a wicked speed and although I opened my mouth no words would come. My shaking legs continued to walk forwards automatically and I climbed off of the bus and into the icy wind that had began to blow in from the hillsides around the little station of Elsecar.

I leaned against the bridge over the platforms as if everything was about to give way and above all the turmoil within me I could not reason why I felt this way? She had a look, she had a strange something, that was not attuned to the world around her. It was not that I was in love with her, it was that somehow she had climbed within me, was trying to communicate with me even now. I knew this, and wondered if I was losing my mind? I had been hiding, bottling up, my grief deep within me for over a year now and I was frightened that my world was beginning to collapse.

Suddenly and sickeningly a strange realisation grew that she reminded me of someone. Not in looks, particularly, or in the way that she acted, or in her age. Somehow though I knew that she reminded me strongly of the person who had walked uninvited through my dreams on so many shivering nights. There was a connection, if only I could find it, to the woman that I had loved and lost. I had buried that woman deep underneath the soil and deeper underneath my cynicism and weariness. Please God, I prayed, spare me from madness.

Chapter Two

I raised my head slowly and noticed that the few straggling commuters stood at the railway platform were looking in my direction. The ice cold wind, surely a harbinger for snow later that day, whistled around my numbing ears and acted to bring me back to my senses. I lifted my reddened fingers from the wall that had been supporting me and making a huge effort, more mental than physical, I steadied my shaking legs and walked with a lack of certainty over the bridge and down on to platform number one. The passengers below looked away from me now, the show was over and they had decided that I was merely another reveller post-party trying in vain to shake off the alcoholic haze before the onrushing return to work.

I shuffled along, conscious of the ice on the platform beneath my feet that sent my foot sliding first right and then left in an attempt to throw my body to the frost hardened tarmac. Finding the Perspex sided shelter, open invitingly at the front to let in all manners of inclement weather, I found a metal grilled bench awaiting me and dropped onto it as though I were already a dead weight. The bench was damp and shudderingly cold but it was a welcome relief as I felt a bead of sweat drip, perversely on such a cold day, from my forehead. The passengers who had also huddled on the blue painted bench in anticipation of the 8.16 service to Sheffield stood up and moved away to the far edges of the shelter, all the while stamping their feet, blowing steam from their mouths and rubbing their hands. They had judged me to be a drunk and didn't want to risk a sudden eruption of vomit that would ruin their new and pristine winter clothing.

I was far from drunk - in fact I had never felt more sober. My senses seemed heightened as if I could smell the dew rising from the dead patches of grass to the rear of the station or could hear the foxes moving stealthily within the undergrowth of the nearby woods. I had always been sensitive of things, as if I could touch people's feelings. My mother once told me that when I was a baby, pushed along in my black hooded perambulator, old women with stooped bodies would stop her and say 'that one's been here before' or 'that's an old 'un you've got' or even 'watch him, he can see things that we can't'. I guess that it was just the way of the times, before science and technology had completely destroyed the old belief in superstition. Nevertheless, I had always had an extraordinarily vivid imagination, recently and painfully manifesting itself in the startling dreams that interrupted my sleep night after night, and would often drift into daydreams that would seem almost to be visions. These dreams felt more real than the world that I would awaken to when a shout in my ear or a quick, heavy push on my arm would bring me back to the external reality that held me. I drifted into one of these reveries now, in an instant as though fingers had been snapped and my head pushed backwards, as once again it struck me that for some unknown reason the girl on the bus reminded me of the woman that I had once loved, the only woman that I had ever loved. If only I could remember what the similarity was or why there seemed to be this connection? In my mind I swam swiftly back to the life that I had shared, until recently, with Lamara.

I had left University with an honours degree of sorts in History. It was a two two, known colloquially as a Desmond and generally acknowledged

24

as the 'Drinker's Degree' for being the grade that those students would invariably obtain who had some degree of ability but had spent their days at parties and public houses rather than at the lecture theatre. My degree had proved itself to all intents and purposes worthless as the only future that it offered me was to pursue a career in teaching: I still believed that children should be seen and not heard and so I was singularly unsuitable for that profession. The main things that University had taught me was never to be sick in taxis, don't give a telephone number to a girl that you have only met earlier that evening and always keep your chips on a winning number on the roulette wheel. These were all valuable lessons but of little use to a man of twenty-one attempting to make an impact on the world.

I drifted into a series of dead end jobs whose financial reward was poor and long term prospects excruciating. I tried shop work and found myself to be spectacularly bored by the constant ringing of the till and the inane chatter of the shop staff. I would see shop lifters dropping items into their shopping trolleys, having been told on the first day that a shopping trolley was the weapon of choice for a thief in a shop, but did not have the heart or the inclination to stop them. They had mouths to feed too and I imagined that their chosen profession, snatching the odd skirt or scarf from a rail, was even less viable than mine.

After my retail years, which had continued for far too long for my parent's approval and certainly ensured that the pride and self importance that I had left University with had all but evaporated, I was coerced into becoming a trainee manager for a leading bingo company. An old housemate from my time at University had rung me up one day to ask what I was doing. I was temporarily between jobs and told him so at which point he proceeded to wax lyrically about his job: he had gone straight from university into the bingo halls and hadn't regretted it for a minute. He was now an assistant manager and soon expected to have his own club and be earning anything up to £50,000 a year whilst in charge of around a hundred staff. I was unsure - the money sounded very tempting but I knew nothing about bingo, beyond the old clichéd image of pensioners shouting 'house' as they waited joylessly for death to arrive. Keith, that was the name of my old housemate, then informed me that the best thing about the job was the women: bingo was a young person's game now, he lied, and some very glamorous young women attended the venues every Friday and Saturday night - a caller or a manager could have their pick of them. And better than the clientele was the staff: ninety percent of them being single, eligible women wearing too much make up and too little clothing. The deal was clinched and I soon found myself making my debut as a trainee manager in the municipal bingo hall.

It didn't take me long, around one hour to the best of my recollection, to realise that Keith had oversold the glamour stakes. When I later discovered that he had received half a grand as bounty for recommending me things began to fall into place.

As a trainee manager it was my duty to learn how each individual department worked before I was allowed any degree of responsibility: it was coal face training as I was thrown in at the deep end and often found myself treading water amongst a collection of sharks with narrowed eyes and fake smiles.

I had been entered onto a fast track course to managing my own club, as my former housemate Keith had been before me, and this created an understandable sense of resentment amongst those who had tried without success to gain some sort of seniority within the company via the more traditional methods of starting at the bottom and working their way up. No sort of meritocracy existed either as the most able were kept in the positions that they occupied, with no obvious chance of progression, in case their replacement could not match their already proven capability. It seemed to many that in the world of bingo clubs there existed a glass ceiling that could only be broken through by those holding a piece of paper from a University.

On my very first day in the job I could feel the frostiness from my new colleagues; as I said earlier I have always been sensitive to people's feelings and inner thoughts but they did little to hide their resentment. The team leaders of the various departments, a collection of middle aged women who all seemed to have worked there for ten years or more, would sit together at lunch and tea breaks whispering to each other behind the backs of their hands. Whenever I tried to sit with them or make any sort of conversation they would swallow their cups of tea and disperse quickly and silently, all the while casting sour faced looks my way. I was embarrassed for them. The general manager, a tired looking man called Colin, was initially friendly but he seemed permanently occupied by ever expanding amounts of paperwork and so I saw little of him.

I got on much better with the general staff, and would prefer to sit with them in their fun and vibrant staff room filled with wooden chairs and loud conversation rather than enter the silent, leather seated tundra that was reserved for management and supervisors.

Amongst the staff were many young women, as promised by Keith, and some of them caught my eye at one time or another. Keith was a charming, salt of the earth type man from Liverpool and his tall and handsome looks and playful Scouse accent made him a hit with the ladies on a scale that I had never seen before and have never seen matched since. I don't doubt that if my friend had been working at this club, rather than the West Midlands outpost that he had recently been assigned to, then he would soon have conquered the hearts of all but the most resolute women that I worked with. I, although not unattractive, had none of his innate charm or way with words, and so I found things to be much harder going.

The first lady that I threw my hat at was a small, black haired young woman called Toria. Before I made any sort of approach I first sought the advice of Kevin, the Regional Director for the company that employed me. It was Kevin who had interviewed me, along with a human resources specialist, and we had immediately hit it off. Halfway through the allotted time for the interview Kevin had leaned across to me and said 'you do know that we are going to offer you the job don't you?' – this had put me at my ease. He also delivered a maxim that I was to hear him repeat on many occasions, he should have had a coat of arms made with the slogan wrapped around the bottom, when he said: 'Don't forget John, it's nice to be important but it's more important to be nice'. Doubtless he said this with all sincerity but then it's easy to be nice when you are already important.

Kevin often visited my club, or I should say the club where I scrubbed the bars, counted chips, sold tickets and helped pensioners to their seats, and he would always seek me out with a friendly word. I felt embarrassed by these visits as he cannot have failed to see that I was making less than the good impression that he had hoped for from me. It was on one of these visits that I chose to speak to Kevin in the office that he had commandeered for the day. I was unsure whether it was in any way correct for a manager, even a trainee one, to make an approach to, let alone date, a junior member of staff. I had the vague impression that some companies may still frown upon that sort of thing. Kevin, in his down to earth way, put me at my ease and positively encouraged me to sow my oats far and wide and as often as possible. He pointed out that my job would entail me working within the club from eight in the morning until eleven at night and so my colleagues were the only women that I was ever likely to see: and the junior members of staff were seemingly expendable. I was a little ill at ease with this viewpoint but took it as the green light that I had been waiting for in order to begin my amorous adventures. Disaster, however, awaited me on that front.

Toria, the young woman who had made an impression upon me, worked 'front of house': her duties varied but included such things as selling tickets, manning the reception and being a 'checker' – this being the name given to those members of staff whose task it was to stand around the auditorium, microphone in hand, looking bored until a customer shouted the magic word 'here' at which point they would sprint over to the lucky player and read their numbers back to the caller who sat on stage behind a console and looked down on his subjects like King Canute surveying the sea. Once the numbers had been checked and verified the caller would run to a supervisor to collect the winnings for the customer: this was all done in swift fashion and with military precision as the golden rule in bingo is that nothing, absolutely nothing, must be allowed to get in the way of the relentless pace of the games. Front of house was perhaps the most junior and unchallenging of jobs in the hall, but Toria had loftier ambitions and had dreams of becoming a club barmaid.

She was small with youthful features and jet black hair cut into a bob. This, along with the short skirted uniform worn by all members of staff who had the figure or self delusion to get away with it, gave her the impression of being a Twenties flapper who might break into a Charleston at any moment: I imagined her as being a timeless beauty who I could whisk away to a better life somewhere and holidays spent sipping cocktails together on the French Riviera.

In truth, though, the primary reason that I began to take such an interest in Toria was that she had acquired the reputation of being an easy conquest: she had relationships of varied lengths with several members of staff and seemed to be on friendly terms with many of the men who came to the hall: they smiled broadly at her but their wives looked at her with pursed lips and furrowed brows. In my relatively young and naïve way I anticipated that the best way to approach her was the direct route. It was common, at the end of a long and tiring evening at work for members of staff to sit in the lounge and relax with a glass of wine or a pint of lager. I went over to Toria and asked if she would see me in the manager's office and she followed me eagerly which I took to be a positive sign. It transpired, however, that she had thought that I had asked her to the office to offer her the chance to work on the bar team and leave the floor behind. Her previously eager and smiling face dropped perceptibly when I told her that I had no decision making powers as yet and little influence over those that had. Her face dropped further when I explained the real reason that I had wanted to speak to her. She remained silent for only two or maybe three seconds and then explained that she was flattered but that I just wasn't her type. She smiled sweetly then and asked me, with more than a hint of condescension in her voice, if I understood and that she hoped that I wouldn't be too hurt. Oh no, I assured her as I ushered her out of the office and shut the door behind her, I'm not hurt at all and I wasn't: I was angry more than anything, angry that this woman seemed to be open to advances from anybody except myself.

I had decided to keep this little failure to myself, but inevitably in the enclosed community that existed within the bingo hall the news of my rejection leaked out. Within a few days of the incident people began to smile slyly at me and even wink at me when Toria walked into the room. In a strange way this did have a positive effect as it seemed to thaw relations between me and many of the staff members: it was as if I had passed some unknown initiation test. A few of the men who had previously thought of me as aloof or snobbish, which is an unfair description of my character then and now, began to take me into their confidence: some would buy me drinks at the end of the day and others would give me tips for the horses that had come from top secret sources with close connections to the big stables.

I also began to notice that I was receiving attention from a new and most welcome source. Jane worked behind the bar but I hadn't seen her as much as many of the other workers because she was only part time, juggling her bar work with a college course studying childcare. In fairness even then she was often absent, regularly phoning up at the last minute with some excuse or other as to why she wouldn't be able to make her allotted shift. When I first saw Jane I had noticed her from a distance and now it seemed that she had noticed me too. She began to buy me drinks at the end of the night, gratefully received by myself even though I knew that I must be earning far more than she was, and took every opportunity to sit near me and engage me in conversation during lunch breaks.

Jane and Toria were complete opposites, and I was later to learn that Toria and Jane had a long held enmity for each other, perhaps stemming from the fact that Jane, although she put such minimal effort into her job, held down the position that her rival so coveted. Looking back, it seems that she courted my attention in a strange and misguided attempt to make Toria envious that she had picked up a prize that Toria had so foolishly turned down.

Jane was only nineteen but looked several years older. She was tall, statuesque even, and had fair skin, long platinum blonde hair and piercing blue eyes. She wore bright red lipstick and would often have lipstick on her teeth, which to my mind only increased her beauty and made her seem even more attractive. She spoke in a broad Barnsley accent couched in deep tones that delighted me. If Toria could have been a Twenties flapper, then I imagined Jane as somebody altogether more powerful: a 'land girl' during the war perhaps although in my more poetic moods I pictured her as a Queen Boudicca cutting her way through life in a chariot.

I didn't have to make any approach to Jane, which was a relief as I had already proved myself to be quite inadequate in such matters, as she, in the liberated style that I had expected from my Icaenian Queen, took matters in hand one night after work.

As you will remember, I had developed an aversion to, perhaps even a fear of, driving and had not stepped behind a wheel since I had first left home to go to University. It was three miles from the club where I worked to the sparse bedsit that housed me at the time and, although I sometimes caught a bus, I often hailed a taxi: this was the best paid position that I had held and, never one for saving for a rainy day, I was loath to economise.

On this particular night, although it is many years ago now I can remember it well, Jane asked me if I would share a taxi with her. I knew that she lived in Grimethorpe and that this was in completely the opposite direction to my small rented rooms on the more acceptable side of town but I'd read between the lines and had enjoyed the book. Little things at work that passed between us, the way that she would stroke the inside of my hand when she handed me change or the way that she would bite through half a biscuit and then hand me the other half, which I accepted gratefully, its end still wet from her red lipped mouth, filled me with unexpected amounts of pleasure and made the days when she worked bearable. We climbed into the back of the taxi together and the blood thumped in my veins like a hammer.

Once the taxi had pulled away from the curb, swerving to avoid the drunken revellers who had stumbled off of the kerb, and started its all too short journey away from the town centre to the crumbling mining village that was home to this broad shouldered beauty she wasted no time in pulling me tightly into her body. I could feel the curves of her breasts against my chest and her body felt taut and muscular. She pressed her lips against mine and removed my tie as I returned her passion greedily.

When I opened my eyes I found hers wide open and staring into me: I knew who was completely in charge of the situation here, that the work roles had been reversed, but I was happy to let myself submit to her powers. The journey, which must have taken around fifteen minutes, seemed to pass in blissful seconds. Jane climbed out of the car and then asked me where I lived. When I replied 'Worsborough', she smiled sweetly at the driver and asked him to take me there. Leaning across to me she planted a kiss on my cheek and promised to speak to me on the following day. The car door was pushed firmly shut and the car continued on its way with its solitary passenger sitting in bewildered frustration in the back seat. The driver, a thick set man in his fifties with a perpetually dripping nose that he kept wiping on the back of his sleeve, said nothing to me but I could see his eyes looking up into his mirror, looking at me. I wasn't in the mood to speak to him I just continued the journey in silence. I didn't even give him a tip.

She was due in at work at six o'clock on the following evening. At quarter to six, as was the regulation for all of the management team, I went to the manager quarters to get changed from my normal day suit, dark blue with a light blue shirt and purple tie, into a formal evening suit, bow tie, winged collars and all. That evening I doused myself, rather too liberally, in the Kouros aftershave that I kept for special occasions and headed down the stairs expecting to see her preparing the bar for its opening. She wasn't there but Toria was stood behind the bar and she was smiling as though it was her Birthday and somebody had bought her a car and a diamond necklace.

"Where's Jane tonight?", I asked her, and followed it up with "Shouldn't you be out there?"

"I think Toria has gone off with Colin somewhere so they've asked me to fill in behind the bar for tonight. This could be the start of something good for me."

"Yeah, great, knock yourself out" I muttered as I turned away from her and headed across to the offices. Before I got there I saw Colin motioning me over. He put his arm around me and whispered confidentially in my ear that he needed me in his office. A great sense of foreboding came over me as I walked through the doors: it seemed that somehow they had found out what had happened and, contrary to the assurances that the Regional Director had given to me, they were unhappy about it. I had not been performing as well as expected in my trainee management role and perhaps they were just looking for an excuse, for any reason, to dismiss me before the company wasted any more time and money on me? Oh well, I thought, at least I can still see Jane if they sack me and I can always find another job somewhere. I was still in my mid twenties and my innocent optimism had yet to be replaced by the world weary scepticism that was to become my companion.

When I entered the office Jane was already sitting there, she had not yet changed into her uniform and was wearing a cream coloured jacket lined with fake fur, blue jeans and brown leather knee length boots with heels that made her look even taller than she already was. Colin sat down opposite her and then motioned to me to sit in the chair that was seated next to his on the opposite side of the desk to the woman that I lusted after. Colin always looked tired beyond his years, although it seemed that he had achieved a pin up status to women of a certain age, but tonight he looked especially faded and weary.

"Thanks for coming John, we need a witness at a disciplinary meeting like this. Jane", here he paused in a struggle to recollect her surname which eventually came to him, "Kirk, you must be aware that your performance recently has been unacceptable. Despite several warnings, informal and formal, you have shown no attempt to make the necessary improvements and indeed you seem to be getting progressively worse." Colin then reeled off a long list of misdemeanours including repeated absences, arriving late and leaving early, dropping bottles of spirits, poor housekeeping and rudeness to customers. As each charge was read out I felt myself shrink within my seat and my eyes were downcast and boring into the linoleum floor.

"And to top it all", he concluded, "your personal appearance is unacceptable. This is a leisure club not a discotheque and yet you always have lipstick on your teeth in a most unappealing manner. I'm afraid, Jane, er, Kirk, we are going to have to let you go."

She didn't say a word as she stood up and walked out of the office but as I finally glanced up in a cowardly fashion I could see that silent tears had been running down her face. I wanted to run after her, to hold her close again, but I just sat there in stunned dejection.

"Sorry to have to get you involved in that, John, but we need to have two people here to dismiss someone in case they concoct some false accusations. What did you think?"

"I can't agree about her appearance, Colin, I always thought that she looked fine" I said in a hushed voice. Of course, I had meant to say that I thought she looked spectacular.

"Well you would, you're young and unworldly. Cheer up - you'll get used to this." I stood up but as I walked out I looked back and saw his hands shaking as he lit a cigarette and I wondered if he would ever get used to it himself? As I closed the door I heard him say:

"What's that shit you're wearing by the way? Smells like you've had a bath in it."

As I walked through the doors into the hall I looked around, all the while knowing that she had gone from my life for good. I should have defended her in the office; I should have offered to resign if she wasn't given one last chance; I should have run after her. I should have done something at least, but I had taken the coward's way out and I never saw her again, although often in future years I thought that I had caught the back of her head as she left pubs and clubs that I'd just entered. It was all I deserved. I spent the rest of the night in a silent daze and was even less effective in my job than I had been in the previous weeks.

I had become disheartened in my efforts to find some sort of partner amongst the staff and began to spend more time within the defensive shell that I had projected around myself. If I wasn't winning hearts and minds amongst my fellow workers at least I had proved to be a hit amongst some of the customers.

We had a regular pair that sat directly in front of the stage every morning without fail. They were two ladies, in their seventies, who would sit in their large woollen coats, whatever the weather, and talk constantly throughout the games – much to the distaste of their fellow gamers. There was a thin white haired woman who was called Emily and remained relatively in order, and her constant companion was a black haired woman called Ada who wore bright pink acetate spectacles and who was loud enough to drown out the sound of passing trains.

Every morning as I went by on my way to introduce the commencement of the day's games, Ada would grab my arm with a firmness that belied her age. She would invariably say:

"Young man, if I win today I'm going to take you around the back and snog you. Don't worry though - I'll put my teeth in first."

I would smile nervously, but I didn't want to put her resolve to the test and always breathed an inward sigh of relief when another day went by without a win for my aged fan.

One morning, I noticed that Emily was sat at home and imagined that Ada had gone on holiday or perhaps been summoned to visit relatives. As I passed the table, however, it was Emily's turn to grab my arm, done with less vigour than Ada managed. Emily said:

"You know my friend – the one I always sit with? She left here with me yesterday and walked down the street and then she just dropped down dead. Like a stone."

She snivelled as she said this, and I offered her my condolences before asking a staff member to bring her a breakfast and pot of tea on the house. It was the least I could do and I was genuinely moved by the fact that a woman that I had seen looking so healthy and full of life could be dead just hours later. Emily continued to snivel throughout the morning but she also continued to dab away at the cards in front of her, never missing a number: it was what Ada would have wanted.

On another occasion, I remember that a large and increasingly voluble queue of people had lined up waiting to use the disabled toilet. Eventually it became apparent that something was wrong and as the incumbent gave no answer to our knocks the caretaker of the building was sent to fetch his tools. When he removed the door from its hinges, there for all to see, although most turned their heads away, was an elderly lady sat dead on the lavatory, skirt around her ankles like Barnsley's answer to Elvis Presley. The ambulance was sent for and I remember that as she was stretchered away, blanket over her face, the crowds sitting at their tables continued to play bingo, moving their chairs in to let the ambulance men carry the lady out on her last dignified journey.

Life and work continued along the same lines for several weeks. I was given new tasks to learn, new departments to supervise, although I had not made any appreciable progress in the previous departments. It had become clear to all that I was not cut out for a life in bingo and I was glad of it: I had no desire to spend the next forty years of my life working twelve or thirteen hours a day in a smoke filled auditorium so that at the end of the day, no matter how many red hot showers I took, I would smell as if I had smoked a hundred Benson and Hedges. I began to look for other jobs.

I had now made the irrevocable decision that I was going to leave the bingo life behind, sooner rather than later, and then as now I never went back on a decision once made: the trait of stubbornness, and its victory over reason, ran deep within me and was carried through my Yorkshire blood. As I now had no intention of completing my training course and achieving the hallowed position of Assistant Manager then I also made the conscious decision to do as little work as possible, without being dismissed, whilst I looked for a new appointment.

One of the ways that I found to avoid any remotely challenging task was to become the ultimate 'meeter and greeter' on the door. This would involve me standing in the reception area and flirting overtly with the aging ladies, sometimes going as far as to plant a butterfly kiss on their wrinkled cheeks, and wishing the men good luck and sympathising with them when they complained that their leg was playing up and that this was a sure and infallible sign that rain was on the way.

If anybody asked me why I spent so much time stood inside the reception hall I would reply that Colin had posted me there to count the footfall and work out trends, thus enabling us to calculate how many staff we needed, and where and at what times we needed them. Word soon spread, in hushed tones, amongst the staff that a major review was underway but nobody spoke of it openly in case this would somehow tempt fate and put their own position at risk: they foresaw a storm coming and didn't want to be the one to rock the boat.

For the same superstitious reason nobody thought to question Colin directly about this and, as usual, he was too engaged with his mountains of paperwork, or speaking to his solicitors and accountants regarding his divorce, to notice what was going on outside of his office. Perhaps I should have felt guilty about the anguished looks that I began to see on my colleagues faces but I was young, with the self centred concerns of youth, and had achieved my goal: I could spend the majority of my days standing around the reception hall doing nothing except pass my time in amiable chit chat.

One of the other tasks that I had taken it upon myself to fulfil, simply in order to pass a little time, was in welcoming prospective members, telling them about the club in glowing terms and helping them fill the application form in. In those days before the gaming laws were liberalised a person could not enter the club until twenty four hours had passed since their application.

It was whilst carrying out this duty, normally of no consequence, that I first met Lamara.

Most customers, during daytimes at least, were elderly. The majority, although not all, of them were perfectly pleasant people and whilst I always loved the company of old people and was effortlessly accepted by them they did not provide the diversion or attraction that young women would. The demographic did change slightly in the evenings, and even more so on Saturday nights when a succession of hackneyed variety acts accompanied the bingo, but the women were loud and often drunk and did not appeal to my sensibilities at the time.

They would throw their shoes at me in some strange courtship ritual and occasionally they would push their telephone number lasciviously into my suit pockets as I stood helpless to stop them with my hands encumbered by trays full of pound coins. Whilst I found their interest flattering I never telephoned them, although if I saw some of them on nights out I would always let them buy me a drink before making my excuses and leaving. I gained the impression that it was not me that they liked but the position that I held, however minor it was in the reality of things.

On this particularly fateful morning, however, a woman entered my life that was to have a profound impact on everything that was to follow: even now I find it impossible to say whether I would have turned and walked away if I could have foreseen how things would develop in the brief years that we would share. All I can say with certainty is that when I saw her strain to push open the heavy set door at the entrance to the bingo hall I was powerless to do anything other than stride over and, opening the door for her, let her walk into my life.

During the handful of months that I had worked at the club only a few women, maybe a dozen or so, had made any sort of impression on me to the extent that I would turn my head or suck in my stomach, which at the time wasn't as toned as it is now, as they walked past. Perhaps they wore large hooped earrings, or had black or purple eye shadow and a star above their right eye, perhaps they had arms covered in tattoos and I longed to see them naked to see if it ran all across their back. At other times it could be a scent that they wore or an unfamiliar accent that grabbed my attention. Occasionally, all too rarely, I would see a woman of obvious beauty that would make everyone gasp when they saw her. Even so, these people would only occupy my thoughts for brief moments and then disappear: they stirred my lust but made no impact upon my heart.

As I opened the door to Lamara I knew that something altogether different was happening. In an instinctive moment I bowed my head slightly and waved my arm before me as if I was a courtier welcoming a Queen into her Palace. It was a foolish movement and I stopped as soon as I realised what I was doing but as I raised my head I could see her dilated pupils registering surprise. For weeks now I had been practising my best Cheshire cat grin in the manner of the new force that had burst onto the political scene Tony Blair. As I walked around the premises every morning I would keep my lips in a wide grin, teeth on show, until my jaw ached and I could take no more but as with every exercise it grew easier by the day. As I looked at Lamara, however, I gave the first sincere smile that I had mustered in a long time and I felt surprised that I could still distinguish it from the falseness that I had been perfecting.

She stood, in her heeled boots, around five and a half feet tall, she was not slim but not weighty either and had what I would describe as a curvaceous body without meaning to imply the common euphemistic use of that word.

She had brown hair running just past her shoulders with occasional dark lowlights hidden within it. On top of her head was a white headband with thin pink stripes at the edges which emphasised the clarity of her skin and the most beautiful eyes of dark blue that I had ever seen. These eyes were large and piercing, and to do justice to them I would have to recall the American poet who said: "I do not know what it is about you that closes and opens; Only something in me understands the voice of your eyes is deeper than all roses."

I opened my mouth to speak, but closed it again in order to compose myself for a few seconds. If I had dared to speak then who knows what would have flowed from my mouth without checking with my brain first? I gulped down air and then gestured her over to the reception table. "Hi, I haven't seen you in here before?", it was the most obvious and the most crass of lines but it was as good as I was going to get.

"Well, I haven't been here before". Her voice had a honeyed tone, with an accent vaguely familiar but not quite in concord with the rough Barnsley vernacular with its elongated vowel sounds and its deliciously descriptive variations. She had an almost sing-song voice which seemed perfectly in keeping with the eyes which sparkled when she spoke. I looked at her deliciously full and inviting lips as she talked and my attention was drawn to a gap between her front teeth and their irregular pattern which seemed wildly attractive to me. I was later to learn that this was a memento from one of many school ground fights that she had found herself in as a teenager, but at the moment of which I now write I remained blissfully ignorant of this volatile side to her nature.

"Never been here? How can you have missed out on Barnsley's premier", at this point I coughed sheepishly as if letting her in on some private joke, "entertainment venue?"

"I've only just moved into the town, I've come from Huddersfield." Huddersfield? That explained the vaguely familiar accent, and as strange as it seems to a man who had spent too long digging himself into a rut in his hometown it gave her a sense of mystery.

"Oh I see, are you studying here then?" In reality I saw nothing, and this was a position that I found myself becoming more and more familiar with during the years that I spent with Lamara.

"No, I just felt that it was time to move away. Make a new start for me and Skye. We've got relatives near here, and they found us a house to move into. Privately rented, lots of playing fields nearby, there are even some swings and a roundabout. The paint's missing from it, but who needs paint?"

"Paint? That's for Southerners! Er, who is Skye then?" I knew at once, of course that it must be her daughter but I felt a burning desire to know if Skye had a father in situ.

"She is my daughter, just turned three – really beautiful."

"Like her mum then." It wasn't my usual style, and I put it down to the nerves that had strangely gripped me, but I found myself uttering corny line after corny line.

"Oh thanks!" She had the good grace to smile after I said this rather than turning around and walking out of the door. How different my life would have been then. "Here, look, I've got some pictures of her."

Like all proud mothers she carried little photographs of her child within her purse and as I saw that she had more than a resemblance to her mother, I had to agree that she was indeed beautiful. I felt an immediate attachment to the little girl that I saw in the picture as if I knew the bond that we were to form in the near future. The thing that had struck my keen mind most was that there was no man evident in these pictures, and that no mention had been made of any man sharing their new future in Barnsley. I was sure that they had left Huddersfield to leave the father behind. I felt a callous satisfaction surge within me.

"Aw, I'm sure you will have a great time here! In Barnsley that is, as well as the club. Although, of course, I want to encourage you to come here and I'm sure that we can find something to amuse you. A young mother like you needs some entertainment in her life."

"Do you say that to all the women?"

"No, no – really I don't." And for once I meant it. I managed to tear myself away from the embrace of her gaze for a few seconds and fetched her membership forms. I remembered every word that she wrote, and it was a measure of how captivated that I had become by her in so quick a time that I loved to see her hand move gracefully across the page as if it were the hands of a virtuoso gliding across a Steinway's keys.

Her name was Miss Lamara Gallagher and she had recently turned twenty one years of age. I imagined how hard life must have been for this woman as an unmarried seventeen year old giving birth to a daughter and raising her, as I imagined, single handed. She had come through her ordeal, if such it was, with an inner beauty and calmness radiating throughout her. I felt that she was capable of anything, and in this at least I was right. Most of all I noted that she had moved into a street that I knew well, and barely two miles away from me.

Reluctantly I explained to her that Britain's archaic gaming laws insisted that although she had signed up to become a member she couldn't enter the actual building until another day had elapsed. She agreed to this without complaint but as she walked out of the building, after having thanked me for my help, I couldn't help wondering if she would return to the club: perhaps I had misread the signals as I seemed to have done so many times before? I resolved that if she didn't return to the club I would check out the address where she lived. I was sure that some sort of accidental meeting could be orchestrated, and I wasn't going to let any kind of pride stop this.

"Well, she made a real impression on you" said Sharon, an oversized woman in her forties who was sharing reception duties. Sharon had taken to wearing her hair in bunches held with bright red ribbons in a forlorn attempt to hold back the advances of time that had already begun to ravage her wearisome face.

"Who? Oh her? Lamara, or whatever? Hardly noticed her, my dear, hardly noticed her."

I slept badly that night, and spent an extra ten minutes polishing my shoes on the following morning. I knew that she wouldn't come, I told myself this over and over again. But I was wrong, she walked into the club at precisely ten o'clock, looking even more majestic than on the previous day, and we were soon to become inseparable, until that day when she finally left me.

It was a huge juddering noise, a metallic scream that dragged me out of the dream that I had been enjoying. The wind was more biting than ever, but there was something else in the atmosphere – smoke and the smell of dust and diesel filled the air. People were suddenly animated and pushing past me.

I looked up at the bridge that I had recently staggered across on my way to the station. A car had crashed into it, seemingly at some speed, and had almost destroyed the whole edifice. People were running towards the vehicle, but I also noticed a figure running away from the car. It was the figure of a short and stocky man, with black hair, dark jeans and a black overcoat. I only saw the back of him as he was exiting the scene with haste but I noticed that he ran with a pronounced limp. The driver's side door was wide open and, amidst the general chaos that seemed to reign, the horn continued to bleat incessantly and murderously.

I knew that there was little that I could do, and was still very much in a daze both from the mysterious sight of the girl on the bus and the remembrance of Lamara that had seemed so real, but I was powerless to stop walking towards the incident.

I pushed my way through the crowd that had quickly gathered, I know not where they had come from, as if I was some sort of doctor: the same people that had shunned me at the train station earlier now moved out of my way. As I got closer I could see that the front and left side of the car had suffered a major impact and had folded like crushed paper. I soon saw that the car had hit not only the wall but had also hit a young woman, who I would have estimated to be of no older than twenty five years of age. She lay motionless on the pavement, half propped against the wall: blood was gathered under her head and her skin had taken on a mottled look, speckled with blood.

"She's dead, she's dead", I heard a man's voice cry. Suddenly the car's horn stopped and an eerie silence filled the cold morning air.

Chapter Three

Shock can hit a person in different ways: some people may break down in tears on the spot with no real knowledge of what they are crying about; some people may feel nauseous, their legs will turn to jelly and their hands will shake so much that they struggle to light the cigarette that they have raised to their thin mouth; others will become angry, aggressive even. Yes there are many ways that shock can hit a person and there are many ways that a car can hit a person, but as I stood there suddenly knocked sober by the shock of the last few seconds I could see that it was better not to be hit at all.

I had pushed my way through the people that had gathered. A light touch on their shoulders or a gentle push was all that was needed for the crowds to move aside. Nobody said a word and the eerie silence that had suddenly descended at the cessation of the alarm still prevailed. The hardy winter birds that had previously been heard singing dolefully out of the surrounding woodlands had somehow hushed too.

People began to creep cautiously out of their red bricked terraced houses, wanting to see what had happened but fearing that they wouldn't like what was about to greet them. Some of them had been caught unawares, and not having had time to get dressed they had simply pulled old tattered dressing gowns on made of blue or pink material. They had towels around their necks in a vain attempt to protect them from the bitterly fierce January wind that whistled around the Pennine foothills. The younger women had dressing gowns that were short and inadequate and goose bumps quickly formed on their exposed flesh, they had slippers in the shape of animals on their feet and already lit cigarettes in their hands. Some people held handkerchiefs over their mouths: whether to keep out the cold, or in readiness to cover their eyes I couldn't say. People continued to gather as if we had gone back to the New Year celebrations of two days previously, but this crowd was hushed and reverent and in no mood for celebration. Doors were opened slowly and shut behind them with the utmost care and precision. Footsteps were cautious as people walked on tiptoe. Silence was general as if everybody was scared to wake the dead – but who can wake the dead?

As I looked round I felt a sense of distaste towards the people who had gathered so silently and yet so swiftly. They were the rubberneckers who slowed down as they passed every accident on a motorway, the people who watched motor racing hoping to see a succession of spectacular crashes and now that a real crash had occurred on the doorstep they were not prepared to miss out on the occasion. Suddenly I remembered that I was no better than them and that I had pushed my way forcibly through the crowds to get as close as I could to the wreckage: like so much that had already happened that day I had no idea why I had reacted in that way.

My head was clear now, the thoughts that had beaten within me in a tumult of violent confusion after I had seen the girl on the bus had passed, as had the visions of Lamara that had returned to me with such familiarity. My breathing was calm and my head was clear, indeed I seemed to see things with an extra clarity as if colours were sharper and every little sound that I heard seemed magnified: I knew that this was the way that I had reacted when shock hit me.

I looked down at the chaos in front of me. The car that was now crumpled had once been a beautiful and sleek sports car. It was a Mercedes Benz CLK 55, and I noticed with surprise that it was the Aufrecht Melcher Grossaspach model: these three letters AMG signifying that this was the very top of the range model, the height of

German exclusivity and not a vehicle I would have expected to see being driven though this normally sleepy backwater of Barnsley.

The soft top roof had torn on impact and the obsidian black paint had fractured and chipped away against the wall. The driver's side of the vehicle had escaped relatively unharmed and this had allowed the driver to extricate himself from behind the airbag, open his door with ease and exit the scene before he could be clearly identified. The car had come to a stop against the bridge wall at a thirty degree angle and from the gouges on the bonnet of the car it seemed to me that it had scraped sideways along the structure before eventually being forced to stop. The front passenger side had suffered a severe impact and the two circular head lights, one large and one small, on this side had been shattered; glass lay scattered everywhere, and the front grille was dented and smashed. The passenger door had caved in upon impact and as I continued to look at the vehicle analytically and dispassionately I thought it unlikely that this door could be forced open. Fortunately, it appeared that there had been no passenger in the car on that fateful morning.

I looked down from the car, and then it became impossible to remain dispassionate and analytical. The woman that greeted my eyes had not been so lucky. Upon closer inspection I would have taken her to be in her early Twenties. She had dark blue, almost black, eyes that bulged wildly. Her eyelids fluttered in slight but rapid convulsions: contrary to the plaintive cry that I had heard when I first hurried to the scene she was not yet dead. Her hair was black and the sun reflected upon it in peculiar ways so that at times I thought it looked streaked in grey and at others vibrant and youthful. Her head lay back horribly against the wall, and I guessed that maybe her neck had broken. Blood continued to ooze from the entirety of her mouth which gaped open in a bloody and toothless grimace. Large amounts of blood had sprayed and congealed quickly across the right side of her face and had matted into her hair.

She lay almost motionless and completely trapped underneath the car, so that all of her body that remained visible was her head, her collar bone which protruded from the torn remnants of her clothing and her right arm which lay jauntily against the pavement. This arm remained undamaged and showed that she wore a shirt of a harsh brown material, which looked both too thin for the harsh morning weather and too dull and lifeless for the prevailing fashion. Her fingers were locked tightly around something, and her knuckles contracted and expanded rhythmically. This and the almost unnoticeable twitching of her eyelids seemed to be signalling to me, and once again I felt a strange unease begin to burn within me as if this dying woman had a message for someone – and perhaps for me in particular. As I looked down on her, at the fragile shell failing before me, I thought that whoever she did have a message for would never receive it.

"She is alive, call an ambulance" I said. I had shouted this simply because although it seemed obvious nobody else had mentioned it. The silence was shattered and I heard greedy fingers pawing at keypads as a dozen different people all called the emergency number. The people felt happier now that they knew that they hadn't been staring so hypnotically at a corpse.

"Thank you, Doctor", a middle aged man in a hastily pulled on tracksuit called out (his Christmas present was getting at least one outing), and I didn't have the heart to tell him what I really did for a living. I didn't want to be standing here any longer and I wanted to run: I recollected the man that I had seen, half running and half limping, fleeing the scene just a few minutes earlier and I knew where I wanted to run to. Somebody had to be held accountable, and the woman who lay crushed and freezing on the blood reddened pavement seemed to be imploring me to be the one to bring him to account. It was as if I heard a silent scream that was echoing across the world. I moved back through the crowds, and this time I had no need to push as they moved away automatically from me as if angry that I were obstructing their view. I no longer felt the cold although when I looked down at my hands I saw that my pale skin had taken on a blue and orange hue. Looking across the street, over the heads of the assembled crowd that showed no sign of dispersing, I tried to calculate which way the man had gone and how far away he could have reached by now. I felt sure that he couldn't have carried on running indefinitely and that the shock of the situation would soon force his lungs to fill and his legs to cease. I expected to find him stooped and crying around some nearby corner but as I remembered the matted hair and the bulging eyes I was in no mood to comfort him.

I looked across the road at the direction that I had seen him take. I tried to trace his flight but the streets were maze like and were crossed by numerous building sites and developments that were now springing up in the village. Elsecar had become prime commuter belt territory with its railway station offering quick and convenient links to Leeds and Sheffield, and from there onwards to Manchester and London, and had close proximity to the M1 motorway.

New housing had begun to spread throughout the area over the last few years and now the pace of these developments was becoming frenetic. All of the buildings looked the same: large, box like houses made of sand coloured bricks with paving to the front and moderately sized gardens to the rear; all came complete with garage space for one or two cars. I suppose it was the old romantic in me that found these houses so aesthetically unappealing when compared to the back to back, cosy, terraced houses that had once dominated the area. It had to be said, I admitted to myself, that somebody was making a lot of money in this village. Unfortunately, it showed no signs of being me.

The crash had made me nervous and I looked several times from side to side before crossing the road although there was no sign of any traffic approaching. After crossing the road I turned around to take a last look at the scene of the accident. The crowd had not dispersed, and had hardly moved, but now the silence had been shattered I could see people in animated conversation with one another. They were all coming up with their theories on how the accident had happened and who was to blame, but from their arm movements, and from the shaking of heads and the general frowns upon their countenances, it seemed that any agreement was far from general. People who had been indoors, or even in their beds with duvets pulled selfishly around their bodies while their partners shivered next to them, at the time of the impact now claimed that they had seen everything and that only their account could be believed. It struck me that situations such as the one that stood so tragically before me could bring out the hero in some people but it brought out the voyeur in all people.

I guessed that some of the crowd must be blaming that poor wrecked young woman, saying that she had stepped out in front of the car without looking, or that she may have been drunk like the man that they had seen staggering down into the train station. Others would then say that that man wasn't a drunk, he was a doctor. Those terms aren't mutually exclusive, I imagined another bystander saying.

From where I stood and reflected, it seemed obvious who was to blame. The woman was crushed between the wall of the bridge, now looking dangerously unstable and showing all of the fragility of its age, and the high performance sports car: she had not even stepped onto the road but rather had been standing on the pavement, probably petrified by the dazzle of the headlights speeding towards her.

Tyre marks were scratched across the road and showed, to my mind, that the car had attempted to brake sharply whilst travelling at an excessive speed. The road was icy underfoot and maybe too icy for even the best traction system to deal with at such velocity. The car had obviously flown out of control and been sent spinning sideways onto the pavement before hitting the bridge, and the woman trapped against it, and shunting and scraping along the wall until it had eventually ground to a halt. The driver must then have opened his door and left in a great hurry without pausing to close his door or check on the state of his victim. I found this as unforgivable as I found it unsurprising and I turned away from the scene that oppressed me so, instead looking ahead of me with a resolute and stony gaze.

I had seen the limping, running man only briefly and would not be able to give an accurate description of him if I was asked to, but I knew somehow that I would recognise him if and when I found him. I was unsure what I would do, having little desire to be a fighter at that point in my life, when we met but I would worry about that when it happened.

I had watched him head along the central arterial avenue that runs though the village cutting across its middle from North to South. I tried to put myself into his situation and imagine what I would do, where I would go? The avenue stretched away into the distance, a straight and unbending road. It would have been folly to keep on running straight down this road as it was easy to see down its entirety from the scene of the accident. I wished now that I had paid more attention to the man but I had been too easily distracted by the crowds and by the desire to see the actual scene of the crash itself.

If he had not continued to run down this avenue then which path would he have taken? There was ample opportunity to turn off onto little boulevards and lanes that ran away from the avenue to the left and to the right. I continued to walk along the street, training every sense to search for clues or signs that would otherwise remain imperceptible. I had a complete confidence that I would somehow be able to hunt him down, but was this confidence misplaced like that of a child who tries to push his Christmas list up a bricked in chimney place?

I had seen him veer right as he had crossed the road and headed onto the avenue and I felt that in his state of mind he would not want to cross a road again and so he would keep to the right hand side of the street. I followed this course as well. After a few seconds walk I came to the first turning but quickly dismissed this path: it was too close to the accident and I would have noticed him turn down it.

After around a hundred yards, by my estimate, I reached another turning which led onto a broader street that ran initially through some bungalows holding an old peoples complex. As I passed through the sheltered housing I noticed that all of the curtains were open and glancing in from house to house the inhabitants were sat, dressed and elegant, in their chairs facing the door, as if waiting for visitors who would never come. I wondered what I expected to see? Whatever I had hoped to find was not to be seen here. I saw no man hiding behind cars that were parked on immaculate driveways and which were as aged as their owners. No doors had been forced and no windows remained half open as if freshly lifted. Not even a curtain twitched as I passed through the complex and as I reached the other side of the sheltered accommodation the houses and bungalows began to thin out until there was a stretch of grass land before the next houses, a series of the new modern but block like buildings that were becoming de rigueur throughout the industrial North of the country, began to appear in more frequent intervals.

I passed a café that catered for the early morning commuter and the burgeoning group of builders and workmen that would normally frequent the area. A sign, hand written in a childish scrawl by a purple felt tipped pen, had had been taped to the doorway and read 'Closed For The Holidays'. The phrasing irked me, it seemed that Christmas had been forgotten, or worse had been outlawed, in the great scheme to produce a new Winter Holiday that people could enjoy without having to think of the meaning behind it.

The cafeteria, called 'Sandie's Sarnies', would have been closed for the week previously and I guessed that it wouldn't open again until the next week sent the majority of the population back to work in a general depression. Despite its inactivity the familiar smell of bacon and stale grease reached my nose and, in spite of everything, the Pavlovian reaction took over and I began to feel hungry. I looked carefully around the perimeter of the building, one of its side walls was covered in graffiti apparently placed there by somebody called Festa and the paint on the door was chipped and faded. Litter lay all around, wrappers and paper bags were congregated in every place except in the waste bin that was provided outside of the shop and which remained, as usual, empty and unused. I tried the handle to the shop, but as expected it was locked and would not yield.

I walked further down the street and as I did so images of faces began to spring to my mind and gradually began to merge and become indistinguishable one from another. The girl on the bus with the aura that seemed to burn into you as you looked at her, the memories of Lamara so young, vibrant and full of life as if ironically mocking the future that had awaited her, the blood soaked woman with the bulging flickering eyes and the hair that seemed first jet black and then streaked with grey and then black again as the weak sunlight bounced off it: all of them sprung to my mind one after another and then they seemed to melt together before my eyes, as if they were all three parts of one person or as if they were all commanding me to do their bidding.

A realisation hit me, like a speeding skidding Mercedes-Benz car, that a feeling had been growing within me since that Boxing Day a year and a week ago when Lamara had finally left me. At that time I was a tumult of emotion veering from despair to dejection and then from rejection to resilient acceptance, but something else had been growing unseen within me and now as I felt it increasing perceptibly minute by minute I realised that it was a sense of deep unease: it was as if somebody was watching me and I span around in a circle but found nobody there.

My heart rate had increased again just as it had when I clutched onto the side of the now crushed and crushing bridge after I had walked unsteadily off of the bus earlier that morning. I walked slower now, with each step planted carefully upon the rime bitten pavement and the frost frozen grass as if I was scared of waking what might be under there. Without warning I heard a rushing and panting noise and felt a heavy blow against the back of my legs. My knees buckled slightly under the impact but it had not been enough to knock me over and I turned around swiftly, my senses now alert and blood pumping furiously through my body, half expecting to see the limping man in the black overcoat.

In a moment of confusion I saw nothing and then looking down I saw a dog staring up at me. It was a pit bull terrier, all white but for a black spot on its back and one black ear, and which looked to be one terrifying ball of muscle. It had scratches and scars along one side of its body. A simple brown leather collar around its neck showed that it belonged to somebody but no voice called to it. The dog's ears began to flick backwards and forwards and as it bared its teeth steam rose from its jagged fanged mouth into the freezing morning air. A growling sound began to rumble from deep within it and I thought that this had become the most inauspicious of starts to a new year.

The dog was staring up at me and its body seemed to be shaking perceptibly as if its muscles were straining and ready to spring. I remembered being told, as a child, that if a dog stares at you and looks as if it is about to attack then the one thing that you must do is to hold its stare: as long as you can return the dogs stare unblinking, as if unconcerned about the challenge that it is laying down, then the dog will become intimidated by the extra size that a man has. One blink, however, and the dog would see that as a sign of weakness and pounce.

It seemed like a childhood myth, a tall story of the kind told by parents, but I had no choice other than to put it to the test.

They say that animals can smell fear, but if that was true then the dog that stood tensed and growling before me would have sprung into action rather than being motionless and threatening. Making a great effort to control my heart rate and to stop the trembling nerves that were shaking my body I kept my gaze fixed upon his yellow tinged eyes and the seconds that passed seemed like hours, my mouth becoming dry and beads of sweat returning to my forehead.

At last the animal blinked and turned its back on me, its head lowered. As I let out a heartfelt sigh of relief I saw the white backed beast move away, at first slowly and then increasing its speed until it was running away from me – I had won the war of nerves but now I began to wonder where the dog had come from? Its collar indicated that it belonged to someone although it was not muzzled or leashed as it should have been. I knew that the dog's owner must be nearby, but looking around I saw no sign of anybody and the dog had now disappeared in the direction of the Scout hut that lay across the scrubby and frost addled patch of grassland in front of me.

Normally I would have counted my blessings, turned around myself and gone home, or at least put as much distance as possible between me and the powerfully set beast that had stood slavering before me seconds earlier with evil in its eyes. On this day, however, I felt compelled to follow it: to find the man that it belonged to, and from him find the information on the disappearing driver. Some innate sense led me to believe that they were intrinsically bound up one with another and this, along with the adrenalin that was still flowing within me and heightening my senses, redoubled my courage.

The wind was rising now as I walked towards the large whitewashed hut, and slight flecks of snow began to fall from the sky which were almost blown away before they could reach the ground. This was the first snow of the year and I quickened my pace in an effort to forget the cold air that was striking at my face with each new gust.

The scout hut had stood at the top corner of this playing field for over fifty years but its glory days were long gone. It still held meetings for cubs on Tuesdays, girl guides on Wednesdays and scouts on Thursdays but the numbers who attended dropped year by year. In its heyday an annual flag carrying contingent would march to the cenotaph every

November in their dozens to lay the troops' poppy wreath, now it seemed a struggle to find two boys or girls who would be willing to give up their Sunday morning sleep to attend.

Emptied tins of glue were strewn around its perimeter along with one litre plastic bottles that had held fizzy orange drinks and had now had their bottom section carefully removed and filled with a plastic carrier bag. Again there was graffiti sprayed in haphazard fashion onto the side of the building by the ubiquitous 'Festa'. The tag, as it was called, was child like in its execution and the spray painted scrawl was repeated in varying sizes across the building.

A jaded looking brass plaque stated "7th Barnsley Elsecar Scout and Guide Group", but it didn't shine with the pride that it once had. To the right of the plaque was the main entranceway, a large blue metal plated door. As I walked closer, my pace increasing along with my impatience, I saw that the door was open.

I had reached the door and stopped in my tracks to try to listen for sounds from within. I thought that I could hear the heavy panting noise of the pit bull terrier that I had encountered earlier but it was hard to distinguish individual noises as they were drowned out by the wind that had now began to whip and howl. Along with the snow that increased in volume I seemed to hear a siren, as if from police cars or ambulances, being blown on the wind and it seemed as if there were several sirens in competition with one another. I looked at the door, it was heavy set and could not have been forced open easily, but there were no markings on it and the lock seemed to remain intact: I concluded that the door must have been opened with a key.

My ice numbed fingers, now alternating between blue, orange and red skin tones, gripped the side of the door and pulled it; the door opened outwards rather than inwards and felt heavy as I pulled at it. I had no idea what I expected to see, and much less what I wanted to see, but I had already been on a long journey that morning and it was too late to turn back. With my hands outstretched in front of me, to ward off any sudden charge from the dog that may have found its courage again, I walked cautiously and deliberately around the door and into the interior of the hall.

It was dark inside as the sun had not yet risen fully in the morning sky and no lights were switched on. As my eyes adjusted slowly to the darkness I noticed that many of the windows were covered with thick black out style curtains. I looked sharply around and then moved my head more deliberately from side to side but at first glance I could perceive of nothing, nobody, being in the hall with me. There was a large main chamber to the hall with a wooden floor that felt sticky underfoot and looked stained in the half light that engulfed me. Sizeable wooden chests were at the rear of this chamber and long wooden benches lined the sides of the halls. Tube lighting hung from the high ceiling and as my eyes became more and more accustomed to the gloom I could make out cobwebs hanging between the roof beams and the lights that swayed in the breeze below them.

There were two internal doorways at the far end of the room. One of the rooms had a plaque on it stating 'General Staff' and the other, to the right of where I stood facing the doors, was fronted by a plain wooden door that had seen better days and now looked chipped and splintered. There was no sign or plaque on this door but as my eyes had now fully adjusted to the lack of light I saw that paw prints led across the wooden floor, and their marks in the dust led from the outer door where I had entered across the middle of the large general hallway directly to the right hand door. I walked with purpose to that doorway, almost on tiptoe to make as little noise as possible. It now seemed to me that besides the dogs paw prints there were here and there marks that could have been mud deposited by the tread of a boot.

I was within ten feet of the door and was about to reach for the rust ridden handle when the door flew open. I jumped back with surprise and the familiar figure of the dog now bounded forward out of the doorway, with a lithe agility that filled me with dread, and once again stood facing me. It bared its teeth as before, and drooled patches formed on the floor underneath its jaws. It looked less certain than before though, as if waiting for instructions before it could act.

"Here, back boy, back", a voice called from within the room. It was a thickly accented but strangely weak voice, and did not seem to carry the authority that the dog was used to: consequently the dog remained where it stood as if not hearing its call.

The door opened again and a tall, gangly figure came around the corner and confronted me. He did not seem surprised to see me there, although I had never seen him before, and stood with his hands tightly in the pockets of the grey tracksuit top that he was wearing.

The man, who in reality seemed little more than an overgrown boy, was easily in excess of six feet tall and was stick thin so that his clothes hung baggily from him. He wore dark blue jeans with orange stitching down the sides and white trainers entrenched in mud and splatters of paint. The pockets of his tracksuit top, where his hands were firmly wedged, both seemed to bulge threateningly. The hood of his tracksuit was pulled over the off cream coloured baseball cap that he wore on top of a head that seemed strangely small compared to his general stature. His tiny bloodshot eyes peered out from beneath thick black eyebrows and the right side of his face was marked and scarred with acne. His lips held cold sores above and below his mouth and his face displayed stubble that suggested that he hadn't shaved in days. He was staring at me and so I decided to take the initiative and break the silence:

"Is that your dog?" I asked him.

"No", was the monosyllabic reply.

"Are you sure that it's not your dog? You were calling to it earlier?"

"What's it got to do with you?", there was ill concealed hostility in his question and his left hand began to fidget within his pocket.

"That dog tried to attack me outside", I countered.

"Well it's a guard dog, you shouldn't be near here should you?"

"A guard dog for a scout hut? And what are you, Akela's little helper?", I remembered the woman lying bleeding under the car and felt as bitter as the morning outside. I was in no mood to be intimidated by a young thug with a squeaky voice, however tall he was.

"You shouldn't be in here. If I was you I'd leave right now. And you'd better not tell anybody that you've seen me here right?"

"It wasn't you, whoever you are, that I was looking for."

"Oh aye? Who were you looking for then?"

"A short, stocky man, a businessman possibly, in a black overcoat. Walks with a limp, probably out of breath." I had decided that honesty was the best policy but it didn't seem to go down well with the man in front of me who walked in a swagger towards me. He removed his right hand from the pocket, and I could see that he wore an oversized signet ring on his second finger. In the pocket I could make out the nozzle from an aerosol paint can.

"I ain't seen anybody matching that description. I ain't seen anybody except you." He was now standing inches away from me, and craned his face downwards into mine. When he talked little flecks of spit shot from the cracked corners of his mouth onto my face and I automatically started walking backwards.

"Are you sure? If you don't recognise the description then why are you so scared?"

"It seems like you're the one that's scared to me" he said quite reasonably and as I continued to back away he followed me with intent; I was being corralled into the General Staff room.

"I know who you are, Festa" I said, the evidence being there plainly before me, "so if you just answer my questions I can let you go on your way. It's not you that I'm after." I tried to remain calm as I said this and attempted to project a false note of confidence and authority into my voice but it really didn't seem to be working.

"You don't scare me. In fact, let me give you some advice: keep your eyes shut, and your mouth shutter", I didn't think that the time was right to give him a lesson in grammar so graciously I let him continue, "In fact you had better be careful that no one is after you, 'cos if they are then nobody will ever be after you again."

I had been so focussed on Festa's speech, delivered all the while in a high pitched Yorkshire whine, that it wasn't until the last seconds that I heard another set of footsteps coming from behind me. These footsteps were sharp and deliberate rather than the soft shuffling noise made by the trainers of Festa and seemed to echo around the hall so that I spent a split second amazed that I hadn't heard them approaching. I noticed that the dog now backed away with a frightened look in its eye and I prepared to spin around to meet the new acquaintance but before I could do so I felt a powerful arm twist my right hand behind my back and apply pressure to it so that I had no choice but to drop onto my knees to the floor. A leather gloved hand then held a handkerchief firmly over my nose and mouth and an acrid chemical smell filled my lungs and made me want to retch. Everything in my vision seemed to turn red as if I was drowning in blood and then within seconds the red was replaced by a growing blackness and I lost all feeling within my body and passed out.

When I came to I was lying face up outside the scout hut. The sky was bright and snow had settled on my clothing; my face was red and raw to touch. I rose unsteadily to my feet but my legs buckled beneath me. I fell onto my knees and my trousers ripped on impact with the gritted tarmac leaving a bloodied graze on my knee that stung as the snow fell onto it. My head throbbed when I moved it as if I was suffering the worst hangover in the world. I lay back and gulped in air, trying to clear my head and remember what had happened. Within a few minutes my senses became more lucid, and the waves of nausea that had been washing over me began to dissipate enough for me to climb once more to my feet and stand upright. Besides the blood that spread from the gash in my knee I determined, by a process of jabbing my face and then examining my fingers, that I had no more cuts on my body. I looked down to where I had lain, where my body heat had melted the snow that had now settled elsewhere, and saw that my wallet lay on the floor. It was opened but a cursory inspection revealed that neither my cards nor my notes had been taken. I felt into my suit's jacket pocket and found my mobile phone still in there. I pulled it out and found that it was switched off: I remembered that it had been switched on in silent mode that morning.

I began to walk unsteadily and my limbs ached at every movement. I blew hot air onto my hands and rubbed them together enthusiastically in an effort to dispel the creeping coldness that seemed to be frozen deep within me. At first I wasn't aware where I was walking to, but I knew that I couldn't remain at the hut. The normal, conventional, thing to do would have been to telephone the police but it just hadn't been a conventional day and I wanted to get my mind, and story, straight before I reported it to anybody: with my tattered clothing and uncertain gait I looked like a drunk, I didn't want to sound like one too.

As I continued to walk along the road, turning left when I reached the end of the sheltered housing complex, I became aware that I was returning to the train station, to the place where I had stepped off of the bus after my silent encounter with that woman who had gripped me so, and to the place where I had seen that other woman lay bleeding, probably dying, underneath a car.

I had expected to see the car still there and to see the area cordoned off by a plethora of emergency vehicles, but the crowds, along with the car and the emergency vehicles, had gone. I looked at my watch, the face of which had been scratched by the fall, and saw that over three hours had passed since the time of the accident. The woman had gone too, but a sign read 'Accident Scene' and blood was still spread in large black patches across the road. Next to the blood, however, I saw something glinting. I walked gingerly towards it and saw that it was a ring.

I reached forward and grabbed the ring as though I was powerless to do anything else and that the ring was grabbing my hand rather than the other way around. The ring was large but delicate and feminine and had a bright green stone set upon it. Beneath the stone lay a snake motif, and the snake was wrapped into the form of the letter X with bands going across its body. It seemed familiar, but then so many things today had seemed familiar. And then it grabbed me with a power equal to, greater than, the gloved hand that had grabbed my face: the snake motif on this ring, underneath the beautiful green stone, had also been on the signet ring of the graffiti artist in the scout hut. I felt certain that, despite being knocked out and losing three hours of the day, my mind was not playing tricks on me and that the designs on the rings matched perfectly.

My mind was occupied and uneasy as I wandered back to the bus stop that lay nearby and sat down heavily upon the seating there. The snow continued to fall on me, in even heavier measure now, but it no longer troubled me as much as the maelstrom of thoughts in my head troubled me.

When I had picked up the ring it had been warm to the touch, even though it was surrounded by snow. I remembered that the woman who had been trapped beneath the car was clutching something tightly within her hand and that it had seemed that she had been trying to signal to me. How had the police who had cleared up the accident scene somehow missed this piece of jewellery? The only woman who could answer these questions was the woman who I had left in such a precarious position over three hours earlier. I had not held out much hope for her, but I had to know if she had any chance of recovery. I had to know if there was any chance that I may be able to speak to her at some indeterminate date, perhaps to return the ring to her and thereby find the missing pieces of information that I felt sure could somehow piece together the crazy events that had been happening around me.

I removed my mobile phone from my pocket again and switched it back on. The battery was full and there were no messages waiting for me. I called directory enquiries and obtained the number for the Barnsley and District General Hospital which was surely the place that the poor woman would have been taken to. I quickly thought of a cover story that would get me past a jaded receptionist and dialled the number that I had been given.

A young and sweet sounding voice answered my call. I hoped that its owner was as naïve and forthcoming as she sounded.

"Hi, my name is John, I work as a reporter for the Sheffield Star"; I lied freely as telling the truth earlier that morning had got me nowhere.

"Oh, right" the young voice replied in a non questioning tone.

"I'm writing up a report about the young woman who was crushed by the car at Elsecar."

"Who?"

"The young woman who got crushed beneath a car in the accident that occurred near to Elsecar train station this morning."

"Oh, right." The voice sounded more puzzled now.

"I wondered if you had an update on the young woman's progress, on her condition in general. Is her condition stable?"

"You do mean that one that was scraped up outside of the train station this morning, the one that they said ran in front of a car? Brown shirt?"

"That's the one", I replied with a sinking heart not liking the description of her as being 'scraped up'.

"Yes, she is in a stable condition, a completely stable condition."

"Oh good, would I be able to speak to her at some point?"

"I doubt it. You see – she's dead. There was never any hope for her. Why did you call her a young woman, haven't you done any research? She was an old grey haired woman, seventy if she was a day. No wonder she didn't see or hear the car."

I hung up and began to take the long walk home through the snow, my feet slipping as they moved across the icy street beneath them. My day had been growing steadily stranger, and I couldn't foresee a return to normality in the near future. I grasped the ring tightly within my hand now, and it still felt as warm as if that poor dead old, or young, woman had just removed it. I took one last look over my shoulder to where the body had lain, the life bleeding out of it, and then turned back with a shudder and continued to walk unsteadily down the hill one foot in front of the other.

Chapter Four

The walk home was going to be a long and lonely journey. It was a distance of maybe two or three miles but the conditions underfoot were becoming treacherous. The snow alternated now between light and almost unnoticeable wisps that melted as soon as they hit the skin and heavy prolonged blasts that pinged off of my face and after five minutes I felt as if I was a boxer in a ring taking a beating. Despite the falling snow the temperature had continued to drop and I pulled the sleeves of my shirt down to cover my hands as much as possible and tugged my collar up as far as possible to protect the back of my neck.

The pavement was icy along some of the more untrammelled side streets and, never having possessed the greatest balance or grace, I often felt my feet slide from under me as I placed them down onto the pavement. I took long striding steps thinking that this might help but I continued to slip and slide and so I then resorted to taking tiny steps and walking in a shuffling gait almost as if on skis. This seemed to produce more successful results but I was too conscious of the impression that I would make upon the few people who could see me, whether from behind the curtains of their invitingly cosy homes, or the people who were brave enough to be outside. They would have seen me walking, in effect half waddling and half sliding, along with shoulders hunched and face red with a hole in the knee of my trousers and eyes downcast.

For the first time that day, and for many days before that, I began to feel self conscious and as it would have taken me twice as long as normal to shuffle home in this cautious fashion I stepped off of the pavement and walked along the road instead. The roads had been gritted during the previous night and this, coupled with the contribution made by the few cars that had passed through on this day, meant that the snow and ice had not had a chance to settle to the extent that it had on the sidewalks. When I did hear cars approaching I stepped as quickly as possible back onto the slush sprayed pavement and every time I saw a vehicle pass I thought of that poor woman who had not been able to get away from the car in time, who in reality would have found it impossible to escape the death that had hurtled towards with a wicked and unavoidable speed.

I tried to keep my mind clear and vacuous as I walked along and I felt glad that the wind blew icy snow and hail my way as the numbing pain that I began to feel in my face and especially on my nose, ears, fingers and feet somehow kept away the painful memories that were entrapped within my head. At first I managed to forget about the girl on the bus ringing the bell in vain, and I forgot about my dreams of Lamara and my life with her that had started so promisingly and ended so wastefully. I forgot about the leather gloved hand that had gripped my throat and the dog that had snarled at me with a murderous intent. I forgot about the woman who had lain crushed beneath the car at the side of the railway station bridge and how her eyes and fingers had been motioning to me as the dark and foul blood seeped slowly from her; her life dripping away surrounded by onlookers in night clothes.

I could forget these for a few steps, for a few minutes even, as one cold and uncertain foot followed another. I tried to sing repetitive songs, nursery rhymes that I had learnt as a child, over and over in my head so that nothing else could take their place. When this stopped working I instead began to count how many cars of different colours I had passed so that after I while I was repeating in my head the phrase 'twelve blue, seventeen silver, nine black, two yellow, eight green, three white, two purple, nineteen red' like a mantra.

Every red car that I passed made me wince, and every Mercedes Benz car that I passed, although of course I saw nothing as extravagant as the AMG sports car that I was trying to forget, brought back flashes of recollections. Eventually the struggle became too much and the memories of the previous few hours came flooding back and began merging one with another inside my head as if they were all inextricably linked in a way that I could not as yet understand.

Resigned to the inevitable, and tired from the struggle that had been raging within my own consciousness, I gave in to these thoughts and instead tried to make some kind of sense of the events. Who was that woman under the car? Like a doubting Thomas, I always preferred to believe the evidence of my own eyes and I knew that I had seen a young woman lying beneath the car hideously twisted and contorted though she was. I could not believe that she could have been anything older than thirty years of age: I had returned the stare from her bulging and dying eyes and they were a young woman's eyes that were to be cruelly closed too soon. And yet the receptionist at the hospital had insisted that it was an old woman who had died in the car crash? I imagined that it might be possible, if not probable, that the winter conditions had claimed two lives that morning in similar circumstances but the description of the old woman's clothing that the receptionist had given seemed to match the dull brown fragment that I had seen. I began to wonder if the bodies could have been switched? This raised more questions than it answered and I didn't see how it could have been done without the knowledge of the police and ambulance services that would have been in attendance. The more I thought about it, the more troubled I became and I realised that the one inescapable fact was that a woman was now dead. Just one more body for the undertaker but a thousand tears for the family, friends, and lovers left behind: years of sorrow to come for the hearts that could never forget this life that had been extinguished like a match thrown to the floor.

As I continued my journey the snow gradually stopped and I returned to walking on the pavements. The landscape was now beautifully and uniformly white and I would normally have been moved by nature's beauty hiding the ugliness that man had created but as the wind also had dropped something else had grabbed my attention. As noted earlier I had, as a result of my heightened senses and my dishevelled appearance, become increasingly self conscious during my walk. At one point a group of men asked me for help to push their car which had failed to start and in which a young woman and child huddled in the back: I had hurried guiltily past without saying a word or raising my eyes.

Now though I began to sense the creeping and unmistakeable feeling that I was being followed. I walked as quietly and deliberately as I could so that I could hear if steps were echoing behind mine and from time to time I did hear tiny and muffled steps as though these feet two were being placed upon the floor in a gentle and surreptitious manner. I began to look glancingly over my shoulder, first left and then right, after every few paces and occasionally felt that I saw somebody quite some distance away duck behind a tree or a bench or a car. I never got a clear view of anybody but I could see a blur of activity out of the corner of my vision that reinforced my sense of being pursued: after all that had occurred to me on that morning it didn't surprise as much as it would have done twenty four hours previously.

After a few more steps I knelt down, on the leg that still had its trouser intact, and first untied and then retied my shoe lace. As I did this I looked up at the wing mirror of the car that was parked directly to the side of me and saw a man, of indeterminate age, walk a few paces and then stop before flattening himself against a shuttered shop front. Although he was quite a distance away I could make out that he wore heavy looking boots and dirty jeans with a white t-shirt topped by a luminous green sleeveless jacket. It was a ridiculous combination to be wearing on such a cold day and even less suitable for a man who was trying to remain inconspicuous whilst following somebody. Nevertheless when I rose to my feet I began to walk onwards with increasing pace.

I again began to look over my shoulders but whilst I never received a clear view of the man behind me I doubted not that he still followed and watched from a distance. As I turned my head back from its over the shoulder view I felt an impact and rocked backwards as I realised that I had walked directly into another man. I apologised immediately and as I looked at the person that I had struck I saw that he had a pitiful look in his eyes, that had been well practised, and he held his hands out before him in a cupping motion.

"Can you help me sir, please say you can help me. I'm desperate you see, proper desperate I am. Don't judge me, I haven't been good but I have changed. Look at this, look at this." He fished a roughly folded and well thumbed piece of paper from the inside pocket of his jacket which was decked out in combat fatigue.

"I know what this is, I've seen it before." It was the truth as the man that stood before me was a familiar sight in the centre of Sheffield, even though I'd never seen him stray so far from the city centre. He was a man of around thirty years of age with a rough and unshaven appearance. He had dirt under his broken fingernails and the sides of his trainers had become unstitched and gaping. On top of his shaven head he wore a black woolly cap that was pulled down over his ears. He looked, all things taken into account, as if he was a man who had reached the bottom of the barrel but I had little doubt that his image was as carefully cultivated as a businessman who shines his shoes for ten minutes and spends another ten ironing the perfect crease into his trousers. Despite my protestations he continued to wave his ragged piece of paper under my nose.

"Look at this, sir, read it but don't judge me. I'm not too proud to say that I could do with your help."

"I've heard it before, my friend, I've seen you before. The games up. You're not going to stop, are you? Go on then, go on – let's hear your story again." The man was relentless in the pursuit of his chosen profession and I knew that whatever I said would be but a waste of my breath as he wouldn't register a word from me until he had finished his well rehearsed pitch. I was growing anxious however, as I still felt that the man in the luminous vest could be close by and I had no desire to have another encounter similar to the one that had left me unconscious near the scout hut. I continued to walk down the street, although the glances over my shoulders now revealed nothing, but as I walked the companion who literally hugged my right shoulder continued with his speech in a whining and pleading voice designed to move a mans' heart with pity and more importantly designed to move a mans' notes and coins out of his wallet.

"Did you see the letter sir? Did you read it? Then you are a quick reader, sir, and I commend you for it. That's what befits a man of your status. I was never any god at reading, you can probably tell that because it shows on a mans' face, and that is what got me into the predicament that I now finds myself in. I was never no good at this schooling, oh no not me. Poor Tommy didn't pay attention in lessons – I only started doing proper reading when they put me inside. Yes – in the nick! I can see that you are looking at me now, is it with disgust or compassion?"

It was neither of course as I was too busy looking over my shoulder to cast the slightest glance in his direction, but he continued his speech apace.

"Yes I did wrong, yes I did, but I have paid my dues to society sir. I am a reformed man! But it's so hard inside, in the nick, there are bullies in there – bad people that prey on the genuine, honest people like you and me. I can't go back inside, if I did it would be hard for me to stay honest, to stay clean. They will beat me up, they will – they all talk about me. Some of them say that I'm a grass – me, poor Tommy, a grass! So I am out and I am keeping my nose clean, that is what I am doing! But now I've got a problem."

"I know, but go on tell me about it again if you must."

"I have to be at my bail hostel by seven o'clock tonight. If I don't make the hostel by seven o'clock I will be reported and they will put a warrant out for my arrest – it will be straight back inside for poor old Tommy," at this the crocodile tears began to drip from his hollow eyes with the precise timing of a Broadway veteran, "But the hostel is in Derbyshire – I need to get to Sheffield and then get another train from there. And do you know what has happened?", I knew what he would say had happened and he patted his jacket's pockets for emphasis, "I have lost my money – lost all of my money. It's this old jacket, you see Sir, it's got holes in the pockets – great big holes that let the money slide through."

"Well I'd better not give you any then in case that slides through as well."

His voice now took on a higher pitch as he took his pleading to an ever more advanced and pathetic level: "Help me sir, help me and I will say a prayer for you and Jesus and all of his angels up there in heaven will surely bless you – he likes those that help poor unfortunates like me who are struggling to keep on the old straight and narrow. All I need is ten pounds for my tickets."

Ten pounds? The going rate seemed to have gone up as to my recollection he normally asked for five but even a beggar has to make allowances for inflation. Tommy talked quickly, without pause for breath, but still I sensed the steps behind me even if I couldn't actually hear them.

"Look, I've got no money. Just go away will you?"

"No money? Why do you say such a thing sir, and you all dressed up like a city gent. It's wrong to lie sir."

"Well you should know all about that. Look at my trousers man, look, I've got a great big hole in the knee that's bigger than any hole in your pockets."

I had his attention momentarily and he looked down at the torn fabric in my trousers and the bloody stain that had spread around it.

"That's nothing sir, just a scratch, slip over did you? You have got to be careful. I can tell you are in a bad mood though, but just think on me! If I don't get back to that bail hostel, and it's all genuine you have seen the letter, then they will lock me up. When you are warm and tucked up in bed with your wife tonight, and I don't mean to be personal there, think

of me thrown back into a freezing cell – and when I have done nothing
wrong too – my only crime being to have lost my fare. Think on!"
He was tugging at my elbow again now so that I had to shake him off.
"Look, as I tried to tell you – I have heard all of this before."
"Have you?"
"Yes. More than once. Get a new story will you? I gave you a fiver last
time just to shut you up and you gave me a kiss on the cheek and then
ran off. I've got to tell you that I don't really approve of that."
Most people would have given up their pretence at this point but Tommy
was made of more resilient material. He looked across at me with a
beaming grin on his face:
"You see, sir – I knew that I had seen you somewhere before. I knew that
you were a kind man and a man that I could trust. You aint one of these
cold ones sir, those la-di-dah types who care about nothing but
themselves, you will help poor Tommy out and may God bless you for it
in triplicate sir."
It didn't seem to have occurred to Tommy that there may be a possibility
that I wasn't going to give him the money that he wanted and if he had
admitted this possibility it would only have led him to redouble his
efforts and enforce his pleas with even more self-deprecating
determination. I was reaching a crossing point in the road now and as I
knew the area well I decided that now was the time to attempt to escape
– not from the man at my side but from the steps that I was sure were
still following at a distance behind me.
I suddenly sprinted around the corner and double back on myself to
where I knew a series of garages were located. These garages were not
attached to any particular houses but were rented out, at exorbitant fees,
by the month to people who didn't have space to park in front of their
houses or who wanted to store things out of sight of their family, or their
neighbours, or the police. There were no questions asked, as long as you
could afford the monthly fee the garage could be yours.
I didn't expect any of the six garages arranged side by side to be
unlocked as that would surely defeat their object and so I turned to the
deliberately dishevelled man who had run with predictable determination
after me: he would have considered it a slight to his professionalism as a
beggar and conman if he had allowed a potential target to simply run
away from him.
"Can you pick this lock?" I said as I pointed to the first garage.
"What do you take me for, I am an honest man?" he protested without
conviction.

"Just do it, and you can have your ten pounds." As I said this I moved the handle on the garage to indicate the lock that I wanted picking and to my amazement it turned easily in my hand: the garage had been unlocked after all. I raised the handle and the door to the garage eased slowly upwards.

It was dark inside the garage but although I could make out the light switch on the wall I did not press it as I was determined to remain as inconspicuous as possible. I looked around and from floor to roof there were boxes of a uniform size and shape stacked on top of each other. One of the boxes was open and I could see that it contained bottles of perfume which were undoubtedly fake but shaped to look like Dior's latest line. I presumed that the other boxes would also contain fake perfumes and aftershaves and that there must have been a substantial value to these counterfeit goods: somebody had been careless but I didn't aim to follow their example. I motioned to Tommy to follow me inside the garage and raised a finger to my lips to indicate the need for silence. He followed me inside cautiously and with some protestation.

"I'm not like that sir, I know that I kissed you – but that was on the cheek sir, and all being friendly like. I was grateful. I have my pride you know, just because I am poor doesn't mean that I will do anything for money."

"You wouldn't be poor if you didn't spend it all on booze, cigarettes and drugs so shut up for once and listen to me."

He stood spellbound and as I talked I could see his stare shift from box to box.

"Did you notice anybody following me?"

"I didn't notice anybody."

"Didn't you? But you notice everything don't you – it's part of your job? It helps you find another poor sap who you can exploit."

"I am normally observant, if that is what you mean."

"But you saw nothing? Nobody following me?"

"Nothing and nobody, I swear it. Though why I should give this information to you for free when it can't profit me is beyond me."

"Well if you listen for a moment there may be some profit in it for you. I believe that I am being followed but I don't know why. Strange things have been happening to me today. The man that I think has been following me is wearing big boots, jeans a white T-Shirt and a fluorescent jacket. Do you recognise the description?"

"Yeah it sounds like Bob The Builder. What kind of description is that sir? It could be one of hundreds around here?"

He had a point. I thrust a ten pound note at him. "Take this and go outside, back the way that we came, and see if you can see a man that matches that description. If you do see him, come back here as quickly as possible and warn me. Then I can get away while you go and try your pitch on that guy and delay him for as long as possible. Get me?"

"You said strange things had been happening – maybe you didn't slip over eh sir? Maybe you mean strange and dangerous? Maybe you have been sleeping with this man's wife and he is out to get you? I can see it all now. Why should I help you, and risk my own neck which I have such a special attachment to, just for ten pounds?"

"That's just a start, Tommy my friend, just a start. When you get back I will give you another twenty pounds – in fact let's make it thirty. And here take this, you can give it to your woman tonight – she will think that you've bought her a present for the first time in your life." I threw a bottle that had stood on top of the open box at him and he caught it deftly.

"What is it?" he pulled a face as he sniffed at the bottle.

"It's Dior – very fashionable, make her smell almost bearable I should imagine." He looked unsure and was still hesitating in the doorway.

"Look, she can sell it down the market alright? Just get out there and look for that man in the luminous jacket; I've got no time to waste. And get back here as soon as you can or there won't be any extra money for you."

Tommy stuffed the bottle of fake perfume into his pocket, seemingly unconcerned about any holes that he had claimed to be there, and exited the garage. I moved into the dark and shadowy corner and awaited his return: I just hoped that he would be returning alone.

Time passed slowly as I waited in the dark and cold lock up, the scent of the cheap perfumes burning my nostrils and stinging the back of my throat when I breathed in. As each second ticked by the feeling of trepidation rose within me. I felt like a man stranded on a rock in the sea watching the tide rise around me. When I looked at the scratched face of my watch I could see that fifteen minutes had passed since I had sent Tommy outside to look for my pursuer. Something was wrong, and I felt that I had to get away as soon as possible.

I crept out of the garage and, so as not to arouse suspicion, I pulled down the garage door and closed it behind me. I walked slowly around the corner back onto the road that I had walked down with Tommy and at any moment I expected to see or hear the man who had walked behind us. As I looked up and down the length of the road I saw nothing: no sign was to be had of either Tommy or the man in the white T-Shirt that was so unsuited to the winter weather. The feeling of panic within me refused to go away, however, but rather it seemed to grow and I just wanted to fly from the scene to my home as soon as possible. I began to run and soon broke into a sprint. I stumbled many times along the way and often felt my legs becoming heavy and weary but the adrenalin that had coursed through me, on and off, throughout the day gave me unknown reserves of energy and after ten minutes of running blindly down the streets, children shouting taunts at me as I ran past and old women cursing me as they moved out of my path with as much swiftness as they could muster, I finally reached my house. The brown wooden door seemed more welcoming then ever and after fumbling for the key I finally managed to turn it with shaking hands. I fell through the doorway onto the carpeted floor and lay shivering as I stared up at the white plastered ceiling. The emotions of the day seemed to flood back to me and press me down with a force greater than gravity while great silent sobs rocked through my body with an uncontrollable ferocity. I kicked the door to with my right foot and lay there shaking on the floor until I felt my strength and reason begin to return.

I raised myself first onto all fours, like the dog that I had become chasing a stick that was forever pulled away from me, and then stood up leaning on the back of the battered brown settee that dominated this entrance room of my house. The day was wearing on and the light outside began to fade. Dark fingers of evening greyness began to creep through the window and I slumped onto the settee, all energy drained, and let it hold my dead weight as darkness began to follow upon darkness. At last I sat there motionless and in a complete blackness save for when cars drove past and the rays from their headlights chased across the walls from one side to another.

The temperature in the room was dropping and I began to shiver as I remained slovenly unmoving. The central heating was controlled by a thermostat located at the rear of the second bedroom but out of a sense of malaise, or sheer incompetence, I had never been moved to learn how to set the timer that controlled it and instead relied upon manually switching it on and off. At last, the piercing chill that was spreading throughout my house roused me from my lethargy. Rising to my feet, passing through two rooms, I climbed the steep staircase to the upper floor. I switched the central heating on and listened until I heard first the whoosh of the pilot flame being ignited and then the initial banging that coursed through the pipes as the heat began to spread thinly around the house.

I now switched the lights on and closed the curtains. I was still wearing my work clothes of black shoes, dark trousers and jacket, white shirt, plainly patterned purple tie and a dark grey overcoat. The bed took my weight as I lay back, still too cold to remove the least item of clothing but considerably more dishevelled than I had been when I had left the house that morning: then my mind had been purposefully empty but now it seemed as if it was full to bursting point and that the thoughts that were crowding in upon each other were all trying to escape through hammer blows pounding within my head.

Where had 'Poor Tommy' gone? He had a reputation, well deserved, of being the most determined and relentless of beggars that festered around the South Yorkshire streets: just about everybody knew his story, and absolutely nobody had any faith in it, and yet nothing distracted him from ploughing the same furrow day after day. It was true that I had already given him money but I had promised him more upon his return and I did not imagine that this was an offer that he would have turned down lightly?

I weighed up the options and concluded that he must have found the sight, and possibly tone, of my pursuer threatening and therefore taken flight (I had seen evidence that he could be deceptively sprightly on his feet) or that he had been working for him all along? But if this was the case then who were they both working for and why hadn't he simply brought the man in the luminous jacket back to the garage to do with me as he intended? Finally the thought reached me that maybe he was dead. Dead like so many others that had gone from my life never to be seen again. Like the woman who had died a slow crushing death beneath the car, and like – like the others that I chose not to think of.

As I contemplated that poor unknown and unheralded woman I suddenly remembered the green ring and found to my amazement that I still held it clenched tightly within my hand and that I had kept it and guarded it within that unmoveable fist through all of the afternoon's tribulations. It seemed that somehow the woman wanted me to have this ring and although I had no real way of knowing that it had even belonged to her I remembered the bulging eyes and the almost imperceptibly twitching fingers and I knew that she had been telling me to take the object and to keep it safe. That would be no easy matter; I no longer felt safe within my own home as it could have been only a matter of time before the person, or persons, unknown that had taken such an interest in me tracked me down and then surely they would come calling?

I began to think frantically of places that I could hide the beautiful green ring with the snake motif beneath it and nowhere came to mind. I turned out drawers and scattered clothing haphazardly around the rooms hoping that inspiration would strike. Returning downstairs I walked into the kitchen, a room that was built for function rather than form and where the fridge, the freezer, and the washing machine were hidden away behind mock wooden doors as if aiming and failing for the pretence of a Provencal scullery.

I opened the drawers of the kitchen rapidly now and closed them just as rapidly as if every second could be too late. At last I opened one of the cupboards that held various bottles of spirits that I had collected on budget holidays across the world as well as various household items that had no other obvious place to store them: such things as balls of string, needles and cloth, glue, blue tak, white spirits, a plunger. The two contrasting groups of products stood incongruously and haphazardly next to each other within the cramped confines of this cupboard but it was at this sight that inspiration finally dawned and I thought of a hiding place that nobody would find.

I pushed my way past the bottles of Greek raki, Czech absinth and Portuguese aguardente and grabbed a half empty bottle of Irish whiskey. Although it felt almost sacrilegious I walked briskly from the cupboard to the sink and removing the pale blue washing up bowl first I poured the drink down the plughole. The pungent stench of strong, stale alcohol began to fill the room and the spirit stung my eyes and made my nose run as the fumes began to circle invisibly around me. I turned the taps on at full blast until steam began to rise from the metal bowl and dissipate the overpowering whiskey smell.

I didn't stop to pause and though the irritation at the back of my throat caused me to cough involuntarily I took the now rinsed and empty bottle back towards the cupboard and placed it on top of the marbled effect work surface. I took the ring from my pocket and took one last, longing look at it. It was only now that I saw how beautiful it was, but the exquisite craftsmanship that had gone in to it seemed to hide an irredeemable sadness within its emerald like stone. The ring still felt warm as if from a heat other than mine and as I carefully wrapped the ring within a torn strip of kitchen roll I offered a silent prayer to the woman that I had left dying at the roadside earlier that day: I promised that I would keep her prized possession safe as I felt sure she was compelling me to do. After covering the ring in this rough white paper I next tore a lump of adhesive gum from the packet of blue tak. I rolled the lump swiftly between my fingers to make it warmer and more pliable and then began to stretch it out and refold it as if elongating pasta dough. Flattening and rolling the gum into a small thin oval shape I placed the paper covered ring in the centre of it and then raising up the sides I formed and sealed a blue protective parcel around its precious cargo. Having done this I placed the lump inside the neck of the empty whiskey bottle and pushed it down with the middle finger of my right hand. Finally I filled the bottle up with cold water, turning the taps off and waving away the steam that now filled the room and which had begun to spread throughout the house, and screwed the top of the bottle firmly on. Taking a length of masking tape I wrapped it around the screw cap of the bottle to ensure that it was held firmly in place.

I carried the bottle, with the ring encased within it, up the steam laden stairs, climbing them two at a time. I entered my bedroom and was surprised to find it the same as I had left it in the early hours of that morning: at least some things had not changed. I walked across the carpet, stepping over the cables on the floor that led from the plug socket to my computer, and walked to the wardrobe that stood majestic and towering in the corner of the room. This grand wardrobe was the oldest thing in the house and had been old when the house was first built a hundred years ago. Its dark wood had blackened with age and its once gleaming hinges and handles were now dull and tarnished but it made me feel as if I was home, as if I belonged, every time that I saw it and every time I opened its creaking doors I smiled and thought that somehow this wardrobe, inanimate and aged as it was, had been waiting for me to use it for more than a century before I was born: I knew that we belonged together. Even on that cruel day five years ago, after I had wrapped the whiskey bottle within an old green Ireland rugby shirt that I never wore and placed it carefully in the far recess of the large accommodating interior, I smiled as I closed the door with a creak upon its new treasure. Suddenly I felt scared and alone, I looked out from behind the edges of the curtains and scanned the road from one side to the other but could see nothing out of the ordinary. I walked with large and quick strides to the rear bedroom and did the same but again could see nothing that would ordinarily have raised my suspicions, but still I felt unsafe. I took my mobile telephone in the palm of my left hand and began to call the friends that were held within its directory: I wanted to be somewhere else tonight if only for a few hours. I tried to hide the panic in my voice

67

whilst hinting that I had remarkable things to tell them but one after another they pronounced themselves unable to come out: they were working in the morning, or it was just too cold to go out, or they were too hung over, ill or broke after the new year to go out yet. In desperation I tried to tell them about the girl on the bus, and the dog and even the car crash but none of it seemed to register with them – any sympathy that I did fleetingly receive was followed by a request to tell them about it next week when they might be ready to go out again. Despite the previous rejections I had high hopes as I called Steven, my longest standing and most reliable friend. I had left him until last to call because I was sure that if all else failed at least he could be relied upon with certainty to come for a drink: he had never been known to decline the opportunity to spend an hour or two drinking thick bodied pints of John Smith's Bitter and had the well developed iron constitution that could laugh off any hang over and rebuff the round of illnesses that swept through the streets in January.

I heard his familiar voice say hello but before I could interject I heard it continue:

"This is Steven, or rather it's not actually. No, actually its his fridge speaking, Steven is out – probably hunting women – and so if you want him to get in touch please write a message on a scrap of paper and stick it on to me, on to the fridge that is, with a magnet after the tone". This message was delivered without any obvious sense of irony or comic timing and as the tone sounded and I asked him to get in touch I felt that this was the worst possible answer machine message and that I had heard it at the worst possible time.

I was not destined to leave the house that night and yet as a new resilience spread within me the lonely sadness grew larger: if only Lamara had still been here then I wouldn't have had to face up to this alone - I wouldn't have had to face up to everything alone. It was time to get drunk and whoever may come for me, let them come.

Returning to the cupboard that had given me such inspiration earlier I removed the barely opened bottle of absinth that had been brought home from Prague: that most alluring and enchanting of cities where ancient streets filled with breathtaking architecture can lay next to gaudy neon lit avenues full of strip bars and brothels. Absinth is a very bitter and savage drink that burns first ones' mouth and then ones' memory, and it perfectly fitted the mood that I now sank into.

I had learnt how to drink it from hollow cheeked Prague residents in the run down bars of Kavalirka, an area that had stood still from its

downtrodden days under a severe Soviet rule. I opened the bottle of
Fruko Schulz Absinth, with the alluring picture of a Parisian style
woman in white bodice beaming out from the front of it as if in an
advanced alcoholic haze, and poured the seventy proof green liquid into
an oversized shot glass. Next I took a silver spoon and dipped and turned
it within the liquid before pouring sugar onto the spoon's recess. Taking
a cigarette lighter, which being a non smoker I kept specifically for rare
guests or for rarer absinth drinking sessions, I then set fire to the sugar
and watched as it melted away to an alcoholic treacle which was then
dripped into the absinth. Finally I stirred the liquid with the heated spoon
and at last the concoction was ready to drink and as close to palatable as
it was ever going to get.
I wanted some music that would reflect the sadness within my soul and I
placed Otis Redding's 'Otis Blue' on repeat play and sat in front of the
speakers listening to 'I've Been Loving You Too Long' and 'Ole Man
Trouble'. After a few shots of absinth the tears rolled down my cheeks as
I listened to 'I've Been Loving You Too Long' but I couldn't say
whether I was crying for Otis, for the old or young woman under the car,
or for myself.
Absinth followed upon absinth and the room began to spin. I still had
enough wit about me to climb the stairs although the stairways now
shuddered and shook as if I was climbing a ships rigging during a
tropical storm. I stumbled but with luck and a drunkard's agility I fell
forwards and not backwards and crawled up the successive stairs on my
hands and knees. Continuing to crawl I reached the foot of my bed and
kicked off my shoes clumsily before pulling myself onto the bed. I did
not have the energy or dexterity to remove my clothing but as the
spinning of the room, which had been racing ferociously, began to abate
I found myself drifting into an uncomfortable and feverish sleep.
Dreams can comfort people and dreams can inspire people but I felt
sympathy with the tragic Dane who said: "to sleep, perchance to dream:
ay there's the rub; for in that sleep of death what dreams may come,
when we have shuffled off this mortal coil, must give us pause." The
dreams that had haunted me for over a year now returned but this time
with new ferocity and a new terror.
I was at the foot of a mountain and looking up I saw a golden light
flowing down from the peak. Birds flew above me shining like gold and
diamonds. As I looked up the peak rose further and further into the sky
and further and further away from me. Suddenly the birds flew down
towards me with their faces changed into deranged and screaming fiends

69

and their talons began to rip at my clothes and to pull at my hair. The light faded and everything became black until a reddened rain began to fall upon me and the ground sank slowly beneath my feet.

Now the dog that had faced me in reality stood before me in my dreams but at twice the size and with three heads, like Cerberus, that snarled at me and snapped inches from my face. It was then that I noticed the baby, a familiar figure from my relentless nightmares, lying in front of bushes of nettles that stood nearby and I saw that the dog growled not at me but at the child. I could see the baby boy kicking his legs in the air and I called out piteously: "Lamara, Lamara, it's our baby – look it's our baby." At this point I often woke up with my body bathed in sweat and my face fresh with tears but tonight the visions continued.

Next Lamara returned before my eyes, but not the fresh faced and zestful girl that I had first met at the bingo hall but a sunken faced woman with tired and broken hair and red blotches on her neck. As she spoke I could see that her mouth was filled with blood.

"Look who I've got with me, John, just look who is with me" she said and I looked at her as if in a trance. Walking up to Lamara and now stood at the side of her was a young woman, around twenty years old, with long brown hair and an almost boyishly slim body. She was naked and her hip and collar bones jutted out at angles from her opaque skin. Stood next to the battered remnants of Lamara she looked impossibly beautiful and as I gazed into her eyes, surrounded by blue eye shadow, I recognised with a start that it was the girl that I had seen on the bus and I thought that I could hear Lamara laughing mockingly. The girl held my gaze and again I felt that I was becoming lost within her stare until she raised her hand to my face and I saw that the only thing that she was wearing was a ring on her finger: it was gold with a green stone that had a banded snake underneath it.

I woke instantly as if from an electric shock and leaped up from the bed, still clothed but suddenly sober. I pulled my mobile from my pocket where it had remained and saw that it was just after eight o'clock on the morning of the third of January. My eyes were wide open and I panted, my pulse racing rapidly. I imagined that I felt a force, almost like a trace of heat, flash before me and a dark streak passed momentarily over my eyes and covered my vision. I then heard a creaking noise and saw that the doors of the large wardrobe were swinging in the corner as if of their own volition before coming to a halt.

I walked over to the wardrobe knowing that I was awake but the horror of my dream had dulled any sense of caution that I would normally have exercised.

Opening the curtains to let in what little light there was from the winter morning and from the thawing snow that still held up in patches on the streets outside I could see that the whiskey bottle now lay smashed upon its side atop the green and sodden rugby shirt. The bottle was empty.

My telephone rang and I pressed the green answer button automatically without looking at it. A familiar voice rang out:

"John, it's Steven, are you alright?"

"Yeah, I'm fine, I'm fine." I didn't know what I was saying; I just kept staring at the empty bottle.

"Well you don't sound fine. And our mates keep telling me that you were phoning them last night saying that you had seen, or been in, some kind of accident. Attacked by a dog or a car or something? Is that true John?"

"Yeah, yeah. I suppose."

"Well why didn't you pin that one on my fridge? Look we need to talk, I've got some news that I think will shock you and it can't wait. I want to see you outside the Red Fountain at one, can you make it or are you working today?"

"Not working today, no. I'll be there." He was my best friend but I just wanted to get him off of that phone as quickly as possible.

"John, what is that noise? It sounds like someone is trying to knock your front door down? What's going on?"

"Whatever. See you at one" I replied and hung up. I had been oblivious to the noise but now I could hear the heavy thudding that was coming from the front of my house. I stepped over to the opened curtains and looked down. There was a police car outside and two policemen were trying to break down my door.

Chapter Five

I looked down and saw two men, in police uniform, standing outside of my front door. A tall and burly man was thudding into the door with his left shoulder whilst a smaller man, who seemed to be giving the instructions, stood behind him and occasionally stepped forward to direct ineffectual kicks at the door.

I opened the window and the icy morning air hit me in the face and made me reel away and cough uncontrollably whilst my eyes filled with water. When I regained my composure I turned back to the window and saw that both men were now looking up at me.

"Open up" the smaller man shouted with unnecessary force and his hands were instructing his colleague to continue his shoulder charges. "Hang on, hang on. I'm going to open up" I shouted back before adding "wait there" as if there was a chance that they might drive away at any moment.

I walked slowly across the bedroom floor and into the bathroom. My body ached and every movement of my head sent a small jolt of pain racing through me. I could still hear the pounding but I was unsure if it was coming from outside of my house or inside my head. Let them break the door down, I thought, but I can't go any faster than I already am. I was still thinking with the absinth rather than my brain.

I was still wearing the suit that I had slept in and I removed its jacket and threw it roughly to the floor as I walked towards the bath. I turned the cold water tap which was located in central position on my large round, white bath tub. I placed my fingers under the water with some trepidation and then splashed the water onto my face. Realising that this wasn't going to bring me back to my senses I placed my head fully underneath the cascade of water pouring at full force from the tap. If the water had been any colder then it would have been coming out in ice cubes and when the first jet hit me stars flashed before my eyes and my breath was ripped from me. It felt like I was going to be sick but I kept my head there for five seconds and then ten seconds before pulling it back sharply, which again sent shooting pains racing along my spine, and closing the tap down.

My hands grabbed a large purple bath towel which had sat drying atop a radiator from the previous morning and I rubbed my face and hair vigorously with it but the water had numbed my skin completely and I felt nothing. My thin white shirt had become transparent from the water and looking across at the floor I saw that water had sprayed off of my face and soaked the top half of the jacket that I had left lying in a bundle on the bathroom floor. I dried it with the towel and as I climbed back into it I was struck by how very different this morning had started to the morning of the previous day and I wondered if I would ever experience a normal morning again.

Looking into the oval mirror I was shocked by what I saw, it was as if I had aged five years overnight. My eyes were bloodshot and sunken and my clothes were crumpled and wet, my trousers were ripped with mud at the bottom of their legs and congealed blood stains near the knee. I looked like a vagrant rather than the low level businessman that I had looked like twenty fours hour earlier.

I walked down the stairs clinging on to the white painted banister as I went to ward off the nausea that accompanied each step. As I got closer to the front door the questions began to grow in my head and I could feel nervous anticipation spreading and fizzing throughout me. I kept telling myself that whatever they wanted all I had to do was to tell the truth, it hadn't occurred to me that some people just aren't after the truth.

I reached the door and as I turned the small silver key and removed the rusting chain that provided extra security the smaller officer was still shouting at me to open up. I didn't know how I was going to explain this one to my neighbours but I guessed that maybe they wouldn't be too surprised: I spoke to them rarely and preferred to keep myself to myself, a trait that arouses suspicions in our increasingly inquisitive society. Having opened the door I gestured the police officers in with a sweep of my hand but before I could speak they had both pushed into the house and the larger man had grabbed hold of me by the shoulders, both of his hands gripping me near my neck and making it impossible for me to resist, and marched me backwards at pace into my living room where I was thrown down onto the armchair that sits facing out of the window. I could feel the power that was contained within his large hands and made a mental note not to upset him in any way.

The two men stood over me and to either side of me now like vultures perched above their prey and waiting for it to expire on the desert floor so that they can swoop down and finish it off. They made no attempt to speak as yet but instead their eyes were sweeping the room as if desperately searching for something. I took the opportunity to look at them more closely and it seemed that there was something not quite right about their appearance although as yet I had not discovered what it was. I first looked at the tall man who had propelled me with such ease to the chair. He was tall, being well in excess of six feet, and seemed almost as broad as he was high. There didn't seem to be an ounce of fat on him and it would have been easy to imagine him in the ring as a heavyweight boxer if the police force had not called him. He had a deep tan and large dark eyes framed with long eyelashes. Despite his gigantic appearance and intimidating physical presence there was an almost feminine quality to his face.

The other man exuded an air of menace as his head moved from side to side in short staccato movements that seemed to take in everything at a glance. I guessed that he was around five feet eight tall but he looked shorter than this when stood by the side of his towering colleague. He was stocky and had a bull like neck and a small faded tattoo of a swallow was visible at the end of his white shirt sleeve. He had taken off his hat and thrown it onto the settee which was arranged at a right angle to the chair that I now found myself on. His head was closely shaved but from the stubble that had grown back it seemed that, as so often, this was done out of necessity to mask an increasing baldness rather than out of choice. He had small hawk like eyes and his face seemed to twitch from time to time. A sizeable scar, around two inches long, was evident on his right cheek and there was noticeable stubble on his jaw: all in all he had an incongruously unkempt appearance behind his immaculately presented police uniform.

The two men now worked their way around the room lifting up magazines and books, bending down to look under chairs and tables and rifling through drawers. They seemed to be oblivious to my presence but the atmosphere was tense and I could almost touch the danger that hung in the air.

"What are you looking for?" I addressed myself to the shorter, more authoritative man, but I got no answer. "Why are you here?"

It was as if he had snapped out of a spell and he blinked and turned to look at me as if seeing me for the first time. "I will ask the questions here" he barked at me.

"Shouldn't you have some sort of warrant to look in my house like this?"

"We will do what we want to do, I'd advise you to keep your mouth well and truly shut or else my friend here might shut it for you." His face was red and his unscarred cheek twitched violently.

"Maybe I can help? That's all I was saying."

"Yeah, you can help alright – that's why we are here. Do you know what this is all about?"

"I haven't got a clue". I was still adhering to my decision to tell the truth.

"Haven't a clue? That's what they all say." He sat down on the arm of the chair that I was sat on and I inched further into the corner of the seat intimidated by his face that was so close to mine that I could feel the heat coming from his rancid breath. The heavyweight moved behind him and stood cracking his knuckles one at a time.

"Do you know Thomas O'Callaghan?" He spat the name at me but it held no familiarity for me. My mouth was suddenly dry and so I just shook my head in response.

"Here's a picture, do you recognise him now?" The officer reached into his pocket and pulled out a small photograph of a ragged looking man standing in a street filled with snow. I recognised him then because he looked exactly the same as he had when exiting the garage the day before.

"Poor Tommy" I said and couldn't keep the note of surprise from my voice.

"Poor Tommy, eh? What's so poor about him – why do you feel so sorry for him?"

"Well that's what he calls himself isn't it, Poor Tommy, it's just a figure of speech. He's always feeling sorry for himself."

"Is he now? Well maybe you should feel sorry for him 'cos he's dead, isn't he?"

"He's dead?" I looked up, first to the man who was sat next to me and then to the colossus who was standing behind him cracking his knuckles. Neither of their faces betrayed any emotion but they continued to stare intently at me.

"Well you should know all about that, shouldn't you Mr Halle?"

"Should I? I don't know anything about it. I didn't know he was dead until you just told me."

"I didn't tell you anything, did I Osbourne?"

"You told him nothing, Sarge." He confirmed the story in a squeaky and lisping voice that seemed to belong to another person altogether. It was easy to see why he was such a taciturn man as his air of menace seemed to evaporate when he spoke. When he closed his mouth and continued to grind his fist into the palm of his hand, the air of menace soon returned.

"What happened to him then? How did he die?"

"We don't know, we haven't even found the body yet – isn't that convenient?"

"Then maybe he isn't dead at all – maybe he's just vanished. That's what people like him do."

"I don't believe in people that vanish, Halle. But I do believe that you were with him yesterday."

"Well, yes, I bumped into him, literally, on the street. That's all."

"Well that's not what I have heard. Osbourne, start looking." At this the hulking officer started to prowl from one room to another but this time his search wasn't carried out as delicately as before. He kicked over

75

waste baskets and threw CD's and books to the floor. He went into the kitchen and I could hear cutlery being thrown to the floor, and then whole drawers being upturned and crockery smashed.

"What is he up to?" I shouted and tried to rise, but the Sergeant pushed me firmly back into the seat with a strength that belied his diminutive stature.

"Just stay there, you don't wanna make me angry. You do not. Now let me tell you what I have heard. You were seen near Hoyland yesterday with this Tommy O'Callaghan. He was seen entering a garage with you but nobody saw him come out. We have located the garage and it's full of contraband perfume and aftershave, isn't it? But of course you already know that, don't you?"

"I think I should have a solicitor here, I've done nothing wrong. Shouldn't you caution me before asking me all these questions?"

The man grabbed my face and squeezed it tightly with rough fingers until I felt the blood rushing to my mouth. He let go and jabbed at me with his finger as he said:

"Solicitor? Where do you think you are? Caution? Just shut up and listen, and let me ask the questions. Don't make me angry, because if I get angry that monster who came with me might get angry and you really don't want to see that."

This day seemed to be staring off even less auspiciously than the last one and so I just nodded as I rubbed my jaw.

"What car do you drive, Halle?"

"I don't drive. You should be able to look that up on your records."

"I have looked it up. I was just wondering why a man who doesn't drive hires out a garage at considerable expense? It was just to put all of that counterfeit perfume in wasn't it? Cheap shit that burns the skin off your face."

"I didn't know anything about the garage until I stumbled across it yesterday."

"So now you admit that you were in the garage?"

"Well yes, briefly. I was sheltering from the snow."

"Were you now? And you knew nothing about that garage or about what was in it?"

"Nothing at all."

"Well then how do you explain the fact that it's been booked out, and paid for, in your name for the last two months?"

I had no explanation, of course, and so I just sat there with a growing feeling of doom within me. My hands felt cold now and it was one of those moments when I wished that I smoked.

"What did you do with Poor Tommy?"

"I don't know anything about any of that. I want to talk to a solicitor."

"You're going to talk to nobody about this, my friend. Nobody. He wasn't in the garage when we got there but we have witnesses who say that they saw you drag something heavy out of there. And we have several witness statements saying that you have been seen regularly coming in and out of that garage, often with Tommy as an accomplice. They say that you were in a heated argument with him and then, surprise surprise, he vanishes. Do you think that you are some kind of Mafiosi, above the law? Is that it?"

I laughed a thin laugh to stop myself from crying. "Look at me, I'm not some sort of crime boss, am I?"

"Aren't you? It's always the ones that you don't suspect."

I heard a crashing noise from upstairs and knew that Osbourne was subjecting it to the same devastation that he had wreaked downstairs. There was a huge thud that seemed to reverberate around the house for seconds and made the ceiling shake beneath its epicentre. There goes the wardrobe I thought.

"Are you going to help us?"

"How?"

"Is there something that you have got for us, did you take something that doesn't belong to you yesterday?"

"What do you mean?"

"I think you know what I mean, Mr Halle. You play dumb, but I don't believe it. I'm an honest man, I don't like liars. Where is it?"

"I haven't got anything." The alarm bells were ringing so loudly within me now that I thought that the whole street should have been able to hear them. Everything suddenly seemed wrong, and I was determined to get to the bottom of it even if it meant that I would receive a beating to remember for a long time.

Osbourne had come downstairs now and the Sergeant rose to greet him. They talked in whispers in the corner of the room and it seemed obvious that whatever they were looking for had not been found. I thought about running for the door but I had nowhere to run to. With their mouths silent it was my time for questions.

"Did you find it? Whatever it was? The ring's not here, didn't you know that?"

They both looked at me as if I had suddenly grown wings and were flying above them. The Sergeant had hate in his eyes but the taller man, although registering surprise, did not seem to have any malice there. "Tell us all about it" the Sergeant hissed at me through his yellowed teeth.

"Well you should know it's not here. Didn't you come and take it in the night? Was it you who broke in?"

"Nobody has broken in here, I was watching the building all last night" lisped Osbourne before his superior, who now turned his hate filled eyes upon him, could interrupt him.

"Well let me tell you that somebody has been here and the ring has gone. So maybe you had better start believing in people or things that do just vanish. And now it's my turn to ask the questions, so just sit down." I was trying to be authoritative but as they remained standing I reeled off my questions quickly:

"Who are you – are you really from the police? If so, why haven't I been taken to the station for questioning? Why haven't I been cautioned and why haven't I been allowed to speak to a solicitor? How do you know that I had the ring and what is it anyway? What happened to the dead woman and the man in the car?" this question seemed to hit home and the short man's face started to twitch and redden and I thought that I could see beads of sweat start to develop on his forehead. Still no answers were forthcoming and so I continued my questioning:

"Who said that they had seen me and Poor Tommy in the garage? How did you know that it was me and find my address?" I realised now what had struck me as wrong about their appearance when they first entered my house: "Why aren't you wearing your epaulettes and why haven't you got your identification number on display. I don't know who you are, but I suggest that you get out of here before I call the real police." At this point the anger that had been boiling up inside of the Sergeant burst out and he shouted in a voice that rocked the ornaments on my mantelpiece:

"We are the police! And if you think that we had broken in here last night then why did you find us trying to break your door down this morning? You want to go to the station? Come on then, let's go for a ride."

He had made a good point about the break in I conceded but I had little time to think about it further as I was forced out of the house by Osbourne and bundled into the back of the police car which set off at pace. I had tried to lock the door behind me as I was pushed through it but the Sergeant had snatched the key from my hand and thrown it down the street. That was the least of my worries.

The two men in the front of the car were whispering to each other again and straining my ears to hear them I surmised that they now believed that I didn't have the ring after all but that my questioning seemed to have unnerved them.

The car now performed a U-turn in the road and began to speed in the opposite direction to where the nearest police station was. We negotiated turns at speeds that were ridiculous for the prevailing conditions and I could feel the car skid as it hit patches of ice. After passing through several side streets the car was eventually brought to a sudden halt and I found that the car had been parked at the bottom of an extended patch of woodland that formed part of the South Yorkshire forest and was known as Shortwood. The two men in the front of the car climbed out and I was soon pulled out of the back seat.

As a child I had often walked through Shortwood and spent many enjoyable hours there picking bluebells or feeding apples to horses that were tethered to trees. It had seemed a remote wilderness to me then but by this time, looking back now to that day five years ago, the woods were beginning to be developed and the trees were being chopped down to make way for business developments and offices.

"Tie him up" was the instruction given by the Sergeant to Osbourne, delivered in a gruff bark, but Osbourne seemed reluctant to follow the order and so the shorter man pushed him out of the way and opened the boot of the police car.

I have to admit that I was scared but in a strange way it was if it was all happening to somebody else: it seemed like everything was happening in slow motion or as if I was in one of those dreams where you are running through quicksand and every step seems to take longer and longer and sees your feet becoming more and more entrenched in the mire. I was surprisingly calm as I was tied up and offered no resistance instead opting to save my energy for a more opportune moment if one was ever going to come along.

Using the wing mirror of the car to look behind me, as I had the day previously when being followed by a person unknown, I was able to see the Sergeant remove materials from the boot of the car that included two thin ropes made of hemp and two large cloths, one of red and one of blue, both of which looked heavily stained. The larger Osbourne remained characteristically mute but he avoided looking at either his

Sergeant or at me and hopped from foot to foot more in nerves than from the cold morning air that surrounded us.

The Sergeant motioned to his accomplice to help him and now that they were fully engaged upon the business at hand neither of them said a word as if everything had been pre-arranged at a meeting that I had not been privy to. Osbourne pushed me forcibly against the car with a strength that knocked the air out of me and made my legs weaken so that I felt like a rag doll that was helpless to resist which in effect I was. One enormous hand held my head down firm against the roof of the car, doing nothing to help the headache that had been pounding within me all day, and the other hand forced my left arm behind my back. I could see nothing now except the metallic white roof of the police car but it must have been the Sergeant who forced my other hand behind my back and tied both hands together with a deft and practised movement. I tried to move my hands apart a little and tensed my muscles as the ropes bound them together but it was to no avail as when I tried to move them apart after the tying had been complete I found no give in the rope at all and every movement seemed to make the ropes cut into my wrists more viciously.

With my hands securely tied and what little threat I could have posed diminished they next took one of the cloths and bound it around my eyes. The pressure from the blinding cloth made my eyes water beneath it and my visibility was reduced to zero. At this point the panic within me began to grow as I realised that I was completely at the mercy of these two strangers.

Another cloth was wrapped around my mouth and then wrapped around again before being tied at the back. A voice which I recognised as the Sergeants had asked me if I had any last words but I had said nothing: I didn't want to give him the satisfaction and found some little comfort in imagining myself as one of those French aristocrats who had smiled on the way to the guillotine. As the cloth was pulled tighter I found my mouth contorted into a tightly bound grimace.

Now I could see nothing and say nothing. A kick was applied to the back of my knees and I fell to the floor banging my head on the police car's door as I fell. An excruciating pain shot through my head and dispersed itself throughout my body as I lay like a worm on the floor powerless to use my hands to raise myself up. A rope was bound around my feet in and out of my legs in a wicked lattice that held me no less tightly than the ropes that secured my wrists. I lay helpless, blind and mute on the cold and wet woodland floor waiting for the coup de grace to be delivered.

The final blow didn't come and I was pulled roughly to my feet and was then grabbed and lifted by the men, one at either end. From the angle of elevation that I was carried at I could surmise that the larger man was at the front carrying me by my shoulders and walking backwards over the frost covered twigs and stones that I knew covered the ground whilst the smaller man had hold of my feet and was struggling to keep up with the younger, stronger man ahead of him.

I could hear twigs snap underfoot and from far off the sound of traffic was caught on the winter breeze and drifted along the woodland air. I thought I heard what sounded like the bark of a dog from some distance away but my senses were confused and I couldn't tell if it came from before or behind me or from my left or right.

The Sergeant addressed me even though there was no way that I could have answered and even had I not been gagged I would have met his questions with a resilient silence. He was asking me where I had hidden the body of Tommy O'Callaghan and how I had killed him and he asked me questions about the garage that had been held in my name and the counterfeit business that everybody knew I had been running. None of the questions made sense to me and I don't believe that they made sense to him either as there was no conviction in his voice.

It seemed to me that we were climbing up hill now as the breathing of the two men was growing audibly heavier and their steps seemed to be getting slower and slower. Both men stumbled at times and the whole sensation was like being on a rollercoaster in the dark without any safety device. I didn't know where I was being taken, or what would happen to me once I reached the destination, but I sure wasn't going to the police station.

It was impossible to tell how long we had been travelling for, two of us on foot and one with his feet suspended in the air, but I estimated it to have been around ten minutes. I tried to concentrate on what I could hear, that being the only sense left available to me, but my mind was distracted by visions that kept bursting into it like fireworks at New Year. Again I thought of Lamara as she had appeared in so many dreams, of the baby and the dog that stood over it, of the woman bleeding to death under the car and now I saw her face change and it seemed that it was my face that I saw and it was myself trapped under the car with my life ebbing painfully away. Next I saw in my mind the girl on the bus, fully clothed again just as she had been when I had seen her so briefly yet so memorably. She was standing in front of a large stone edifice and it was as if her feet were bathed in flowers. She seemed to be beckoning to me and then it seemed that she was pointing to something and I was drawing ever closer to it but before I could see what it was I was thrown unceremoniously to the cold and stony ground.

I was half rolled and half dragged across the floor and was positioned with my back against a hard and uneven surface that I took to be a tree. The Sergeant, his name still unknown, was bent down towards me as I could smell his breath next to my face again.

"So you won't tell us anything, eh? Well you had better make sure that you don't tell anything to anybody. Maybe you are as stupid as you make out and maybe you're not but for your sake you had better make sure that if it is an act then you keep on acting. Get me?" He asked questions but I could neither reply nor nod my head in acknowledgement. This didn't deter him as he continued: "I am gonna be watching you, Halle. Watching you like a hawk, and if I hear that you have said anything, or find out that you are up to anything that you shouldn't be then next time I won't be so nice to you. Do you understand me, Halle?"

I understood nothing. It was hard to avoid doing anything that I shouldn't when I had no idea what it was that I should avoid. In a moment of relief though I realised that he intended not to kill me but to scare me: he had done a good job but as yet I still didn't know what I was being scared away from. I felt a hand rummage in my right hand jacket pocket and then a foot connected with my ribs. The kick was painfully received but it seemed to me that whichever man had aimed the kick at me had held his blow back rather than give me the full force of his strength.

I could hear their steps walking away into the distance now and then the footsteps stopped and the Sergeants voice shouted:

"Be careful around here, it's so easy to have an accident."

I heard a clicking noise that, from the films that I had seen, seemed to resemble the cocking of a trigger on a gun or the release of a safety catch. My heart began to race again and I was unsure whether the bullet would take me before a cardiac arrest did. Another clicking noise was heard and then once again I heard the steps recede into the distance.

I began to wriggle around in snake like fashion and made vain attempts to stand on my feet. Stones and ice covered brambles and twigs ripped at my clothes and skin as I writhed. I fell away from the tree and rolled a few feet before being brought up against another hard and cold object. I spent what seemed like hours in this most uncomfortable of positions although in reality only a few minutes had passed.

With my sense of hearing heightened by my otherwise sensory deprivation I began to hear the sounds of more footsteps approaching, but it seemed to be from three people. As the sound grew nearer and more audible I could hear a shuffling, snuffling noise as well and guessed that it was one person and a dog, maybe the same one that I had heard barking from a distance away earlier.

If I had been able to I would have shouted for all I was worth but now my sense of relief was surpassed by a fear that they would pass by without knowing I was there. The woods were relatively deserted at this time of year, before the industries that had begun to take route there had reconvened, and I didn't know when my next opportunity to be saved would come. What I did know was that I was becoming colder and colder and the ropes were beginning to dig deeper into my skin. I again tried to rise to my feet, but each attempt was becoming harder and harder and using more of my reserves of strength. I managed to raise myself up onto my knees but then fell backwards again with my bound legs flying up from beneath me.

The noise that I made as I fell attracted the attention of the walkers and I heard the dog barking and then a pair of footsteps rushing towards me as if running. A woman's voice cried out to me:

"Don't move, whatever you do don't move." It sounded like the voice of a guardian angel that had just descended from heaven and I was in no position to ignore its instruction. The dog reached me first but although I could hear its panting breath near to me it did not approach me directly but waited until its master got near.

"What's happened to you? Who has done this?" I lay still and thought how I would answer her questions and thanking God that I would be alive to consider them. The woman pulled at the ropes but was making slow progress with the knots. I next felt the cloths being removed first from my mouth, allowing me to draw in great gulps of the freezing air like a man who has been drowning, and then from my eyes. The dazzling winter sun blinded me for a few seconds and I felt the blood rushing back to my face where the circulation had been impeded by the bindings. "Hop this way if you can" she said and led me by the elbow up an incline and then over the brow with her dog following behind.

I looked behind me now to where I had been lying and a cold chill ran through my veins that had nothing to do with my exposure to the winter elements. There was a steep drop below me interrupted at rare intervals

83

by a couple of sickly looking trees and a large boulder that I had fallen against. The drop fell for around fifty feet into a foul looking expanse of water of a yellow ochre colour. I recognised this location instantly as the Devils Pool that I had been warned about so often in my childhood.

The Devils Pool was surrounded by stories that were designed to keep young and inquisitive minds and feet well away from it. It was said firstly that the devil himself would come to visit it at full moon to bathe in the water or that stray dogs were brought there to be drowned and you could hear their pathetic howls on a still night. Some children were told that drunken men had become confused by the shadows cast by the trees and out of their mind had fallen to their death in the muddy waters. It was also said that the pond was of a deceptive and unimaginable depth and that hidden within it was an unexploded bomb that had fallen into its waters during the blitz on Sheffield during the Second World War and that sixty years later it could still go off at any moment.

What was certain was that smoke rose constantly in diabolical fashion from the treacherous and muddy inclines surrounding the pond as it did from the land stretching away past the woodland beyond it. This was the result of underground fires that had started in the coal workings under Shortwood: coal workings that had long been abandoned but which still burnt with a savage ferocity decades after all the miners had gone. As I took in this terrifying vista it seemed to me that I had been placed deliberately so that one false move could have sent me plummeting to injury or death. Anger burned within me and dispelled the coldness that had crept over my skin.

I had hopped further inland onto the main path, which in reality was a roughly hewn walkway through the overgrowth eroded over the years by boots and trainers, and away from the precipice which had veered so dangerously before me unknown to my blinded eyes.

The Good Samaritan eased me gently onto a tree stump and set to work again trying to loosen the bonds, this time concentrating on the ropes that were tied in and around the lower extremities of my legs. I could only imagine what I looked like but the pictures that I had in my mind were outstripped by the gruesome reality that was facing this young woman. For all she knew I could have been a killer, like the policemen had accused me of, and I was certainly a man who found himself in a large amount of trouble yet not once did she pause for a second to consider any danger that she may have been in and nor did she stop to ask me the questions that she had such a right to ask: questions such as who was I, how had I got in that situation and what was I going to do now? These questions were to come much later but to her eternal credit at that moment she kept working her cold and delicate fingers until they were raw and blistered in an attempt to free me from the ropes.

I was embarrassed to look on this woman who it seemed had arrived so miraculously to help me and I could imagine her fighting feelings of pity and terror as she continued to push and pull at the rope. In order to avoid her gaze I looked at the dog that was stood patiently nearby, its tongue hanging out and clouds of breath tumbling from its open mouth. It was a Springer Spaniel and it had an immaculately preserved golden red coat that marked it as a dog of some pedigree. It showed no signs of impatience, not even a bark or a growl escaped its lips, but simply stood at guard awaiting his mistress's instructions.

Brief and furtive glimpses of the woman who had rescued me revealed her to be of an indeterminate age in the region of twenty to thirty, possibly more or possibly less, of diminutive stature at not much more than five feet tall and what would be called a comfortable build. She wore a padded winter coat in a dark blue colour and her blue jeans were tucked into black leather boots that came up to her knees. A woollen hat, in a dark blue colour that matched her jacket was atop her head and wisps of red hair escaped from underneath it. She had been wearing gloves at first but these had been removed and stuffed into a pocket of the padded jacket so that she could get more grip upon the twisted ropes. I saw that her hands were not only becoming raw from the cold but that the skin was beginning to rub off of her own fingers from her efforts. I wished that I could have been more help but I had to sit there, unspeaking and eyes downcast, as she worked away at the bonds beneath me like a servant attending her master.

She had tried her best, and had given more than anybody could have expected of her, but it quickly became evident that she would be unable to remove the ties by hand alone. I stood up and found that although the ropes were still intact, and the knots still in place, they had been loosened enough for me to move my legs along in a shuffling gait. I took a few small and pathetic steps but then by increasing the speed at which I shuffled my feet I began to cover the ground at a more reasonable rate. This little triumph brought an amount of confidence flowing slowly back into me like the circulation of blood that began to flow back into my feet as I turned to address the woman.

"What's your name?"

"Rosa" she replied in a voice whose accent seemed to be a strange but yet melodic mixture of Yorkshire and South East England tones. On a good day I would have probably smirked and made a comment about how a Rosa by any other name would smell as sweet, but this had been far from a good day.

"Thanks, Rosa, thank you so very much. I'm John, John Halle."

"It was a pleasure John John Halle, what else could I have done – leave you there?" It was a good point that she made but I preferred to think that she had done it out of the mercy of a helpful heart or because she had sensed some innate goodness in me rather than from practicality and necessity. "Where do you live, John John?"

I was impressed by the way that she spoke with some levity in her voice even in such an unnerving situation and I replied: "It's just John, thanks, and I live in Birdwell. It's near here."

"I know it is, I used to live around here too – although I'm in Sheffield now."

"I know, I can tell by your accent." It was a little joke, if it was a joke at all, but it was the best that I could manage and it seemed to bring a playful smile to her lips.

"With wisecracks like that I'm not surprised that you were tied up. No, sorry, I shouldn't joke about that."

"Don't you want to know what happened to me and why I was there?"

"I don't know."

"No, I don't know either."

"Well let's forget what we don't know and concentrate on what we do know. I know that we need to get you to a house – you live closer than me so let's go. Come on shuffle along as best you can, I know that it must hurt but the sooner we get you indoors the sooner we can get you cleaned up. My cars parked nearby."

"Have you always been so practical?" I asked but she had already marched on ahead and I had to shuffle quickly to keep up. "I'll have to take you for a drink one day – just to show my appreciation" I called after her as I struggled along in her wake. The timing was bad, but from my bingo days onwards I had learnt that you have to grasp every opportunity that comes your way and maybe pity can be an aphrodisiac as much as power can.

"I don't drink" she shouted back and despite everything my heart sank. "Come on Tramp, keep up" she shouted. I was thinking that that was a little insensitive until I saw the Spaniel answer her call and race to her side. So now it was two tramps and an angel struggling through the woods until, after an age of her marching on almost out of sight and then stopping until I caught her up by a painful combination of shuffling and hopping, we came to her car.

She drove a two doored Ford Fiesta, in the old style, and the dog jumped eagerly into the backseat to be followed by me clambering in ungainly fashion into the passenger seat assisted by the ever helpful Rosa.

The journey was passed in almost surreal fashion as I still felt uncomfortable looking at this woman who had so surely saved my life and our conversation skirted around the issue that we must face eventually.

She narrated a potted account of her life story, although I was to learn later how abridged it was, and told how she had grown up in a village nearby but her family had moved down to London while she was still young. Her mother and father had both died and left her alone in the world when she was in her late teens and so she had grown up incurably independent and practical. She was now in her late twenties like me but unlike me she was beginning to make real strides in her life having set up her own company specialising in design. It was early days yet, hence the Ford Fiesta rather than a TVR, but she had made projections that would see her become a financial success within two years.

My plans for the next two years had consisted of keeping my dead end job and managing to pay the rent while leaving enough for regular nights out at the pubs but the way that things had developed I had formed a new two day plan which involved doing my best to stay alive. I sympathised with her over the loss of her parents and told her that I had lost mine too: what I didn't tell her was that I had lost them to the Algarve where they had emigrated and where I occasionally joined them for rounds of golf in the Portuguese sun. Occasionally I felt the dogs tongue licking at my cheek from the seat behind and I felt glad that the pitbull terrier that I had encountered on the day before hadn't had the opportunity to develop such a taste for my blood.

We reached my house and I indicated to her where to pull up. I told her that I could cope from here on in but, as I had expected and as I had fervently hoped, she insisted in coming in with me. Tramp followed behind her, ever the good and faithful servant.

I shuffled along to the door and was wondering how to reach my key when I remembered that the Sergeant had thrown it down the street anyway. My neighbours across the road were peering out at me from behind thin net curtains and I thought that I saw them shaking their heads with bemused sadness.

"Please open the door for me, Rosa, it's not locked."

"Not locked? You don't know what could happen to you" she said in a shocked voice that betrayed no sense of irony before she pulled down the handle and forced the door open allowing us to step inside to a hellish and chaotic scene.

The house was in worse condition than I had remembered: everything had been upturned or kicked over. I tried to explain that, even though I was resolutely a bachelor, my house wasn't normally in such a distressed state but she had already walked through to the kitchen to find a knife. It wasn't a hard task as they were scattered across the kitchen floor and she returned with my largest and sharpest bread knife to saw away at the ropes that held my legs. I stopped her and advised her that it might be better to cut through the ropes on my arms first. It took around five minutes of frantic sawing before my hands were finally freed and then she rubbed them tenderly until the feeling began to return to them. I took the knife from her now and began to saw through the ropes that bound my legs. Rosa went back to the kitchen and fetched a smaller knife which she used in conjunction with mine to sever the ropes. All the while the dog sat mute and magnificent in the corner of the room.

The ropes were eventually cut through and Rosa embraced me in triumph. Tears fell down my cheeks and I would have held her in my arms for ever but eventually she pulled away and ordered me to run a bath and get changed whilst she made some attempt to tidy the rooms. When I reached the bathroom, after making slow steps up the stairs which sent shocks of pain through me at every jolt, I looked in the mirror and saw that I was in much worse shape than I imagined and it was only then that I realised how wonderful that woman must have been to have embraced the monster that I had become.

The mirror had a large crack running across its middle but I could see that my head, indeed my whole body and clothing, was covered in mud and blood was still dripping from black mud infested cuts on the side of my head and had encrusted at the side of my mouth. I stripped the wet and tattered clothing from my body and every time that I raised my legs to climb out of my ragged trousers it felt like I had been shot. My knees were still gashed from the day before and now I could see a large bruise had already begun to spread over the side of my ribcage. I looked like a man more dead than alive.

Eventually the bath was full and I had used the time whilst the water ran to stretch and massage the cramped muscles on my body. I climbed into the bath and as my cold and beaten body hit the steaming hot water I almost fainted with the pain and bit deeply into my lips to stifle my scream.

My whole body stung as the water entered cuts and abrasions that I had not known were there but I forced myself to scrape the mud off of my body with a sponge that felt like a razor blade being plunged into me over and over again. The water quickly turned a heady mixture of black and red but the heat that was spreading through my body eventually began to ease the pain that had held its power over me in such an excruciating fashion.

I climbed out of the bath and having endured the pain and come out again at the other side I began to feel more alive. I stood naked in front of the mirror secretly admiring the body which had proved to be so resilient and mopping away the gatherings of blood with cotton buds that had been soaked in antiseptic liquid. Every slight touch of the cotton bud brought a fresh wave of pain but I found that the bolder I was in pressing the bud to my face then the less shocking the pain became.

Living alone I had never had a lock fitted to the bathroom door and suddenly I saw the door open and thought that I glimpsed a figure in the cracked mirror. I automatically reached for a towel to cover myself up but before I could do this the door was closed again.

Having dried myself as carefully and delicately as I could I opened the bathroom door and peered around the side of it. There was nobody to be seen and so I walked still naked across to my bedroom. Everything in my bedroom was overturned or had been kicked around in haphazard fashion. The large wooden wardrobe lay horizontally on its side and the smashed whiskey bottle which had alarmed me so early in the day was on the floor next to it. Opening the wardrobe door I searched for clothes that looked to be less creased and entangled than the rest and pulled on a pair of jeans in stonewashed denim, as were popular at that time, and a brown short sleeved shirt with the Joe Bloggs insignia stitched into the upper corner of the breast pocket. I pulled on a pair of white Nike trainers, rubbing at my deeply marked ankles as I did so. Feeling at least superficially respectable again, with the clothing hiding the worst excesses of my battered body, I walked back to the bathroom to remove my mobile phone from my jacket pocket. The water, which was now a muddied pink colour, was still gurgling down the plughole. I pulled out my phone and placed it in the right hand pocket of my jeans but noticed that behind the phone was a piece of paper that I hadn't seen before: it held a mobile telephone number that was unknown to me and was written on a torn fragment of paper that had four letters in red spelling 'ices' emblazoned on its reverse. I tucked the paper into my pocket as well and walked back down the stairway: the tidying of the rooms could wait.

"Why, who is this? Do you know where John is?" announced Rosa as I entered the room and once again I was struck by how cheerful she was in this strangest of situations. She had unzipped her jacket and removed her woollen hat which rested upon the armchair where I had been thrown earlier that morning. Her body looked curvaceous and inviting and I saw now that she had sparkling green eyes and red hair that cascaded around her beautifully pale face. She had started to tidy the room up but the heavy work was still to be done.

"I'm sorry that I was naked when you burst in on me, not that I'm ashamed of my body or anything you understand, but I haven't got a lock on the bathroom you see."

"What are you talking about?" she countered, "I've been down here all of the time that you've been gone."

She looked at me seriously now and as the dog padded past her and, judging by the sound of its footsteps, on up the stairs her voice took a more commanding tone:

"Look lets just talk about what happened here shall we John – from the start. Maybe you should call the police? In fact, forget that – you should definitely call the police."

"Maybe it was the police that did it" I responded in a meek voice. I thought about telling her the story from the start, and in reality I wanted to so that I could have been held in those rescuing arms again, but didn't know what to tell her and all of the events rushed into my head in a mad jumble: there was the girl on the bus of course but I didn't know why that still held such significance to me, the dreams of Lamara alongside her, the young woman who had been crushed by a car and seemed to have died an old woman, the chase after the driver and the encounter in the scout hut which had left me unconscious on the floor, the walk through the snow pursued by an unknown man and my meeting with the beggar who was now missing presumed dead, the ring that people seemed to want but which had vanished in impossible fashion, my kidnap by two men who seemed to be police officers and then my rescue by the vision that now stood before me expectantly.

I took a deep breath and tried to think of a story that she might have believed but suddenly the dog that had hitherto been so well behaved started barking with manic ferocity. Tramp bolted down the stairs and reached the living room with lightening speed before rushing through it, ignoring his mistress Rosa, and standing in the hallway with his tail curled away between his legs. He was both barking and whining now and was scratching feverishly at the front door.

Rosa rushed over to her dog with concern on her face. "I've never seen Tramp like this before; I don't know what's got into him." The more Rosa tried to placate him the more frantic the dog became until she had to turn to me and say with resignation:

"Look John, I'm really sorry about this because it's been great meeting you. No that's not right at all, it's been strange meeting you. No, I didn't mean that either really. Look I can't leave it like this can I but I do have to go before my dog breaks your door down? Here's my card, I will be in touch soon and we can talk then. Take care, John, I'm worried about you" she shouted over her shoulder as she ran after her dog that had sprinted to her car and had jumped my gate on the way. She waved as she pulled away from the kerb with her dog pacing restlessly around in the back seat.

I was worried about me too but I closed the door and sat on the armchair next to the blue woollen cap that she had left behind. I hoped that she might return to collect it some day but I couldn't have blamed her for keeping as far away from my house as possible. I would have invited her across to the public house where I was still intent on meeting Steven at one o'clock but she didn't drink and I didn't think that she would understand.

I looked at the card that she had thrown to me: it seemed to have been a morning for people to give me their numbers. Above her number was the name Rosa Galloway Design Consultant and running around the edges of the small gold card was a design that reminded me momentarily of the banded snake motif that I had been seeing.

I suddenly noticed that my phone had been vibrating in my pocket and I pulled it out to find that Steven's number was calling me but he rang off before I could answer. I was placing the phone back into my pocket when I felt it ring again and looking at the screen I saw that it was the unknown 'Ices' that was ringing me. I pressed the green answer button: "Hello? Hello?" no reply came although I could hear breathing. "It's John Halle here" I said and then the line went dead.

I sat on the chair for a minute or two just staring at the blank screen and wondering whether to call the number back when a familiarly irritating beeping noise announced to me that I had received a text message. I looked at the display to find that I had received a message from the

number that I knew only as Ices and the message that had been sent to me simply read:
"Meet me in the cemetery."

Chapter Six

I looked at the text message again, still saved on my phone: "Meet me in the cemetery". The message raised more questions than it answered, but that didn't surprise me – it was just the way that my life had been going in the last twenty four hours. I longed for a return to my previous, boring, unfulfilling existence: I had been on a long, seemingly endless road to nowhere and with no obvious prospects of leaving the mundane oblivion that I existed within but at least I wasn't being chased by unknown men in luminous jackets, at least I wasn't being kidnapped by policemen intent on killing me and at least people weren't dying around me like flies.

But who can turn back the clock? I had met a beautiful caring young woman, admittedly with a dog who had taken an almost instant aversion to my house, and I had a feeling that at last I was doing something with my life that mattered. Looking back now I can see what it was all leading to, but at that moment five years ago I sat in the chair in a state of frightened ignorance staring at the screen on my mobile telephone and wondering whether to send a message back.

I didn't know who the message had come from other than that the number that had sent it was the one that I had found in my pocket on the back of a tattered piece of paper bearing the single word 'ices'. The only possible answer was that it had been placed into my pocket at some point during the previous day or that it had been placed there on that morning by one of the policemen but I couldn't imagine why they would have done that when they had left me, tied up and as good as dead, above the Devil's Pool in Shortwood?

There were two cemeteries roughly equidistant from my house: a small and ancient one at Worsborough and a much larger municipal cemetery at Hoyland. The text message that I had received indicated neither which of these locations I was being asked to attend, in reality it seemed being ordered to attend, or what time I was supposed to be there.

I decided to ring the number again, although the mysterious messenger had chosen not to speak on the last call, and my finger hovered above the recall button as conflicting emotions of fear, curiosity and anger fought within me. Eventually the curiosity within me won out and I pressed the green button decisively and held the telephone to my ear. The ringing tone began to make a trimming noise and as the ringing went on and one I transferred the telephone from my right hand into my left but still the ringing continued unanswered. I would have expected the call to have been forwarded to an answering machine by now and at least the voicemail's introductory message might have given me a clue to its owners age and sex, there was even a chance that the voice might have been familiar to me thus allaying all my concerns, but as the ringing continued for one minute and then two minutes I reluctantly pressed the red button and hung up with my questions still floating unanswered in the air.

I counted slowly to ten and then pressed the redial button again and it was just as I expected: the line was now dead. The person who remained known only as 'ices' had been listening to their phone ringing for over two minutes and had chosen deliberately not to answer it, as soon as I had hung up they had switched off their mobile phone to ensure that I couldn't contact them. The facts were that a person, or persons, unknown had invited me to an unspecified cemetery at an unspecified time and were reluctant, indeed more than reluctant they were unwilling, to talk to me and clarify the instructions. If they thought that I would head straight to one of the cemeteries for an immediate rendezvous then they were gravely mistaken: I had more concrete plans for that afternoon. I knew somehow, though, that this meeting with the mysterious 'ices' would happen sooner or later – it was to be sooner than I had expected.

Feeling the telephone in my hand reminded me that I had another call to make: one that seemed insignificant in the maelstrom that I had found myself in but I still need to put bread on the table. I telephoned my manager at work and his familiarly pompous voice droned back at me with his normal detached intonation:

"Halle? Is that you? Where have you been – you were supposed to be here yesterday?"

"Yeah, sorry about that – there was an accident, a car accident."

"You don't drive, Halle?"

"No, but I was getting a lift you see and there was lots of ice, you know and – and we hit a bridge."

"Are you okay?" His normally emotionless voice struggled to hide his suspicion at my story.

"Well yes, er well not really. I had to go to the hospital for some tests. I had concussion – that's why I couldn't call."

"Right – are you back this afternoon then?"

"Well, of course I'd love to but I'm not allowed to on doctor's orders – I've got whiplash and I've got to rest fully for a week."

"Concussion and whiplash? You have been unlucky, Halle. Well if you're off for a week or more you have to bring in a signed doctor's note. Don't forget that."

"Don't worry boss, I will bring it in with me next week. The pain in my back is pretty bad but it's made worse by thinking about how extra hard you will all be working this week in my absence." I said this with all the insincerity that I could muster, in imitation of the cynical and sneering manner that had been mastered by my manager. He was a stern faced, balding, man with no interests in life outside of the company that he lived, worked and breathed for. He had failed at University but had a first class honours degree in sucking up to his superiors and he affected an unconvincing air of superiority by calling all of the directors and senior managers by their first names and everyone else by their surnames. I owed him and the company nothing and resolved not to return until I had sorted out the chaotic situation that I had somehow become so entangled in. The demand for a doctor's note didn't worry me unduly as I knew enough would be forgers with a computer and a printer who would produce a convincing fake for me in return for the price of a pint or two or a packet of cigarettes.

Looking across at the clock which stood on the centre of the mantelpiece I saw that it was two minutes before twelve o'clock which gave me five minutes before the next Sheffield bus was due. If I caught that then I could still meet Stephen at one o'clock at The Red Fountain in the centre of the city. I rose from the chair and walked slowly to the broom cupboard that was positioned between the living room and the kitchen. My jackets and coats were contained within this cupboard among other things that had been pushed in there when they didn't seem to belong anywhere else in the house such as my set of golf clubs and a remote controlled blimp. The items were still positioned exactly as they had been when I had last opened the broom cupboards door two days previously – it seemed that the police hadn't been as thorough in their search as they would have liked but I was thankful that their general level of incompetence had also spread to their efforts to dispose of me unnoticed within the woods.

I grabbed my dark brown leather jacket with blue piping down the sleeves and a blue band across the chest. It was a retro style biker's jacket and spoke of my frustrated desire to be a motorcycle rider: whilst cars had never held any appeal to me, even more so after my abortive teenage attempts to join the car driving majority, I had always loved motorcycles and the two-wheeled lifestyle had always held a glamorous allure for me.

I picked up my weekly bus pass, which of course lasted eight days for me and for many others who had noticed that bus drivers paid no attention to what had been scratched from the passes surface, and my bank cards and placed them into the inner pocket of my jacket before walking out of the door into the weak winter sunlight.

Out of habit I turned to lock the door behind me before realising that I no longer had the key. Taking into consideration the previous twenty four hors it didn't seem that locks had been very effective anyway and so I simply pulled the door to behind me and made a mental note to get in touch with my landlady and a locksmith upon my return.

The snow had almost completely melted now but had left icy pavements and a dirty sludge had congregated at the sides of the road and would spray muddily up onto unwary pedestrians when cars drove amongst it. I walked slowly along the pavement to the bus stop and at first every step was painful and every footstep put an agonising pressure onto my ribcage. After a few steps had been taken the aching that coursed throughout my body seemed to subside a little and my muscles which had been as tight as the knots on the ropes that had bound me began to loosen up sufficiently for me to hide from the few people that I passed the fact that I had just received the beating of a lifetime.

The bus turned up, as happened less and less frequently, perfectly on time and I flashed the bus pass to the driver who looked at it for less than a second with the usual bored indifference and then climbed stiffly onto the bus. This was the X10 bus that ran directly from Barnsley to Sheffield and was an altogether different journey from my abandoned journey to work of Tuesday which would have involved the short journey to Elsecar and then a train from there to Meadowhall and finally another short bus journey from Meadowhall to my place of work. It was a large double decker bus in an all red livery and the seats were made of leather and were spotless when compared to the graffiti strewn seating that was assembled within the 265: for a bus commuter it was like the difference between travelling business class and economy.

The driver was another of the taciturn fraternity who considered that his job was simply piloting his vehicle rather than having any interaction with his passengers. He hit the accelerator pedal almost before the doors had closed and I lurched forward at the gathering momentum forcing another shot of pain to spread from the side of my body. I walked towards the back of the bus, hoping that I might be able to close my eyes and gather some much needed sleep, when I saw to my surprise that Paul was seated in his usual position on the back seat dressed in his regular business attire, waist coat, silk tie and all.

I sat down gingerly in the seat in front of him and wondered if Paul had noticed the wince of pain that had crossed my momentarily contorted face as I positioned myself into the hard leather backed seat. If he had noticed he certainly didn't mention it but then in truth I think that Paul never noticed anything unless it was female and under twenty five years of age.

I was desperate for a few precious minutes of sleep but first I wanted to know why Paul was on this midday bus to Sheffield rather than the early morning bus to Elsecar that we had shared on Tuesday. I smiled at him to attract his attention away from the book that he held to the side of his face and greeted him with a feigned attention. He put his book down as if noticing me for the first time and returned my greeting.

"It's not like you to be on this bus Paul, you usually get the early morning 265 to Elsecar like me?"

"What's that John? 265 – you mean the fox mobile? Yes, well I'm not working today. Got a days holiday so I thought that I would spend some of the day just cruising along at the back of this bus on the route to Meadowhall Shopping Centre – lots of young women will be travelling to the January sales there all dressed up in their finest - start the year as I mean to go on."

"Not working? Why are you dressed like that then?"

"It's all part of the image isn't it? You are what you wear, John, not that I'd expect you to understand that. I dress like I mean business, like I'm a success and so success attracts success: money, promotion, women they can all be yours if you dressed sharply. Well, maybe not in your case you are a bit of a lost cause. I mean, just take a look at yourself, John, you're dressed like you're the sole member of the Hell's Angels bus riding chapter. I say this as an old friend of course, no offence meant."

"None taken, old chap," I replied grim faced as I imagined grinding his offensively smug face into the back of the seat in front of him.

"That's why you haven't had a woman in so long, you just don't dress well enough. What was that last one you had, Tamara was it?"

"Lamara", I corrected him and tried to block the familiar memories from running back into my mind.

"Yeah, Tamara – what happened to her? Oh, yes, sorry about that. Sorry, I just forgot, no offence." I would have wondered why the most offensive people were always the first to protest that they meant no offence, but he continued: "Well anyway that's over a year ago now. You need to get off of the singleton's bus and onto the party bus, put yourself back on the market. Some women are completely desperate, you're bound to find someone eventually if you dress a little better."

He looked as though he had grown tired of mocking me and was planning on returning to his book but I continued the conversation and steered it into the line of enquiry that had been at the front of my mind since I had first noticed him on the bus:

"Well, there was a woman on the bus that interested me yesterday in actual fact."

Paul looked at me with interest now and a sparkle came into his eyes as we discussed his favourite subject – women.

"Was there now? Surely not that badger haired woman, she is misery on a stick my old friend. If she is that miserable now then just imagine what she would be like after going out with you for a while. No, John, it's nice to see you paying some kind of interest to the opposite sex but I think that your radar has gone a bit rusty."

"Not the 'badger one'", I spat the name out as if I found it unnecessarily cruel conveniently ignoring the fact that I had already christened her with the same name in my mind, "there was another young woman on the bus."

"Was there? Are you sure?"

"Yes, of an altogether different calibre. Long brown hair, the most piercing eyes I've ever seen – green and flashing they seemed to just eat into me. She wore a pale blue shirt and suede jacket, dark lips that drew you into them."

"Well, she certainly seems to have made an impression on you."

"Yes she has, Paul, she really has. To tell the truth, I don't know why but I've not been able to stop thinking about her since that moment." It was a truth that I had not even admitted to myself and now I found myself pouring it out to a man who I held in little affection.

"I'm sorry but I really didn't notice her at all – and I notice all the girls. Where was she sat?"

"Around the middle of the bus and on the left hand side as we look down it from the back, probably around seven rows back."

"On that bus yesterday morning – the ramshackle old thing that they foist upon us every day? Those seats are broken in the middle of the bus, nobody can sit there! I think you've dreamed her up my friend, it's about time you got out there and found yourself a real woman. I think the lack of sex is driving you mad."

I thought of this sad specimen dressed like a business man and spending the day going backwards and forwards on the same bus hoping to spend the day looking unnoticed at women who had dressed in their finery for a shopping spree. If he was lucky maybe he could listen to them tell their girlfriends about the purchases that they hoped to make at La Senza. One of us may be going mad, but I was still confident that it wasn't me. I had seen the girl on the bus as clearly as I saw Paul now, but I must have miscalculated where she was seated. It had been unlike Paul not to have noticed her but I was glad that she had escaped his predatory eyes.

I was suddenly tired of listening to Paul and his delusional tales of the world that he imagined he lived in where he was always just one step away from a huge bonus or a night out with a top model. I closed my eyes and rested my body sideways along the seat. I tried to sleep but each jolt of the bus along the uneven roads sent the familiar shots of pain across me and stopped any hope that I harboured of spending a restful half hour on my way into the city. I kept my eyes firmly closed however to discourage any thoughts that Paul may have had about restarting his conversation with me.

I thought again about the brown haired woman in the pastel blue shirt with the sharp collarbone poking out from under it. In my mind she seemed unhappy that I was travelling on a different bus, and on a route that headed away from where I had seen her. I made a silent promise to make it up to her and screwed my eyes closed tighter now in a vain continuation of my attempt to sleep.

Familiar thoughts began to run through my head as they had done over the past day and a half on so many occasions. I tried to hold them at bay but eventually they began to wash over me. I was glad when the bus finally shuddered to a halt and the engine fell silent. I opened one eye cautiously and saw the bus emptying and Paul leading the other passengers off of the bus. As I sat up in the seat, with a welcoming stretch of my arms and a stifled yawn, and then stood and walked off of the bus at the back of the queue of departing travellers I saw him head to the sandwich shop to buy refreshments before embarking again upon his return journey. I wondered what he listed as being his hobby upon his curriculum vitae?

My limbs were beginning to ache again now, the jolting and shuddering ride had irritated my bruised frame and as I walked I put each foot on the ground with tender care as if I walked with a limp. I saw the back of Paul as he stood at the sandwich and pasty concession and I hurried past him with as much speed as I could raise in my delicate position.

The automatic doors of the Sheffield transport interchange swished open as I walked through them. Outside of the doors was a man selling the Big Issue magazine with a mournful eyed dog at his side but I walked past him with the familiar feeling of guilt that I had failed to support him in his laudable enterprise.

I continued now to walk up the steep hill that led from the central bus and railway stations to the main consumer areas of Fargate and High Street. I passed the super loo, which the benefit of hindsight showed to have been ironically named, where it was initially planned that passing shoppers or commuters with disposable incomes could pay a pound to spend a few minutes in luxurious contemplation. Now the mechanically operated sliding doors were broken and perpetually open to the elements, the sides were daubed with graffiti and worse and specially designed strip lighting with an ultra violet hue had been installed in the roof of the toilet thereby ensuring that passing junkies would be unable to locate their veins under the lighting and use the super loo as a shooting house. As always it seemed to me that this pathetic looking receptacle was a perfect example, in minutiae, of what happens when a planner's ambition exceeds the requirements and desires of a cities populace.

I continued to walk up the increasingly steep hill and pushed my hands deeper into the pockets of my tightly fitting jacket. Only now did it become apparent that I had dressed lightly for the winter's day and the creeping coldness began to spread over my body again causing my teeth to chatter involuntarily within my mouth.

Why, I wondered, had I travelled into Sheffield when I could easily have postponed or cancelled my meeting with Steven with a phone call that would have lasted just a few seconds and left no hard feelings on either side? The answer was that, despite all of the incredible and terrifying things that I had witnessed in the past thirty or so hours, and which were so extraordinarily different to the life that I had been living up until that point, I longed to return to some sort of normality and the thought of seeing my closest and oldest friend promised a return, at least for a few brief moments, to the life that I had been leading, in a happy kind of oblivion, before. A return to the past where I could guarantee to get through a day with nothing more taxing than the threat of a bus not turning up or somebody fetching me a cup of coffee rather than my usual cup of tea.

The problem of how much to tell to Steven, and then of how much he could possibly be expected to believe, was at the back of my mind and for now all I concentrated on was hauling my protesting body up the steps and then underneath the subway and across Tudor Square to Fargate before finally reaching The Red Fountain which was cosily hidden away amongst the incongruously cosmopolitan Orchard Square.

I passed through the subway, which smelled more than ever of urine and stale takeaways, carefully avoiding eye contact with the busker tunelessly plucking his guitar and trying to wrap his strangulated vowels around a Neil Young song. From past experience I knew that any kind of eye contact or any movement of hand towards pocket would have been enough to stop the busker from playing – this in itself would be a good thing but would invariably be followed by pleas for money and then muttered oaths when no money was forthcoming.

I passed by the theatres that were gathered at either end of Tudor Square, the once futuristic theatre in the round of the Crucible, now more famous for drama on the snooker table than on its stage, and the renovated Victorian delight that was The Lyceum where crowds of parents were gathered for the afternoons matinee production of the pantomime with children in tow already straining at their mothers arms like foxhounds waiting to be unleashed.

I turned right now, away from the matinee crowds, and passed the Roman Catholic Cathedral whose modest exterior belied the hidden yet substantial beauty that waited within to be witnessed by the cities large Irish and Polish communities.

The post midday temperature seemed to be rising slightly but perceptibly as I entered onto Fargate, the cities main pedestrianised shopping street that whilst modest in length had attracted a large and vibrant crowd which had flocked to the January Sales being offered by the large retail chains that populated its stores.

It was as true then as it is now that a large majority of January bargain hunters congregated in the sprawling Meadowhall Shopping Centre that lay outside of the city centre and had rejuvenated Sheffield's previously derelict East end. There was however still a significant number of shoppers who shunned the chaotic melee of Meadowhall and the half hour queues that went along with its claustrophobic shopping experience for the more airy and bearable prospect of al fresco bargain hunting. These shoppers were still gathered in large enough numbers to make it hard to walk more than a few yards at a time without having to take evasive action to avoid women with double push chairs or pensioners walking in synchronised fashion two or three abreast at half a snails pace – the whole area was a haven not only for bargain hunters willing to spend an hour or two looking for last years coats with a five percent reduction but also for pick pockets. Gangs of youths congregated near the end of the street that held both a record store and a fast food outlet: the girls plastered in make up to conceal their acne and with mini skirts failing to conceal the goose bumps arrayed on their too exposed legs and the boys wearing hoods and sullen looks that had been practised in front of mirrors.

A street preacher was stalking the precinct haranguing the shoppers and warning them of the hell that awaited those who had been seduced by worldliness and the golden calf that was commercialism: her voice quivered with rage and her face twisted in scorn. Whichever Bible she was quoting from seemed to have omitted any mention of a God of love but preferred the wrathful deity whose vengeance would strike everyone down imminently. Some of the more daring youths were swearing at her or throwing litter that had over flown from the waste bins that had been neglected over the festive period, but like a modern day Ezra the mockery only spurred her on to louder and louder denunciations of modern society.

I ignored the unedifying spectacle as best I could but after the events of that morning it was hard to stop myself nodding ruefully in agreement as I heard her shout that the hour of judgement was at hand and none of us could know the moment when we could be called to our fate.

At the other end of Fargate a wooden table had been placed with a large white tablecloth draped across it. A middle aged woman with curly and unkempt hair fastened behind her head with a doubled up elastic band was holding a megaphone in her right hand while in her left she held a petition that she urged everyone to sign. I walked past with head and eyes cast down, in the studied fashion that I had also used to effect in the subway, but when I had got safely past the stall without having a pen thrust into my hand I allowed myself a quick glimpse over my shoulder to find out which protest group I had successfully evaded today.

The table was covered with pictures of badgers and dogs that were in a bloodied and pitiful state. The battle against fox hunting had almost been worn, in the publics heart at least if not yet in a parliamentary vote, and so the league against animal cruelty had now turned their attention to the underground pursuits of dog fighting and badger baiting. I had read that these sports, if they could possibly be called that, were once again gaining popularity in Yorkshire and it sickened me to think that the county of which I was otherwise proud held increasing numbers of men and women whose idea of fun was watching animals forced to kill or be killed for their vicarious entertainment. I was almost tempted to turn back and sign the petition but I decided that becoming a do-gooder was a dangerous precedent to set so early in the year and so I carried on, head down in contemplation now, into Orchard Square.

Orchard Square was rectangular in shape and had never seen an apple tree in living memory but it held a small corner of Sheffield that considered itself to be a bohemian retreat from the bustling commerce around it. As I heard the clock strike one I looked up at the Orchard clock that marked the centre of the square. Two steel forgers moved robotically out of the clock and danced in mesmerising fashion around a furnace as they beat out the time: if it was hardly on the scale of the astronomical clock so rightly prized in the original Bohemia but it was at least a touching reminder of the industrial heritage that seemed to have been readily abandoned by large swathes of the city.

Directly across from the clock was The Red Fountain, the only public house on the square and where in Summer large crowds would gather outside, with standing room only, their drinks in hand to discuss the latest band to make an impression on the cities thriving music scene or to stoke the rivalry between rival groups of football supporters – the red faction supporting Sheffield United and the blue faction supporting Sheffield Wednesday.

It was much too cold for any soul to be brave, or foolhardy enough, to stand outside and most people had either already spent their money over Christmas or were busy spending it now in the January sales and therefore the inn, whilst having a fair number of customers scattered across its large interior, was not full to bursting point as it often was at later points throughout the year.

The Red Fountain was a glass fronted public house of modern design and arranged on two levels. It had eschewed the traditional entertainment of pool tables and darts boards, still readily to be found in pubs that were further from the city centre, in favour of video jukeboxes that would play ten minutes worth of music for one pound and a Weakest Link quiz machine where a computer generated Anne Robinson would wink at the gamers as they tried and failed to answer her increasingly hard questions.

There were three fruit machines situated around the venue whose flashing lights would entice the drunk and the gullible to empty their pockets along with their minds.

I looked from left to right around the building searching for my friend Steven. I was, rarely for me and especially remarkable when considering the circumstances of the day, more or less on time but Steven had a reputation for being early so that he could look at his watch disdainfully if anyone arrived more than a few minutes beyond the allotted time.

I saw a familiar array of characters, the kind that could have been found during the daytime in any of the city centre establishments: students talking loudly and drinking sambuca and brightly coloured cocktails; lawyers and would-be city gents who had come for a liquid lunch and had removed their ties to signify that there was to be no business talk for the next hour or so; shoppers who needed a quick stiffener to help them overcome the strain that they had forced upon their credit cards; office parties where the women outdrank and out laughed the men who sat meekly in a corner discussing the weeks sporting action sotto voce.

At one of the tables sat a man with a deck of cards, his sleeves were rolled up and he was showing to everyone who would look that he had nothing concealed in his hands. I had seen him before and had been impressed by the card tricks that he pulled off so effortlessly and more impressed that he always refused to accept money or drinks for the entertainment that he dispensed so freely.

There was another man going from table to table who I had not seen before and who looked strangely out of place in The Red Fountain. His face was lined as if he had spent many years worrying or in deep meditation and much of his face was obscured by a beard in salt and pepper tones. He wore a dark green oilskin jacket atop a large grey and baggy jumper and a ragged looking pair of jeans that had stripes of varicoloured paint across them as though he had been wiping a brush among them. He held a large sketch pad across his chest and a packet of charcoal pencils of different colours. Although the man was for the moment engaged in talking to people sat around tables at the far extremity of the inn I could see from his actions and from the smiles and reactions of the people that he spoke to that he was offering to draw their portraits: everybody has to make a living somehow I reasoned but I was unsurprised to see that he was not having much success on his intended sitters that afternoon.

At the other end of the room, still on this ground floor, sat Steven at a table and as I caught his eye he raised a glass to show that he had already bought me a drink and then looked conspicuously down at his watch with a little shake of his head. I was two minutes late, three at the most, but I smiled involuntarily at his familiar action and began to feel safe again for the first time since I had boarded that fateful bus to Elsecar on the Tuesday morning.

Steven was a tall man and of thicker build than me, he had dark hair and permanently tanned skin and although he was a computer technician by trade he could easily have passed for a builder or a road layer, or at least somebody who spent most of their days labouring outdoors rather than being stuck inside doing nothing more physical than tapping key after key on a computer keyboard. He was inordinately successful with the ladies, and was often quick to remind me of this, but our friendship was an old and strong one and left no room for jealousy on my part at any success that he may have enjoyed.

I walked across to the table now with careful strides trying to conceal my injuries from him. I had staunched the blood that had flowed from my head and cleaned myself up thoroughly, at the cost of temporary agony, in the bathroom of my house and so I was confident that I could more or less conceal the extent of the injuries that I had received at the hands of Osbourne and his Sergeant. Steven had always thought of me as a dependable man who had led a resolutely quiet and boring existence since Lamara had gone so suddenly from my life at the Christmas of 1999 and I would have felt embarrassed to try to explain the remarkable chain of events that had somehow engulfed me. My aim was simply to spend a short period of time with an old friend and talk about matters of no consequence so that I could put all thoughts of the girl on the bus, Lamara, the dead woman underneath the Mercedes and the host of people who suddenly seemed to have the worst of intentions for me to the back of my mind: if I had thought that I could spend an afternoon in The Red Fountain without such things being brought back to haunt me however I was sadly mistaken.

I sat down at the table and raised the pint glass of sweet cider to my lips. The alcohol in the drink stung my mouth, which had been tied so roughly with the cloths, as I drank but each gulp seemed to breathe new life in to me and I drank quickly and greedily. I had emptied half of the pint in a matter of seconds before I finally placed the glass back on to the black wood-effect table and wiped my mouth with the back of my hand. I looked into the eyes of my friend who was sitting opposite me and saw that he had wide eyed astonishment registered on his face.

"Whoa steady down, John, steady down." He was always full of advice, well meaning and usually well received, but Steven Carter always saw the world in terms of black and white where something was either right or it was wrong, and where if something was wrong then he was the man to sort it out. My life had increasingly begun to take on various shades of grey.

"Sorry, mate, it's been a rough day."

"Yeah? Heard you had a rough night as well – what were all those telephone calls about last night? People have been telling me about them – they were worried about you, John. I wasn't of course – I know you better. Nothing happens to John, I tell them, well not since Lamara anyway."

"Well I had a bad day yesterday. There was an accident yesterday, did you hear about it?"

"That one down near the train station? I heard something about it – wasn't it an old woman who stepped out in front of a car?"

"That's not how I remember it, mate. Well, I don't know – maybe I'm wrong about it all." I had tried sticking firmly to the truth earlier that day with disastrous consequences so now I had decided to embark upon the path of least resistance and just go with the flow of the conversation, I had somehow found myself in more trouble than I could handle and I was going to do all that I possibly could to ensure that my friends didn't get dragged into it as well, "I was there anyway, I saw her life draining away. It shook me up."

"Well that's understandable, so that's what you wanted to talk about is it?"

I thought for a few seconds before answering and as each second passed I could see an anxious expression spreading across Steven's face as if he could feel the pain and the turmoil radiating out from within me. Eventually I chose again to follow the path of least resistance: "Yeah, that was it, that's all. A bit silly really I suppose. A grown man like me. Anyway, I drank a shed load of absinth and that seems to have done the trick."

"Absinth? Is that the one where you drink it with salt?"

"That's tequila – you melt sugar into absinth."

"Sugar? Shit, you should stick with the cider mate, you can't go wrong with that. Stick to what you're good at."

They were wise words from Steven, as always, but the problem was that I no longer knew what I was good at. I had a vague feeling that my life had taken a strange turning and there was no way back. Thinking was as painful as the jolting bus ride had been for me and so I just raised the pint glass in answer and continued to drink.

Steven continued talking in his deep voice that was so resonant with the Yorkshire spirit that ran deep within him like the coal, now unmined and uncared for, that still ran in deep veins under the earth. I caught occasional words from him now and then, and nodded my head or shook my head as I thought was appropriate, and he seemed to be discussing old friends and some sort of get together. I gathered that everything seemed to revolve around our old school friend Richard Clay, Little Dicky as was, but in truth I was paying little attention to his speech as my eyes were caught on the bearded portrait painter who still seemed to be plying his trade around the tables with little effect. The unnerving thing was that it felt like the man was paying even more attention to me than I was to him, and as my eyes looked up they were often met directly by his eyes before I cast my eyes down coyly like two lovers unsure of what to do next.

I felt a hand shaking my arm now. I snapped out of the trance like inertia that I had been captivated in and saw Stevens face looking with disappointment at mine.

"Have you been listening to a word that I have said?" he asked with an unusually accusatory inflexion in his voice.

"Yes. A few. Look, sorry – I'm just tired. I guess it's the cider bringing the absinth hit back into my system. I'll focus don't worry. Just carry on, no forget that – can you just sort of précis the conversation up to this point. Sorry."

I knew from experience that if I apologised enough then Steven couldn't stay angry at me for long and eventually, after a deep sigh full of reluctant resignation, he explained what he had been talking about.

He too had seen Richard Clay quite a few times recently and had been deeply shocked at his haggard and unkempt appearance. Having always been a closer friend to him than I was, he had attempted to engage Richard in conversation but it was a fruitless effort: Richard's very voice seemed to have taken on the listless quality that had gripped his body and it was all that he could do to croak out an answer.

"You know what's up with him don't you John?"

"Me? How should I know?"

"Mate, you should know the signs better than anyone. Sorry about that - I shouldn't have brought it up."

The truth was that I did know what was wrong with Richard Clay from the moment that I had seen him on yesterday's bus, but I had made a conscious decision not to admit it to myself. The truth hurt but I was a Barnsley man and the thing that I had been taught more than anything as a child is never to look weak in front of a friend, and so I choked back the emotion that had suddenly welled up within me and waved my hand at Steven as though his words had had no effect on me.

"He's an addict, John", he continued his story and was becoming more and more impassioned, "he's on that junk shit isn't he?"

I just nodded quietly lest my voice should give away the tears that were falling inside me and Steven carried on his story to explain how yesterday he had followed Richard back to his ground floor flat at Hoyland. Richard had been oblivious to everything as he shuffled along and into his house. It had been evening and a light had been lit in the front window of the apartment and Steven, who had taken shelter from the sub-zero night air under a large tree across the road, could see clearly into Richard Clay's living room.

The room was chaotic, boxes were piled everywhere and the walls looked filthy with peeling paper hanging from them. Another man was in the room with Richard, a thin dirty looking man who never remained still but walked in circles around Richard. Eventually a package was exchanged between them and two strips of foil were produced from which the two men proceeded to smoke the substance using a cigarette lighter to heat the foil from below. Steven said that he had seen enough then and had headed home cold and dejected, the saddest thing of all, in his opinion, was that Richard was so far down the road of addiction that he couldn't even take the precaution of turning the light out or closing his curtains. Maybe he didn't have any curtains left.

Something in Steven's story interested me immediately and I questioned him further:

"Could you see clearly into the flat then?"

"Oh yeah, I could see into the flat as clearly as I can see you really. Clearer than I can see that painter guy over there who keeps looking this way. I was straight across the road, and my eyesight's fine – I'm not as old as you."

He was just two months younger than me but I let it pass:

"And what did this guy look like, not Richard of course the other one?"

"Quite tall, dirty looking is the best way to describe him. He had a combat jacket on."

"Black woollen cap?"

"No, he had a shaved head. Do you know him?"

"How could I, mate, how could I? What sort of time was this?"

"Yesterday evening, it was more night really – around eight o' clock."
 The alarm bells were ringing again and it seemed that I was trapped inescapably. Steven kept on talking, with animation in his voice and his arms now, but again although I tried it was hard for me to concentrate on what he was saying.
"So are you in then?", he asked and it was hard to give the correct answer without knowing what I was in for. I hazarded a guess:
"Yes, of course I am."
"So you're in for the intervention? Great, I knew I could always rely on you."
I had guessed the wrong answer and my heart sunk. I knew all about 'interventions' where friends, relatives and concerned professionals would burst in upon an addict without warning and by persuasion, mental and physical if required, would force the addict to seek immediate treatment. I had never heard of a case where this method actually worked but it seemed that in the black and white world inhabited by Steven this was the only path open to him: to sit idly by while his old friend slowly killed himself with his addiction was not an option that Steven would ever have considered. And now, somehow and against all of my instincts, I had volunteered, or been volunteered, to be one of the concerned friends.
It was at this point that a drunken woman, who had detached herself from one of the office gatherings staggered across to our table and sat woozily between us. Steven would normally have been delighted by this situation but for once he had more weighty matters on his mind and he became more and more frustrated as the newcomer talked over the top of him and began to tell us in a loud voice how her boyfriend didn't understand her and wouldn't allow her any freedom: it became clear from her inebriated ramblings that this extended to sleeping with whomever she wanted whenever she wanted but for some unfathomable reason her boyfriend wasn't too keen on the idea.
She was a woman in her early thirties, with blonde hair that showed darkly black at the roots. She had tried to make herself look younger with large amounts of make up and by wearing short black skirt and knee high boots but the overall effect was vaguely depressing.
She offered us both cigarettes and looked offended when we declined, although Steven would normally have accepted a cigarette from a woman just to impress her and would struggle through it trying to keep his coughs down. As she put the cigarette packet back into her gold and glittery handbag her elbow caught the near empty pint glass of Steven

and knocked it onto its side emptying its contents over his lap. She righted the glass, which thankfully had not smashed, and her hand stretched eagerly to my friend's groin where she pretended to mop up the drink with a napkin that was in a cube on the table.

Steven stood up with a look of rage on his face that I had rarely seen and as he disengaged himself from the partying woman he stalked over to the door. Looking back he shouted across to me:

"Sorry about that, John, I've got to go. Things to organise. Thanks for agreeing to help, I'll be around soon to tell you all about the intervention. It's got to happen soon though – we've not got time to waste." He waved as he walked through the door and I had neither the inclination nor the energy to follow after him. The woman shrugged her shoulders at me and then slumped back into the seat, she was asleep almost before her head hit the leather.

It hadn't been much of a session with my friend Steven and rather than take my mind off of recent events, a distraction that I would have welcomed, it had increased the sense of anxiety that continued to grow within me. The woman who was now slumped to the side of me had not knocked my glass over but only the dregs of the drink were left anyway. I raised the glass and tilted my head backwards to drain every last drop and it was an easy decision to walk across to the bar and order one for the road.

The barmaid flashed a winning smile at me as I handed her a five pound note in exchange for my second cider of the day. As she handed me the change she ran her fingers across my palm and winked at me. She was small, blonde and incurably beautiful and I thought for a moment that as my luck in life was running out my luck with women seemed to be improving rapidly but then she ruined everything by saying:

"That artist bloke, the one with the beard and paint on his trousers, was asking about you earlier. He said that he had something that would interest you."

"Unless it's your telephone number then I very much doubt if he has" I ventured but the gambit failed and the barmaid simply flashed her sweet smile once again, a smile that could have melted the ice cubes stacked in boxes across the bar, and walked away to her next lucky customer. I turned round and as I walked back to my table I saw that the portrait hawker was now standing next to my table evidently awaiting my return. I thought for a moment about turning round and heading to another table on the upper floor but people had displayed a habit of finding me recently and so I gave in and returned to my seat.

I sat down without looking and immediately proceeded to drink my pint in silence as though completely unaware of the presence standing over me. He was hard to ignore and he seemed somehow bigger and broader now as if he was taking up the whole room. He was first to break the silence and when he spoke it was in a mild Geordie accent that nevertheless betrayed his north-east origins:

"I've got something for you."

"A lot of people seem to have things for me. Either that, or I have things for them." I answered him in a wearily brusque manner.

"It's a picture. That's what I do, I paint pictures. I'm very good."

"Really? Well when I was younger I used to paint model aeroplanes, and I was quite good too, but I don't go around telling everyone."

"It's a picture of your woman. I think that you'd like to see it – it's a surprising likeness."

"No, sorry. I've no money, and I'm just not interested. I'm sorry if you've already painted it but you've been wasting your time. Anyway, she's not my woman – I've only seen her once." I gestured with my thumb to the woman who had been slumped beside me and who had now roused herself from her brief sleep. She seemed to be listening intently to every word.

"Have you now?" he asked, in a voice which was compelling rather than threatening. There was a strange kindliness hidden deep within his soft voice which I found almost hypnotic.

"Just once, that's right. Well, I'm sorry but like I said, take it away."

"I want to see it. I want to see it." The woman had sprung fully to life now and seemed to be on the verge of violence if she didn't get a chance to see the picture that the man had seemingly drawn of her.

The painter gently tore the uppermost sheet from his large sketch pad and handed it to her. At first she looked inquisitive, and then confused and finally angry as she threw the portrait onto the floor.

"That's nothing like me. That's not me. That's not me!", she shrieked in a voice that could have cut glass.

I picked the page up from the floor as if unable to do otherwise, although I felt reticent to do so. I only needed to study the picture for a second and then I rose quickly to my feet bringing another sharp rush of pain to my chest and knees. I looked around, from left to right, up and down and twisted around as if I was spinning on the spot but to me it felt like the room was spinning, and wherever I looked the man who had stood before me a matter of seconds before was now nowhere to be seen. I sat back down in the chair. The drunken woman had swung her handbag over her shoulder and risen and left me without saying a word as if she had been mortally offended.

The public house was beginning to fill up now with more and more people coming noisily in who had either been triumphant or had become exhausted at the sales that raged on in the nearby shops. Still, I felt alone with the picture that was before me on the table now and which I looked at unable to tear my eyes away.

It was not the faded woman with an orange tan and died blonde hair, but rather it was a young woman with a face pale and intoxicating, her green eyes shining under delicate blue eye shadow and her brown hair falling down around her shoulders. She was stood in front of a building that looked vaguely familiar as so many buildings do and on which the word 'Elektra' could be picked out. It was a portrait of the girl that I had seen only once and on the bus and it was more than a portrait, it was incredibly lifelike in its brilliance and it mesmerised me and drew me deeper and deeper into the picture. And yet the thing that drew my attention more than anything else, and made all of the action around me seem less important and less of a reality than the charcoaled image before me, was the fourth finger of her right hand on which was pictured, with incredible clarity, a golden ring with a green stone set atop a banded snake.

Chapter Seven

I sat motionless, slumped against the back of the chair, staring wide eyed at the charcoaled picture until my eyes lost focus. Eventually, with a startled blink, I shook myself out of the trance that had overcome me and looked around the public house that I found myself in as if seeing everything for the first time. I saw the bar and the varied and ever increasing number of patrons and wondered how I had come to find myself there as if a loud noise had just wakened me from a deep sleep. It was, in truth, a loud noise that had wakened me from the trance: not from the jukebox, which as my senses returned I realised was playing an old Nirvana song, or from the crowd beginning to congregate in a jostling throng at the bar but rather it was coming from within me as if a drum was playing in my head and the pounding was getting louder and louder. I breathed deeply and purposefully and closed my eyes for a brief period before opening them again, studiously avoiding looking at the picture that still lay on the table in front of me, until the heart beat that had been thudding within me began to calm down to a more manageable level. My senses and memory had fully returned now and I looked with purpose around The Red Fountain and received stares from a number of people which seemed to convey a mixture of concern and fear. A quick glance at my watch revealed that I must have sat staring at the picture for almost ten minutes. The bar had become uncommonly busy for a midweek afternoon and many of the newcomers in the crowd were stamping their feet or wiping snow from off of their shoulders; all of the chairs and settees around the large seating area were occupied except the ones next to mine and I felt a self conscious moment of shame as I realised that my strange behaviour had scared people away from sitting near to me.

I had barely touched the pint of cider that I had bought before the painter came to talk to me and had produced the drawing that had affected me so deeply but I had an unshakeable desire to get out of The Red Fountain and away from the prying and accusatory heads that I imagined were still focussed upon me from all directions. I gulped the drink down as quickly as possible until the sudden intake of liquid, still as ice cold as when it had left the pump, made me cough with a sudden rush of air that shot up from my lungs and I sprayed some of the cider back out of my mouth which shot embarrassingly onto the front of my jacket.

I rose now and walked out of the pub leaving the remainder of the drink to be poured away like the life of the woman under the car had been poured away on the previous morning. Before walking away from the table however, I took one further glimpse at the picture, now removed from the element of surprise that had shocked me so much, and rolled it up carefully before placing the thin tube of paper that it formed into the deep inside pocket of my leather jacket.

A cold blast of air hit me as I walked out of The Red Fountain and onto Orchard Square. I zipped my jacket up and pushed my hands deep into the pockets but the temperature had dropped sharply during my short stay in the pub and I shivered underneath the thin and inadequate clothing. Snow had been falling again and had quickly settled so that already everything was covered in a thick white layer of snow and people were holding onto each other for stability as they walked cautiously across the slippery streets.

I wanted to get home and just climb into my bed, pull the duvet up around my face and sleep for at least twenty four hours. I thought that if I got a proper rest I could somehow piece together the madness which had been happening in my life and find a solution that would allow me to return to the mundane reality that I had been living in and which held such an appeal to me at that moment.

I walked back through the streets to the bus station as quickly as I dared to go on the treacherous city streets. My head was cast down to keep the snow out of my eyes and my neck was pulled in to my collar with my shoulders hunched up around it. I had an unreasonable dislike of umbrellas as I hated the way that water would drip off of the ends and onto my knees and I dislike the way that I had often had to take evasive action to avoid other peoples umbrellas as they walked along seemingly oblivious to anyone who may be in their path. As the snow began to gather icily atop my head I thought, not for the first time, that maybe it was time to invest in a good hat.

The streets were clearing quickly and the shops were emptying as people headed to bars to pass the hours until the snow stopped or made dashes for their cars hoping to beat the jams that would block the cities roads as snow brought them to a slow and grinding halt. The animal rights display had been dismantled before the snow destroyed their petition and even the preacher, who had stalked the street with such manic energy, had left now so that the few straggling shoppers still struggling through the snowy streets could continue their journey without fear of being harangued or made to face their prospect of eternal damnation.

It was a downhill journey all the way from the centre of the city to the transport interchange which made the conditions underfoot even more precarious but eventually I reached the entrance to the bus station. Two women were stood by the automatic doors looking up with arms folded at the snow that continued to fall in big flakes from the sky. As I walked past them one of them grabbed me by the arm and told me not to waste my time waiting for a bus at the station as the roads were already becoming blocked and so the bus companies would be taking all of their buses off of the road. She said this with a joyful glint in her eyes and her companion shook her head dolefully as if there was nothing that they enjoyed more than being the harbingers of bad news. They had positioned themselves by the doors so that they could pass this information on to everyone who walked by and whilst I am sure that they thought they were providing a service to the passing public it seemed to me that they had missed their calling in life and would have been more suited to earlier times being sat in the front row by the guillotine shaking their heads and knitting furiously.

Normally I would have greeted such advice with healthy suspicion and waited at the bus stop for ten or fifteen minutes to see if the buses had indeed been called back to their depot: it was a regular and predictable occurrence in Sheffield, nestling between the hills of the Pennines and the Peak District, that as soon as snow settled the buses would be called in and passengers would be left stranded and shivering but sometimes a brave driver would ignore instructions and battle gamefully on.

On that bleak January day five years ago, however, I was in no condition, mentally or physically, to waste time standing in the station waiting for a bus that may never arrive. I went to the cash machine that was placed inside the bus station temptingly close to the newsagents, the sandwich shop and the travel agents. Placing my card into the machine I tapped the four digit number onto the keypad, carefully shielding the combination from any prying eyes, and withdrew fifty pounds which I slipped into the pocket of my jeans. I walked past the posters warning commuters to beware of pickpockets and not to leave luggage unattended in case it was taken away and destroyed (I always thought it was more likely that it would be taken by the pickpockets) and made my way through the doors to the side of the interchange which led to the taxi rank.

The physical exertion of trying to keep my balance as I walked swiftly across the icy snow bound surface of the streets as well as the chill wind that was howling again and carrying fresh assaults of snow into my face had caused my bruised and battered ribs to ache anew and every breath that I drew in sent a little spasm of pain shooting through me. I was longing to feel the relative warmth and comfort of the taxi and was prepared to pay their exorbitant charges to gain this.

Four black cabs were lined up along the rank and their drivers were huddled together under the shelter of an overhanging roof. They were holding cups of coffee to keep their hands warm and one of the drivers was passing around a newspaper and discussing the day's sports headlines. The taxi rank was unusually free of passengers queuing for a ride but I noticed that a woman was walking just behind me and was evidently heading for the taxis as well and so with a smile and a wave of my hand I gestured her past me and into the taxi at the forefront of the queue. She neither spoke nor returned my smile but climbed haughtily into the back of the taxi without even looking at me. I would have been offended but I reasoned that I had only let her past because she was young and pretty so I guess that pretty much evened the score out.

I climbed into the back of the cab and noticed from a sign that was pasted onto the back of the front passenger seat that my driver for the day was Ashraf Saddiq licensed to drive hackney carriages by Sheffield

City Council. Ashraf turned around and asked me, through the grill on the plastic partition that separated the front of the vehicle from the back, where I was going – it was a question that I had been asking myself for the last two days but I put those questions to one side and asked him to take me to Birdwell. As usual when I had to take taxis from Sheffield this produced a bemused look on the drivers face and he had to phone up two of his colleagues to get the directions. Whenever a driver asks me how to get there I always say that I'm not sure: my navigational skills are non existent at the best of times and the journey was expensive enough as it is without the extra miles and diversions that might have been necessitated by following my route.

The car pulled away and began its journey that would take it out of the city through Hillsborough and onto Tankersley before finally reaching my home village. I could feel the taxi's wheels slipping from time to time on the roads surface but the driver seemed unconcerned and handled his car with unperturbed ease. The snow had wreaked its usual havoc on the roads and the traffic had become congested and in many places came to a standstill for several minutes at a time. I just slouched back into the leather seat and let the heat from the air conditioning blow over me little caring about the clock at the front of the car adding money on to my fare at an extortionate rate minute by minute.

I was in no mood for a conversation as I had talked enough in the last day and a half but the taxi driver was relentlessly chatty and sought my opinion on everything from the festive football results to the demands and restrictions that the city council were making on the taxi drivers (unfair in Ashraf's view and certain to lead to a strike by the black cab drivers sooner or later). He complained about the racism that he had to endure and told how if he picked up passengers who had given him trouble in the past, who were always too drunk to remember their previous encounter with the driver, he would drive them along their chosen route until he came to a remote spot on their journey and then press a button which would cut the taxi's engine and bring the car to an immediate stop. He would then ask the passenger to get out of the car and give it a quick push to help start it again at which point he would restart the engine and drive off leaving his passenger in a remote limbo. I praised him for his actions and he seemed to like this and saw it as a green light to try to involve me in more conversations. My answers became more and more monosyllabic until eventually he left me alone to concentrate on his driving.

I was heading in a relatively sedate and cautious fashion towards my house. An Englishman's home is his castle it is said but I felt like mine was increasingly under siege. I didn't know what to expect when I got back to my house, but the inexplicable meeting in the Sheffield pub, and the picture that had resulted from it which was still tucked carefully into the inner pocket of my jacket, seemed to confirm that I was not going to return to any sense of normality for the foreseeable future. I had somehow become entangled in a web which was growing stickier by the moment. I had taken my usual option of following the path of least resistance but a feeling was growing within me that the only way I was going to break out of the web was to track down the spider before I became another fly on its menu. There must be some logical connection between all of the events that had happened to me and around me, although it eluded me at that moment, and only by realising the connection could I hope to find a solution that would allow me to carry on my life in the boring and non-threatening way that I had been living it before that fateful Tuesday.

The taxi was nearing my home village now and as it grew closer to Barnsley and further away from Sheffield the snow was growing less fierce and the roads were noticeably clearer and more negotiable. The taxi pulled to a halt outside of the shop that stood across the road from my house. I looked at the clock and saw that it showed twenty three pounds and forty pence. I gave Ashraf twenty five pounds and told him to keep the change: it wasn't a generous tip but I wasn't paid enough to be generous. The driver remained magnanimous enough to thank me for the tip and after I climbed out of the back of his cab he waved at me cheerfully before turning the car around and heading back towards the white hills of Sheffield.

I looked across the road at my house half expecting to see a figure lurking in the shadow of the alleyway that ran to the side or to see someone moving around in my living room but everything looked calm and as normal as it could look after the battering and destruction that my home had taken that morning. I put the twenty five pounds that remained into my pocket and felt there the two numbers that I had been given that day: one on a carefully crafted business card and one on a hastily torn scrap of paper; which number, if any, would contact me first?

I looked to the left and right but the roads were quiet and so I crossed uninterrupted to my house. Once again as I reached the door I felt in my pocket for the key to open it before remembering that I no longer had a key for my own front door. I pushed the handle down and opened the door cautiously. I put my head around the door and listened for any possible movement but all I could hear was the gentle thudding of my heart and so I walked back into my cold house and closed the door firmly behind me before sliding the security chain into position.

I walked into the living room and then into the kitchen but my caution began to subside as it became apparent that everything was in the same dishevelled state that I had left it and that nobody had been into the house in my absence. I walked up the steep staircase and checked all of the upper rooms just to make sure that my instincts were correct but I was soon satisfied that I was alone in my house. There was a major clean up operation to be done - that could wait until later in the day or even later in the week if necessary but there was one item that I wanted to restore to its rightful place. The large old wardrobe was still stranded on its side and I resolved to try to push it upright again and then position it back in its rightful place in the corner of the bedroom, the position that it had occupied so imposingly since the early days of the house. I was used to lifting weights as part of my daily fitness regime but as I crouched in front of the wardrobe and placed my hands underneath the exposed edge of its frame it seemed folly to attempt to lift it; it looked enormous from this unusual side on perspective and as I flexed my arms and knees in preparation I felt sure that it would have to remain where it was until I could recruit extra muscle to help me. To my surprise, however the wardrobe lifted off of the ground with relative ease and was much lighter to lift than I had imagined: I knew that the secret to lifting large weights was to gain momentum and to keep pushing until the arms were fully extended and so I did this and then used my body weight to push the wardrobe back upright. I was surprised that I had managed the job so easily; it was as if somebody else had been pushing the wardrobe with me but I chose not to dwell on this as I rocked the wardrobe from side to side and backwards and forwards until it regained its rightful position. I looked with satisfaction on my work and saw that although the front panelling had been chipped the damage was only superficial and could easily and inexpensively be remedied.

I allowed myself a few seconds to stand happily in front of my work and then returned back down the stairs. I removed my jacket and threw it casually over the back of the settee. Having done this I rummaged into the pocket and drew the rolled up tube of paper that contained the picture of the girl that I had seen on the bus to Elsecar. The likeness was uncannily accurate, although now she was stood in front of an unspecified building rather than seated on the run down bus, and it seemed impossible that the man had drawn this picture without me describing her in any way. I imagined that maybe she was a model and that she had posed for this painter or maybe even she had been in that same pub earlier in the day and the painter had merely a copy of the painting that she had neglected to buy from him? Many solutions came into my head as I threw the portrait, now unfurled, onto the seats in front of me but I considered every possibility except the obvious one that as yet I was not ready to face.

My telephone rang again and as I looked at the display it contained the answer to my earlier question as to which of the two numbers would ring me first – it was 'ices'. I thought for a second about leaving it to ring but then I remembered that I had resolved to take a more active approach to the puzzle that I found myself engaged in and I pressed the green answer button before lifting the phone to my ear. I said nothing and again there was silence from the other end. I was about to end the call when suddenly a thick and deep voice spoke which sounded as if its owner was speaking through a cloth or was deliberately trying to hide his voice:

"You're back at last" it said and I moved across to the window to see if I could discern anybody looking in at me but the street appeared to be deserted.

"Go on", I replied trying to sound unconcerned and unsurprised.

"Why weren't you at the cemetery?"

"Where do you want me to start? I didn't know which cemetery or at what time and I don't know who you are."

"You do know who I am, you just don't realise it yet. I'm surprised at you, Halle, I thought that you were brighter than that?"

"Well, life's full of disappointments, my friend, just chalk another onto the score." There was nothing that I wanted more than to find out who this man was that was ringing me and what his purpose was but I wasn't going to let him know this without a fight.

"Well we need to talk – believe me, you need to hear what I've got to say. I will be at St Peters Cemetery, Hoyland in five minutes and you'll be there too if you know what's good for you."

"And who are you? How shall I recognise you?" I asked.

"You won't have to recognise me, just be at the cemetery in ten minutes and I will find you. And as to who I am? I'm a friend, that's all you need to know for now Halle – a friend."

I needed all the friends that I could get, even the mysterious and menacing ones, and so I had no option but to agree to the meeting:

"okay, I'll be there, but it won't be in ten minutes. It's at least a thirty or forty minutes walk up to there."

"I'm sending a car for you, it'll be there in five minutes. Oh, and don't ask the driver anything because he doesn't know anything. Five minutes – be ready." With that the line went dead.

The voice had sounded familiar and although it was heavily disguised it seemed that the callers' natural voice was on the verge of breaking through at moments of the call into a gentler and less threatening tone. I had five minutes to get ready for a journey to meet a person or people unknown but at least this time I felt that I had the promise of information dangling before me: perhaps I was finally getting somewhere. On the other hand, I reasoned, I could have been five minutes away from another trussed up ride to the Devil's Pool. Waiting around my house for the next unwelcome caller didn't seem like an option and so I was prepared to take a chance on the car and the cemetery.

I took the leather biker-style jacket that I had been wearing earlier in the day and placed it back onto its coat hook before removing a large blue parka style coat with a snorkel hood which seemed much more suited to the weather outside. The snow was not falling here as it had been in Sheffield but still as I looked out of the window I could see that a few flakes fell from the sky and floated down to the floor where they placed a thin white coating over everything that glistened in the icy evening air. It was not yet five o'clock but darkness had already descended and the street lights that reflected off of the icy streets gave a serene appearance that seemed strangely out of kilter to the world that I had been experiencing.

I thought about sending a brief text message to a friend letting them know that I was going to be at the Hoyland cemetery and to come looking for me if I didn't get back to them within an hour but I quickly dismissed this idea as to do so would only have led to the raising of questions that I was not yet ready to answer. The voice on the phone had insisted that it was a friend and I had decided to trust this man, to follow my instincts, for better or for worse.

The minutes ticked slowly by as I stared eagerly out of the window onto the road outside. The street was practically deserted and the few cars that drove past showed no sign of stopping. The fifth minute came and went and I was in the process of sending a message to 'Ices' saying that I wasn't prepared to be messed around by him any longer when a car pulled to a halt in front of my house and flashed its headlights.

I removed the security chain and walked outside feeling surprisingly calm. The car that was waiting for me was essentially a Ford Escort but it had been modified to within an inch of its life. The large exhaust spewed gases into the winter air and the windows had been blacked out at the sides and the rear. Drum and bass music was blaring out of the car at such a volume that it seemed to rock the car from side to side as it stood stationary at the side of the road. I opened the rear passenger door and climbed in to be greeted by an overpowering noise and the smell of stale cannabis smoke that was not masked by a cardboard pine tree hanging from the rear view mirror.

The driver was a small wiry man wearing navy blue tracksuit bottoms and a grey coloured fleecy top. He wore a battered old baseball cap and a frayed Barnsley Football Club scarf was wrapped around the lower half of his face so that all I could see was a pair of blue eyes that looked young and lacking in any sort of emotion.

As the car set off in the direction of Hoyland I decided to question him. Raising my voice in an attempt to make myself heard above the incessant monotone thumping that was coming out of the speakers I asked him: "Who are you? Who has sent you to collect me?"

"Look – don't ask any questions alright? I don't want any trouble. I'm just doing a favour for a friend – for somebody, alright? That's all you need to know. Just shut your mouth, sit tight and we'll get along fine."

At least I think that was what he said, it was hard to tell as his voice was muffled beneath his scarf and his voice was delivered with a curiously passionless delivery. The driver turned the music up even higher now, a feat which I would not have thought possible, to signify an abrupt end to what I could almost call our conversation. My ears were taking as large a battering as my ribs had been earlier that day but as I placed my hands over my ears I noted with content that the car was heading in the right direction for the cemetery and so I sat back in my chair and waited for the unknown ordeal that may lay ahead.

The car had been travelling at indecent speed and the accelerator seemed to be pressed in line with the breakneck pace of the music although when I glanced occasionally into the mirror the driver's eyes were always fixed firmly straight ahead as if oblivious to anything else that may have been on the road. As we approached St Peters Church the car was brought rapidly to a halt and it was all I could do to stop from crossing myself or kissing the snow lined tarmac as I stepped out of the smoke filled car. The car sped off into the darkened streets barely giving me time to close the passenger door and although the vehicle was soon out of sight I could hear the music fade into the distance for many moments afterwards.

The church stood in front of me and the large outstretched cemetery lay beyond it but as yet I could see nobody waiting for me. I passed the parish church of St Peter. It was a moderately sized Church of England chapel and looked imposingly stern and beautiful outside but I had attended a wedding there two years ago and knew that it was disappointingly plain and undecorated inside with none of the golden grandeur and aesthetic glory that was to be found in the Catholic church of St Helen further into the town. A large wooden cross was stood outside of the church and as I hurried past it loomed up like a large white spectre in the blackness that had descended over this starless evening. I came to the central iron gates for the cemetery now and they creaked and groaned upon the gravel as I pushed them open and entered the graveyard waiting at every moment for a hand on my shoulder.

I wandered in what I at first thought was a random direction along the many criss-crossing paths that ran through the necropolis all the time looking round to see if I was being watched and followed but all I saw were the eyes of cats that had grown feral and spent their days scavenging among the gravestones. The cemetery contained many hundreds of gravestones, some more than two hundred years old and with the carved writing weather worn away from the roughly hewn stones. Alongside these were modern monuments with multi coloured pebbles stretching out in front of beautifully crafted marble headstones. Some of the graves were fresh dug and had floral arrangements that were shaped to form words such as 'Dad', 'Grandad' or on sadder and smaller mounds of frost bitten earth the floral tributes said 'Son' and 'Grandson'. The saddest sights of all though were those graves that over the years had become neglected and overgrown with weeds as if time had finally condemned them to be forgotten and uncared for, those people who had once been so vibrant and a central part of so many peoples lives, who had laughed and cried and breathed and hoped like you and I, were now merely wasting space amongst the weeds of the overcrowded cemetery, even their names hidden away from prying eyes.

I had always felt at home within the cemetery and a strange sense of energy filled me as if being surrounded by so much death made me feel even more alive. When I was a child I had often taken the long walk here to spend summer afternoons amidst the stones, reading the inscriptions with more interest than I read any book and watching the white winged butterflies duelling in the skies above the headstones. In those far off and fondly remembered days every stone had seemed to sing out to me as I walked past them but now it had been a year since I had last visited and as I came to a halt with a startle before a relatively new monument the memories that I had hidden came flooding back.

It seemed inevitable that the path would lead me back to this graveside that I had so fastidiously avoided for the past twelve months. The monument was of a modest size fashioned in a black stone with golden inscribed writing. I was pleased to see that flowers had been laid there recently, probably over Christmas, although they had withered and died in the snow. I had only seen the inscription once before but I still knew the words by heart as I read:

"Here lies Miss Lamara Gallagher, beloved daughter and granddaughter, went to sleep 26th December 1999 aged 25".

I had spent a year turning my heart to a stone that was harder than the black headstone that faced me but my eyes betrayed me and a solitary tear slid down my left cheek. I felt guilty that I didn't know who had brought flowers for her, guilty that it wasn't me and guiltier still that I had spent over a year too sunk within the pit of my own mourning to visit the grave of the woman who had lived with me for over four years leading up to that final day. The overriding emotion that burned within me as I looked at the words again however was the same feeling that had been killing me from within for the last twelve months: a bitter resentment and a hidden fury that she couldn't even have lasted another week and made it into the new millennium with me, with the man who had loved her so much that he spent every night wishing he had died instead.

A sudden bustling movement grabbed my attention and I thought that I saw a gathering of cats moving towards me but as my eyes focussed in the snow highlighted darkness it seemed that they were not cats at all but a collection of youths. The sound of footsteps approaching quickly behind me seemed to catch their attention and they faded away into the background as quickly as they appeared. I turned around and saw a familiar figure standing before me.

The man was as huge as he had been that morning but he was out of his police uniform now and wearing a black rain jacket over a polo neck jumper and black jeans. Only his bulk stopped him disappearing completely against the night sky, but as he moved around it was as if a gigantic black shadow was crossing over the earth. I was surprised that the man that I had known to be ices turned out to be Osbourne, the police officer who had assisted his Sergeant in an apparent attempt on my life that morning, but with the benefit of hindsight it seemed that I had detected a lisping quality to the deep voice that he had affected during our telephone conversation. He had said that he was a friend but his actions had been far from friendly on the occasion of our last meeting and so I stood nervously before him wondering how I could outrun him if and when he chose to attack me. At least they wouldn't have far to move me afterwards I thought with my customary black humour that I used as a defence mechanism to keep my real emotions in check.

"I thought I would find you at this stone, Halle", he said in the lisping, insipid voice that he had reverted to and which seemed so incompatible with the man that it came from.

"Did you?" I managed to spit out from my increasingly dry throat.

"Yes I've read all about you in your file. It wasn't much of a file to start with but it's been added to considerably recently. Of course, hers was much larger" he explained as he pointed to Lamara's grave with an insolent finger.

"You said you were friendly – you didn't seem so friendly this morning?" I hit him with the truth from the start and my muscles were taut and ready to spring into action at any moment, although of course they were primed to run rather than to fight.

"Halle, believe it or not I am your friend and right now I'm the best one that you've got. Look, we can't stay here all night; we've got to move around so that nobody can overhear us."

Osbourne moved away with long but silent strides and I followed him after throwing one last glimpse towards the grave that I vowed to visit again as soon as I could. Once more I imagined that I saw eyes watching us from the periphery of the cemetery.

"Who would be listening to us?"

"You really don't know anything do you? Sarge thinks that you're pretending to be dumb; maybe it's better for him to think that and maybe not? There's a lot for me to tell you so just shut up and listen."

People had been telling me to shut up all day now but none of them carried the latent threat of the hulking Osbourne and so I heeded his counsel and followed him around the cemetery like a silent and obedient dog listening to his masters' whispered words.

Osbourne seemed nervous as he began his story and I reasoned that whoever it was that scared him was not somebody that I would ever want to meet:

"All is not as it seems around here, my friend, but you have somehow got mixed up in something that is way out of your league. You could, and should, have kept your mouth shut and your head down but you didn't do that and now you have brought yourself to the attention of a pretty nasty person. Bad mistake." He shook his large head mournfully and against my better instincts I asked who this man was.

"Are you really mad?" he countered, "Do you think I would tell you that? It's better that you don't know. But just let me fill you in on a few things that might make it all a little clearer for you."

"Go ahead."

"Yesterday there was a car crash, it was an accident. There were many people at the scene after the event but it seems that nobody witnessed the incident. Or maybe somebody did witness the incident, eh? It's been brought to our attention that you ran after the driver of the car for reasons unknown and tried to confront him. We have reason to believe that you later returned to the accident scene and found an object there that is of some importance to the man in question."

"Well you've hit on a few half truths there, Osbourne," I conceded, "but you're more cold than warm really."

"Half truths are safer than the full truth for you, Halle. A lot safer."

"I didn't see the car crash you know?"

"The accident where the woman stepped in front of the car? You didn't see it. Good."

"No, I didn't see it, but I know that it wasn't an accident, well at least I know that the woman wasn't to blame."

"How do you know that if you didn't see anything? Start talking sense, man, because I am on your side but the next person asking you the questions might be much less benevolent." He raised his voice above a whisper as he said this as if to emphasise its importance.

"I don't know. Well, I do but I just can't prove it. Have you examined the car?"

"We can't examine the car, it exploded."

"Exploded?" I struggled but couldn't keep the note of incredulity out of my voice, "How did it explode?"

"I'm not a mechanic am I? I'm not forensics – don't ask me. All I know is that it caught fire and then exploded. That's what happens to cars when they've been in an accident. All of the evidence was destroyed."

"That can't have happened! I saw that car after the accident and there was no way it was going to catch fire. And if it exploded why wasn't there any debris at the sight or any impact damage from the explosion? You know that it didn't happen, Osbourne."

"What I think I know isn't important, nor what I believe to have happened. All I do know is that the official report states that the car exploded before we could carry out a forensic examination on it. Case closed, and if you have any sense you'll let it stay closed."

The events of the previous two days were beginning to become connected in my head, and I didn't like the pattern that was emerging. "But there was a life lost – doesn't that mean anything?" I turned to Osbourne with an accusatory look on my face. We stopped walking now as he looked me square in the eye.

"Lives have been lost throughout the ages, my friend. We can't investigate them all now can we?"

"Well, yes you can." I didn't know whether Osbourne was a friend or foe but I needed to find out and so my voice became more aggressive.

"Well then maybe we should investigate the death of Tommy O'Callaghan? I don't think that you would like that Mr Halle."

"I had nothing to do with that and you know it. And I've heard from sources that he isn't even dead."

"It's dangerous to be a source like that. Haven't you understood yet that what is known isn't important – it's what seems to be known. Your name is on the leasing agreement for the garage where you and Tommy O'Callaghan were seen –"

"It can't be. That's absolutely impossible" I objected.

"Well I tell you honestly that I have seen that document myself and your name is on there with a signature right next to it. So you and Tommy were in a lock up belonging, in all intents and purposes, to yourself. We have reports that you were seen arguing with Tommy and that you left that lock up alone. We know that the garage is used for concealing illegal goods, we've been watching it. And believe me if certain people want to find Tommy's body then they will find it and that's going to be a black day for you my friend."

I looked at the headstone in front of me where lay the good father and husband Mr Pat Marsh but at that moment it felt like the ground was going to open up and pull me in there with him. The jigsaw was still missing pieces and I had no idea what the final picture would look like but I had to test my theory on Osbourne. I didn't expect him to admit that there was any truth in what I was saying but I hoped that I could catch him out from a look on his face or the widening of his soft eyes.

"I think I'm beginning to get the picture Osbourne, so just listen to this and let me know what you think. A woman was knocked down, maybe accidentally and maybe deliberately I don't know as yet, yesterday morning and some people think that I was the sole witness to the event. I blotted my copy book by chasing after the driver who then left me unconscious on the floor outside the Scout hut. Whilst I was knocked out he, or his accomplice Festa, rummaged through my pockets and took note of my name and address and other such details as they could find. It turns out that this driver was some shady Mr Big figure who even has police officers like you doing his dirty work for him. They fix it up so that it looks like I murdered Tommy O'Callaghan, a man who is still alive but probably being kept in a safehouse somewhere until he becomes less useful or until his body really needs to turn up. So you and the Sergeant were dispatched this morning to scare me, to get information from me or to kill me – which was it?"

"Does it matter", Osbourne replied nonchalantly.

"It matters to me, yes. It's my life and I'm pretty attached to it."

"Don't think that me and the Sergeant are the same. That's why I said I'm your friend and that's why I'm here talking to you now. Sarge would have killed you on the spot but I persuaded him to scare you into keeping quiet. He only agreed to that on condition that we left you in a position so precarious that you might kill yourself of your own volition – that's his idea of a game. I went back to look for you at the first opportunity but I saw that you had already gone. I don't know how and it's best that I don't know but I put myself at risk by going back to look for you and I'm putting myself at risk by talking to you now."

"So what do I do now?"

"You need to learn to keep silent, to keep a low profile. Say nothing to anybody about anything."

"I've been trying to keep a low profile all year but things don't seem to have worked out that way."

"And of course there's the item that you took from the scene of the accident, scene of the crime as you would call it. Nobody knows how it was missed but it's of the utmost importance that it's returned and it needs to be done right now because these people aren't going to go away Halle. You want my advice? Wrap it up and post it through the police stations letterbox. Nice and anonymous and then if you're lucky and keep your mouth shut nobody should bother you again – you might even see the year out."

"What if I haven't got it anymore?"

"That's not even an option my friend. Find it, find it quick."

"Why are people so interested in this ring?"

"Do you want to know? It's too dangerous for you to know because it would lead you right to him." I was trapped between a desire to know who this 'him' was and a desire to keep my head on my shoulders. I

126

looked deep into Osbourne's eyes and it was as if he wanted to answer and almost as if I could sense his answer without any need for him to articulate it. His lips trembled and he was about to speak when suddenly a fresh look appeared on his face, one of almost amused surprise which quickly turned to sheer terror.

"Run," he said but no longer in a whisper, "just run."

I turned to look in the direction of his gaze and saw what at first I took to be a black cloud moving slowly towards us along the floor. Now I saw that it was a group of people, maybe six, seven, eight or more, all dressed completely from head to toe in black and wearing balaclavas over their faces. The blood ran cold in my veins and a huge shiver ran through me causing my knees to shake and almost give way underneath me. The sense of menace increased now as a strange rhythmic banging nose began to sound from the group and I saw that they were all carrying some kind of baton which they pounded on the gravestones that they passed at precise and synchronised intervals. My legs had turned to stone and although my mouth gaped open the rest of my body was frozen in fear.

"Run! Run now, get away from here!" The gigantic Osbourne pushed me which caused me to stumbled and almost fall but the impact had freed me from my inertia and using the momentum that I had been given I sprinted towards the cemetery gates knowing that my life depended upon it.

I reached the gates and by placing one foot on top of a metal bar that ran across the main gate and gripping the spikes that were on top of it with my hands I vaulted the gate and landed heavily on the other side sending a wave of pain shooting up from my heels. For the first time I allowed myself the luxury of looking around and I expected to see Osbourne following me with the gang close behind. Instead I saw with horror that Osbourne had stood his ground and was engaged in a vain attempt to fight off the assailants who attacked him from every side. At last I saw him sink to his knees under the blows which kept raining down on top of him.

It was a horrible sight, something akin to a bear being pulled down by a dozen tearing terriers. I didn't know whether to continue running or turn back and try to help him although I knew that this would have been in vain and could only have ended in disaster for me. A sudden screeching of tyres accompanied by thudding music made up my mind for me.

I turned away from the cemetery and back towards the road to see the same blacked out Ford Escort that had brought me there. The front passenger door was pushed open and my survival instincts took over, although some may call it a cowards way out, as I climbed in to the car which promptly sped away carrying me ever further from the cemetery and from the man who had seemed on the verge of revealing some sort of truth to me.

I turned to look at the driver now seated at the side of me and although only his eyes were visible I had no doubt that it was the same man who had fetched me from my house. I spoke to him in an agitated voice:

"You're friend is being attacked out there. They are going to kill him." His eyes betrayed no emotion and he remained silent and so I tried again: "Don't you care about that? Shouldn't we call the police?"

"Why should I care? Who said he was a friend of mine? I was just returning a favour and now I've done it."

The rest of the journey continued in silence, if it could be called that amidst the relentlessly pounding music, and we soon pulled up outside of my house. I turned to look at the driver again but his eyes barely registered recognition and he made no attempt to speak. I opened the passenger door and climbed out with my mind hurting just as much as my body. As I was going to close the door the driver gave me a parting piece of advice:

"Oh, and if I was you I wouldn't think about calling the police. You know that there not going to do anything and it might be you out there next."

I slammed the door of the car shut with as much power as I could muster so that the thud of the door momentarily drowned out the muffled thud of the music's beats. The car pulled away with its obligatory screeching of tyres and I turned towards my house just in time to see its front door being closed from within. I stood immobile for a few seconds and it was long enough to see the lights come on within my front living room.

I had passed the point of no return now and a weary apathy gripped me. Whoever it was, they were going to track me down so it might as well be today as tomorrow. I walked into my house with stooped shoulders and an air of resignation. I didn't know who I would find inside but my mind kept picturing a marble headstone reading:

"Here lies John Halle, went to sleep 3rd January 2001."

I walked through the lobby into the living room and the eyes that met mine seemed equally startled, but I was so pleased to see them.

"You look a lot better than when I saw you this morning" said Rosa, who now stood before me wearing a long white coat trimmed with fake fur on top of a white dress decorated with a red rose pattern that came down to her knees. I had seen her twice now and both times she had seemed like a guardian angel. She smiled at me and maybe it was the sense of relief that made me think that she looked astonishingly beautiful. She was dressed to kill in an altogether more acceptable way than the men that I had escaped from in St Peter's cemetery.

It struck me that she had asked me a question and was expecting a reply and so I ventured:

"Do I? That's funny, because I don't feel any better."

"I'm sorry if I startled you! After I left you so abruptly this morning I just had to call and see how you were. I thought that you might have telephoned me? I had a missed call but it was an anonymous number."

"Sorry, it wasn't me. I would have called but I've been a bit busy."

"It seems to me that you're always busy. I'm going to have to get used to that if I get to know you, I can see."

I hadn't considered that she might get to know me but as I looked at her mischievous smile the idea appealed to me and I vowed that I would try to stay alive long enough for it to have a chance of happening.

"So you just thought that you would come in and wait for me, eh Rosa?" I asked the question in a tone that I hoped wouldn't sound too accusatory or dismissive.

"Well I was standing outside when one of your neighbours, the long haired guy from three doors down saw me and passed this key to me." She held up my front door key. "He says that he found it on the road and had tried a few locks before finding that it fitted yours. He locked it and was holding onto it for you but he said that seeing as I was your girlfriend I could have it."

"My girlfriend? Why did he think that?" Again I tried my hardest not to sound as if this idea was somehow incredulous.

"He says that he saw me leaving the house this morning. I guess that he's a curtain twitcher."

If he had been peering out from behind his curtains that morning he would have seen a lot more than Rosa leaving behind her frantic Spaniel but I felt grateful for an act of kindness from a man that I barely knew. He had moved into the street around two months previously and I sometimes heard him playing an acoustic guitar as I passed by his window but we had never really had a chance to speak.

I was still standing in the same position that I had occupied when I entered the room with such fear and trepidation but Rosa had moved across to the settee now. She reached down and with one smooth movement lifted the charcoal picture from the seat; as she looked at it briefly I saw a tired look come into her eyes and her face grew visibly paler.

"What's this?" She asked.

"It's just a picture that some strange man gave me. Don't you like it?"

"Is this some kind of joke" she asked as she dropped the picture back onto the settee. Her voice was quivering with barely concealed emotion.

"A joke? Why should it be?" I asked. She didn't answer me but instead reached into her coat pocket and pulled out a red leather purse which she opened. With shaking fingers she pulled a small photograph from a concealed pocket and threw it down on top of the charcoal picture of the girl that I had seen on the Tuesday morning bus.

I walked closer to the settee so that I could see the photograph under the lights and all the while Rosa stood silently looking at me. As I approached the photograph I could finally see that it was a faded picture of the exact same girl, wearing the same clothes, as the girl in the portrait. It was as if another blow had been landed upon me and I mumbled, almost inaudibly:

"I'm sorry, I don't understand. Who is it?"

"Who is it?" Rosa spat back, "That's my sister. And she died ten years ago."

Chapter Eight

Where do you start when a woman finds that you've got a freshly drawn charcoal picture of her dead sister in your house? That morning I had been tied up, blindfolded and left lying at the top of a slope that led right down into the deep, stagnant waters known locally as The Devil's Pool but although I was now stood in my living room it seemed that once again I was on the edge of a precipice and it was going to be no easier to get out of this one.

Rosa was still standing nearby with arms folded across her chest and her beautiful face displaying a mixture of anger, hurt and expectation. I had only known the woman for a few hours but I already owed my life to her and so I knew that I had to give her a response, it was just a matter of judging how much to tell and how much to leave out.

"Your sister? And she's dead? I didn't know anything about that – I'm really sorry. Look – here's the truth and I'm going to level with you. Lots of strange things have been happening to me: you can tell that from the situation that you found me in this morning."

"Go on" Rosa encouraged me in a voice that was sterner than I had previously heard it.

"Well, this afternoon I was in Sheffield – at a pub called The Red Fountain. I know what you're going to say – how could I go for a drink after all that had happened to me that morning? That is what you were going to say isn't it, Rosa?"

"Yes it is" she replied.

"Well I had a pre-arranged meeting with my best friend and I just, well I just needed a drink. I guess that I've been drinking too much for this last year or so. There was a guy in the pub, he was painting portraits and hawking them around the customers. I didn't ask him to paint anything, I swear, but he pushed this painting on to me and insisted that I take it. And he didn't charge me anything for it either come to think of it. So that's it – that's the truth."

"Is it?"

"Yes, I swear that it's the truth. I wouldn't lie to you after what you've done for me."

Rosa sank into the armchair which faced the large front window. The look of anger had gone from her face and was replaced by a weary confusion which seemed to age her in seconds. Tears were collecting in her eyes and she dabbed at them with the white fur trimming that ran around the edges of her coat sleeves. To see her upset made sadness well up inside of me and I felt protective of her in a way that had been alien to me for far too long. I wanted to hold her close and comfort her but I had forgotten how to do it so I just stood looking at her and feeling strangely guilty. At last she looked up and spoke in a soft voice that was barely audible but full of sorrow:

"I know that you're telling me the truth. But I know that you're not telling me the whole truth are you?"

"No, I guess I'm not. I just didn't think that you would believe the whole truth. I can hardly believe it myself and I'm the person that it's happened to."

"Tell me the whole truth, John, I deserve it. I need to hear it: you can't imagine how I need to hear it."

I sat down as well now on the settee that was next to the armchair in which she sat. I turned my body so that it was facing her but as I began to tell my story I turned my head downwards to avoid looking into her eyes. I was scared that I might find hatred there or find a look on her face which meant that she thought that I was half mad. I took a series of deep breaths and then began a brief outline of the story that related to the woman that now appeared, incredibly, to be Rosa's sister.

"Well, my dear, you've asked to hear the story and so I'll tell you. But take this caveat on board, that this story seems fantastical to me so I don't know how you will receive it and if it hurts or saddens you too much just let me know and I'll stop."

"I'm a strong woman. I've had to be strong, growing up on my own. So go ahead, just tell me the whole story this time."

I began the story, somehow hoping that in the telling of it I may pick up things, clues, that I had missed at the time and that would bring everything into some sort of sense:

"It all began yesterday morning when I got the bus to work. Well to be more accurate the bus to Elsecar where I was to catch the train to Sheffield where I work.

The bus was emptier than usual, not everyone's back at work yet I suppose. My fellow passengers seemed an unremarkable bunch, allowing for a couple of people that I knew, and the journey was progressing as expected until the moment when I saw – well I saw her. I don't know who the woman was, and it may well have been somebody completely different, but I swear that she looked just like the woman in the portrait and the woman in your picture. Yes, the one of your dead sister. I'm really sorry about this."

My voice trailed off now, and I kept my head lowered and eyes to the floor as I was suddenly overcome with a spasm of emotion. I could hear Rosa encouraging me to carry on, in a gentler voice now, and so I continued my story:

"She was wearing a blue and white striped shirt and a sandy coloured jacket and something attracted my attention so much that nothing else seemed to matter. It was as if she was talking to me inside my head but I couldn't make out the words and her dark lips never moved. At one point she seemed to look at me and point to something out of the window but I forget what she was pointing at, maybe I wanted to forget? I saw her press the bell but I guess it wasn't working as no sound came out and the bus just drove on. I thought, well I thought that she said 'here' to me but not in words if that makes any sense to you? It makes no sense to me but if it didn't happen then I guess that I've gone mad already.

I got off of the bus but she didn't look at me as I walked off. I never got to work either, there was an accident at the train station, and then all hell seemed to be let loose. I don't know what's happened, Rosa, I just don't know but it's as if somebody is playing tricks with me and I lurch from

132

one disaster to the next. People have been chasing me, following me in the streets. The police have said, in so many words, that they are going to frame me for the murder of someone that I don't even know and then they beat me, tied me up and left me in Shortwood. Only your intervention saved me from death, Rosa, I really believe that. And they, whoever they are, are still out to get me – I've just had to escape from a crowd of men armed with batons in a cemetery. Everybody is after my blood but I swear that I don't know why: I don't think that I've done anything wrong?

And the rest you know, kind of. The story that I related about The Red Fountain is true: I didn't ask for the picture and I certainly didn't describe this woman, sorry maybe I should call her your sister? No, I didn't describe her, didn't ask for the picture and yet somehow here it is just in time for you to find it. I looked for the painter but he'd gone before I could question him. And that's the truth for what it's worth. I suppose that you'll want to go now? You can take the portrait with you, please do."

I finished my story with a thumping in my head and a dry mouth. I sat with my head downcast expecting to see Rosa's feet walk past me on the way to the door and then out of my life but when I finally raised my head I saw Rosa's eyes looking directly at mine and a sweet look had returned to her face. I had been so focussed on telling my story that it was only then that I noticed that during my monologue Rosa had taken my hands in hers and was gently rubbing them with a comforting affection.

"I'm not going anywhere without you" she said.

I looked into her eyes again and they were still moist with tears that had softly fallen but it was then for the first time I realised the startling truth that had been literally staring me in the face since that morning: Rosa had the same brilliantly luminous green eyes that the girl on the bus had possessed. I knew now without a doubt that it had been her sister, but the acceptance of this threw the reasoning and beliefs that I had clung to through all my years into chaos and I finally knew that I had started a new journey in my life. It was a journey that would lead me to a new life altogether, the one that I am living now five years on from these events.

"Do you believe me?" I asked her more in hope than expectation.

"Of course I believe you. What did the painter look like? No, don't tell me. That's for another time."

We just sat silently on our separate chairs facing each other and time ticked past unnoticed as we looked into each others eyes yet all the while seeing nothing except the thoughts that were running through our minds.

Without warning, Rosa gently pulled her hands away from mine and stood up. Once again she was taking charge of the situation as she asked me:

"We're not safe here are we?"

"Well, I'm not safe here. People could be on their way over right now for all I know. I don't really know if I've got the strength left to fight them anymore."

"Don't you? Well I have and so I'm telling you that you're going to keep fighting too. You've just told me that you can see my dead sister, my dear Georgie, that I haven't seen in ten years and you think that I can walk away? I need you around me."

I winced when she said that I could see her dead sister. Yes, it seemed that, somehow, I had seen her once but I'd not seen her since, discounting the dreams that regularly tormented me, and had no expectation or desire to see her again. I was still shying away from accepting the truth.

"Well, what do I do then Rosa?" It felt good to place myself into her hands and I felt safer when she was around.

"It's obvious that you can't stay here. And your house is completely wrecked anyway."

"Yes, it's not looking good is it? I think that I may have lost my bond on this place – the landlady isn't going to be best pleased when she sees it." I returned to the gallows humour that I had favoured down the years.

"Pack some clothes into a bag as quickly as you can: don't bother with anything else – I've got all you need."

"You've got all I need?"

"I believe so, so hurry up and get some clothes packed. You're going to stay at my place for a few days until all this blows over." She said this with such imposing finality that I didn't pause to say a word or even to consider her proposition. I knew in my mind that I had to leave this house and yet again she had come up with the best possible solution. I hurried upstairs fearing every second that a bang on the door could signal an end to our escape.

I ran up the stairway two steps at a time. The confusion, mixed with the adrenalin that was flowing through me, made me oblivious to the pain that had been shooting across my body since that morning. I reached my bedroom in record time and from the newly righted wardrobe I pulled the large holdall type bag that I used for my holidays: I hated waiting at the luggage carousel at airports – my luggage always seemed to enter the carousel last and as every minute passed I would wonder how I was going to cope if it had been lost, destroyed or forwarded to Kuala Lumpur whilst I was in Barcelona. For this reason I preferred to travel light whenever possible and I knew that this bag could contain enough tightly packed clothes to last a week whilst still being compact enough to be used as hand luggage.

As I carried the holdall across to my bed I stepped over the glass of the broken whiskey bottle that still lay scattered on the floor. It had been in the early hours of that morning when I had found the bottle without its hidden treasure but already it seemed a world away. As my mind jumped momentarily back to the ring though it seemed that there was something else about the girl on the bus, Georgie as she seemed to be called, that I should remember but it just wasn't coming into my mind. I realised also that, unintentionally, I had missed the story of the ring from the version that I had related to Rosa and wondered whether to tell her all about it: or at least the little about it that I knew. After a few seconds deliberation, which was all that I could allow myself in the circumstances, I decided against this course of action for now, instinctively feeling that the less that Rosa knew about it the less danger it could bring to her. It seemed that a little knowledge could be a dangerous thing in the brave new world that I had stumbled blindly into.

In the opposite corner of my bedroom was a set of three oak drawers on top of which stood a once beautiful and intricate mirror arranged in three separate panels which could each be moved independently of one another. One of the panels had now been smashed and so with the bathroom mirror I guess that it meant that fourteen years bad luck was on its way to somebody. I remembered then that it was Osbourne that would have smashed the mirrors and hoped that his fourteen years of bad luck hadn't all visited him at once this evening: I made a resolution to myself that somehow I would find out how he was but in my mind I was trying to hide the fear that I would really be finding out not how but if he was. The drawers had held a collection of my clothing that had been washed, ironed and neatly folded ready for the week ahead. Most of that clothing had now been thrown into a jumble that surrounded the oak dresser but I gathered up the clothing that seemed to me to be the least creased or trod upon.

I packed three T-shirts and the Celtic football shirt that I liked to wear in summer with the name of Henrik Larsson printed proudly on the back: that soccer genius who had thrilled fans of the green and white hoops north and south of the border. To this I added another pair of jeans and a pair of black casual trousers, in case I need to go anywhere formal during my exile from this house that I loved so much, and two long sleeve shirts and a jumper that was a dull mixture of many colours in rustic fashion. I took three pairs of boxer shorts and an equal number of socks and folded them into the bag alongside my other clothing. Ignoring Rosa's instruction not to pack anything else I walked swiftly to the bathroom and in a side compartment I placed a bottle of aftershave, a spray deodorant and a handful of disposable razor blades. On top of these I placed a purple bath towel: I didn't mind staying at other people's houses when necessitated but I had a strange aversion to using their towels, even when they belonged to somebody as angelic as Rosa.

I ran down the stairs and stopping momentarily by the lobby I packed a pair of shoes into the side of the bag and then pressed the whole contents down allowing me to zip the cover snugly over my collection of clothing and toiletries. As I walked back into the room I saw Rosa looking at her watch worriedly as if I had taken an hour rather than the two minutes that I had estimated had passed, but then the worry lines disappeared to be replaced by the beautiful smile that I already loved.

"Let's go" she said and opening the door walked outside into the cold night air. I followed behind her with my meagre belongings packed into the bag that was carried in my left arm. I closed the door behind me and walked on after Rosa but she stopped me by making a gesture as if turning a key and pointing to the door. I felt foolish as I realised that I had constantly attempted to lock the door when I was without my key but had not even thought about locking the door now that the key was back in my possession.

I saw now that Rosa's white Ford Fiesta was parked a short distance down the street although I hadn't noticed it when I had exited the taxi. I hoped that if anybody had been watching my house then the fact that the car was not parked directly in front of it may have helped it to escape their attention. As Rosa and I marched quickly to the car the long haired neighbour came outside to greet me:

"Hi, neighbour," he shouted in a jovial fashion which nicely evaded the fact that neither of us knew the other ones' name, "did you get the key then?"

"Yes, thanks a lot. Very kind of you." I answered in a voice that I forced to sound friendly and unconcerned.

"Going away then are you – you and the missus?" he seemed keen on conversation for the first time in the two months that he had lived near me and I felt guilty at having to curtail his conversation so abruptly.

"Yes, that's right – something like that. Just going away for a few days, bit of a break. I don't even know where we're going yet, but please keep an eye on my house for me while we're gone will you? Oh, and if anybody comes looking for me or asking about me while I'm away then just tell them that you haven't seen me in days and that you don't know where I am. I'm sure you understand, is that okay mate?"

"Message received and understood" he said and saluted theatrically with his reply. Rosa had started her cars engine and as I climbed into the front seat she sped off towards the junction with the motorway.

The air freshener that was stuck onto the dashboard could not completely disguise the smell of wet dog that lingered in the air but it was a much more comfortable journey than the one that I had endured earlier that day when my arms had still been tied behind my back. I looked in the mirrors at regular intervals and my paranoia seemed infectious as Rosa cast nervous glances at them too but there was no sign of any vehicle following us and so we soon settled into a more relaxed journey.

We had weightier issues to discuss but after the emotion of our earlier conversation I wanted to enjoy a more normal discussion and so I asked Rosa where she lived.

"Well actually I've bought a little pad in Camden – it's a lovely area not too far from the lock. Like everywhere in London it was over priced and it's not very big but it's in a great location and I managed to secure a loan on the projections for my design business."

London was certainly far enough away to keep me out of danger, I imagined, but it was a ridiculously long journey to make at this time of night. Rosa must have noted the concerned look upon my face for she laughed and said:

"Don't worry, John, we're not off to Camden now. The flat there won't be ready to move into for another month or so yet and so in the meantime I've rented a flat in Sheffield. I love to be back in Yorkshire, it reminds me of where we grew up, mum, dad, Georgie and me: it's not all sad memories you know? That's why I was walking through Shortwood today, I used to do that every day when I was a child and so whenever I can I take Tramp down there. He'll miss that when we move down to London permanently, poor old thing."

It was strongly out of character for me, especially considering that I had spent the last year deliberately hardening my heart and concealing any emotions, but I had already formed a strong attachment to the woman alongside me and I began to feel that maybe I would miss her too when she moved down to London.

She had raised the matter of her family, and her sister Georgie in particular, and so I wondered whether I should ask for more details about her or ask Rosa if she had any idea why I had seen a vision of Georgie on the bus that had seemed so lifelike. I decided to leave the final decision, as before, to Rosa:

"Do you want to talk about Georgie?" I asked and then wished I hadn't as I saw the sadness reappear on her face. She bit her lip for a second before replying:

"Not tonight, John, not tonight. We will talk about it tomorrow; I think we both need a good sleep after today. I've got someone that I want you to see tomorrow, is that okay?"

"Yes, that will be fine. If you think that it's someone I should see then I'm sure that it will be okay."

I didn't know who she wanted me to meet but I was happy to back her judgement. In the back of my mind I felt that she may be planning to take me to a doctor or a psychiatrist but if it would help bring the banal normality back into my life then I would readily go along with it.

We drove on down the motorway and through the streets to Sheffield neatly reversing the route that I had taken in the taxi a few hours earlier. The snow was no longer falling and although there was substantially more snow covering in the city than in nearby Barnsley the gritting lorries had belatedly done their job and the roads were much more passable now.

As we journeyed we discussed trivial matters as if to take our mind off of the crazy events that had overtaken us both that day. We talked about music and books and Rosa seemed pleasantly surprised that I could shake off the philistine exterior and admit to a love of classical literature and even opera: although I preferred the modern daring of Puccini while she championed Monteverdi and the early Operatic pioneers. We even played I Spy and I managed to stump her by saying that I had spied a zebra. When I explained that I had seen it on an advertising billboard she accused me of cheating but I still put it down as a Halle victory.

The journey continued in this manner and now that we were both convinced that nobody was following us Rosa drove at a more sedate pace which was a welcome respite from the breakneck rides that I had been taking that day. I was glad that Rosa had made it clear that she didn't want to talk about her sister because it gave me a chance to put the events of the last two days out of my mind and feel relaxed and safe, contented even, for the first time since that fateful bus journey had set my nerves on edge. Under normal circumstances it would have taken a real effort to keep the thoughts out of my head and I would have had to count numbers over and over or repeat silly meaningless mantras in my head but on that night forgetting came easy as I was carried along by listening to the beautifully insubstantial conversation of Rosa.

We drove on through the centre of Sheffield now, skirting around the pedestrians only area that held The Red Fountain and travelling down West Street which was still full of revellers braving the cold and wintry conditions to enjoy the last remnants of the Christmas and New Year festivities. West Street was the party capital of Sheffield being a long road full of large gaudy bars and restaurants of both low and high cuisine. In the back streets that ran off of it a handful of prostitutes would gather in dingily lit car parks risking hypothermia and worse to earn the pittance that they craved.

Trams ran down the centre of West Street and onwards onto the far reaches of the city: they trundled slowly down their tracks bringing chaos to traffic and danger to inebriated students from the nearby Universities who would stumble across their paths when staggering drunkenly from the many emporiums' delights.

We made steady progress along West Street, slowed by a procession of trams and buses and revellers who ran across roads without looking. The clear night sky had sent temperatures plummeting again but many of the party people were content to wear outfits so skimpy that they would have been dismissed as impractical by the hollow faced women who hid around corners on the sidewalks that concealed another world. Rosa seemed to pay them little attention but my inherent fascination for people watching meant that I spent happy minutes watching the young men and women that we passed and somehow, for a few brief but happy minutes, I forgot the troubles that were pressing down upon me.

We reached the end of West Street and drove on past the University and past Hallamshire Hospital until we reached the suburb of Broomhill. Broomhill is a large village, if an urban environment can be referred to as such, lying on the outskirts of Sheffield's city centre itself: it is a place of contrasts whose populace is made up of a heady, at times bohemian and at times decadent, mixture of students past and present, university lecturers, doctors and semi-successful businessmen on the road to more salubrious areas such as Dore and Fulwood.

Its streets seemed to be an overspill from the gauche city centre and contained a succession of supermarkets, bars, coffee shops, takeaways and restaurants. The prevailing culture in Broomhill though seemed altogether different to the city centre a mile or so away. It was as close as the hardy Yorkshire city got to a Greenwich Village kind of atmosphere and here people could, and did, wear what they wanted and behaved how they wanted without anybody seeming to pay them any attention.

Rosa announced that we were nearly home, I found it strange but yet reassuring that she was referring to it as my home less than twenty four hours after she had first met me when I was bound and gagged in the woods, and then turned right down a leafy tree lined street that extended behind the main row of shops. The houses on this street were large white fronted Georgian buildings that had once been home to the most affluent members of South Yorkshire society but were now each divided up into three, four or five self contained flats that were rented out to students or young professionals at exorbitant rates. Rosa pulled up outside the fourth house down and as I stepped out of the car I knew that as long as I stayed here I would be safe.

As we walked along the path to the communal hallway that led to her flat Rosa continued the inconsequential but touching conversation that we had been engaged upon for the last half hour in her car. It had been a short journey but already I had learnt that her favourite group was The Smiths, her favourite number was seven and her favourite colour was purple: I had stored this information deep within my mind under the heading of 'may prove useful later.'

Rosa unlocked the door and ushered me into the hallway, she followed after and locked the door behind her. The hallway was on the same grand scale as the house itself and was immaculately white and breathtaking in its uncluttered simplicity. A large staircase, wrought of black iron, led in a spiral to a first floor and a second floor but Rosa indicated that she had secured the prime ground floor apartments and I followed her through another door into her self contained flat.

I understood that this Broomhill lodging was only a temporary arrangement for Rosa, and imagined that the Camden flat would be a more spacious affair decorated in the colourfully modern style that seemed to be de rigueur at the time, but she seemed very proud of the flat and showed me around every room as if she was an estate agent eager to impress a potential buyer.

The whole flat adhered strictly to the all white scheme on view in the hallway and was decorated in a minimalist fashion which served to heighten the simple beauty of its Georgian design where everything had been created on a sweeping scale. The only concession to colour in the rooms, and indeed the only attempt that Rosa had made to personalise the flat, were the sprays of flowers that were in every room in combinations of purple, white and red and two large prints that she had framed and mounted. The living room housed a reproduction of the painting 'Big Blue Horses' by the German artist Franz Marc and the wall to the left hand side of Rosa's bedroom held an abstract but stunning picture by Kandinsky which was apparently called 'White White' although the only portion of white in the picture was a small blank circle floating amidst a riot of colours. I supposed that these had been placed to emphasise her chosen career in design and to indicate that she had an immaculately highbrow taste in art but I found myself wondering where she would hang the portrait of her sister which fortune had placed into her hands that evening.

The flat was deceptively large and felt warm and welcoming from the first moment that I had stepped into it. It contained four rooms, the central one of which was a large open plan living room with black leather armchairs and a large black leather sofa facing a wide screen television with the other end of the room holding a large mahogany effect table with enough space and chairs to hold small dinner parties. A neatly compact but expensive looking music system was situated against the far wall and two towers of compact discs rose up from besides it.

A large wicker basket was situated near to the sofa and Rosa's dog, Tramp, was curled up inside it. As he saw me he rose from the basket, tail wagging behind him, and walked over to me as if I was an old friend. I patted his head with enthusiasm and turned the palm of my hand to his face which he sniffed, a gesture which I had always been taught shows a dog that you are its friend. Satisfied as to my identity Tramp padded back to his basket and positioned himself comfortably within the tartan blanket that lined it.

The kitchen was situated across from the living room and the whole room was so spotlessly clean that I wondered if it had ever been used but then maybe I had just been living on my own for too long?

Further down the corridor was a bathroom where the white walls had been replaced by paint of a pastel lemon colour. A small looking bath seemed to give precedence to an enclosed Perspex fronted shower unit that was situated alongside it and the whole room smelt of the white and red roses that were situated in vases placed in all four corners of the room. During the last forty eight hours I had become accustomed to taking note of the littlest things around me and I immediately spotted that next to her bathroom sink was a container which held both a pink and a blue toothbrush and my heart strangely sank as I realised that I had not yet asked Rosa if there was a significant other in her life – indeed it was only at this point that I realised that I was beginning to care if there was a significant other in her life. She seemed to follow my eye line and sensed that there was an unasked question hanging in the air but she put an end to any awkwardness by explaining:

"While you're my guest in this flat please treat it as your own, John. What's mine is yours so to speak. There are towels in the Ottoman basket over there and I always have a spare tooth brush handy in case any visitors come round. I use the blue one by the way, so it's the pink one for you I'm afraid."

We smiled to each other as the momentary tension evaporated and I followed her into the fourth and final room of the flat.

Rosa's bedroom was large and free of any clutter which made it seem even more spacious than it was. A large double bed lay in the very centre of the room which seemed to radiate out from it and was overlooked by the Kandinsky painting that hung on the far wall. There was a double wardrobe, in the ubiquitous white, with a mirrored front and two sets of drawers. A set of bookshelves were well stocked with a mixture of books: from a series of books on design to biographies of pop stars, horror books by Steven King, collections of poetry and an old but obviously well loved copy of Little Women. Next to the doorway was a computer desk which was home to a new desktop computer and a top of the range printer and scanner.

Rosa led me back into the living room and I sat on the sofa as she walked across to the kitchen to make me a drink. I was impressed that although she had only been living in the flat for a short while, and would be moving out of it in the near future, she had really made it her own and the whole building seemed to glow with the effortless style that I had so quickly come to associate with the woman who had proved to be a guardian angel to me.

I bounced quietly up and down on the sofa, trying to avoid being heard by my host across the hallway, in an effort to judge how comfortable it would be for me tonight. I had no objection to sleeping on the sofa; I had spent nights in many worse places in my time including foyers of banks, and even outside in gardens during the excesses of my student days. The sofa was indeed very comfortable and although I would have to sleep with my knees tucked under me in a foetal position or with my feet hanging over the edge of the sofa's arm I was confident of sleeping well there for as long as necessary before I could return from my exile to Birdwell with the certitude that things would be normal and safe for me there again: I had no idea how long it was going to take to reach such a situation or how it would come about but I was filled with a new found confidence that made me believe that anything was possible.

Rosa returned from the kitchen with a light step and I was pleasantly surprised to find that in each hand she was carrying a large glass filled with red wine, one of which she handed to me before sitting down besides me.

"I thought that you didn't drink?" I asked her.

"Well, I don't, not really. Well, what I mean is that I don't drink alone – but I always keep a bottle of red handy in case a friend or business acquaintance comes calling and I figured that you could do with a glass." She sipped timidly at her drink as she said this and I took a large gulp in reciprocation. I could have done with a whole bottle in truth but a glass was better than nothing. So now I was learning a new side to Rosa: she did drink, albeit occasionally, and she didn't always tell the whole truth. I was perversely pleased at this revelation and happy that she felt comfortable enough in my company to let this side of her character out.

"Do you like movies?" she asked before answering for me, "of course you do: everybody does. I will watch absolutely anything but especially comedies. They're showing 'Stir Crazy' tonight – you must have heard of it – it stars Gene Wilder and Richard Pryor? Do you know it?"

I had seen it at least half a dozen times and could probably have recited most of the dialogue if pushed but I didn't want to dent her enthusiasm and so I just nodded and added vaguely that it sounded familiar.

My non-committal answer seemed to please her and so she continued: "Well it's just about to start, so let's watch it, with another glass of wine if necessary, and then we can go to bed."

I remained calm as if nothing unexpected had been said but when she said that after the film we would go to bed that little word 'we' had exploded like a bomb within my head. I tried to convince myself that she meant our respective beds, including my sofa on that score, but as the film progressed it seemed to me that the atmosphere in the room was becoming more tense and it took me back to nights in my distant past when the promise of sleeping together had hung heavily in the air between myself and a succession of women and it always seemed to turn into some kind of stand off to see who could delay it the longest before dragging the other one off to the bedroom.

I had already developed a great affection for Rosa, and the feelings that were growing in my previously hibernating heart had surprised me with their swiftness. Those feelings had now been replaced by butterflies in my stomach as if I was sixteen again and a faint sense of nausea grew within me. My feelings of trepidation had nothing to do with Rosa, but I had been badly damaged by the end of my relationship by Lamara, by the death of Lamara that the gravestone had brought so vividly back to me earlier that evening, and I was not ready to be rushed into anything. I knew deep down though that once again I would submit to the will of the woman who had served me so well on that first day that we had known each other.

As the film progressed I forced myself to laugh when Rosa laughed alongside me but in truth I was finding it hard to concentrate on the antics of the two men and their efforts to escape from their prison: instead my focus was on the clock which was ticking down towards the end of the film with what seemed to me to be an alarming speed. At last the moment arrived when the laughter stopped and the credits rolled. My companion pressed a button on the remote control and the screen faded into blackness. She rose from the sofa but I tried one last gambit:

"I thought that I could stay on here tonight, I've got really comfortable. Fetch me a blanket and it will be fine."

"Don't be silly", she replied, "We're both adults and I'm not leaving you freezing on the sofa here when I've got a large bed that's plenty big enough for two. I really trust you John, do you know that? And I promise that I won't bite."

She smiled gently at me and I felt all of my misgivings melt sweetly away. She held out her hand to me and I took it and let her lead me into the bedroom.

"You can use the smaller of the sets of drawers for your clothes John, we can get you some more clothes later in the week if you need some, I don't really use that one. I'm off to get changed so just make yourself comfortable and I'll try not to wake you up with my cold feet when I climb in. Do you snore?"

"I don't know" I replied.

"Well, I'll let you know in the morning." She walked out of the room carrying a bag of toiletries and headed for the bathroom where I heard her switch the shower on. I quickly got undressed feeling bashful in a way that I had never felt before and climbed under the king size gold and ivory patterned duvet wearing my boxer shorts and Celtic football shirt as nightwear. I reached over and switched off the light that stood on a bedside table and illuminated my side of the bed.

I closed my eyes but my mind was racing so much that sleep was impossible. After a few minutes the noise from the shower stopped and a few minutes later I saw Rosa walk through the darkness to the bed. My eyes adjusted to the darkness quickly and I saw that she was wearing a long dark T-Shirt, of indeterminate colour at that point, as a nightdress which stopped above her knees. She was wearing slippers which seemed to be in the shape of cats, or possibly rabbits, and these she kicked off before climbing under the duvet alongside me. She said goodnight, to which I didn't reply as I had now half closed my eyes in a pretence at being asleep, and as I opened my eyes again I saw that she had turned on her side away from me with her left hand tucked under her head for support and her knees raised slightly towards her chest.

It was the first time that I had shared a bed with a woman for over a year and I was surprised at how natural and good it felt. I spent minutes just staring at the beautiful young woman sleeping besides me, for she had already entered the realms of sleep, and felt a strange comforting strength grow within me as I watched with delight the slight rise and fall of her shoulder blades as she breathed and the gentle sighs that accompanied them.

It was as yet a curiously platonic ardour that gripped me and I had no desire to see Rosa naked, nor to hold her in my arms and make love to her but I was so happy just to be alongside her that I would have liked to spend all night in contemplation of her while she slept. The ease that I felt at that moment however began to succumb to the stress and the physical and mental attacks that I had suffered that day and fatigue began to press down on me again. Although I fought against it I was eventually powerless to stop myself falling into a deep and troubled sleep.

It seemed as if lights were flashing in my head and a cacophony of noises began to crowd onto one another until they became one huge thudding sound. Suddenly I found myself falling through the air and I tried to fly but the more I flapped my arms the quicker I fell and then I realised that I was falling towards a freshly dug grave that was awaiting me. I stretched out my arms and managed to grab hold of the headstone before I plummeted into the pit that now seemed to be bottomless. I pulled myself to the surface and found myself in a cemetery. As I looked at the stone that I had clung onto I read: "Here lies John Halle, soon to be dead." I looked around and Lamara was standing before me dressed in heavy winter clothing to protect her from the mist that gathered and swirled around us.

"I see that you're coming to join me then, John. Won't be long now", she chanted repetitively. I tried to back away from her but was pushed forward by many hands and looking over my shoulder I could see black clad people whose hoods contained no faces just an empty nothingness until suddenly they all vanished and only Lamara was stood before me. "You came to visit me today. At last! Come again, and next time bring something for me. How can you expect me to give you anything when you won't give anything to me?" She looked at me in the offended and accusatory way that I had seen too many times in our years together but now the earth began to shake around me and I fell to the floor. Arms were breaking through the soil around me and it seemed to me that they were the arms of children.

I jumped up in the bed with a groan and eyes wide open and was met by a pair of green eyes watching me. At first I thought that it was the girl on the bus who had appeared in my dream of the night before but at last the visions faded and I realised where I was and saw Rosa's concerned face looking at me:

"Shush, shush, it's just a nightmare John, it's only a nightmare."

"I keep having them. I just can't stop having them" I whispered back to her.

"Well, I'm going to take you to see someone tomorrow and she will make it all alright."

Rosa cradled my head in her hands and then rested it against the crook of her neck as she gently stroked my hair. Held in this position I soon surrendered to sleep again as she cradled me. I spent the rest of the night in a peace that had remained alien to me for too long.

When I awoke the light from outside was streaming into the room and Rosa was nowhere to be seen. I heard her voice speaking into the telephone that was positioned on a small wooden table that was kept in the central corridor. She seemed to be fixing an appointment of some sort but as yet my ears had not adjusted to the new day and I only caught fragments of the conversation.

Rosa walked back into the room and fixed me with a huge smile that made it seem as if the Sun had broken through the clouds. She was wearing a close fitting knitted top of black and white hoops on top of a dark pair of jeans and her hair was tied back. It was the first time that I had seen her without make up on and yet she seemed prettier than ever.

"I'm sorry about last night. About waking you up like that."

"It's okay, don't mention it. That's what friends are for. Look we have to be out of here in half an hour so grab a shower and meet me in the lounge."

I walked across to the bathroom and took a long warm shower. As I relaxed in the hot water I noticed that the beating that I had received the previous morning had taken its toll and bruising was beginning to come to the surface of my skin covering my ribs with colours black, purple and yellow. There was no interruption to my routine this morning and I headed back to the bedroom wrapped in a towel and feeling revitalised. It seemed that Rosa had decided on the clothes that I should wear that day and I found that on the bed were laid out a white long sleeved shirt and my black trousers. Next to the bed were my shoes which had been freshly polished.

I dressed quickly and walked over to the living room. As I entered the room Tramp passed me and I saw him push open the kitchen door with his nose where two red bowls awaited him – one filled with water and one with dog food that he began to eat with noisy appreciation.

In the living room Rosa was eating too: she nibbled on a slice of toast which had orange marmalade on it and with her other hand she handed me a slice of toast with strawberry jam upon it.

"You look like a jam man", she said, "Well I keep finding you in jams anyway."

I smiled back appreciatively and quickly devoured the sweet toast while it was still warm.

"I'm sorry that it's not a proper breakfast but we've got to get a move on if we're to get to Irina's in time. We can get something more substantial later."

Rosa switched off her music system that had been playing rock music at a subdued volume and she walked out of the door with a dark grey woollen jacket neatly folded over her arm. In the corridor she knelt down and whispered words into Tramp's ear upon which he dutifully returned to his basket in the living room. Rosa straightened up from her kneeling position and walked to the door with me following behind her like another obedient dog as if me and Tramp had become soul brothers.

As Rosa locked her door and we headed out of the large communal house I asked her:

"Who exactly is this Irina then?"

"She is a very busy woman, it's really good of her to see us at such short notice – but then again maybe not, she sounds really keen to meet you John."

That hadn't really answered my question but Rosa added:

"You know who she is really don't you John? Don't look blankly at me because I know that you do. Come on, let's get in the car and I will tell you more on the way."

The reality was that I didn't have a clue who Irina was or why she wanted to see me but I didn't know if an admission would offend the woman who had been so good to me and so I maintained an enigmatic silence. I was pleased to note, however, that this Irina woman didn't sound like she was going to be a doctor or a psychiatrist.

"What do you know about me John?" she asked when we were driving back across the roads of Sheffield. She supplied the answer herself as seemed to be her way: "You know that my name is Rosa Galloway, I'm 28 years old and I am a design consultant, whatever that is. I had a sister and parents who are all dead and besides my dog and this strange man that has dropped suddenly into my life I'm all alone in the world. That's it isn't it?"

"I'm not that strange am I?", I replied but then remembering the circumstances that she had found me in I thought it better to leave this question unanswered and so continued: "Yes, I know that about you. But I know more as well."

"Such as?"

"Well, I know that you are a beautiful, independent and strong woman and above all that you are wonderfully kind."

"Thanks, John it's nice to hear that but really I'm just as fragile as the next person. I know that you've lost your parents too –", as she said this I thought again about the golfing holiday that I planned to take when I visited them in their Algarve home that Autumn, "but I lost everything within such a short space of time. I don't like to unburden myself to people, I like to keep up a pretence, but I'm going to tell you the truth now so strap yourself in."

I pulled at the seatbelt automatically when she said this and felt foolish as I did so but then I sat back and listened to her story as we wove through the early morning traffic:

"We were a close family, the Galloways. I always looked up to my sister Georgie, idolised her really: she was five years older than me and was all that I ever wanted to be. She used to read me stories and I loved to listen to her sing song voice as she became more engrossed in them. She read 'Little Women' to me one summer week from beginning to end and I still treasure that book now.

When she hit her mid and late teens she got in with what they called the wrong crowd and began to drink and stay out all night. Much worse was to follow but my parents shielded me from it as much as they could. I went to University at eighteen becoming the first member of my family ever to do so, my sister had always had more potential than me but she never applied herself.

Shortly after the start of the second semester in my first year as a student I got a terse phone call from my parents who passed the telephone alternately between themselves. From their fractured words I heard that my beautiful sister Georgie had been found dead in the early hours of that morning, dumped by the roadside. I tried to get more information from them but they didn't seem able to tell me anything.

I returned home for the funeral of course but things had changed completely: my parents who had once been so kind and bubbly were now understandably sullen and uncommunicative. At the funeral, and at the wake afterwards, I got the sense that people were hiding things from me but everybody stuck to the official line that my sister had died of a sudden heart attack. I don't believe it, John, I just don't believe it.

Anyway a week went past and I felt that I had to return to my studies: I kidded myself that it was what Georgie would have wanted but in reality I couldn't take any more hours trapped in that silent house of mourning where my parents spent all day staring at the linoleum on the floor.

I had arranged to return back to them for a few days a month later but three weeks after I returned to University I received another telephone call, this time from my Uncle Pat. My mother and father had both been found dead in their house: it seems that it was some kind of suicide pact. They had left a note for me, I guess trying to explain things, but when it was handed to me unopened I ripped it into little pieces before I had got two lines into it.

So there I was, eighteen and all alone in the world. That's how I've turned out like I am. Maybe things would have been different, maybe not. All I know is that not a day goes by when I don't miss Georgie, my parents too I guess although I still feel angry at them for what they did, but my how I miss Georgie. I heard someone say once that mourning can last between a week and two years but I've been mourning for her for ten years now and it's not getting any easier. I wish I had dreams, I wish I could think about her. I try so hard but nothing comes: all that I have left of her is that faded photograph."

She grew silent now, lost in her thoughts, and I was so moved that I had to battle back the tears that had risen up tentatively in my eyes. I wanted to hug her but she was driving on resolutely and so I stroked her leg tenderly.

She turned to me again now and to my surprise she announced:

"You can help me, John. I know that you can help me." She noted the quizzical expression on my face and so she explained: "For the last twelve months I have been seeing a woman called Irina who lives in a flat near the City centre. I had her recommended to me. She is a psychic John, a medium as people say. She can speak to the dead, but only when they want to speak. I need to know how she died and if she is okay, and then maybe I can rest too. I've been seeing her once, twice, sometimes three times a month now, travelling from London when I had to, and sometimes I feel that there is going to be some kind of breakthrough but then nothing happens and I go home feeling worse than ever.

John, I believe in strange things – I believe that there is more to this world than we can ever know. It wasn't just chance that led me to you yesterday. You are psychic too aren't you? You've seen visions of Georgie and I think that you can find the truth out for me, for Georgie. You're my only hope, John."

Her words had left me speechless. Was I psychic? It had never occurred to me and it was not something that I had ever believed in but what other explanation was there for the things that I had been seeing and for the remarkable events that had overtaken me?

I didn't want to know if I was psychic or not and the only medium that I wanted to see was on the label at the back of my T-Shirts but then I remembered how much Rosa had done for me and how it had felt as I lay my head next to hers that morning. Above all I remembered her tragic story and I resolved to do all that I could for her.

Rosa's car pulled up now in front of a grotty looking old building made of blackened stone. We were in Pitsmoor, one of the less glamorous suburbs of Sheffield where the choice of gangs was more important than the choice of subjects for its schoolchildren and where the trials of poverty were a reality for too many of its population.

Rosa pushed a button on the outer door; it had a sign next to it which read 'Flat 1 – Madame Irina Markova'. As the door was slowly opened I didn't know what to expect but I felt uneasy. A stooping grey haired woman with a deeply lined face who could have been aged anywhere between fifty and seventy opened the door to us and beckoned us in to her flat. A crimson carpet covered the floor and numerous sticks of incense burned in holders that were placed carefully around the periphery of the room that we were ushered into.

A small table was situated in the middle of the room which was surrounded by four stools and upon the table lay a pack of cards, a candle and a kitchen knife.

Neither myself, Rosa nor Madame Irina had spoken since we entered the house which felt colder than the air outside and the silence added to the unease that was growing inside of me: if I was being honest with myself then I would have realised that I was uneasy at the prospect of discovering the truth about John Halle; the truth that I had been struggling to hide within myself for too long and at too great a cost to myself.

Madame Irina reached a thin hand out to me and I thought that she was going to show me where to sit but as her hand clasped mine she shouted out in a voice still heavy with a Polish accent:

"John Halle! John Halle! I can feel the power rising strong within you! I've never felt one like this before. Watch out, Halle, watch out! I can see the flames all around you, I can smell the smoke. Beware of the flames that grow nearer and nearer or else you will be consumed!"

I was truly scared now and I wanted to shake my hand free of hers, although she held me in a strong grip that belied her outward frailty. Despite my inward promise to Rosa I wanted to run and denounce Irina as a fraud and a charlatan. I looked away from Madame Irina but suddenly and unavoidably my eyes were drawn to the corner of the room and I saw to my horror a figure standing there that banished all thoughts of flight from my head.

Chapter Nine

When my alarm had rudely awakened me two days ago I had nothing more to worry about than how long it would take to get rid of my hangover and whether or not I would get to work in time for the start of another year chained to my old familiar desk in the soulless office that was home to me from Monday to Friday. A little more than forty eight hours later and somehow I was in a red carpeted room filled with the overpowering smell of incense and standing alongside Rosa, a beautiful woman to whom I owed my life and Madame Irina, a medium from Poland who was going to use me to channel the dead. It seemed that she might be successful in her attempts because in the corner I could see, as clearly as I saw the two people alongside me, Lamara Gallagher – the love of my life who had died more than twelve months previously. Things had certainly changed over the course of two days.

Madame Irina held on tightly to the hand that I had tried to wrench free from her a moment before. She led me over to the table that was positioned in the centre of the room where Irina lowered her old hunched body down onto one of the four stools whilst Rosa sat on the stool that was directly to the left of the one occupied by Irina. I was now faced with the choice of which of the two remaining stools I wished to take. One stool was directly to the right of the aged psychic and the other available seat was to the right of Rosa and facing across from Madame Irina. This would have been my preferred choice, the presence next to me of Rosa would have calmed the nerves that were racing within me, if it hadn't meant that I would be looking straight into the face of Lamara and so I took the seat next to Irina which meant that the vision of my ex-partner was now positioned behind me and over my right shoulder.

I kept my eyes fixed firmly on the table as I shuffled nervously on the stools hard wooden surface. I could no longer see Lamara and by a great effort of will power I forced myself not to look around. Still I could sense that Lamara remained standing behind me and if I should happen to cast a glance over my shoulder I would see her again.

Questions ran through my mind now: was I mad? Had it been a trick of the light or was the charged atmosphere playing tricks on a consciousness that had been strained to breaking point over the last two days? Had I seen her at all? The only answer that I could truthfully give to myself was that yes, somehow, I had seen her. I had seen Lamara in dreams that had occurred almost nightly since she had passed out of my life but now I could not doubt that I had seen her again not in a dream but in a reality: a reality that very was different to the one that I had existed in previously but one that I now realised I was to inhabit for the rest of my life.

In my dreams her appearance and actions changed regularly, night by night. Sometimes, on happy occasions, I would see her as the fresh faced and smiling young woman that I had first met in the bingo hall so many years ago but more frequently I would see before me, as I slept, the faded, tired Lamara that had ended her life with such pathetic tragedy. Sometimes she would laugh and talk with me as if we were still together: we would discuss holidays that we planned to take or I would ask her how Skye was doing at school; at other times she would look at me with anger, accusation or even hatred in her eyes; on the darkest of nights I would see her as if she was a rotting corpse rising from the earth and she would stare at me with empty eyes that saw nothing – on those nights I would jump out of bed with sweat dripping from my forehead and unable to get back to sleep, I would pass the hours until daybreak rocking self consciously on the edge of my bed with the radio and lighting on as if to drive away the demons.

The Lamara Gallagher that I had seen in the corner of Madame Irina's room, and the one that I could still sense standing behind me, seemed to be a dreadful composite of all the Lamaras that had haunted me so relentlessly over the previous twelve months: she looked young and beautiful and her clear white skin showed no traces of the scars and lines that could be found on it in its later years, her brown hair shone brilliantly rather than being unkempt and greasy. She was wearing a vest top in the Brazil football colours and a pair of white jeans that had become black and dirty in the creases that ran through them, her feet were uncovered: this more than anything had sent a cold shiver running through me as it was the clothing that she had been wearing when I had found her dying. Her lips were closed hiding the gap toothed smile that I had loved so much and her large blue eyes that had once sparkled like the most exquisite sapphires were now dull and unfocussed as if they saw and registered nothing. She had been staring directly at me but no sign of emotion or recognition had been visible on her face. Every sinew within my body was straining to turn my head sharply to its right and an incessant voice was in my head telling me to look over my shoulder but somehow I kept my head down and focussed on the card table in front of me until the worst of the madness seemed to pass from me.

Rosa and Madame Irina were silent as if they sensed that I had seen something and no efforts were made to rouse me from my miserable inertia. The only noise in the room came from cars that drove past outside and the shouts of youths who seemed to be in competition with each other to see who could talk in the loudest and quickest fashion. Eventually the noises from the world outside seemed to fade away until the room that we four were in seemed to become the whole universe and all that I could hear was the ticking of a clock that appeared to grow louder and louder until each little tick of the finger sounded as if it was a hammer blow being landed upon my skull.

I took deep breaths now and as my heart beat began to slow down and the ticking began to return to normality I raised my head and looked at the two women who were sat down with me. Madame Irina was holding Rosa's right hand in her left hand and now that she saw me raise my head Irina held out her right hand expectantly. Rosa was looking at me with intense concentration on her face but as I looked at her she threw me a warm smile of encouragement that renewed in me the resolve to help Rosa in any way that I could, whatever the cost to me may have been.

Everyone remained silent but I nodded my head as if to show my acquiescence and I took Madame Irina's hand that was still proffered before me. The hand was dark and worn and the skin was stretched tightly across it showing the raised blue veins that ran markedly over it. Her fingers now clenched tightly around my fingers and her long white fingernails dug into the fleshy palms of my hands as if she was trying to squeeze the strength out of me and draw it into herself.

Madame Irina addressed us both now:

"My friends, it is good to have you both here today. Miss Rosa, when you telephoned me this morning it was as if I had been waiting for that call for all of my lifetime – I have not known this man but somehow I knew that he would be drawn to me."

Rosa smiled at both of us in turn now, as if she felt confident that the answers that she had been seeking were finally to be brought within her grasp, but I sat quiet and stony faced, still uncomfortable with the new turn that my life had taken and the revelation of the new and strange powers that it seemed I possessed.

"Mister John, John Halle – that is your name isn't it?" Irina inquired with relaxed informality as if she found nothing exceptional in the circumstances or in the conversation that we were having and my grim faced nod gave her the answer. She continued:

"John Halle, Miss Rosa has told me all about you and about the remarkable story that you share. I was intrigued, I was excited, I had to meet you. Let me tell you that I am not disappointed, when I first saw you enter my flat I could see what you are and when I touch your hands I can feel what you are. I can see what even you cannot see about yourself – am I right?"

She liked to ask questions and so I answered:

"Yes, I suppose that's right. I don't know why I'm here really and I don't know what's been happening to me in these last couple of days."

"But it hasn't been just for the last two days has it John? It's been a lot longer than that – since you were a small child I imagine. But all your life you have been fighting to hide it – you should know that when you fight against yourself it is a fight that you can never win. The last two days have simply brought the truth to the front of your consciousness and forced you to acknowledge it."

"And what is the truth, then?" I asked sharply, although as Madame Irina had guessed I knew the answer before I asked the question.

"You have a great psychic ability – let me explain. I have trained as a medium all of my life, I have practised daily and honed my skills first in

Poland and now here, but all I can do is attempt to talk to those who have passed over to the other side. Sometimes I am lucky and I get a message and sometimes there is nothing there, but you – you can actually see the people who have crossed over to the other side. You see things that nobody else can see, you can look into the past as though it were happening right now. Does this make sense to you?"

Madame Irina fixed me with a penetrating stare and I felt powerless to resist any longer. It was time to admit the truth that I had been hiding deep within me for so long.

"Yes, it makes sense. I didn't realise it, but yes I guess that is exactly what I do."

"And then you can help me, John – help me contact Georgie?" Rosa interjected with an excited smile upon her face.

"I don't know, Rosa, I just don't know. If I could then I would, but well I don't know. I don't seem to have any control over what I see – it just happens to me whether I want it to or not."

"You are a channel, Mister Halle," said Madame Irina, "the spirits are using you to send a message to people who are still living here in our mortal world."

"How can we use this channel, Madame?" Rosa asked with a voice that betrayed the years of despair and longing that she had suffered since those fateful weeks had robbed her in her youth of a sister and parents. I didn't like the way that I was being de-personalised and referred to as a channel as though the human side of me had ceased to exist but I waited to hear how Madame Rosa would respond.

"We shall see, my child. We shall see. I have tried to contact your sister on many occasions now but all without success. We know for a fact that your beloved Georgie has chosen to contact this man before and so I believe that this time I will be able to make contact with her."

I looked at their faces from one to another and saw that Rosa now had a look of grim determination on her face and her eyes were closed and lips sealed tightly as if to aid her concentration. Madame Irina had a calm and relaxed air but it seemed to me that I could feel energy building around her. She looked directly into my eyes and I started to look away but pulled my head back to her gaze as I remembered what was standing behind me, or should I say who was standing behind me. I could feel her presence as if she was breathing down my neck.

Madame Irina tightened her grip and started to rock on her stool pulling my hands forwards and backwards as she did so. I was unfamiliar with the procedures of a séance and my knowledge of such things was limited to watching snatched moments of Most Haunted on television as I flicked through the channels but I was filled with a mixture of fear and amusement as I watched the aged woman rocking backwards and forwards on the flimsy stool that teetered on three legs and then two as if it was going to give way beneath her at any moment.

I could not take my eyes from Madame Irina as she continued her rhythmic convulsions. Her face, which had appeared indelibly lined at first glance was now furrowed even deeper as she contorted her face from some great pain or some great effort or, as I thought, some great artifice. Her arms were sinewy and bore the marks of age but she had a wiry strength that ran tangibly through her. I thought that she was probably younger than she appeared to be but that a lifetime of worries had pressed down upon her.

I had now admitted to myself that I did possess some rare parapsychological ability and that this hidden talent, if such it could be called, had coursed within me since childhood. Since my earliest days I had seen glimpses of things out of the corners of my eyes and even in daylight I had experienced moments where it was as if I was suddenly walking through a sheet of blackness before entering back into the sunshine seconds later. I was a committed rationalist and therefore I was left with little option but to believe that the girl on the bus was Georgie, the sister of Rosa, who was hidden from the vision of everybody else who had been travelling with us. I also realised, however, that these visions came on their own volition and I had no means of controlling or summoning them. It was for this reason that I remained sceptical about Madame Irina, rocking backwards and forwards before me with her head staring up at the ceiling, and wondered whether her powers simply extended to taking money from gullible and mourning people. It struck me that the woman who I still felt standing behind me was there because of my latent psychic ability rather then anything that the Polish medium had achieved and the fact that Irina seemed oblivious to her presence made me question her credentials even more.

Madame Irina then began to move her head up and down and from left to right in random spasmodic movements and a low groaning noise began to come from her that sounded as if it was not of this world. My curiosity was roused now as to what she would do next but at the height of her movements she suddenly stopped and sat bolt upright on her stool. A calmness descended upon her and she began to speak:

"Are you there? Georgie Galloway can you hear me? Make you presence felt."

I looked across at Rosa now and while her head remained downcast and her eyes closed I could see that the knuckles on her right hand had turned white from the pressure with which she was gripping the older woman's hand.

"Georgie – your dear sister Rosa is here again. She just wants to know that you are okay, that's not too much to ask for is it? Please send us a sign – all we need is a sign."

The room went quiet now and as Madame Irina remained silent for minute after minute I could hear the ticking of the clock growing louder again. I felt somehow disappointed in myself, as it was a failure on my part more than anything else that meant that Georgie was once again choosing not to communicate with her sister.

Without warning the door opened slowly and I looked towards it with a curious reluctance. I could see nothing initially but I heard a soft padding across the floor and then I jumped backwards with fright, pulling my hand from Irina's in the process, as a small figure suddenly jumped onto the table in front of us.

Madame Irina fixed me with an icy stare and I realised that it was only a cat that had entered the room: and not even a black cat at that, but a rather scrawny looking tortoiseshell creature that had seen better days. Madame Irina shooed it from the table and I rejoined my hand with hers, a foolish half smile of apology upon my face. She started to speak again: "Georgie, are you still there? I could feel your presence drawing nearer and nearer before the chain was interrupted. Can you still here me?"

I didn't like the way that Irina was shifting the burden onto me, and hoped that Rosa wouldn't be swayed by the old woman's opinion. I was becoming more and more convinced that Madame Irina's powers, if they existed at all, were much less potent than she liked to pretend and wondered how much she charged her visitors to subject them to an hour or so of frustration.

"Please send us a sign to show that you are here" pleaded Madame Irina, now with a hint of desperation in her voice. The cat, after being shooed away by its owner had shuffled from the room again as if embarrassed at its actions but soon a different disturbance altogether happened.

A pack of cards had been placed in the centre of the table, at first I had thought that they were an ordinary deck of cards but now I saw that they were what I imagined to be tarot cards although I had no experience of using them or seeing them used. Madame Irina had gone into silent reflection again and Rosa looked at her with sad eyes which suggested that once again she had resigned herself to having made another wasted journey to Pitsmoor. I knew that she would try to hide it but her downcast face seemed to say that the faith that she had shown in me had been misplaced.

Without warning the women saw the cards rise from the table and they were dispersed around the table one or two at a time, falling in random fashion onto the table top or onto the floor. One of the cards landed on my lap but I paid it no attention for I could see what the women couldn't see: the cards were not flying across the table of their own accord but rather they were being thrown around by Lamara who had now abandoned her position behind me and having walked over to the other side of the table, unseen by Rosa and Irina, was looking defiantly in my direction.

Rosa stifled a scream that had been raised in her throat; she looked terrified as if she could cry, but whether she would have cried from happiness or fright I couldn't say. She had longed for a sign from her sister, and spent large amounts of time and money in her pursuit of it, but her reaction now showed that deep down she had never expected it to come. Madame Irina remained as calm and collected as she had been throughout the séance and she spoke again to the spirit that she wrongly imagined was that of Georgie:

"You have come, my girl, you have come. I thank you for gracing us with your presence. Do you have a message Georgie, do you want to speak to your sister Rosa through me?"

Irina went silent again but the cards lay where they had fallen. Irina began to talk again and my ears caught mere flashes of her words that appeared to be imploring Georgie not to remain silent now that she had manifested herself. I lost most of her words as I was too busy focussing on the vision before me. Lamara had lost the dullness that had been in her eyes when I first saw her in the room and now she looked more alive than she had when I first saw her in the Barnsley bingo club. She kept her eyes fixed on me and I could not pull myself away from then. It seemed to me that when Madame Irina asked Georgie if she would speak, Lamara answered for her with a vigorous shake of her head. I sat unblinking in my chair as if I had gone into a trance but this spell was broken as Madame Irina now extracted her hand from mine and as I finally looked away from Lamara I found that the two women were now looking intently at me.

"I. I'm sorry. I'm not feeling very well" I offered to the two women by way of explanation although I didn't know what I was apologising for. I placed the palms of my hands onto the table and raised my shoulders as I prepared to stand up and leave the room but Irina pushed me back onto the stool, once again demonstrating the strength that was belied by her fragile appearance.

"Stay here, John, just a while longer" she said before addressing Rosa alongside her:

"Rosa, my darling girl, would you please leave us alone for a short time. John has seen something and I can still sense the presence here. Maybe Georgie is reluctant to speak in your presence at the moment or maybe she has already been speaking to Mister Halle? I would like to have a private chat with him if you don't mind?"

"That's fine" replied Rosa and I thought that I could discern a hint of sadness to her voice as if she was upset that her sister would choose to talk to a stranger rather than to her but as she was walking out of the room she turned to me and said with a sincere enthusiasm:

"John, please do anything you can – don't be afraid. Please do this for me."

"I will do anything that I can for you, Rosa" I mumbled back.

"Help yourself to a cup of tea my darling", Irina shouted to her. It was a gesture that seemed strangely incongruous in our present setting where there was a palpable tension hanging heavily in the air.

Rosa had left the room now but my eyes were once again turned to Lamara. She turned to walk out of the door now but as she did so she walked over to my stool and standing right next to me she whispered in my ear:

"Next time you visit me John, please bring something for me. I deserve that don't I? And, who knows, maybe I have something for you?"

She stroked my neck tenderly after she said this and if I had been surprised at seeing her in the room it was nothing when compared to the heart stopping shock that hit me when I found that I could physically feel her fingers caressing my neck just as if she was still alive and living with me.

She walked towards the door now and I had to restrain myself from shouting to her to stop but I blinked my eyes in disbelief and when I opened them again a fraction of a second later she was gone. I looked around the room hoping to see her standing in some corner but she had vanished completely and returned to the unknown place that she now called home.

It would have been impossible to describe the emotions that I was feeling as I didn't understand them myself but I held my head in my hands and silent tears began falling from me causing my shoulders to heave up and down.

I felt the thin arms of Madame Irina around me and she held me in her grip to comfort me whilst making shushing noises like a mother would make to a young and upset child. She raised me from the stool and as she did so the card that had landed on my lap fell to the floor by the side of one of the stools four wooden legs.

Guiding me by the arm the Polish matron led me over to a frayed brown coloured armchair that reclined in the far corner of the room next to the window. Grey curtains had been drawn across the window which had lent the room a dark and gloomy aspect but Irina threw them open now letting the sharp January sunlight flood into the barely furnished room. Irina looked into my eyes, which were tinged with red and at which I dabbed with my fingers to remove the wet remnants of my tears, and said:

"She is gone now isn't she? I can feel that her presence is gone."

"Yes, she's gone."

"You have a power, an ability, such as I have never seen before: that is why it has drained everything out of you. I could feel a presence, but I know that you could actually see her. Am I right?"

"Yes, that's right."

"Did she say anything to you?

"Yes she did." My answers were terse and to the point but I was still confused from my encounter with Lamara.

"What did Georgie say? Please take your time." Madame Irina spoke to me in a soft and coaxing voice and I noticed that her East European accent was much less prominent now than it had been when she had addressed both me and Rosa together.

"It wasn't Georgie at all. It was somebody else."

"Somebody else?" asked Irina with disappointment in her voice.

"Yes, it was Lamara Gallagher."

"Does this Lamara know Georgie perhaps?"

"No. Well, I don't think so. Not as far as I'm aware. We used to live together. She died."

"Have you seen her before, since she passed to the other realms?"

"Only in dreams. I see her every night in dreams."

Madame Irina spoke to me in soothing tones now:

"John, you are a good man and this is all new to you, and we all know that new things can be frightening. I can help you, John. Tell me all about this Lamara, and what happened today, and then maybe I can tell you what she wants. Would you like that?"

I had to think for a while but then replied: "Yes, I suppose that I would."

"Then tell me everything that you think that you need to say. Unburden yourself; I won't say a word to anyone – living or dead. You have a rare talent, but a raw one and you don't yet know how to interpret the messages that are being sent to you. That is how I, with my little talent but large experience, can help you. So speak, John, and I will remain silent while you tell me all that you want to tell me."

I had stored feelings up within me for over a year now and had talked about Lamara to nobody in all that time. My friends sensed that I didn't wish to talk about her and rarely mentioned her as if the past that we had shared together had never happened at all. It felt strange that I was going to tell her story to a woman that I barely knew but in other ways this allowed me to be brutally honest in my telling of it. I took a deep breath and began her story although in all the time that I spoke I kept my eyes fixed on the old crimson carpet rather than looking my listener in the face:

"I first met Lamara Gallagher many years ago now. I was in my early twenties and I had been stumbling from one dead end job to another since I had graduated from University. At this point I'd managed to secure myself the position of trainee manager at a bingo hall, it could have had career prospects I suppose but I was inherently unsuited to it and it was just another stepping stone on the rocky road that I suppose you could call my career. Have you ever been to bingo? I think you'd like it."

I threw the question out as a means to delay the need to talk about Lamara but Irina, true to her word, remained silent and so I continued:

"I was only at the bingo hall for a short time and, taking everything into consideration, I disliked that job more than any other that I've held and so it would have proved to be perhaps the most inconsequential phase of my life if it wasn't for the fact that it threw Lamara into my life.

I had rapidly grown tired with the world of bingo, where the retired and unemployed grew addicted to betting on random selections of numbers and spent their days moaning that it was either too hot or too cold. I took every opportunity that I could to stay out of the way of any actual work in the hope that I could pick up my pay cheque without doing anything for it.

One fateful day I had retired to my preferred hiding place of the reception area where my duties were nothing more strenuous than looking smart while I said hello and goodbye to people and occasionally showing prospective customers how to fill in application forms. A stream of customers had gone past, dozens and maybe even hundreds, with no consequence to me when suddenly I saw a young woman walk through the doors who looked so beautiful that it was as if I had been hypnotised by her. This was, as you can guess, Lamara.

She was twenty one years old, and I just a few years older, but it seemed that she had so much more experience of life than me: I had had an easy ride; school was followed by University which was followed by jobs that brought in regular salaries that more than met my requirements. She had been a teenage mother who had brought up her daughter Skye single handed and had now moved to Barnsley to make a new life for herself and the child that she loved.

I'd had a series of one night, or when lucky slightly more than one night, stands and a semi-serious affair whilst a student that had lasted two years but was never going to survive our respective graduations. I had considered myself to have fallen in love with all the shallow frequency that young men and women across the world have always done: the love that is like a balloon where it seems to be growing and growing and getting more and more exciting but if the surface is scratched just once it become apparent that there is absolutely nothing inside – it's all surface and hot air. From the first second that I met Lamara though I knew that this was something completely different and, happily for me at the time, I soon found out that she felt the same way.

She came into the club for the next three consecutive days and on each occasion we spent more time in each others company until she barely played the game at all preferring instead to spend her time chatting to me. She was absent on the fourth and fifth day and I began to feel that maybe I had misread the signs, as I was wont to do, and that she hadn't formed the same sort of attachment to me as I had to her. At other moments I would imagine that some other, more attractive, man had come along and won her heart and in a jealous rage I would rail against myself and my spineless inaction around her.

On the sixth day however, as I was walking around the club in a general mood of despondence having all too quickly given up on the idea of seeing her again, I saw her walk through my doors again and speak to one of the ticket sellers who stood by the doorway. It seemed that she had been asking where I was because he pointed at me and then she walked quickly and purposefully over to where I was. She explained that her daughter, Skye, had been ill and that whilst she was a lot better now she had to rush back to see her again and so couldn't stop. I wanted to believe her, and had no reason not to other than the pessimistic cloud that hung over me, but I found it hard to be convinced that she wasn't using this story just to brush me off once and for all. I told her how much I had missed her and to my surprise she kissed me on the cheek and replied that she had missed me too. She handed me her telephone number, which was written on the back of a folded bus ticket, and told me to telephone her that night. As she walked back out of the door I kept thinking back to that peck on the cheek which seemed to be worth more than all of the kisses I had received before and it was as if the gloomy artificially lit club was bathed in glorious spring sunshine. I'm sorry to get so florid in my descriptions here, Irina, but when I think back it's as if it had all happened today – I didn't know how quickly the sunshine was to be eclipsed.

I telephoned her that night with a sense of panic within my heart. This was in the days before mobile phone usage had become endemic and so it was her landline that I had to call: I worried that she might be out when I called or that it might be an inopportune moment that would put her in a bad mood or, worse, that I would telephone and have nothing to say to her. The only telephone calls that I usually made were either to my friends or parents and I liked to keep them as short as possible so I was unsure how to begin my conversation with Lamara and how to keep it going if it began to lag. After putting the call off a number of times I finally rang the number and as I listened to the ringing noise with a heavy heart I calculated that if the call lasted ten minutes I would have done well and there was definitely a future together for us. She answered quickly and when I heard the cheery note in her sing song voice all of my fears were instantly allayed. I was surprised to find that our conversation flowed easily and when I finally said goodbye I was surprised to find that I had been on the telephone for more than fifty minutes which was easily a record for me. More importantly than that was the fact that I had arranged, well the truth was more that she had arranged it for me, to meet Lamara at a town centre pub for lunch and a few drinks on the forthcoming Saturday when I had a rare day off of work.

When the big Saturday came I was nervous in a way that I had never experienced before and instead of throwing on the first shirt that came to hand, as I would normally have done, I tried on four or five different options and agonised over which one best suited the occasion. I was at the pub early, having a drink for Dutch courage, when Lamara came in and said that there was somebody that she had to introduce me to:

163

following behind her was a small and beautiful child with long blonde hair, a colouring that I assumed was a trait from her father, and large sparkling eyes that she had inherited from her mother. Lamara explained that her baby sitter had let her down at the last minute and she hoped that I wouldn't mind that she had brought Skye along. I didn't mind at all, I liked children and it was a joy to see the mother and daughter together who were obviously so happy in each others company. I quickly finished the drink and we three headed to a child friendly pub nearby where Lamara and I sat sharing drinks and conversation while we watched Skye happily playing in the ballpit or drawing pictures with crayons. It was an idyllic first date and it seemed to me as if we had been a family for years. When Skye grew tired from her exertions I booked mother and daughter a taxi home and after Lamara ushered her child into the back of the vehicle she turned and, hidden from her daughter, placed her arms around my neck and gave me a long lingering kiss that seemed to transport my soul from my body until it felt that I was floating above myself and looking down upon the happy scene.

We started seeing each other regularly after that, and I soon went to her house every evening after work where she cooked me a meal with more skill and love than I could ever have managed for myself. We had our usual furtive kisses when Skye went to bed, at a frustratingly late hour for a young child, whenever we could but we always ran the risk of a shout from upstairs putting an end to our intimacy and so for the first three weeks it remained a sweetly chaste affair. Lamara then announced that her mother was taking her only grandchild, Skye, to a caravan that they owned in Mablethorpe on the Lincolnshire coast. I asked the bingo company for the weekend off at short notice and, as was their right, they refused and so I handed in my notice and phoned in sick so that I could spend the weekend alone with Lamara. We embraced as soon as I walked through the door and taking each others hand we walked up to the bedroom without saying a word. We undressed quickly and I stood in front of her in speechless awe at her naked beauty. We made love with tender slowness and it was as if the world had ceased to be and that all there was or had ever been was me and Lamara: it was a moment in my life that I felt would never be surpassed, and as I'm being unflinchingly truthful here I have to admit that it never has.

That weekend changed us and although we hadn't known each other long it was clear for all to see that we were painfully in love with each other. I worked my notice at the bingo club without enthusiasm and quickly replaced it with a job at a bank that whilst being mind numbingly dull was easy and unchallenging work. My new job paid more than my trainee managership had and I found myself with an increasing amount of spare cash that I was happy to splash on Lamara and Skye. Looking back now it seems that I should have noticed how profligate Lamara was and how quickly she was willing to spend other people's money as well as her own.

It was barely three months after that day when she had first walked into the bingo club that I invited Lamara to move in with me: I had a disposable income and had just moved into decent sized privately rented house that was plenty big enough for us all; Skye had grown as attached to me as I had to her and we could be a real and loving family unit together. I put the case to Lamara and waited for her answer but it didn't take long for her to say yes and within a week we were all living under one roof.

I had never lived with a partner before and raising a child was a completely new concept to me: but whilst I had difficulty at times in disciplining Skye, which sometimes infuriated Lamara as she came across as the bad parent who had to say no and administer telling offs whilst I was the good guy who said yes and bought Skye little presents, it was on the whole an easy and happy adjustment and our first few years together were as pleasant as I could have hoped for.

Skye was at school now and although I wasn't her father I treated her as I would a child of my own. I was so proud at the little achievements that she made at school and read to her every night whilst her mother would be sat downstairs enjoying a cigarette whilst she watched one of her soap operas. We hired babysitters whenever we could and spent many nights at the cinema or at a pub or club. I liked to have a drink and could hold a reasonable amount but for a moderately sized woman Lamara could drink me under the table: she was unable to have just two or three and then call it a day but instead had to drink until she was drunk. At times she would get aggressive with people that she had imagined had thrown a catty comment her way and she got involved in fights on more than one occasion. From time to time her old friends would visit her from Huddersfield and they were a very loud and extrovert bunch: I would dread their visits as it always ended up with me going to bed and then being woken at four or five in the morning by the sound of drunken arguing from below. I tolerated it all, however, because Lamara said that it made her happy and on the whole our relationship was still a strong and loving one."

I fell silent for a moment as I approached the traumatic end to the story and looked up at Madame Irina who sat next to me on the sofa that appeared to be as old and worn as she was. She remained silent but her eyes urged me to finish and so I continued:

"Now that Skye was at school Lamara said that she wanted something to occupy her during the daytime and, with the help of her old friends, she obtained a job in a factory that packed frozen poultry. The job was based in Huddersfield but she insisted that she could easily commute there and that her friends would drive her home when they could. I was unsure of her friends and wanted somehow to keep Lamara all to myself – I was insecure and felt that if she became more independent it would only be a matter of time until she would find somebody else. I was secretly happy, however, that Lamara would be bringing her own wage in as she had been spending my money at a rate that couldn't continue indefinitely.

At first things went smoothly but within a few months she spent more and more time with her friends in Huddersfield, sometimes crashing at their houses for days at a time leaving me to look after her daughter on my own.

When she did come home she was often drunk or aggressive or sometimes it was as if she was in a world of her own and the words that I said were floating over her head. Although we still shared, all three of us together, happy moments from time to time the situation began to deteriorate over the next couple of years.

Lamara had always smoked cigarettes, Embassy Red as I remember, but shortly into our relationship I found that she liked to smoke cannabis joints at the weekend: it didn't appeal to me but I was happy to let Lamara enjoy this harmless diversion.

Now that Lamara had her own job, and her own income, it was becoming apparent that she had moved onto stronger substances. She would come home at all hours of the night with glazed eyes and rapid, incoherent talk. I confronted her on many occasions but finally Lamara admitted that she liked to take ecstasy and amphetamines. She convinced me to try these products with her and occasionally, when her mother was looking after Skye, we would meet her dealers in bars and then Lamara would pass the wrap of speed from her mouth to mine in a passionate kiss. We would return home and make love for hours on end and then the next day it would feel as if I was dying and the dryness of my mouth would choke me.

In truth though, Irina, I only partook on rare occasions and preferred to stick with alcohol which was my drug of choice. Lamara, on the contrary, was becoming more and more dependent and would often take days off work as she recovered from her excesses.

On one night I went to Huddersfield with her but rather than going to clubs or visiting friends we spent hours trawling seedy crack houses where the iron fronted doors would be opened cautiously until they saw Lamara and then we would be admitted into filthy hovels that stank of stale cigarettes and vomit. I refused to touch the drug, attracting contemptuous stares in the process, but watched in horror as Lamara expertly placed a small stone of crack into the bottom of a modified jar and then mixed it with cigarette ash before lighting the pipe and breathing the fumes. I remember her telling me that the secret was to take in the fumes but then expel them again before they were inhaled because the fumes were so bitter that it was impossible to inhale them without gagging. I knew, during those endless and horrifying hours, that I had to end our relationship but I had grown so used to her company that I was scared to do so and I kept giving her one more chance.

She grew less concerned about her appearance and about Skye, and eventually Lamara's parents came to collect their granddaughter and take her to live with them: Lamara seemed completely unperturbed at this event but I'll never forget the looks of accusation that they directed at me as the three of them walked out of the door.

We were arguing regularly now and when Lamara informed me that she was moving into a squat in Huddersfield I didn't try to stop her. I was living alone again, and regaining the strength that she had drained from me, but some strange, seemingly unbreakable, ties kept us together and on alternate weeks I would travel to spend a night with her or she would travel to see me.

I had travelled to the one bedroom flat that she now called her own when she disappeared into the kitchen for five minutes and then ten minutes. When I went to find her she was lying prone upon the floor and barely breathing with a syringe next to her arm. I telephoned the ambulance in a strange calm as if I had expected this to happen and as if I had known that she had become a heroin addict. The ambulance men came and after checking her pulse and breathing they injected a shot of adrenalin into her: the result was astonishing and she came round almost immediately. The ambulance was waiting to take her to the hospital but she insisted that she was fine again and ushered them out as if nothing had happened. I left with them without saying a word. How I wish now that I had said a final word to her.

Two weeks passed and as the age of mobile phones had by now arrived I spent those two weeks ignoring her calls and text messages. It was Christmas time but I had decided to make a clean break and had returned the gifts that I had bought for her to the shops while posting Skye's presents to her grandparents' address.

On Boxing Day it was a Halle tradition to go out with my friends and get as drunk as possible and this year I felt like drinking more than ever both to forget the dreadful year that I had endured with Lamara and to celebrate the new opportunities that the end of our relationship had given me. My friends had never liked her and congratulated me on the new lease of life that I had found.

When I eventually staggered home on the Boxing Day evening I knew immediately that something was wrong. The front door was open, although I had locked it behind me earlier in the day, and a strange and cold calmness seemed to fill the house. I knew instinctively that I was in the presence of death and when I pushed open the living room door I saw Lamara lying there hollow eyed and bare footed without a trace of life left in her. I still don't know why she travelled to see me on that day: maybe she wanted to die at the closest thing that she had to a home? Maybe she had become angered at being ignored by me? Maybe she had brought me a Christmas present? At the inquest it was found that Lamara had been pregnant with our child, I know that it was my child. I can't forgiver her for that."

I would have cried then but the tears over Lamara had long since dried up within me. I turned again to Madame Irina:

"So that's it – that's my sordid little story. And that's the Lamara Gallagher who I saw here in your room today."

Madame Irina remained silent for a while longer as if in deep thought but then she took my hands softly in hers and spoke to me:

"Yes you have had a hard life, but then we all have hard lives. A man like you, who can sense what others never know, must feel it more than anyone. But do you know why you have seen Lamara, and why you have seen Georgie?"

I shook my head and mumbled that I didn't know.

"If you look within yourself then you will find that you do know, John Halle. You have a power that is so rare that I have never seen its like before but yet you are scared of it and wish to hide from it until it goes away. Let me tell you that it is never going to go away but that it will get stronger and stronger – you need to embrace it and master it for you are its master. Bring your powers to the front of the mind and listen to the messages that the dead are giving you.

Lamara and Georgie are both contacting you because they are not at rest. They need somebody to find out why they died, how they died, and then at last they can return to peace. You are that somebody, they have chosen you because they have faith in your ability to help them. I can sense it – they need you to find out what happened to them and it is more than that: they are crying out for vengeance."

I sat there with a maelstrom of thoughts running through my head: did Lamara want revenge and if so who from? From me? Madame Irina had said that I needed to know how and why she died but as far as I was concerned that had been put beyond doubt at the inquest over a year ago: she had overdosed on a self administered cocktail of drugs and choked on her own vomit. And then it seemed that Georgie wanted me to bring some sort of justice for her as well but why had she chosen me and why now? Irina seemed to sense the questions in my head and she said:

"Those cards that flew across the table didn't move of their own accord did they? I couldn't see anybody but from what you've told me I can guess that it was Lamara who scattered the cards to draw your attention. Find the card that she threw at you and bring it to me."

I obeyed without question or comment and rising from the sofa I walked slowly to the stool that I had occupied whilst my mind was deep in thought on other matters. I remembered where the card had fallen, face down, and picking it up from its position next to the rear right leg of the stool I brought it across to its owner. Madame Irina looked at the card and then turned it with deft fingers so that it faced me. The card meant nothing to me and so Irina explained:

"This is the Five of Swords. It represents dishonour and loss and betrayal by a friend. Look inside yourself because this is the message that Lamara wanted to pass to you, if you search hard enough you can find its meaning. Know also, that it won't be coincidence that both of these women have chosen to contact you at this time. If you can't bring rest to these women then how will you rest and how will Rosa rest?"

I could not deny that I had seen visions of two dead women that were so realistic that it was impossible to tell them from the living people around me and it seemed plausible that they had appeared for a reason and did want to convey some message to me but I was far from convinced that Madame Irina knew more about the meaning of their apparition than I did. It still seemed to me that she could be a charlatan feigning a

mystical air to make a living out of the gullible but she could feel my uncertainty and what she did next dispelled these doubts from my mind. "I can sense that you are unsure of me, unsure even that I have any craft at all. Well come to me now and let me lay my hands upon you, John Halle, for I have a message for you too. What it will be I don't know, but it is irrevocable, a prophesy of the future that can not be changed."
She reached out her bony arms towards me and although I was reluctant to let her touch me I needed to know if what she had said was true. I bowed my head before her and she placed her fingertips on my temple. It felt as if I had placed a battery on my tongue and I could feel a blast of energy jolt through me. The room seemed to darken and then fade until I was no longer in the room at all. Smoke seemed to be all around me and I was retching as it filled my mouth and my lungs so that I had to pull my arm across my mouth to stop it. I could see a wooden floor before me but the way in front of me was completely blocked by fire and the blazing heat forced me back. I saw a figure crouched and then crawling on the floor but then an oak beam that was fiercely ablaze fell on top of it and pinned it to the ground. Fire was consuming everything now but as I backed off I discerned the face through the smoke and my stomach churned as I recognised the face that was so very familiar to me.
Madame Irina removed her hands from my head and the vision faded instantly as I found myself knelt in front of the sofa in her Pitsmoor room.
"Doubt me no longer, John Halle. Do what you have to do, but you have to help Lamara and Georgie – you are the only one who can help them and who can help yourself."
I fell onto the floor and lay there with my knees tucked underneath me as if in the recovery position. Irina called Rosa back into the room and after she had whispered in her ear they lifted me back to my feet and Rosa walked me out of the room and from the building to the cold street outside. Rosa seemed concerned but had a steely determination in her face. She embraced Irina and passed money from her hand to that of the Polish woman. I stumbled towards the car in silence and Rosa opened the white door and helped me into the seat. A group of youths who had been watching the car intently now scattered and ran away down a side street. I was still sat in shocked silence as Rosa reached across and fastened the seat belt around me.
"Madame Irina has said that you will have a lot to tell me but that it's taken a lot out of you and I have to be patient with you. We're going to drive home and then if you want you can have a nice long bath or sleep

for a while, or do whatever you want. We can speak when you've rested a little. Is that okay?"

I said nothing but Rosa stroked my leg again tenderly and pulling away from the kerb started the journey back to the Broomhill flat.

"I'm so grateful to you, John, for all that you're doing for me!" She looked at me and smiled as she said this and as I began to pull myself out of my daze I gave her a weak smile back.

Yes, I would certainly have some talking to do with Rosa but what had affected me so deeply and shockingly was something that I felt I would never be able to explain to her: I had just seen my own death.

Chapter Ten

I was lost in silent thought as Rosa drove us through the streets of Sheffield and back to her ground floor flat on an elegant side street of Broomhill. Rosa cast sideways glances at me from time to time and I gave weak smiles in return to allay her concerns.

The visit to Madame Irina, the Polish medium whose house we were returning from, had lasted less than an hour but it had given me plenty to think about and for a while I forgot about Georgie, the girl on the bus, and Lamara and the mysterious people who seemed to have spent the last two days attempting to kill me. I was lost in a moment of introspection as I realised that Irina had revealed the secret that I had been hiding from myself all of my life. I had finally admitted, in a moment of self awareness and awakening, that I had psychic abilities that were alien to most people: even more than that it seemed that I could actually interact with dead people, not just through dreams or voices in my head but actually face to face – they had chosen to visit me so that I could help them achieve the justice that had been denied them beyond the grave. It was as if Madame Irina had provided me with the key that would unlock the rest of my life, but it seemed a huge burden for me to bear.

As this thought ran through my head I found myself wondering how long the rest of my life would actually be: decades, years, days, hours? As soon as we had entered Madame Irina's flat she had shouted at me: "Beware of the flames that grow nearer and nearer or else you will be consumed!" I'd put this down as the rambling of a charlatan, or a madwoman, but try as I might I could not forget the vision that had hit me when she had placed her hands on my head: it was more than a vision it was a reality – a glimpse into the future that awaited me. I could feel the heat of the flames around me and the smoke entered my lungs and choked me as I saw myself, my future self, lying prone on a wooden floor, trapped by a burning beam, and about to be swallowed by the flames. So this is what it would all come down to – that was the horrific end that awaited me and there was nothing that I could do to stop it. And yet hope springs eternal in the human soul, although Irina had said that this was a definitive vision of the future that could not be altered I clung onto a hope that somehow, somewhere, I would be able to escape this fate. It was only by clutching at this straw that I managed to keep myself sane.

By the time that the car pulled up outside of the large Georgian building that had become my temporary home in exile I had managed to convince myself that not only could I escape, but that I would escape. I didn't know how it would happen but I could not bring myself to believe that each man's fate stretched out unalterably in front of him. Madame Irina had marvellous powers that had hitherto been hidden from me but I believed her to be wrong on this point and it was my firm conviction, then as now, that we make our own way in life and that the actions we make today determine the future that awaits us. I felt a new courage begin to rise within me: yes, one day I would meet my fate and yes that day could be soon but until that moment came I was going to do everything that I could to help Rosa, and Georgie, and solve the puzzle that had enveloped me.

I followed Rosa into her flat with a calm heart and conscience and she seemed to notice the change that had come over me during the short journey. We both gave each other broad smiles now. I sat down on the black leather sofa and Rosa walked across the corridor into the kitchen to make us warming drinks. Tramp rose from the basket where he had been resting and walked across to me. He stood in front of me, a magnificent, beautiful and proud creature, wagging his tail as if we were already firm friends. I smiled at the dog and patted the palms of my hands onto my knees before stretching out my arms before him. At this signal Tramp jumped up onto the sofa and lay down contentedly on my lap where I stroked and smoothed the hair on his head.

Rosa had returned from her kitchen now and handed me a delicate blue china cup that had steam rising seductively from it. She placed herself into a leather armchair which was situated adjacent to the matching sofa and warmed her hands around her mug as she spoke to me:

"It looks like you've made a friend for life there. Tramp is very perceptive you know, spaniels always are, and he knows that you're a good man – he feels comfortable in your company."

I was happy at this compliment, especially since I felt that it told me more about her feelings rather than those of her dog. I sipped at my tea, which was still boiling hot so that I had to blow on the surface before taking another mouthful, before Rosa spoke again:

"Is that tea okay for you?"

"Yes, it's great – thanks. I can't help noticing though that I've got a dainty little china cup and you've got a great big mug for yourself." I chastised her in jest and the twinkle in her eyes told me that she took the comment in the spirit in which it was intended.

"This isn't any old mug – it's my ET mug!" As she said this I noticed that the mug was indeed shaped like the cute extra terrestrial of movie fame and the handle took the form of one of his arms. "I've had this mug since I was a little girl, my dad took me to see the film at the local cinema, it was the first that I ever saw, and I fell in love with the little thing – I had ET duvets, ET books, an ET sandwich box but all I have left is this lovely old mug. So the tea is to your liking then, John?"

"Yes, don't worry I would have let you know if it wasn't but you've made it just the way that I like it – nice and milky with one sugar. Good guess, or are you sure that you aren't a bit psychic too?"

She laughed and replied: "No, no – I'll leave all of that to you. If I was psychic I could have saved myself all of the money that I've spent on that Madame Irina over the last few months. Are you okay with being a psychic though, John, it scared me to see you curled up on the floor like that and then you were so subdued in the car on the way over here?"

"To be honest, Rosa, it was a huge shock to me and it took a hell of a lot out of me, mentally more than physically. Yes, I'd always felt that there was something different about me and all through my life strange little things had happened to me that I was at a loss to explain but when Irina, with your help, revealed the truth to me it came like a bolt from the blue. And some of the things that I saw, well I won't go into them because I don't know how you could believe them, but they were touching my past and my future and it was all a bit too much to take. But I'm fine now; in fact I've never felt better."

Rosa grinned at me and took an appreciative slurp from her mug before asking:

"And do you think that you can help me John, help me find out about

Georgie I mean?"

"Yes", I answered with confidence, "I'm absolutely sure that I can." Looking across at Rosa I felt humbled that she had placed such hope, such trust, in me. The death of her sister had haunted her for ten years and the pain of loss had only grown sharper down the years rather than diminishing. Outwardly she had become something of a success in life but her inner heartache had made this success seem insignificant – until she could find out why her sister had died nothing else in her life would be of any import. She had saved my life and now she sheltered me and cared for me when it seemed that the rest of the world was conspiring against John Halle, now it was time to start repaying her kindness. As I continued to pat the head of the loyal and faithful dog that was resting on my lap I knew that he would never let Rosa down and I resolved to be just as helpful. I didn't want to be insensitive to her feelings but the only way that I could help her was by being direct:

"Rosa, what do you know about your sister's death?"

"Nothing. Absolutely nothing."

"Nothing?"

"No, well only what the family told me at the funeral – that she had a heart attack and I just don't believe that."

"Why don't you believe it?"

"She was only a young woman in her early twenties, yes her lifestyle was a bit messed up but I can't believe that she would just have a heart attack and die. It just didn't seem to fit, but that's what they all told me happened. My family that is."

"Why would they have told you that if it wasn't true? I'm not doubting you, you understand, I'm just trying to put everything in order."

"I think they were trying to hide the truth from me; the trouble is that they hid it so well that I never did find out what it was. Whatever it was, it was something that they, my parents, couldn't live with. It sent them to their grave too and now, some days, it seems that my life is a living death as well. You're so lucky you know, John, being able to see her – I just wish that I could see her again."

I hadn't felt particularly lucky over the last two days when I'd been drugged or when I'd been beaten and left for dead, or when the police had threatened to frame me for a murder that had never happened but I kept this thought to myself. The dog had jumped off of my knee now and was circling the floor in front of his mistress who was sat forward in her chair with a playful smile on her face and a glazed look in her eyes that suggested that her thoughts were on happier days.

"When I was speaking to Madame Irina, whilst you were out of the room, she said that your sister had chosen to contact me because she needed my help – that she wanted justice or revenge of some sort. Does that make any sense?"

"Yes, yes I feel that it does. But I don't know how it makes sense, it's just a feeling that I've had too. If we could only find out how she died then maybe everything else would fall into place. I wish that we could turn back the clock ten years but even you can't do that can you?"

"No, even I can't do that." I looked at Rosa and wondered how she had looked ten years ago when she had been part of a loving family, just starting University with the whole world in front of her: now only Rosa remained. No, I couldn't turn the clock back ten years but I wasn't going to let that stop me getting to the truth of how Georgie had died and more importantly why she had died.

Rosa stood up as if she had just awoken from a deep sleep. She walked across to Tramp's basket and pulled out a lead. Rattling the lead in her hand produced a ringing sound from the metal fastening attachment at the end and this sent the spaniel into rapture so that he jumped into the air barking happily as he did so.

"Come on Tramp, it's time for walkies. I'm just taking Tramp for a quick walk down to the local woods and back, the fresh air will do him good and it will give me time to see if I can think of anything else that might be of use to you. Do you want to come?"

"Er, no thanks – I've had enough of woods for a few days so I'll give it a miss if that's okay. By the time you get back I'll have thought of what to do next, just wait and see."

Rosa smiled and nodded and I was glad that she hadn't taken slight at the fact that I hadn't wanted to share her walk into the woods, but as the last time she had seen me in the woods I had been bound and gagged and covered in mud and blood I felt that she had understood my reluctance. I patted Tramp's head once more as he walked past me and Rosa kissed me gently on the cheek before she left the room. It was a chaste kiss, such as might pass between a brother and sister, but it brought a pleasant flush to my cheeks that I hoped had passed unnoticed by her.

I rose from the sofa now and paced up and down the room hoping that inspiration might hit me. I had promised Rosa that I would have formed a plan of action by the time that she returned from her walk in the woods but I had little idea what that plan would be. How much did I know? I had lots of little pieces of information but I didn't see how they all fitted into place and without the missing information that would bring them all together they could be half clues or pieces of nothing.

Ten minutes passed and then twenty and I realised that while I had been pacing around in ever decreasing circles, wearing out her carpet, I had been thinking of nothing. Soon thirty minutes had passed and I was beginning to become concerned at Rosa's prolonged absence. I walked out of her flat and into the communal hallway and then out of the grand front entrance to the building.

Another group of youths, hooded tracksuits pulled over their faces, were gathered across the street. There was nothing unusual at that but it seemed to me that they too were looking at Rosa's car just as the group in Pitsmoor had been. I walked over to the white Ford Fiesta to see what was so interesting to people but as I did so the group ran off in silence towards the main street of this Sheffield suburb. I paced carefully around the vehicle but could find nothing amiss and no sign of any attempt at breaking and entering.

I had come out into the street with the intention of walking towards the woods where Rosa and her dog had gone but as I looked up and down the length of the street I realised that I had no idea in which direction the woods lay or the route that she would have taken to get there. I didn't like the idea of leaving my hosts flat unlocked and unattended and so with reluctance I headed indoors, still with no idea what to do next in my mission to bring Rosa the truth about her sister's death.

The minutes ticked past now and I felt the anxiety growing within me as each one came and went. Forty minutes had gone now and I worried that Rosa might have fallen into the same trap that I had found myself in twenty four hours earlier: it was irrational to think this way, I admitted to myself, but things hadn't been too rational in my life lately.

Another three minutes past and as my fears were growing to their worst and strange ideas had entered my head I saw the door open and the Spaniel ran towards me with his owner following behind him.

"I thought that you were only going for a short walk?" I said and instantly felt foolish for scalding her this way as if I was a father talking to his small child.

"That was a short walk for us. Were you missing me?" Rosa pouted in a kindly mocking manner.

"Yes, I suppose I was actually." I said this as I thought it to be a less embarrassing answer than the truth. The dog had climbed onto its back legs now and had placed his front paws onto my leg leaving wet and muddy prints there.

"Get down, Tramp" Rosa commanded and her dog obeyed. He had obviously been having a delightful and energetic time in the woods and was covered in mud and rusty coloured leaves. Rosa picked the spaniel up carefully in her arms and carried him out of the room. From the sounds of barking and running water that followed I could tell that she was subjecting her pet to a well warranted shower. She soon returned with Tramp looking like a new dog and with splashes of water across her clothing where she had stood too close to Tramp as he had shook himself dry.

"Seeing that I was gone so long that you were missing me, so I'm led to believe, I suppose that you must have decided what we have to do next?"

"Well, I have actually Rosa, yes" I lied. I remember hearing an extract from the bible when I was a child that had read 'On the mountain God provides' and whilst at the time it hadn't made much sense on many occasions since then I had put this statement to the test. I had no clear plan in my head but I decided to open my mouth and see what came out and once again I managed to pluck an answer seemingly out of thin air:

"You wanted to turn the clock back ten years and I'm afraid that none of us can do that, but do we really have to? We don't have to actually be there ten years ago to find out what happened – a beautiful young woman found dead in the street one morning is bound to have been reported on in the local media. I suggest that our first port of call should be the central library in Barnsley – they keep copies of all the papers going back a hundred years. I can feel this voice within me and it's telling me that we will find something there that's going to be very useful. What do you think?"

The only voice that I had heard was the one that had leapt into my head while I spoke but it seemed to meet Rosa's approval as after a few seconds thought she replied:

"Well at least it's a starting point I suppose. Back to Barnsley again? I'm glad that I filled up with petrol yesterday - I've never driven the little Fiesta as much."

She filled the dogs' water bowl and brought it from the kitchen to place it next to the basket where the exhausted Tramp was now asleep: from the twitching in his legs it seemed that he was dreaming about running through undergrowth or chasing cats and a contented smile had formed on his sleeping face. Next she fetched two unused notebooks, ring bound across the top, and a couple of blue biro pens that she handed to me for safe keeping. I felt that with a combination of Rosa's methodical approach and my intuition we would find some useful information from the library archives but I was to be surprised by what we did discover. Soon we were in the little car again, the one that seemed to be catching the attention of the cities youth that day: car crime was widespread across much of the country and I guess that car thieves would consider an old and poorly secured vehicle like this Ford Fiesta an easy target. Soon we had crossed the city centre and were on the M1 motorway heading north towards the town of Barnsley.

The northbound section of the motorway that we were travelling on was unusually quiet and the only hardship was keeping within the seventy miles per hour speed limit that seemed inadequate and antiquated in the present conditions. The south bound carriageway, on the other hand, was heavily bound in traffic heading back to the January sales at Meadowhall and to a lesser extent the city itself. Roadworks had reduced the carriageway from three lanes down to two, a situation that had been pretty much constant since the motorway had first been opened although it was hard to know what the workmen were doing and harder still to find them working at it.

As we passed junction 36, the turning for my home village of Birdwell, I wondered when I would be able to return safely to my home but I knew somehow that this wouldn't be possible until I had solved the mystery of Georgies' death and maybe that of Lamara too. Rosa looked at me as we passed the junction as though guessing what my thoughts were but she said nothing and kept the pedal to the floor until we turned off at junction 37 of the motorway and headed into the centre of Barnsley.

Barnsley was a moderately sized town that would have been much the same as many other Northern towns but for the binding sense of community that still reigned there. Yes the town had been in decline for many years now and the only industry that seemed to be thriving was crime but many of its citizens talked with pride of coming from the town as if it had made them hardier and better people. There was a growing sense that the scars of the Eighties miners strike, that ugly conflict that had decimated and divided the town so much, were finally being shaken off and a new optimism seemed to be growing in the town for the new century. Shops that had been boarded up were opening again but now the shops were internet cafes instead of pawnbrokers or delicatessens rather than laundries. I wasn't at all comfortable with a lot of the changes that were taking place, being worried that my hometown would lose some of its rough charm and individuality that marked it out from other towns of similar size, but even I had to admit that change was preferable to the slow death that had seemed to grip Barnsley during the previous decade. Although Rosa had often visited Shortwood, Hoyland and the areas around it that brought back happy memories of her childhood spent there she had not been into the Barnsley town centre itself for many years and she seemed surprised at the changes that were taking place. As we walked along the streets people would smile at us as if recognising that we too belonged in this town and mixed in amongst the thick Barnsley accent, that can seem almost impenetrable to newcomers to the town, could be heard accents from all corners of the British Isles as people were now travelling to the town rather than leaving in one long exodus from it as had been happening in the years since the coal mines, which had once promised jobs for life, had been closed. Here as well as in the surrounding smaller towns and villages building and construction work was visible everywhere and as we walked to the central library we passed scaffolding on every corner.

Barnsley's town hall dominated the urban landscape around it. A pre-war building constructed in overly grand fashion, George Orwell had devoted a significant portion of his documentary 'The Road To Wigan Pier' to denouncing the huge costs that it had taken to build the towns' hall while large portions of its population were starving or living in squalor. Those arguments, and the suffering of the townsfolk during the depression years, had been long since forgotten and the good people of Barnsley looked on this building with pride as it shone like a beacon of beauty surrounded by a drab forest of greyness.

The central library was situated a short throw away from the town hall on the aptly named Shambles Street but architecturally and aesthetically it was a complete opposite to the overbearing Town Hall. Built in an almost prefabricated style it looked like the sort of flat topped box shaped building that could have been expected to hide the secret police headquarters in some Eastern European capital. As I walked in, with Rosa striding purposefully beside me, we were hit by a blast of warmth from the radiators that were positioned strategically around the building and appeared to have been turned up to their very maximum setting: it was a welcome contrast to the cold conditions and icy air outside, but the shock of heat upon my face made me think again, momentarily, of the flames that I had foreseen blazing around me. I steeled my nerves and brushed all thoughts of my mortality aside; I had a promise to Rosa to uphold and somehow that seemed more important to me then.

This was the first day that the library had been open after the Christmas and New Year holidays and because of this it was unexpectedly busy. A large queue had developed at the checking in counter as people were eager to bring back the books that they had borrowed in the previous year: it was just twenty five pence fine for each day that a book was late but these soon added up and each pound was important to people who were so famously careful with their own money although I had always found them to be unfailingly generous in their treatment of others.

The library was arranged on three levels: the ground floor held the non-fiction and fiction books; the subterranean level held the children's library and small cafeteria that offered a choice between weak tea, weak coffee or weak soup; The upper floor contained the music and video library, a large and diverse selection of reference books and the local history archive that we were seeking.

Rosa had not been to this library since she was a child and at that time she had confined herself to the delights of the lower ground floor that held tales of hungry caterpillars and barn owls that were afraid of the dark. The library had remained the same on a superficial level, the décor had not changed since the day that it had opened, but for those who looked hard enough significant changes had begun to take place. There was now a large multi media library: originally this had contained vinyl records and then cassettes and eventually compact discs as well but now it was beginning to house DVDs and computer games. Further to this it seemed that the library had become a focal point for the local communities and the walls were covered with advertisements for various groups along with public information announcements. Every sign and poster had its writing translated into a selection of different languages in small print that was hidden under the main message – I thought it was slightly extravagant to translate the messages into Welsh, a language which was not particularly widely spoken in this corner of Yorkshire, but I didn't see that it was harming anyone and I suppose that it might have warmed the hearts of any stragglers from Tonypandy or Aberystwyth who might pass through.

The well worn and slightly battered looking chairs on this ground level had all been occupied by people who held books up close to their faces and had positioned carrier bags or folded newspapers by the sides of their chairs. I imagined that many of these people were not here to read but simply to escape the pitiless cold outside for a few hours: they were the army of unemployed people who had been sent forcibly out of their house at first light with orders to spend the day job seeking or they were pensioners who had also been banished from their houses by dominant spouses who were loath to have them around in case their brooding presence began to make the place look untidy.

We pushed past these people and ascended the large staircase that rose from the centre of the ground floor. Out of force of habit I had been moving my head from left to right and indulging in my pastime of people watching but Rosa had paid them no attention and walked impassively by my side as if fully concentrated on the job that lay ahead. She had bought into my story that I had heard voices compelling me to bring her to this library and I offered a silent prayer that my last second hunch would not let us down and that we would find some tangible new evidence about the hours leading up to her sisters death.

The upper level of the library was not as densely populated as the ground floor; people were unwilling to make the physical effort of climbing so many stairs when the upper reaches only held the promise of volumes of Yellow Pages that missed entries which had been torn out and books on esoteric subjects such as psychology and astrophysics. A large glass fronted room that was situated in the top right hand corner of this floor held the local studies and media archive, however, and this seemed to draw myself and Rosa to it like a magnet so that even I stopped noticing the people who were around us.

Rosa was unsure of the layout of the library but she had followed at my side unquestioningly as I led her towards the promised land that held the newspaper archives from the fatal night. As she caught sight of the impressive looking room, whose glass had a dark tint to it, she took my hand and squeezed it reassuringly but I could feel a slight tremble in her fingers as if after years of not knowing she was scared at what she might find to be the truth.

We walked hand in hand into the archives room and it felt good and it felt right to be so close to a woman again after suffering an over long period of cold loneliness. The room was darker than the open plan floor outside and it took my eyes a few seconds to adjust to the subdued lighting. As I squinted I saw a woman walking towards us who looked from a distance to be every inch the archetypal librarian. She was wearing a grey tweed jacket over a pink knitted top and a grey skirt extended to just below her knees. I would have sworn that she would have had a string of pearls around her neck or horn rimmed glasses on a golden chain but when she drew closer I saw that she was much younger than I had taken her to be and that her dark hair had pink highlights flashing within it that seemed to match her top.

181

The librarians name tag introduced us to Sharon Wells and she placed a book onto the counter that we stood in front of and told us where to sign in. Rosa signed first and then I followed and listed my name as being John Galloway. Rosa looked at me with wide eyes and raised eyebrows as I did this but she caught a quick hand signal that I made as if to gesture to her not to say anything and that I would explain everything later. The truth of the situation was that I was scared of them looking under my real name of John Halle, although I didn't really imagine that they would, and finding that I still owed them the return of a guidebook to Portugal and a compact disc that contained the Greatest Hits of Blondie – both items that I had borrowed more than two years previously. I had of course intended to return these items at the time but I had long since lost them and the letters that they had sent asking for their return had ceased to flow some time ago. I wanted to keep it that way and the events that had happened over the week had taught me to be cautious in all things.

The library boasted that it kept all copies of local newspapers and periodicals going back for more than a hundred years and you may imagine, as I had, that these copies would be stored as computer files contained upon DVDs. This may be the case now, for all I know, but at that time the information was stored on individual microfiche sheets and the library had a huge collection of these records. The slides were then placed upon a glass panel which when pushed into the microfiche viewing machine would carefully hold the slide in place. The viewers themselves were large screens that looked like they could have belonged to a computer from a Seventies science fiction movie. There was no way of performing any search on the data that was contained within the microfiche record as the viewing machines only function was to magnify the miniscule writing that was densely copied onto the slides.

Rosa informed the librarian that we wanted to see local newspapers dating from around the 29th of January 1991 and Sharon returned with a handful of slides that met this criteria. I positioned myself in front of one of the viewers, with Rosa sat in front of the adjacent machine, and together we began the painstaking effort of searching for a needle in a haystack.

It was a long and laborious task with the only way to navigate around the information on the screen being to make slight adjustments to the glass plate that could be moved around underneath the viewer. A tremble or a twitch in the hand could cause the information on the screen to jump and skip two or three pages at a time. As the minutes dragged slowly on I felt my frustration growing.

I was flicking through pages at a rapid rate hoping that somehow a word or an image on a page would draw my attention to it but all the while I risked missing out on a small collection of paragraphs that could have proved vital. My attention wandered now and I found my gaze straying from the screen to the large round plastic clock and then to the posters that were displayed on the wall: apparently the Mexborough Morris Men were planning a large display of their traditional dancing on February 1st – I made a mental note to be as far away as possible from Mexborough on that day. Next to this was pinned a small card which in hand written green ink asked for the return of a black cat with one white foot which had been missing since late October and answered to the name of Lucky. From these posters I found my gaze straying to the calves of Sharon Wells: it wasn't that her legs were particularly shapely, although they were in no way unpleasant to look at, but rather that her left leg showed the design of a blue dragon that rose from her ankle and travelled up the back of her leg for a good five inches; it was a beautiful tattoo but seemed quite out of place with my first impression of her as a dour librarian who had devoted herself to cataloguing books.

Time had ticked on as always and I felt guilty that I had not had the patience or discipline to stick to my allotted task. A pang of shame gripped me for an instant and I hoped that Rosa had not noticed that I had been less than diligent in my search. I looked to my right and saw that Rosa was engrossed in her screen and doubted that she would have noticed if I hadn't been sat there for the last hour. She was biting her lip though and the incline of her head that drooped forward from her shoulders told me that her search had been equally as unsuccessful as mine.

I tried to put myself in Rosa's position and wondered which would be worst: continuing to live in ignorance of the circumstances surrounding my beloved sisters' death or to find the truth in all its potential sordid squalor. I think that the coward within me would have preferred the former option but Rosa was made of sterner stuff and had made her decision: I turned back to my screen now and resolved to concentrate solely on the news print that rolled endlessly in front of me.

I read each story now, or at least the first few words of each story. I read about post office closures and new road extensions, about meetings with the mayor of our twin town in Germany, I read about the Barnsley in Bloom competition and about bonny babies and cute dog competitions.

The pages revealed to me a whole host of crimes large and small from the theft of mars bars from a working men's club and the local youths whose new hobby consisted in pushing sheep over so that they couldn't climb back up again to the petrol bomb that had destroyed a police car and to the post office raiders who had bludgeoned an old woman to death while she queued for her pension. What I didn't read about, though, in any way shape or form was the death of Georgie Galloway.

The tattooed librarian with the tweed jacket and pink hair came over to us now. In a voice that was barely above a whisper, although there was nobody else in the room to be disturbed, she informed us that it was half day closing today and that the library would be shutting in ten minutes. Rosa stood up instantly as if to leave and I could see that tears had formed in the corners of her eyes. It had been an emotional morning for her and it seemed that it would end in disappointment.

"Wait, Rosa, wait. We've got ten minutes yet" I counselled her and somehow as I said this I felt a strange confidence rise within me and a tingling sensation within my stomach as I knew with a sudden certitude that I would yet find the information that we had been looking for.

I crossed over to the chair, made of an uncomfortable plastic that seemed designed to stop people loitering for too long, that Rosa had vacated and sat within it. I moved the slide a page to the right and two pages down as if drawn there instinctively or as if I was being guided there and as I felt Rosa's hand on my shoulder the headline jumped out at us for all to see: "Hoyland woman found dead in street – tragedy strikes local beauty." Underneath this headline was a photograph of Georgie Galloway, aged 23, and I recognised again the girl on the bus staring back at me but to Rosa this meant so much more. I turned to look at her now and I saw her legs buckle slightly as if she would faint; I jumped out of the chair and quickly placed my arm around her to steady her, guiding her by the elbows I led her gently to the chair. She sat looking at the screen for a few seconds but then it seemed that she became conscious of the time constraints that had been placed upon her and snapping out of her lethargy she took the pen and notebook in her hands and began to transcribe the information that was on the screen in front of us.

The information seemed at first to be vague and unremarkable to me. Georgie's body had been found at five o'clock on the morning of 29th January 1991. The cause of death had not been ascertained as yet but foul play had neither been ruled out nor seriously considered as yet. It seemed that one of the contributing factors could have been exposure to the elements as it had been a bitterly cold night and Georgie's body had been found wearing only a thin white t-shirt, a pair of blue jeans and green converse trainers; it was noted that no money or valuables had been found on her person and I found myself wondering why they had reported on this fact. Locals reported that Georgie had been a very popular and gregarious girl who was often seen in the bars and clubs of Hoyland and Barnsley and was generally regarded as the life and soul of the party. Lately though, a source had said, she had become more introverted and had been spending more time with an older boyfriend and less time at her old haunts. There were conflicting stories about her personal habits with one source saying that she drank heavily and another unnamed source claiming that she had given up drink and hadn't touched a drop for weeks even during the Christmas celebrations: everybody though was in agreement that it had been a tragic waste of a beautiful life that had once seemed so promising.

Rosa scrolled down to the next page now although the shaking of her hand meant that she shot down two pages instead of one and had to adjust the glass slightly upwards again. She continued to take notes but I was paying little interest to the news that an inquest would be performed shortly or that the parents had been informed but that this unknown boyfriend had yet to be traced. My gaze had instead become firmly fixed upon a small photograph next to the story. It was a picture of a face that was familiar to me although it appeared to be younger and cleaner that I knew it – it was the face of the young man who had found Georgie's dead body lying in the street and who was named by the Barnsley Star newspaper as being one Thomas O'Callaghan, presumably in the days before he became widely known as Poor Tommy.

I was still staring at the screen when Sharon retuned to us and told us that we really had to leave now. This time Rosa had a contented look on her face and she hugged the notebook to her breast as if the four pages of notes that she had quickly scribbled down contained sacred writings. I walked alongside her and she grabbed my hand again as she walked. On the way to the large graffiti strewn car park that held her car Rosa talked happily and excitely of the information that she had already gained and seemed to think that this would be a good starting point for our investigation; I had to agree because although I was as yet no closer to completing the puzzle I had an unshakeable feeling that I'd just found a few more pieces to the jigsaw.

Rosa continued to chat excitedly as we drove out of the car park and away from Barnsley's town centre. To me it seemed as though the task was just beginning but Rosa, full of exuberance and enthusiasm, seemed to think that we were already nearing the end. She had an excited smile on her face and I imagined that this must have been how she looked on Christmas Day mornings with her family before it all went wrong.

As we conducted our way through the sparse morning traffic I tried to piece things together in my head. Poor Tommy had found Georgie dead, it seemed, but what had he been doing wondering down an otherwise deserted street at five o'clock in the morning on a freezing winters day? Fast forward ten years and the same Tommy O'Callaghan, now in very different circumstances, is walking along the same street with me – I send him out to check on a man that I believe has been following me but I never hear from him again until two policemen turn up at my house and practically state that they are going to frame me for his murder. The other thing that had grabbed my attention was the older boyfriend who could not be found – it was easy for me to jump to the conclusion that Tommy and this man were linked then and were possibly still linked now. Poor Thomas O'Callaghan had jumped to the top of the list of people that I wanted to see, but I had to get him before he really was murdered.

"Wait, slow down a minute", I called out to Rosa beside me. We were passing close to Birdwell again and I felt an urgent desire to check on the house that I loved and that I had left in such haste. "Can we check out my house just for a second please? I want to make sure that it's still standing, basically, and if we see anything untoward then you have just to drive on is that okay?"

Rosa looked worried for a second but, as was her way, she hid the worry deep inside of her and her face soon resumed its calm and cheerful exterior. "Okay, let's go", she said, "but don't hang around in there okay John?"

The car pulled off of the motorway and taking the first exit drove down the high street that ran through the length of my home village. It had been less than twenty four hours since I had last travelled down this road but it seemed like a lifetime away. As Rosa pulled up just outside of my house I looked anxiously at the building but could see nothing that looked out of the ordinary. Rosa agreed to wait in the car with the engine running and I promised her that I would be gone for no longer than two minutes.

I entered the house cautiously but with less trepidation than I had on the previous evening when I had found Rosa Galloway in my house as an unexpected but not unwelcome presence. Even before I had turned my key in the lock and entered into the old familiar building, wiping my feet on the doormat out of habit, I had a sense that I would find nobody home and after my visit to Madame Irina I was already beginning to trust my instincts with more confidence.

The whole house seemed to be at rest and as I walked from room to room I felt calmer and calmer. I made brief attempts to straighten some of the carnage that was still left from the raid by Osbourne and his Sergeant that had happened yesterday but I spent no serious time or effort on this as I didn't want Rosa to be sat in her car worrying about me. Entering my bedroom I found glass, that had once been an emptied bottle of Irish whiskey, still strewn on the floor and so I picked this up carefully and placed it into a carrier bag which I then carried downstairs and placed into the Silver coloured swing bin that was situated in the kitchen. Somehow it seemed that the ring that I had instinctively hidden inside that bottle held the key to everything but I was, for the moment, at a loss to explain who had taken the ring or even how they had taken it without attracting the attention of me or of the police who had been watching my house like hawks.

How had the police been watching me and was it only the police that had been watching me? For the last two and a half days it had seemed that everybody had been a step ahead of me, or at least alongside me, so that they always knew where I would be and when. Thinking of this made me hurry back to the car outside as I was determined not to let Rosa, the beautiful and caring woman that I had already grown close to, become as hunted as I was. I locked the door behind me and headed for Rosa's car with a vow in my heart that soon, very soon, I would be doing the hunting.

I had reached the car, which still had the engine purring, when a voice cried 'hi' from behind me. I turned around not knowing what I would find but to my relief it was my guitar playing neighbour that had come to his gate to meet me.

"I thought that you two were going away, neighbour?" he said to me.

"Well we are, we are, but I just had to collect a couple of things. We'd better be going now, in a hurry – you understand."

"Have you any forwarding address?" It seemed out of character for him to be so inquisitive.

"No, not really. The thing is we don't know where we are going yet – or even for how long. I'll tell you all about it when I get back."

"I'll hold you to that – and bring me a bottle of wine back."

"I will", I said and my fears vanished as I chalked it off as another attempt by the man to make the acquaintance of the people who lived near him. I had turned again to climb into the car when he stopped me by saying:

"It's just that somebody was asking about you this morning. Wanting to know where you had gone. A short, squat fellow he was."

"Oh yes, what did you say?" I asked without turning around again and trying to hide the anxiety in my voice.

"Well I just said that you had gone away. With your girlfriend. In her little white Fiesta."

"Oh thanks, thanks. I'll see you later." I waved at him without turning around; I didn't want him to see the look in my face which said that I was not at all happy with the news that he had given to me. I climbed into the passenger seat and Rosa drove away back to her flat, our flat, in Sheffield.

I wondered whether to tell Rosa what my neighbour had said but after a moments deliberation I decided to keep it to myself: she was in a happy mood that seemed to light up the whole car and I wanted to keep her that way for as long as possible. When she asked me if the house had been okay I simply replied that everything was fine and there was nothing to worry about it but all the time I was keeping an imaginary pair of fingers crossed in my head.

The journey back to her flat took significantly longer than the journey from it as we became snarled up in the traffic that was still queuing for the monstrous shopping centre at Meadowhall. Cars beeped their horns with frantic impatience as the season of goodwill was brought prematurely to an end. I asked Rosa what she had thought of the information that she had found in the newspaper.

"Well, there are lots of questions", she replied, "Yes it's definitely raised lots of questions in my mind. And that's good because you can't find the answer unless you know what the question is."

I liked this positive attitude but I would have expected nothing less from her.

"What questions has it raised then?"

"Well, the whole tone of the article seemed to indicate that the police thought that the death was suspicious. And the stories didn't really add up – those so called friends of hers don't seem to agree on whether she was an angel or a devil. I suppose that the truth is that she was somewhere in between like most of us are."

She had spat that word 'friends' out as if it was a terrible insult that had stuck in her throat.

"What about this boyfriend then, did you know him?" I asked her.

"No, I never heard about an older boyfriend before. Yes, I mean she was always very popular with the boys and the men too but I certainly wasn't aware that she had a serious boyfriend at the time of her death. And my parents never mentioned it to me. But then again they didn't mention much of anything to anyone after her death."

Rosa went silent again now and as she concentrated on the road ahead I saw her white teeth bite into her lower lip in a movement that I had grown to love and which signified that she was deep in thought. We had broken through the traffic jam now and as we grew closer to home she turned to me and asked:

"And you – what did you gain from the report? I suppose that you wouldn't have known anybody in it really?"

"Oh I wouldn't say that. Did you see the picture of that young man Thomas O'Callaghan who found your sister's body?" I felt callous referring to Georgie in that way but Rosa nodded her head and so I continued, "well I do know him – in passing. In fact I passed him on Tuesday."

"Really?" She looked me square in the eyes then before turning her attention back to the road but her voice had betrayed the excitement that she had felt at this news.

"Yes, really. Unfortunately, just yesterday I was informed that he was dead."

"What?" Her previous enthusiasm had now been replaced by a depressed sigh that seemed to suck all of the life out of her face. I hastened to reassure her:

"I don't believe it though. I really don't believe it at all – and what's more I think I know exactly how to track him down. It's not going to be pleasant but I promise that I'll do whatever it takes." I added the words 'for you' under my breath but when I turned to look at her she was concentrating on the road again and her teeth were biting into her lower lip once more.

With the traffic jams successfully negotiated we soon found ourselves back in the tastefully designed flat that was the temporary domain of Rosa Galloway and which had become the even more temporary domain of John Halle. I rubbed my hands to warm them until the central heating began to reach my bones but the house seemed quiet, too quiet.

Rosa walked briskly from one room to another and I could hear her throwing things to the floor as she went. She had already completed one circuit of the flat and now she began to look in the living room again. I followed her into the room and saw that she had a concerned look on her face and lines had appeared on the brow of her forehead.

"What's wrong?" I asked her as she turned from one corner of the room to another.

"It's Tramp. He's gone. He's not here." She rushed over to the dog basket and whilst the dog was no longer there it seemed that something had caught her eye. Reaching into the blanketed basket and moving aside the towel and squeaky pink bone that were contained within it she reached down and picked out the card. Rosa looked at it with wide eyes and an ashen face and then she began to weep great big sobs that shook her shoulders.

I ran over to her and placing my arms around her held her tightly against me. Her sobs now turned to wails and then her shoulders began to heave silently; as I held her tighter I felt the silent weeping spasms race violently through her body. She had grown silent now and hung limply in my arms. I stroked her back and then prising open her fingers I took the card gently from her hand.

The card had been almost crushed in her clenched fist and her nails had dug deeply into it. I managed to unfold it enough to read what was written on there and when I read it I cursed the guitar playing neighbour who hadn't known when to keep his mouth shut. Dropping the card to the floor I rocked Rosa gently from side to side as she continued to weep silently in my arms.

Chapter Eleven

It was incredible to think that I had known Rosa Galloway for less than forty-eight hours: already she had become an essential part of my life and I felt like we had known each other for many years. She had been a rock and somehow it seemed that she was the foundation that I could build my life upon; the new way of life that had opened up in front of me. Well, I guess that was the dream I had at that point but sometimes dreams just don't work out.

It would be no exaggeration to say that she had saved my life when she had first encountered me on the previous morning and since then she had been at my side when I needed her to comfort me and advise me. She had provided a roof over my head, a sanctuary when my own house had become unsafe and I had nowhere else to turn. When faced with situations that would have made most people turn away and flee Rosa had proved steadfast and loyal. Now, as she stood silently shivering in my arms, it was my turn to be strong for her.

I directed Rosa, still cradled within my arms, gently across to the black sofa so that I was leading and she was taking little backwards steps as I guided her. As soon as the back of her legs hit the front of the sofa she began to fall backwards and taking her weight within my arms I lowered her gently into the chair. She was still in a shocked daze and it was as if I had been moving a dead weight that saw and felt nothing.

It seems a peculiarly English thing to do but in situations like this but I have always found that a hot cup of tea is invaluable. When, as a young boy, my favourite Uncle died I remember my father breaking the news to me by bringing me my first cup of tea and I sipped it with tears dripping from my cheeks and making little splashes in the cup. When I had found Lamara dead in my house on that terrible Boxing Day I sat crouched on the floor next to her immobile body until the police and ambulance had arrived to carry out their pointless formalities: even on that day I had a cup of tea next to me when the authorities arrived, although I had no recollection of having made it.

Leaving Rosa on the sofa, alone with her thoughts, I crossed into her kitchen and seeing the kettle by the side of the sink I pushed the plastic switch down and turned it on. The kettle had a clear panel running along its side and this showed that it had been filled with water to its maximum limit; not having the time to wait any longer than was necessary I lifted the kettle up and poured its contents down the sink until the bare minimum remained before placing the kettle back upon its stand and starting the boiling process again.

I realised now that I had never used Rosa's kitchen before and as the first wisps of steam had already begun to issue from the spout I began a rapid search through the wall mounted cupboards for the necessary ingredients.

The cupboards were packed full of various consumables: fresh herbs and spices mingled with pre prepared sauces and little containers that contained multivitamins, iron supplements and St John's Wort: Rosa had never struck me as the depressed type but I suppose that this could have suggested that the wort was fulfilling its purpose.

Eventually, amongst the myriad of cans, jars and packets, I found the tea bags and a packet of sugar both of which bore the fair trade mark. The fridge was easy to spot, although it was white to match almost everything else in the flat. Pulling open its door I found a carton of full fat milk and placed it on the work surface next to the sugar. Rosa's ET

191

mug was hanging from a hook underneath the cupboards and so I took it down from the hook and placed the tea bag into it before pouring the now boiling water. I placed the milk in next followed by two generously portioned spoonfuls of sugar. I didn't know how Rosa took her tea but I always found that milky and sweet was best in these circumstances.

I turned to carry the drink out of the kitchen when my right foot struck something and looking down I saw it was a dog bowl that had been filled with water, most of which was now spread across my foot and the laminate flooring of the kitchen. Seeing the bowl made turned my thoughts back to the card that Rosa had found in the empty dog basket and which was now placed in my trouser pocket.

It was a card that measured about three inches across and two inches up and was in a light blue colour with a dark blue line just down from the top edge. Thin lines were drawn across it and it appeared to belong to some sort of filing system. The words that had been inscribed onto it read:

"We have your dog. Ask lover boy to give us what we want before midnight on Friday or it dies. And then on Monday we are coming for you."

The writing was quite measured and carefully scripted with a style that seemed somehow familiar and elaborate capitals used on 'Friday' and 'Monday'. There was, however, no name or number given and no further clue as to who had sent it or what they wanted.

Shaking the water from my foot I walked back into the living room and, sitting next to Rosa, I passed her the cup of tea that I had made in her favourite childhood mug. She sipped at the tea automatically as first but the warmth seemed to spread through her and at last she looked back into my eyes as if she had returned to the land of the living.

"What does it mean?" she asked and her voice sounded monotone and unemotional, robotic almost.

"I don't know what it means."

"You do know what it means" she insisted and although her voice still sounded detached its volume was raised considerably on the word 'do' as if she was trying to control her anger. I felt guilty for having lied to her then and earlier and expected a cockerel to crow at any moment.

"Yes I suppose that I do, sorry I don't know why I said that. Well the fact of the matter is that I don't know but I can guess."

"Go on then, your guesses seem to be as good as another person's facts so let's hear it."

"Well here goes," I began, "On Tuesday, shortly after seeing your sister on that bus journey, I was standing by a train platform not feeling at all well when I heard a crashing noise rent the air. There had been a car crash and I walked up to the scene to find a young woman crushed and dying under the wheels. It seemed that she was trying to say something to me but couldn't.

A large crowd had gathered by this time but I was the only one who had seen the driver flee from the scene and so I followed after him. I thought that I had found where he was hiding but then I was attacked, well drugged really, and left unconscious on a cold grassy floor. I staggered back to the scene of the crash and was surprised to find that it was completely deserted now and then even more surprised to find a ring on the floor.

I took the ring and began the painful walk home but it seemed that somebody was following me on the way. It was at this point that I met Poor Tommy, who it seems was the man who found your sister by the roadside ten years ago. Eventually I got back to my house and, following my instincts, I hid the ring securely. On the next morning two policeman kicked open my door, assaulted me and left me tied up in the local wood – which is of course where you came in.

Later in the day however, after I had been given the portrait that you found at my house, I was summoned to a meeting at the local cemetery. It was with one of the policemen but he insisted that the morning's attack had been against his will and that he wanted to help me. Apparently some mysterious person, not to be messed with, knows that I had taken the ring and was desperate to get it back. Before he could tell me anything else we were surrounded by a group of men who attacked the policeman, Osbourne was his name, but allowed me to escape.

So it's not too difficult to put these pieces of the puzzle together. We were either followed from my home to here or somebody gave enough information for us to be tracked down. I don't know who these people are except that they appear to hold some sort of influence or power to the extent where the police, or at least some of them, are under their control and they seem to be able to find out information on people at will. Osbourne had told me, as a friend he said, that I had to hand the ring in to the police station as soon as possible and I guess that they, whoever they are, have now taken your dog to use as leverage."

"But Tramp – why would they take Tramp?"

"I don't really think that they're animal lovers."

"So you have to do it then, you have to give that ring to them."

"Yes, that would have been my preferred option Rosa." I paused here unwilling to give her the sad news that I was unable to return her beloved dog to her but she seemed to have second guessed me again as she asked: "What's happened to the ring then, John?"

"I don't know, Rosa, I just don't know. I took pains to hide it within my house but when I woke in the morning it had gone. I know that the police didn't take it, or the unknown person who is controlling them, because they are still trying to hunt it down now and as far as I can tell nobody had entered the house during the night. It just seems to have vanished into thin air."

It wasn't the answer that Rosa would have wanted to hear but it was the truth and it was all that I could give her. The news that I thought would devastate her again seemed instead to galvanise her into action and I could see the colour, an angry flush now, begin to return to her cheeks. "What did this ring look like?" she asked with her old vigour returning to her voice.

"Well it was quite large and had a striking appearance: it was gold with a large green stone set within it; underneath the stone was a banded snake that was wound into the shape of the letter X – it was all quite beautiful but it seems that to somebody out there it's so precious that it's worth killing for."

"I know that ring" Rosa replied and of course this didn't surprise me. "Yes, I thought that you would."

"Georgie, as a young woman, had a brilliant and creative mind – she got that side of her character from our father. She liked anything that was beautiful; I suppose that was because she was so beautiful herself. So she got the looks and the talent in our generation, I just got the drive to succeed that comes from being the youngest sibling always trying to climb out from the shadow. I don't begrudge her of course, I love her."

I looked into her eyes as she said this and wanted to tell her that she was just as beautiful, in her own way, but I let her continue her story:

"Because of her love of pretty things she spent much of her teenage years designing clothes and designing jewellery. She never actually made them of course but she just drew the most exquisite pictures of her designs and then it was almost as if they were already real in her head. Her favourite design by far was this ring that you have described. Georgie had drawn it many times, each time more perfect than the last. She said that the green stone had to be large and dazzling like our eyes; she never did explain what the snake was for. And then one day, I remember vividly the happiness that radiated from her, she came home wearing that ring. We asked her how she had got it but she just wouldn't

194

tell us, instead letting a smile form on her face whenever she was asked. There was no way that she, or anybody that she knew, could have made it as it was just absolutely perfect, as delightful a piece of jewellery as you could ever see. She wore it rarely but I knew that she always kept it with her until, well until that day."

A smile came briefly to her face as she remembered happier days when her sister had spent hours making drawings of jewellery and clothing. My mind, however, was on different things: I didn't doubt that the striking green ring had belonged to Georgie and that was the reason why I had seen her wearing it on the bus and in the dreams that I'd had of her but how had I come to find it by the roadside and what link, if any, did it have to the unknown woman who had been crushed by the car two mornings ago? More importantly I wondered who or what had taken the ring from my house – it was going to prove difficult to get the ring back when I didn't have a clue who had got it. These thoughts were interrupted by Rosa who now asked:

"So how are we going to get this ring back then?" Not having an answer I remained silent and so she added imploringly: "We have to get it back, I can't just leave Tramp."

"I know, Rosa, I know. But I just don't see how we are going to find it again. I think that our only hope is not to find this ring but to find Tramp. This whole crazy thing is linked together somehow – me, you, your sister, the ring, the police, your dog, Tommy O'Callaghan. If I can just piece it together then I'm sure I could find out where they are keeping your dog."

"And then what?"

"And then I'll rescue him of course."

"How are you going to do that? These people are heartless, they could be killers. And what if you do rescue him – they'll only come looking for you instead."

"Yes, I suppose they will. But I'll deal with that when it happens because one thing's for certain, Rosa – I'm not going to let you down."

Rosa's beautiful mouth upturned slightly as I said that but it was a weak smile as if she wanted to encourage me but didn't really have any confidence that I could succeed in what she seemed to think was an impossible task.

I climbed from the sofa and began to pace around and around in a small circle which was a habit of mine when I needed to think. Rosa remained silently seated but I can only guess how irritating my circling must have been to her. I had been pacing restlessly for only a few seconds when my phone rang. I took the phone from my pocket and looking at the display saw that the call was coming from Steven Carter. I pressed the button and held the telephone to my ear.

"Hi Steven."

"Hi John, it's Steven – oh you know that already don't you? Is it a good time to talk?"

"Not really, I've not had many good moments to talk for a while actually, so you'd better just continue."

"Right. Where are you?"

"I'm at Rosa's"

"Who is Rosa?" My friends' voice registered interest.

"Oh, she's a good friend of mine – lives in Sheffield."

"I see, I see" he replied but of course he didn't see at all, "you'll need to get over here pretty sharp then."

"Will I? Why?"

"The intervention – you know, the one that we were talking about at The Red Fountain yesterday. Richard Clay. You were really keen on the idea."

I hadn't been keen on the idea at all but that seemed to have escaped Steven's notice.

"Yeah, the intervention. What about it?"

"It's tonight. I called round at your house about twenty minutes ago but you weren't there."

"Did you notice anything when you went to my house, Steven?"

"No, only that you weren't there. Of course, I know why now – you were too busy doing the horizontal lambada with this Rosie."

"It's Rosa not Rosie and – oh well, never mind."

"Anyway, pal, get over here as quickly as possible. I've lined a few other people up as well but the more people who turn up the better. And we've got no time to waste if we want to help our old school mate. Can you meet me at the cenotaph in an hour?"

"Yeah, I'll be there." I pushed the red button and slipped the mobile phone back into my pocket. It might seem as though I was abandoning Rosa in her hour of need or that I was allowing myself to become distracted from the task that lay ahead but things were beginning to make sense to me now and I felt that I needed to return back to my little corner of Barnsley, back to the scene of the crime so to speak, if I was to have any hope of solving the puzzle that stretched out before me.

"Who was that?" Rosa asked and she seemed more lively and attentive now.

"That was my good friend Steven, the guy that I met at the Red Fountain yesterday. He wants me to meet him in Hoyland in an hour. Ordinarily I wouldn't of course but –"

"But you think that you might find some more information out about Georgie, or the whole imbroglio around her anyway?"

"Yes, that's right. How did you know that?"

"Well I know you, John. And I know that you wouldn't go there now unless it was absolutely essential."

"You know me indeed, Rosa. But, look, I can't ask you to come as well. Stay here, you need to get some rest. I won't be gone too long."

"And how are you going to get there in an hour – run?"

"Taxi"

"Don't be stupid, you don't get rid of me that easily. I need to get out of the house, John, I need to keep myself occupied. And if you can find something out that might help me get Tramp back then I'm coming too."

I looked at Rosa still slouched tiredly upon her black leather sofa and wished that I could persuade her to stay behind. I didn't know what was going to happen when I got back to Hoyland but it was odds on that it was going to be dangerous and I wanted to keep her as far removed from that prospect as possible; I saw the sense in her argument though and I admired her resolute courage. Rosa rose from the sofa now and a new sense of strength and determination were evident upon her face. I nodded to her:

"Okay, Rosa, let's go."

As she reached over to her car keys I saw once again the picture, now in Rosa's possession, which had been given to me in The Red Fountain. Lifting the picture up I held it towards Rosa and said:

"Look, she's even wearing that ring in the picture."

"Oh, yes. And she's standing in front of the Elektra Palace."

"What's the Elektra Palace?" I asked although the name seemed vaguely familiar.

"You must remember the Elektra Palace – you're even older than me. It was the cinema down Elsecar way, that was the place where I went to watch ET. It's been closed for years now. All of the old things are gone."

Yes, I thought, all of the old things are gone but some of the old people still remained. The Elektra Palace - now that Rosa mentioned it the memories came flooding back. I had known it by its local nicknames of The Bug Hut or The Flea Pit and had spent many happy childhood hours there. What this information didn't answer though was how the cinema came to be in the portrait and how the artist had known Georgie enough to paint her wearing her beloved ring.

Rosa hadn't seemed at all surprised at the detail contained in the portrait but I supposed that her mind was still preoccupied with thoughts of her faithful and much loved dog. We had walked out of Rosa's flat and she turned to lock her front door behind us when it struck me that she had also locked the door when we had left the apartment to go to the library that morning and yet there had been no sign of forced entry into the flat. We were soon driving back through Sheffield and towards the motorway that led north to my hometown. It had begun to seem as if Rosa had become more than a friend but that she was practically my chauffeur too until I reminded myself that I wasn't going to Hoyland to help Richard Clay, or even just to please my friend Steven, I was really going there to help the woman alongside me and to start paying back some of the debt that I owed to her.

It was mid afternoon as we drove along the motorway but already the first signs of darkness had begun to descend. As we travelled I explained to Rosa that we were going to an intervention being carried out on my old schoolmate Richard, known as Little Dicky, Clay. She seemed puzzled at this and so I explained that an intervention was where a group of friends and associates would forcibly remove someone from their home in an attempt to stop their addiction to drugs – it was an attempt to save somebody who had become powerless to save themselves. I also explained to her that normally I would have had no desire to take part in such an event, believing that it is up to everybody to help themselves rather than rely on others to clean up the mess of their own creation, but on this occasion the words of Steven had attracted my interest: Steven had described seeing a man, a fellow addict, with Richard in his flat and from the description that Richard had provided it seemed very likely to me that this man had been none other than Poor Tommy O'Callaghan himself. I had a strong belief, or more accurately I should have said a strong hope, that Richard Clay could lead me to Poor Tommy – a man who seemed to be strangely central to this whole mystery.

Rosa seemed very interested in this information so that I, poor driver as I was, had to keep reminding Rosa to concentrate on the road in front of us. It was almost as if she believed that we would find Tommy, and maybe even Tramp too, at the Hoyland flat that we were going to but whilst I was reluctant to dampen her enthusiasm I knew that things were going to prove much more difficult than she imagined.

Rosa turned off of the motorway again as we neared our destination but, having covered many more miles than she had anticipated that day and with the return journey to come, she first pulled into a petrol station to fill her car's tank up. As she stood by the side of her vehicle, pump in hand and her eyes fixed on the reading in front of her, I headed into the shop at the top of the concourse.

A sudden and persistent rumble from my stomach reminded me that I had eaten nothing but toast that morning and with this realisation hunger began to grip me. I took and paid for a large 'grab bag' packet of ready salted crisps and while I waited for Rosa to queue and pay for her petrol I leafed through that days edition of The Barnsley Star. It seemed to be less sensational than the one that I had studied in the library, and the main stories were split between a new manager coming to the football team and elaborate and exotic looking plans for even more new housing to be build in what the newspaper called the 'necessary expansion and rejuvenation' of the town.

As we climbed back into the car I looked down at my watch and found that there was still twenty minutes until the designated meeting time. I had shared my packet of crisps with Rosa but this had only served to remind us how hungry we really were; at my suggestion we drove to a takeaway that was just around the corner and en route to the cenotaph where we were meeting Steven. The takeaway offered a large variety of food none of which could have been described as haute cuisine and most of which would have struggled to be described as edible cuisine. I opted for a cheeseburger, which came with an overwhelming amount of tepid fries and which by appearance and taste could have been cooked the day before, and Rosa had a spicy chilli burger which had been made extra hot to hide the cardboard-like taste of the meat inside it. We sat on a bench that ran by the side of the counter and ate our plastic food with little enthusiasm.

A large man was sat on the bench at the opposite side of the shop eating slice after slice of Hawaiian pizza; chunks of pineapple fell from the pizza onto the floor every time that he raised a slice to his mouth. He was tall with a stocky build and a perpetually puzzled look on his face that seemed to say that thinking tired him out and made him angry. At times I felt that he was staring at me but maybe he was looking at me simply because I kept looking at him. It was hard to tell. He ate rapidly, as if he had taken the wise decision not to savour the taste in his mouth for too long, and soon he had risen to his feet and wiped the back of his hand across his mouth. Before he left the shop he turned around and asked the bored looking man behind the counter if he knew how to get to the cenotaph. The instructions were given and the man walked out of the shop leaving Rosa to look at me with a puzzled expression.

"Do you know that guy?" she asked.

"No, and I don't think I'd like to" I replied. I laughed the matter off but the incident had me feel ill at ease again.

We finished our meal, or as much of it as we could take which for me meant leaving at least a couple of dozen cold chips in the plastic tray, and drove to Hoyland's war memorial to await the arrival of Steven. I hoped that the brute that I had seen in the takeaway wouldn't be there and as we left the parked car and walked across to the cenotaph I was pleased to see that he was nowhere in sight.

The cenotaph stood in the centre of the small suburban town of Hoyland and its striking monument contained a long list of the town's heroes who had fallen in action during World Wars one and two. A cold November Sunday every year saw the memorial covered in poppy wreaths but year upon year the number of veterans grew smaller and smaller and the wreaths were now provided by Boys Brigade groups, pubs and working men's clubs, churches and local businesses who were in the market for a little bit of free advertising.

Thinking back to that fateful bus journey, which had been three days ago but which seemed like more than three years ago, it struck me now that this was the spot that I had seen Georgie indicate to me by a silently mouthed 'here'. It was also a possibility that she had been indicating the sprawling cemetery, scene of my meeting with Osbourne, that lay further up the road just beyond the local comprehensive school that pushed out children with a handful of qualifications and a headful of hopelessness.

Rosa seemed to be deep in thought again as if just standing in this place was bringing back memories of her childhood. Whether they were happy memories or melancholic ones was hard to say and before I could ask her I saw a group of three men heading towards me. Two of them I knew as Steven and our mutual friend Ed and with them came the large man who had asked for directions in the takeaway.

I introduced Steven and Ed to Rosa and she smiled sweetly at them as if she hadn't a problem in the world. They seemed to be suitably impressed and I saw Steven's eyes broaden involuntarily as if he was impressed yet surprised to see me with such a woman. It was now Steven's turn to introduce the man that he had brought along and with a sweep of his hand he introduced Dr Rob Mitchell. I shook the hand that the good doctor offered and thought again how deceptive first appearances can be as I imagined that Steven had brought Dr Mitchell along to provide any medical arguments or expertise that may be needed.

It was a short walk from the cenotaph down the hill and towards the housing estate, a neglected relic from the Sixties, that contained the flat occupied by our erstwhile schoolmate Richard Clay. On the journey we passed the garage that I had took shelter in with Tommy O'Callaghan: it appeared to be locked and lifeless but I had to battle to control the urge that I had to run back to it and try its door again. The garage could wait, I decided. After all, it seemed that somehow I was the person who was renting the premises.

The estate was a collection of back to back houses that had now been turned into self contained flatlets and studio apartments, and houses that had been previously belonged to the council but had now been bought by their tenants who had then watched their property buck the national trend by plummeting in price. A maze like warren of streets and tight alleys, known locally as ginnels or snicketts, ran between the houses and the whole estate buzzed and teemed with life that was surviving hand to mouth. Speed humps had been placed at regular intervals along the main roads but they did little to prevent the joy riders who spent every night racing past assembled crowds as if in a modern day courting ritual.

I was unsure as to which of these flats, which all resembled each other and were often unnumbered to add further confusion to the senses, was home to Richard but Steven led the way with confidence and we all followed silently behind lost in our own private thoughts. Rosa was holding my hand as we walked but I could not have said if it was I that had sought her hand or Rosa that had grasped mine.

We soon reached a particularly inauspicious section of the housing estate. Windows were boarded up with pieces of chipboard and the gardens were overgrown with weeds that hosted empty cans and empty packets of cigarettes. Steven stopped now in front of one of the flats. A small oval sign on the outside of the fading yellow front door displayed the number one but it seemed as if there had once been another number alongside it that had now fallen off. He motioned at us, with an outstretched arm, to keep quiet and then knocked loudly on the door before stepping back a couple of feet. No answer came and so Steven knocked louder and more persistently and this time we heard the sound of footsteps from within coming to answer the call.

The door was opened cautiously and I saw Richard's head peer around the door. He looked at Steven for a few seconds and my friend looked firmly back at him. It seemed as if Richard was having problems identifying his visitor and so Steven helped him out:

"Richard it's me. It's Steven – Steven Carter. You remember me don't you?"

"Yeah, Steven I remember you" came the wheezed reply that seemed to carry no conviction.

"I'm your friend."

"Friend? What are you here for?"

Richard still had his hand wrapped around the door and only his head peered cautiously around it. In contrast with most of the houses and flats in the vicinity however he had not slipped the security chain on the door before opening it, as if he was past caring about personal safety, and Steven took advantage of this by pushing Richards head backwards and then pushing the door open. Ed and the doctor rushed after him and I followed behind at a more sedate pace with Rosa. I was in no hurry to see the pantomime that would await us inside.

As I sometimes like to use the pretence of being a gentleman I ushered Rosa into the flat before me and being the last to enter closed the flimsy plastic door behind me. The first thing that hit me was the smell: it was a stench that I had encountered many times before but the year or more that had passed since I last encountered it only seemed to make it more unpalatable. It was a powerfully acrid smell that seemed to be a cross between human excrement, rotting food, sweat and stale smoke. All junkies seemed to smell of this to some extent or another as if they were already rotting from the insides out.

The room that we had entered into now was woefully shabby and had no ornamentation or carpet on the floor. Old scraps of paper were strewn everywhere and empty chocolate wrappers and a large bag of sugar were on the floor in testimony to the heroin addicts overwhelming desire to eat sweet foods and nothing else. It seemed as if Richard lived in this room alone as a large cocoon style sleeping bag, with a faded brown stain across it, was stretched across the corner of the room. A work suit was hung up on a coat peg attached to the back of the room's door and it seemed amazing to me that whilst reaching this level of degradation Richard Clay had still managed to hold onto regular employment of some kind. An old fashioned looking television, in a fake wooden style cabinet, stood against the back wall but the dust that had gathered thickly upon its screen showed that either it didn't work or that it wasn't watched.

My eyes turned now to Richard himself. He was standing against the same wall with his back pressed against it as if he would retreat still further if he could. His bloodshot eyes were wide open and his face showed a terrible fear upon it. He was wearing nothing but a pair of white boxer shorts that hang loosely on his bony frame. He was painfully thin in the flesh, much more so than he appeared to be when hidden within the confines of his baggy work suit, and his greasy hair hung dirtily over his glistening forehead. The skin on his face had a distinctive yellow tint to it and this seemed to have spread to his arms as well. Bruises covered his arms and small sores and marks were prevalent across his lower legs and on the insides of his elbows. It was impossible not to feel sorry for the man who had been such a misfit at school but had risen to some level of success in his life before sinking to this all time low.

"What do you want?" he repeated and although he was trying to place some authority in his voice it came out as a frightened croak. Steven, who had appointed himself ringleader in this affair, approached him now and spoke to him as if he were addressing an ill child:

"We're here to help you Richard."

"I don't need any help."

"Don't you? Look at you, man. Why are you practically naked in here?"

"I was hot. I was trying to cool down."

"Cool down? It's the start of January man, it's minus two outside!"

He snapped his fingers and Ed and the doctor left the room as if had all been carefully choreographed beforehand. I had imagined that they had gone to find him some clothes to hide his pitiful body from our eyes and as I glanced at Rosa I saw that she was looking firmly at the dirt riddled floor.

The crashing sounds from the rooms that the two men had gone into however indicated to me that clothing Richard was the last thing that they had on their mind at that moment. I began to wonder what their plans were but I had decided to stay in the background and do and say as little as possible. I was only here to get the information that I needed and callous though it sounds I had no interest at that time in whether Richard cleaned his act up or injected himself into an early grave just like so many others who didn't know what to do when their dreams died.

The banging and crashing noises continued now and it seemed small comfort to think that at least the items that they were smashing would be of little or no value. Richard shuffled on the spot from one foot to another and although he writhed and sweated he did not move his back from the wall, it was as if he was caught in the unflinching stare that Steven held him in.

Steven lived according to his own strict morality – people who agreed with him were right and people who disagreed with him were wrong and there was nothing more to it in his eyes. He had lived an easy existence and had never had to worry about money or women or prospects or illness in the way that wears down the majority of people. He had no comprehension of the torture that he was putting Richard through and I felt that he was driving him to the grave quicker than any of his drugs would have done.

Doctor Mitchell and Ed returned to the room now. Ed was a largely silent man, a deep thinker but a man of little words. He was generally apathetic to most things and conversely could easily be brought around to agree with another's point of view. He was acting now not out of any deep conviction but simply because Steven had called him and he had nothing else to do on that cold dark night.

It was Ed that held out a small sealed plastic bag that contained a brown powder. Uttering his first words of that evening he told Richard that he was doing all of this for his own good. Taking the packet to the sink he pierced it with his thumb nail and then ripping it open he poured the contents down the sink before rinsing it away as the horrified addict looked on.

Richard sprang to life now and with a strange shrieking noise that seemed to come from deep within him rather than from out of his mouth he raced towards the sink with his arms outstretched. Before he could reach the sink, or Ed who was still standing over it, the doctor grabbed Richard roughly by his scrawny arms. Richard struggled wildly so that scraps of skin came off underneath the doctor's fingernails but he regained his grip harder now and then wrestled Richard to the floor. Kneeling down beside him the doctor kept his considerable weight pressing down upon him to prevent any escape.

Steven addressed our old schoolmate again and a fire burned within his eyes as if he was an evangelical preacher. He believed that he had studied his subject carefully but it seemed to me that his stories and statistics had been culled from some of the more sensationalist pages of the tabloid newspapers. He started by telling Richard of the health dangers that drugs could bring on: overdose, cardiac arrest, liver damage, thrombosis, and coma. He then tried to press upon him, whilst Doctor Rob more literally pressed upon him, that he was letting his friends and family down and how his poor mother would be crying over him every night. I knew that it was a wasted speech: health dangers of the future mean nothing to an addict when placed against the exhilarating but momentary pleasures of a score that would send a warm rush of tranquillity to blot out the agonising cravings. Family meant nothing to an addict and his only friends were the needle and the spoon. I had thought that the talk of the gently weeping mother had been crassly offensive but I guess that Steven had forgotten that Richard's mother had died whilst he was still a child and that this had been one of the reasons why he had been teased so mercilessly at school. Richard Clay still struggled on the floor with a madman's strength and Steven, seemingly bewildered that his well rehearsed and well meaning words had made no visible impact on his audience, now turned to me:

"Have you anything that you want to say to him, John?"

I was waiting for him to add that I had some experience in this area but he seemed to think better of it now and nodded at me as if to reinforce that it was my turn to talk. I crouched down to the floor near to Richard and asked him in a calm but firm voice:

"Who do you get your drugs from?"

There was no answer and the man on the floor didn't even attempt to raise his eyes to meet mine. I tried again:

"You were seen here with another man two nights ago. Who was it?"

No answer came.

"Who was it, I asked? You had better tell me."

Still no answer was forthcoming and although I tried to remain calm it was hard not to raise my voice.

"Tell me, Little Dicky, tell me. Well forget his name, just tell me where I can find him?"

Richard hissed at me after I said this as if he suddenly blamed me more than all of the others. I felt an urge rise within me to swing my boot into his face and it became harder and harder for me to resist this temptation. Steven placed his hand on my shoulder and led me away to the corner of the room next to the sleeping bag.

"You got a bit off message there, John" he said to me in a voice that almost seemed angry. I was in no mood to explain and so I replied:

"Look, you do it your way, and I'll do it mine. What are your plans anyway? I don't know why you wanted me here?"

"You've experienced it all, with Lamara. I'm sorry to bring it up mate but I thought that you would be able to get that across to him."

"Lamara is in the past you know, Steven, and I don't like the way that you keep dragging her up."

Of course the whole problem was that Lamara wasn't merely in the past but that I had seen her in a very real sense just that morning. Steven

205

patted my back though and I accepted the apology that my old friend offered.

"Okay", I said, "what are your plans for him now then?"

"I'm going to take him back to my house. Ed and Rob are staying over too and we are going to sweat it all out of him and then start all over again. Tough love, that's what he needs mate, tough love."

As he said this it seemed that the doctor had let his grip or his concentration falter for a moment for Richard somehow slithered to his feet. Ed and the doctor both grabbed him together now and in the melee that ensued the well worn boxer shorts were ripped off so that Richard stood pathetically naked in front of us. Still the struggle went on and was only ended when first the doctor and then Ed landed hard and meaningful blows to Richard's thin ribbed stomach that sent him crashing to the floor where he vomited up a darkly bilious and foul stinking liquid.

Rosa, who had said nothing since entering the flat, had now edged towards the door and taking her by the hand I led her out of the flat and into the bitter air of the late afternoon. We left the madness behind us and as we walked briskly through the streets we did not glance over our shoulders. For too long as we walked we could still hear a shrieking and howling noise which grew fainter and fainter.

Rosa followed my path as we walked through the confusing maze of streets, many of which had not been built when Rosa had lived in the area, towards her car which had been parked underneath a street lamp near to the cenotaph.

She was silent for a while but when I glanced back at her I saw that she was biting her lip with the look of concentration that I had already grown familiar with. She could sense that I was looking at her and at last she broke her silence.

"Well, that was really something John. I'm not sure what it was but I know that it was really something."

"You can say that again."

"Have you seen anything like that before?"

I had kept hidden from Rosa some of the excesses of my youthful days, and in particular the drug fuelled death of Lamara, preferring her to think of me as I was now – firmly on the straight and narrow. I brought to mind now the naked bag of bones running around shrieking and answered Rosa truthfully:

"No, Rosa, I've never seen anything like that before."

206

"What good did it do us though, John, **what good?**"
I felt that Rosa had approached this enterprise with an unreasonably optimistic view but even I had half expected to find Tommy still ensconced in Richard's flat or at least to **have** gained some tangible pointer to where he might be found. There was more than one way to skin a cat however and I was determined **that** I would have found Tommy and the dog Tramp well before the next day's deadline arrived. "I picked up a couple of things, Rosa, that I can work on. Don't you worry – I promise that I will get your dog back to you if I have to stay up all night." It was a heartfelt promise but I didn't realise at the time how much of this bargain I would have to keep.
The evening was darkening rapidly around us and the younger children were beginning to clear the streets to make way for the older children, the forgotten youths who would rule the streets from now until sunrise on the following morning. I remembered my happy childhood that had been spent playing football and cricket in the streets until it was too dark to see the ball or playing at cowboys and Indians as we ran home from the school, taking cover behind cars that had become giant cactus plants in our imaginations. Those days had long gone and I found myself wondering what was more of a threat to our children: the imaginary abducting ogres who were said to lurk on every corner and hang around every playing field or the adults, parents, teachers, and media who no longer let their children enjoy their lives worry free? So in these streets that I walked through at night significantly large gangs of children, barely into their teens, would spend their time smoking, drinking, sniffing solvents, smashing, grabbing and generally destroying anything that crossed their paths. People said that there was nothing else for them to do and (besides their computers, internet, bikes, music players, games machines, mobile telephones, hundreds of television channels, after school clubs, skate parks, indoor football pitches and foreign holidays) they were probably right.
Rosa had sunk back into silent mode now with her hands thrust deeply into her coat pockets to keep out the freezing chill that would attack you in blustery blasts and set your teeth chattering. I could tell that she was disappointed and I felt sorry that she'd had to witness the shockingly squalid scene that we had found in Clay's flat. She had become accustomed to the finer things in life and it would take a long time for her to remove the memory of that foul stench from her nose.
We had reached the old white Ford Fiesta now that remained gleaming underneath the streetlamp on the main road that ran through the small

town. I climbed into the car alongside Rosa and uttered some comforting words designed to make her think that it was only a matter of time, of hours, before I would be able to return Tramp to her unharmed. I hoped that she didn't guess that I had said the words more in an effort to convince myself than her.

There was little traffic on the road as most of the evening's joyriders would be congregating at the other side of town. Rosa rubbed her hands vigorously to warm them up, blowing on them all the while, before starting the engine putting the car into first and then second gear and turning the wheel to perform a u-turn in the road and lead us back towards the motorway. As the car was performing this manoeuvre the vehicle's headlights, which had arced in a semi-circle, picked out a familiar looking figure from the shadows before it returned to darkness as the car continued to turn in the road. My heart skipped a beat and I banged on the dashboard as if I was a driving examiner on test day.

"Stop here, Rosa" I practically shouted at her and she obeyed as if carrying out the instruction automatically. I undid the seat belt, which had only seconds before had been fastened around me, and opened the door of the now stationary vehicle.

"Wait here just a couple of minutes if you will please" I said in a lowered voice before closing the door behind me as quietly as possible. I walked with brisk but carefully picked out steps to where I had seen the figure which had been momentarily exposed to the revealing light. As I got closer I could see that the tall thin figure was still in the same location and his right arm was moving up and down. I had managed to creep to within a few metres of him now and I could see that my first instincts were right. The man that I had first seen on that Tuesday morning in Elsecar suddenly wheeled around as if the hairs on the back of his neck had warned him of my approach; he held a can of spray paint in his right hand but instead of fending me off by spraying it in my face his feeble reasoning decided to throw it at me instead, I ducked and the can hit the floor with a clanging noise before rolling on down the street. This time there was no pit bull terrier to growl at me and no unknown accomplice hiding in a back room: it was just me and Festa and I was determined that this time I was going to come out on top.

I had known from the first second that his distant figure was caught in the light that this was Festa and now as I surveyed his handy work scrawled upon the wall I realised why he held such significance in this matter. His tag was as childlike and without merit as ever but, as always, the capitalised letters were carefully scripted and given flourishes around the edges – the F looking particularly familiar to me.

"How is the filing Festa?"

"What do you mean? I aint done no filing?" he replied in his weak and monotone voice.

"No? Well you've been using filing cards haven't you? I saw one of them this afternoon – I'd recognise that scrawl anywhere. And I had you down as such a dog lover as well."

It took a while for the signal of panic to pass from his brain to his feet or his fists and I saw at last that he was ready to either run or throw a punch and then run. I had been taught to fight as a young man and whilst I was now to all intents and purposes a respectable pillar of society I was still confident that I could put the techniques that I had gained into good use. The first tip was always to throw the first punch and to throw it quickly, power comes from speed and why wait for your opponent to strike first when he might only need one punch? The second technique was the most important one and one that had helped me through many difficult situations as a young man. I had been taught it by a neighbour called Bill who although old was still a formidable looking man, he had been a bare knuckle fighter in his younger days and the tip that he had given me was this: most people when they punch someone only hit the surface of the target in front of them and no more; the secret to hitting someone so that they don't get up is to imagine that the person is standing two feet further back and punch for that imaginary spot – don't pull your fist away when you feel the impact just carry on punching through until you hit your imaginary target.

I channelled the anger that had been flowing through me since I had been in Richard Clay's flat and in one quick and fluid movement I punched solidly into Festa's stomach causing him to crumple to the floor with a wheezing sound as the air was knocked out of him. I suppose that I should have left it there but the adrenalin that raced me through me had to be sated. Cowardly though it was I kicked him once in his ribs and once in his face as he lay curled on the floor.

Grabbing the hood that had been pulled over his face I flipped him roughly over so that he was now lying on his back. Blood was pouring from his mouth and as his mouth gaped open pulling in air I saw that at least two teeth were missing: I didn't feel guilty, he wasn't going to win any modelling contracts anyway.

"It's time to talk Festa" I told him and he stared up at me with a mixture of hatred, fear and above all incomprehension in his eyes.

"I know that you took Tramp", I continued, "and that has made my friend very unhappy which, as you can see, has made me rather unhappy too. Who ordered you to take him?"

Festa said nothing and I realised that he was more scared of the possible retribution that his master might meter out to him than any imminent beating that he might receive from me. I changed to a question that he might have been willing to answer:

"Alright then, forget that. Just tell me where the dog is?"

"I don't know" he shouted and his rasping voice had an undeniable honesty to it.

"How can I get him back then?"

"The ring, you know. That's all I know, boss, I don't know anything more."

"I don't believe you" I said and raised my leg theatrically as if I was about to launch a conversion attempt with his head. It had the desired effect.

"Alright", he said, "look just be at Shelby's Shack tomorrow at midnight – you'll see the dog then alright."

"Where?"

"I can't say anymore, just be at Shelby's Shack – oh you'll see the dog alright!" A sly grin seemed to flicker over his face at this and I tried to resist kicking him again. I tried and I failed. The fresh blow that I now landed caused him to turn back onto his side groaning with pain. I knelt down and whispered into his ear:

"Oh, I'll be there alright. And do you know what? I'm going to bring that ring as well. But you tell your boss, whoever he is, that I'll only give him the ring in person – and if he's hurt a hair on that dog's back then he can forget all about it. Do you hear me?"

He said nothing but continued to whimper in suppressed pain; it was doubtful how much he had heard but it made me feel better as if I was somehow still in control of the situation.

I walked back to Rosa's car not caring whether anybody had seen me or not. I knew what I had to do next and it would involve me returning to the streets and haunts that I had thought I had left behind me long ago – I wasn't proud of what I planned to do next but I was ready to do anything for Rosa, no matter who I hurt along the way.

Chapter Twelve

I clenched and unclenched my fist as I walked back to Rosa's car. I had not thrown a punch in anger in a long time and although I had caught Festa sweetly enough to send him crumpling to the floor the impact had left my knuckles feeling bruised and painful.

It would be worse for the graffiti artist though, I had left him curled on the floor with blood trickling from the corner of his mouth where I had kicked him in the head. In a moment of bravado I had left him a message to pass on to his, as yet unknown, controller and it had been a message of defiance. As I neared the car I could see Rosa's eyes upturned towards the rear view mirror anxiously watching my return. What future was there for us now? We had been brought together by a force from beyond the grave and increasingly it seemed that we were pawns in a deadly game being played from beyond the grave. I had been warned previously that we were messing with a powerful and callous man and it seemed that he thought nothing of killing people to get his way – and now, foolishly, I had thrown down a challenge to him. He had already sent police officers to kidnap me and now he had organised the taking of Rosa's beloved dog but these were just warnings – I knew that now it was our very lives that were at stake and that every second that ticked by could be bringing us closer to our fate – a fate that would see Rosa and her sister Georgie reunited permanently.

I climbed into the car and sat down next to Rosa whilst carefully shielding my red and swollen knuckles from her sight. She looked at me with her beautiful green eyes wide and sparkling with expectation.

"There is a man called Festa, well at least that's the name that he goes by, and I think that he was the one who took your dog this morning. I saw him up the road there and I managed to ask him a few questions."

"Go on" said Rosa in a voice that seemed to signal that she was fearing the worst and that Tramp was already dead.

"Festa is a low grade criminal who gets his kicks from scrawling his nom de plume, his tag, on any buildings that he can. He doesn't have two brain cells to rub together. Yes he took your dog alright but there is no way that it would have been his idea. I asked him who was behind it all and where the dog was kept but he was too scared to answer. I tried my best to coax it out of him, and I can be a very persuasive person when I need to be, but his mouth was firmly shut."

"So you got nothing out of him?"

"Oh, I wouldn't say that Rosa. Like all of this low level lowlife he was quick to boast and to threaten. He told me that I could see your dog if I was at Shelby's Shack at midnight tomorrow."

"Shelby's Shack?"

"That's what he said – do you know the place?"

"Well maybe. I think it was a garage in Elsecar that I used to see sometimes when I was a girl. I'd be surprised if it was still there though – it was falling to pieces twenty years ago."

"The name rang a bell with me too but I couldn't quite remember where I had heard it. Look into it will you, pet, and if I don't see you beforehand I will see you near there at twelve midnight tomorrow?"

"What do you mean if I don't see you before then? You're staying at mine remember John?" Rosa asked the question but I think that she already knew the answer that was coming.

"Well, hopefully I will see you later, Rosa, but midnight tomorrow will come around all too soon and I've got a lot of work to do before then. First of all I've got to go round to Steven's house – there was something that I forgot to ask him over at that rancid flat and then there is another old friend that I think may be able to help me not to mention Tommy O'Callaghan to track down."

"Well let me come with you then, you've got to let me help you John. It's you and me now; you don't have to do everything on your own anymore."

I was surprised and happy to hear her speaking like this but I knew that the hours that lay ahead would be even more dangerous than the ones that had preceded them. Rosa had only wanted to find out how and why her sister had died and I had already exposed her to more danger than she knew, this time I couldn't allow her to get dragged into the fires with me.

"We are still going to be a team, Rosa, but I can't be in two places at once. I'm expecting an important phone call from a guy called Matt and I've given him your house number to call – he's looking into something for me that could really blow this thing wide open. He could call at any time and so I need you to be in your flat the whole time waiting for that phone to ring. Have it by your bedside when you go to sleep, Rosa, it could ring at any moment."

"Matt? What's his surname?"

"Er, it's Sinclair. He's always known as Matt though, just Matt. When he calls make a note of everything that he says, and when I meet you tomorrow let me have the notes. Can you do that for me?"

"Of course I can, John"

"Great. You're the best Rosa, a real rock. Steven lives around a mile from here and so if you could drive me over there on the way back that would be great. And whatever happens, tonight and tomorrow, keep your door locked and open it to nobody."

I had made the story about Matt up in a ruse to ensure that Rosa remained locked in the relative safety of her house. I had delivered it with as much sincerity as I could muster and my acting had passed the test because there was no way that Rosa would have left my side unless she thought that she was doing something equally useful.

Rosa had put up no argument and it took only a matter of minutes to drive through a selection of back streets to arrive at the house of my friend Steven Carter. It was a large house, one of the recently built homes that had been springing up in ever increasing numbers across this area of Barnsley. It's immaculately manicured lawn, even during winter, was a result of his fathers weekly visits with a lawnmower and a pair of shears and an imitation wishing well stood at the side of his houses main entrance. A cluster of elegant yet identical houses were gathered around the cul-de-sac and were home to middle class families with aspirations of building a leafy suburb here just a stones throw from the back to back terraces that had once been the sole housing option in the area. I wondered what the quiet neighbours, busily living their peaceful and uncomplicated lives, would make of the noisy drug addict who had been brought forcefully into their midst?

Rosa brought her car to a halt at the foot of his driveway and her aging white Fiesta seemed ill at ease amongst the Range Rovers and newly bought Volvos that made up the majority of vehicles parked around the nearby properties. I undid my seatbelt and turning to her said:

"Don't forget to keep the door locked at all times and only to answer it to me. And if I don't see you before I will definitely meet you near Shelby's Shack at midnight tomorrow."

"Okay, John, and don't worry – everything's going to be okay." I felt that it should have been me comforting her but it seemed that she was always the strong one. What happened next surprised me as she leaned across to me and, placing her warm hands tenderly around the back of my neck, kissed me on the lips in a long, sweet and tender moment that made me forget, for a blissful moment, the trials that awaited me. It was the last thing that I expected and it signalled a change in our relationship that until then had been somehow like brother and sister. As I closed the car door behind me I had a smile on my face and a warm glow within me: yes, now I really had something to fight for.

We waved warmly at each other as Rosa drove away and the playful smile that I saw flit across her face seemed to suggest that she had been surprised by her actions as well. I walked up the gravel covered driveway to Steven's house convinced that whatever awaited me I could and would overcome it but as I neared my friend's house I could hear shouts and the sound of altercation coming from inside.

I knocked on the door but it seemed that the general mayhem from within the house had drowned out my knocking because nobody came to answer it. I pulled my coat around me to keep out the increasingly bitter evening air and knocked again in a louder and longer fashion. At last the hallway light was switched on and I heard steps walking briskly towards the door. The security chain was moved into place and the door was opened fractionally. Steven's head peered around the corner and upon seeing me he nodded his head removed the safety catch and ushered me quickly inside before closing the door behind me.

"He is in here" was all Steven said as he led me through his house and upstairs to his second guest bedroom. I had been in the house on many previous occasions and had always found it to be immaculately preserved for a bachelor pad. Although Richard Clay could not have been in the house for more than a few minutes the building already had a different atmosphere around it and I dreaded to think what the house would be like after he had been in it for a few days while he experienced the terrible pains of withdrawal.

Steven pushed the door open and we entered the room. It was deliberately Spartan now and everything had been removed except for the single bed with its plain white sheets that would soon be filthy beyond recognition. Richard was thankfully fully clothed again and was surrounded on either side by the Doctor and the taciturn Ed. They were performing some kind of good cop bad cop routine and while Ed, when he spoke at all, whispered soft words of encouragement the Doctor spent his time shouting at him and when Richard seemed to be paying him no attention he would slap him harshly around the face with the open palm of his hand; the force knocked his head back from his shoulders and while he looked to be on the brink of tears he instead contented himself with shouting obscenities at the two men with him.

"Is all of that necessary?" I asked Steven.

"Oh yeah absolutely, John my old mate. Tough love, that's what he needs – it's the only way that we can get through to him. It's already working – he's starting to get some self pride back, some hatred back – some emotion back. He is already starting to become human again."

214

I wondered what sort of animal he thought that Richard had been before but I knew that Steven meant no malice – it was just the way that his black and white world worked. I winced as I looked back at the bed and saw the Doctor land another blow to the side of his face. If they knew what I was planning now it could have been me that would be the target of his fury.

"What kind of doctor is your friend anyway?" I asked Steven while noting that the guy seemed more suited to hurting people than healing them.

"Oh I don't know actually John. He just calls himself Doctor and nobody dares ask him why. I brought him along because he is the biggest and most uncaring bastard I know – just perfect for this job."

"Very commendable" I replied in a dry tone that I hope conveyed my disapproval of the process that Steven had started. I took my friend to one side now and whispered conspiratorially to him.

"Look Steven, I know you mean well and you can probably tell that I'm not wildly enthusiastic about your treatment here but we are old mates and I can see that something needs to be done to help Richard. You were right, as always, when you spoke to me at Dicky's flat: I do have a lot of experience of the hell of living with an addict and I should have spoken to Richard about it. I just got a bit intimidated by the whole situation."

"That's understandable mate. Look, none of us really know what you went through with Lamara and I can appreciate that what happened at the flat, and what's happening here as well in all probability, upset you. But it really is the best thing for him."

"Yes I see that now. I only wish that I'd managed to speak to him at his flat, really speak to him I mean."

"Well it's not too late, John."

"I just don't think I could do it Steven, not with all of you about. I just respect all of you too much to lay myself open before you all. Sorry."

"No need to worry about that" Steven said and gave a sharp whistle that pierced the air and made all of the men, even Richard, turn around in silence to look at the person who had made it.

"Let's give John here a little time alone with Richard. They're old friends and I think he's got a very special message that he wants to give to him. We could all do with a rest anyway." With that he made a gesture with his hands as if he was a general signalling his troops to make a tactical withdrawal and the three men filed past me out of the room. I imagined that the doctor gave me a dirty look as he walked past me but from what Steven had said he was probably like that with everybody.

215

Steven had fallen for the spiel that I had given him and I had gained exactly the result that I had so deviously hoped for. The door was closed gently behind us and I waited a few seconds until I heard their three sets of footsteps descend the stairs. Richard had laid back on the bed now in apparent exhaustion but his head was raised up on the pillow. The left side of his face was a large red mark with a faint black outline around it and I could tell that it would be swollen in the morning. His sunken eyes peered weakly at me and he watched in silence as I approached him. The air in the room was a heady mixture of stale sweat and lemon and lime that was being pumped from an air freshener which was plugged into the wall socket. I thought that it was remiss for Steven to leave this here when everything else had been removed from the room but I guessed that they wouldn't be leaving their poor guinea pig alone for a second during the next forty eight hours or so.

I approached the bed with a sense of trepidation. A cornered man can be dangerous and I had already seen that his wizened frame concealed a wiry strength that could be roused into desperate fury. He continued to watch me closely and I could sense that his terrified mind would be wondering what new tortures waited. I reached the bed and sat down beside him, all the while watching him and ready to jump out of the way at any sudden movement that might come from him. We watched each other silently for a few seconds and then I began to speak to Richard:

"Richard Clay, well here we are. Who thought it would come to this eh? Do you remember me? I'm John Halle, I went to school with you. Wasn't a happy time for you, school, was it? I had nothing to do with all of that bullying did I? You can't remember I suppose but take my word for it. I wasn't a bully then and I'm not now. Never was and never will be." Here I leant in further towards Richard and practically whispered to him:

"Which is why, old school pal, I do not like the way that they have treated you tonight."

Richard's dark eyes widened at this and he replied:

"Don't you?" His voice was thin and reedy but already it had gained some normality to it that made it seem a hundred miles away from the hissing that had come from him earlier in the evening.

"They are well meaning fools, but fools none the less. Yes, they want to help you but you're a man – you're holding down a job. Yeah, things may be a little tricky at the moment but things are going okay for you. That's right isn't it?" Clay's head nodded at the suggestion that I was feeding him and so I continued:

"You can make your own decisions; you can help yourself if you want to. You could kick your habit anytime that you wanted to – but it's up to you to decide when you want to, not them! What they are doing is nothing more or less than kidnap and holding you against your will. That's a serious offence."

"Yes it is" he rasped in a voice that was too loud for comfort so that I had to put a finger to my lips and wave my other hand downwards to signal that we needed to be quieter.

"They have had easy lives, not like you and me my friend. They don't know what tortures are going to happen to you."

"Tortures?"

"Oh yes, tortures. It will take days for the heroin to get out of your system and during that time you will sweat so much that it will be as if all of your body had dried up and your bones were turning to dust. And you will see horrible visions, you want to sleep but every time that you close your eyes it gets worse. And then there is the physical pain – all of your body will ache as if you were being attacked by a baseball bat until your body was one broken, bloody sore. One moment you will feel as if you are on fire and sweat will drip like molten lava from your eyelashes into your eyes and then the next minute you will be cold and shivering. And after all of that what is the net result? Absolutely nothing. If they let you out, assuming that you have survived it all without your heart giving out, you will just buy some heroin again sooner or later. And why shouldn't you – it's a free world after all."

"A free world" he repeated parrot fashion.

"Yes, Richard, they are doing this because they say the drugs are killing you but hey we all die in the end. And the drugs may kill you but trying to give them up when you're not ready for it could kill you quicker. I only wish that I could help you."

"Help me" Richard echoed but this time it wasn't a question it was a request.

"If only I could. What could I do?"

"I'll give it up, I will give it up – but not right now. I need just a little something, not much really, a little medicine to get me through the next few days."

I pretended to be deep in thought at this and I rose from the bed and paced up and down in front of his eyes. With my eyes turned downwards I shook my head from side to side as if I was arguing with myself or was victim to an inner turmoil. When I estimated that I had tortured Richard enough I turned back and sat beside him once more.

"Look, if they find out what I'm going to do they will absolutely kill me. So why should I? Put it this way Richard – if I help you then you have got to help me."

"How can I help you?" he asked with a new light of hope shining in his deep set eyes.

"I know who you were with the other night – it was Poor Tommy O'Callaghan wasn't it?"

Richard Clay remained silent just as I had expected him to but a nervous twitching erupted at the corner of his right eye and when I said the name he had flinched in a way that he hadn't when facing the slaps and punches of the self titled doctor.

"Okay don't tell me. You don't have to because I know that it was him. I'm not as stupid as people think I am, Dicky, and I know a lot of things. So let's take it as read that it was Tommy and let's take it as read that you know where he is, or at least where he can be found. I need to know that, my old friend. It's a personal matter, that's all that you need to know but rest assured that I am going to find him."

"Why do you want him?"

"Like I said it's a personal matter and the less you know the better it is for you. I'm not going to harm him I just need to talk to him. So where is he?"

I had leaned close to the spectral figure of Richard on the bed now and the rotten smell of his breath made me want to be sick.

"I can't remember" he answered, "how can I think straight when my mind is messed up like this. But if you bring me some medicine then I'm sure that it would jog my memory a little."

I had expected this answer from Richard and while a guilty conscience was already troubling my mind I was prepared to overcome it if it meant that I could find the information that would bring some sort of hope for me and Rosa. I rose from the bed and walked to the door without saying a word. When I reached the doorway I turned around to find Richard's hungry eyes eating onto my back.

"Okay. I'll fetch you what you want. But be assured, my friend, that if you don't tell me what I want to hear when I get back then you won't see a grain of it."

Richard was rocking backwards and forwards now and mumbling words of gratitude to me but I let them wash over me and walked out of the door to find the doctor and Ed stood at the other end of the upstairs landing.

"You can go back in there now gents" I said and they pushed by me, the doctor with a fierce glint in his hard eyes and Ed looking sheepish and flashing me an apologetic grin as he passed me.

I walked down the stairs and Steven came to greet me at the foot.

"How is he?"

"A bit better, pal, a bit better. You're doing a good job there I think – but if I was you I'd tell that doctor bloke to lay off him a bit. At least until tomorrow morning. Yes, all in all it was very productive – he seemed really interested in what I had to say."

Steven had a broad grin as I passed my judgement on his patient upstairs and before I had the chance to move my right hand out of the way he had grasped it between his sweaty palms and was shaking it vigorously. As the spirit of brotherly love seemed to be in the air I took advantage of it and asked him for one more favour.

"Oh by the way Steven, I'm supposed to be meeting Rosa for a drink in Barnsley tonight. She's gone home to get changed but I said that I'd meet her there, can you give me a lift into town?"

"Aren't you going to get changed as well?"

"Me? No point, mate, you can't do much to hide the ugly mug that I've got can you? No, I'm just going to go in like this."

Steven smiled again and I followed him out to his car, a new Ford Mondeo that was painted in British racing green livery, and on through the ever darkening roads to the town centre.

As the car purred through the streets I tried not to think of Richard and to speak of him even less and it seemed that Steven was happy to change the subject as well because he spent the journey discussing my luck, or lack of it, with women and how he was amazed that I had found someone as nice as Rosa. I remembered with happiness the kiss that I had recently shared with her and I too found myself slightly amazed.

I asked Steven to drop me off at the Courthouse pub and he obliged after telling me that he regretted that he wasn't able to share a quick drink with me but rather had to return to see how his new housemate was doing. He sped away into the night after giving me three farewell blasts on his car horn and I found myself hoping, above all else, that he would manage to stop his doctor friend from killing Richard Clay before I got back to him with a supply of heroin.

I kept up the pretence of walking into the bar but as soon as Steven's Mondeo was safely out of sight I turned around and sprinted across the road to my real destination of Barnsley railway station.

The station had seen better days and its main function was to provide shelter for the homeless on winter nights and a convenient place for drunks to urinate on their way home – not in the designated lavatories which were invariably out of order but in the darkened corners of the station itself.

Looking at my watch I found that I was eight minutes too late for the hourly Huddersfield train that I had wanted to catch and I cursed my luck volubly causing a drunken reveller to wake momentarily from the sleeping position that he had adopted along one of the cold metal benches. The screens that had been placed around the station buzzed and flickered so that it was hard to read the information that was displayed on them but looking up at one I managed, by screwing up my eyes in concentration, to make out the figure of eleven next to the departure time of the Huddersfield train. Eleven minutes late! I heard it rolling slowly down the track towards my platform and thought that at last my luck was changing.

The train shuddered to a halt in front of me and I climbed onto it along with four other passengers who had been waiting on the platform. There were two carriages to choose from and so I made my way down the first carriage to the rear of the train. The two carriages were very sparsely populated and I wondered why they could find two carriages for little used routes such as this one when the main commuter service in the morning normally consisted of one carriage where people were crammed in and jammed together like sardines in a tin.

I had a lot to think about during the journey: would Rosa be safe in her flat on her own while she waited by the telephone for a call from a person that I had made up? How was I going to find the much sought after green ring and if I couldn't find it then how was I going to get Rosa's dog back? Who was the mysterious figure behind everything that somehow seemed to link Georgie and Lamara? All of these questions were at the front of my mind and along with them was the growing feeling of guilt as I travelled towards Huddersfield with my self appointed mission of getting enough heroin to tempt an addict into revealing the whereabouts of Tommy O'Callaghan. The train jolted up and down as it rattled along the rickety old track and I let myself escape from these questions by concentrating on the noise that somehow soothed me as the train rolled on through a succession of nondescript villages of South and West Yorkshire.

From time to time I glanced down at the mobile phone that I held firmly within my grasp. I was hoping for a call from Rosa just to hear her comforting voice, with its winning combination of London and Yorkshire tones, but no call was forthcoming and I felt that she would be too anxiously waiting for the incoming call from Matt to attempt an outbound call. I would have to wait until I saw Rosa in person to hear her reassuring words but as the train continued its journey I had little idea how much I would have to go through before I would get that opportunity.

A group of teenagers, noisy and drunken, clambered onto the train at the agricultural village of Penistone and their loud and wanton behaviour put an end to the hopes that I had harboured of passing a peaceful hour or so on the journey. There were three girls, aged around thirteen or fourteen, and two boys who were maybe a year or so older. They had secreted cans of Carling lager in brown paper bags and swigged from them routinely only pausing to hide them under their seats when the ticket inspector passed by. They were already inebriated and their intoxication grew progressively worse as we continued the journey.

The girls clambered on and off of the boys' knees as if on a merry go round and they giggled as they did so whilst the boys made lewd comments in deep and monotonous voices. They had now taken to ripping up the newspapers that lay scattered around the filthy carriage and they were folding the ripped paper into balls that they placed within their mouths to bind together with their saliva and then threw around them in random directions. A soggy paper ball whizzed passed my ears and stuck with a splat onto the black streaked window beside me. The girls giggled uncontrollably at this and the boys gave me what they hoped were fierce looks from their small narrow eyes that peered out from underneath the rim of their oversized baseball caps.

The inspector came past again now and I grabbed his sleeve as he past. It has never been in my nature to tell tales or to 'grass' on people but my nerves were already becoming shredded by their loud drunken boasts and ear piercingly hysterical laughter. I pointed out to the inspector that these children were drinking alcohol on the train but he showed little interest in what I said and walked away leaving the teenagers to giggle and flash two fingered salutes at me as their repost.

They had picked the wrong day to annoy me and whilst the inspector had been too scared to confront the gang of children I, with the adrenalin from my encounter with Festa still flowing around me, certainly wasn't. I walked down the carriageway, which had now been abandoned by the handful of passengers that had shared it with us, and confronted the group who looked through me with drunken disinterest.

"What's so funny?" I asked.

"You are" said one of the boys as the girl on his knee popped a bubble of gum that she had blown.

"Wrong answer" was all that I said and with a swift movement I grabbed the paper bags that were assembled on the floor of the carriage. Opening the window next to their seats I flung the drink out of the window and onto the side of the track where it exploded in an alcoholic spray on impact. The group looked at me open mouthed incredulity but I saw the larger of the two boys make a movement as if to punch me. Before he could raise his arm I pushed my right hand into his throat and pinned him to the back of the chair. He was soon making spluttering noises but I waited until his face had turned a deep shade of red before I loosened my grip and walked slowly back, unchallenged, to my seat.

The five rose from their seats and walked through the divide into the front carriage swearing at me as they did so. I said nothing and was simply happy to have the whole carriage to myself so that I could relax and let my mind empty of everything in the few minutes that remained before the train reached its destination of Huddersfield.

All too soon the train pulled into the railway station and I stepped off of the train along with the small number of passengers who had collected onboard during the journey. The teenage gang had stumbled off of the train in front of me but they neither looked at me nor uttered a word until, having walked a distance along the platform, they burst into an uncoordinated sprint shouting curses at me as they went.

Huddersfield is a moderately large town nestled amongst the Pennine hills that mark the border between Yorkshire and Lancashire. It's large and impressive baroque style railway station is a lasting reminder of the importance that this town once possessed when it had been the centre of the woollen industry and one of the hotbeds of the industrial revolution. The town had once had more millionaires per capita than any other town in Britain but the other extreme was that it had a large amount of suffering and poverty as well. The woollen factories had largely gone now and their millionaires had migrated to the nearby cities of Leeds and Manchester but the enclaves of poverty still existed and indeed flourished with the influx of migrants from Asia, Africa and Eastern Europe to the area.

Walking out of the railway station, and down the hill into the town centre, I passed on my left the George Hotel which had been the birthplace of Rugby League. Things had turned full circle now and the

Rugby League players were being poached by their Rugby Union counterparts for the lure of greater salaries.

I had walked these streets on many occasions with Lamara who had originally hailed from Huddersfield. It was here that she had taken the inevitable progression from an occasional user to a full blown drug addict and I was now attempting to find one of her friends, any one of her friends, that might be able to help me to source some of the poison craved by Richard Clay without asking too many questions.

The public houses that lined the centre of the town in such proliferation were large and light buildings often populated by the young office workers of the town and its ever increasing student population. The University of Huddersfield had left its polytechnic roots behind and now offered refuge to a large number of students who didn't have the brains or work ethic to make it to one of the older and more established Universities of the cities nearby. Consequently the town's student life revolved far more around the many identikit theme pubs rather than its libraries and lecture theatres.

I was looking for an altogether different kind of public house, the seedy back street inns where anything could be obtained for a very reasonable price and the only thing that needed to be left at the door was a sense of morality. With my hands placed tightly within my pockets for warmth, and a sense of foreboding in my heart, I continued my walk through the streets to the less salubrious side of town.

Just beyond the fringes of the town centre itself lay a series of factories and industrial units, many of them abandoned now or never taken up in the first place, and beyond them lay the suburbs of Birkby and Fartown which housed many people who preferred to live in the anonymity of their flats and terraces, with windows boarded up, rather than the glare of the spotlight that fell upon the town centre and the leafier suburbs that spread to the west of the town. These desperate suburbs, shanties by any other name, were where Lamara had retreated to when we had finally parted and this was where I would find her friends if they could be found at all.

Night had descended now and the street lamps that stretched out were often out of operation or had been deliberately smashed so that for large stretches it was pitch black and at each step that I took it felt as if I was being watched.

I had just passed underneath an archway that served no apparent purpose anymore, when I felt a hand on my shoulder. I turned around sharply unsure of who I would be faced by but found myself looking at a thin faced woman with sad grey eyes and bright red lipstick. The make up that was plastered thickly across her face served to mask her real age but whilst in the half light you could have guessed her to be in her thirties the small and delicately framed woman seemed to me to be barely out of her teens.

"Are you looking for business mister?" she asked in a voice that carried more than a hint of desperation.

"No, no I'm not" I replied.

"Are you sure?" she said disappointedly and it seemed that she had become used to punters changing their minds and feeling their ardour waning once they had taken in her unappealing form.

"Quite sure. I am looking for something though."

"Oh yes?"

"No, nothing like that – nothing kinky you understand." She looked downcast again as she began to realise that I wasn't after any of the services that she might offer and would therefore have to keep walking these cold and threatening streets. I tried to recall some of the names of Lamara's friends and I threw them at her now:

"I'm trying to find some people that I think might live around here. Do you know them? Sophie Taylor, Hannah Cochrane, Melanie Siddall, Vicky Gallagher."

The previous names had produced no effect on the young woman but at this last name she nodded.

"Yeah I know Vicky. She's working at The Nelson's just up the road there. It's a Thursday so you can probably catch her tonight if you're lucky." She was pointing to a street that ran uphill from where we stood and in the far distance I could see a light shining through the darkness that I took to be The Nelson's that she had mentioned.

"Thanks, thank you very much, And good luck tonight." I don't know if that was the right thing for me to say but, as is often the case with me even today, I had said it before I thought about it. I shook her hand, which was rough and freezing to the touch, warmly and as I did so placed a ten pound note that I had fished from my pocket into her hands. She looked down with surprise at the note and a genuine and wide smile lit up her face making her look younger than ever.

"You can have a hand job too for that if you want?"

"Very kind of you, but I must decline. Got to get going." With that I set off at a brisk pace up the hill before she could catch me up and make any more offers that would be all too easy to refuse.

As I continued to climb the hilly street I looked back over my shoulder but she was nowhere to be seen. I wished that I had given her twenty pounds rather than ten but what would she have spent it on anyway, it didn't seem to be food? What kind of country do we live in that criminalises hopeless waifs like this while ignoring the brutal uncaring men who exploit them in mercenary fashion before returning home to their wives?

The full darkness of night had descended now but as I walked up the steep incline of the street I passed between rows of flats that shed light from their windows onto the street below. A cacophony of noise came at me from either side that was a mixture of blaring televisions, the thumping basslines of oversized sound systems and the raised voices and tears from domestic arguments. People that passed me in the streets threw me looks of suspicion but I kept my gaze fixed firmly on the lights that were coming from the public house which was situated near to the hills summit.

The road became even steeper as it progressed and although it had been only a short walk from the archway down below I was already breathless by the time I drew near to the pub. The exertions of the day, and the two chaotic days that preceded it, were beginning to take their toll and my legs felt heavy and unwilling as I dragged them step by step towards our destination. The noise that could be heard from the flats that surrounded the area had receded now or, to be more accurate, it had been drowned out by the noise that was coming from The Nelson's Arms. It was a noise which suggested that a large crowd were gathered inside and were fully intent on enjoying themselves.

The Nelson's, as it was known throughout the town of Huddersfield, was famous locally as being the sort of bar where stolen goods could be readily purchased but where it was of paramount importance to hold on to your wallets and mobiles at all times. On my previous visits to the town I had heard it mentioned in hushed tones many times and I knew it was a place where the police feared to tread and no questions were ever asked. It had gained a reputation as a drinker's pub, a fighter's pub, a pub where people could go when they no longer fitted in anywhere else – I was about to discover whether its reputation was deserved.

The pub itself was a flat topped one story building that took the shape of a large rectangle. The outer walls had been freshly whitewashed and a large wooden board covered one of the windows. A brass plaque above the door announced that the licensees were Mr & Mrs Derek Edgehill. I pushed open the door, which creaked forward with some reluctance and entered the sensory overload that was The Nelson's Arms on a Thursday night in the Huddersfield suburbs.

The first thing that hit me was the noise that blared out from two large speakers that were held on poles at the far end of the pub. The sound system, positioned behind the bar, was playing that metal classic 'Run To The Hills' by Iron Maiden and never before had it seemed so appropriate. The whole room, which was large and comprised the entirety of the pubs' public area, was covered in a smoky fog that issued from a hundred cigarettes and caused me to blink my eyes that were stinging under the smokes influence. The room was crowded in a way that I would not have expected for a provincial pub on a cold Thursday night: every seat was taken and the bar itself was lined two deep with people either still queuing for drinks or clutching their drinks proprietarily to their chests as they guarded their spaces with fierce looks.

I pushed through the crowd before me and this was a hard task in itself. Careful judgement was needed as to which people it was safe to push physically past and whose shoulder you could place a firm hand upon to guide them out of the way and which men, and women, it was important to avoid coming into contact with as much as possible. The noise from the speakers continued to blast out their rock music but in my mind for a second it seemed that the whole bar had gone silent as they turned to look at the stranger in their midst. The general consensus seemed to be that I wasn't that worst of things, an undercover policeman, and so I continued to navigate my way through a sea of people to the bar.

The bar was a long counter that held a number of mast heads advertising the lagers, bitters, ciders and stouts that were for sale. It seemed that Joshua Tetley's finest had already been popular tonight because bar towels had been draped across the bitter pumps to show that this option had now run dry.

There were three bar staff on duty tonight all of whom were busy serving the endless and vocal crowd waiting before them anxious for another pint. A girl with spiked hair and large hoped earrings who looked around fifteen years of age and was plainly too young to be working there legally flirted with her customers at the far end of the bar and the middle was occupied by a man with thinning black hair, which he compensated for by wearing a large bushy moustache, and who wore nothing more than a pair of jeans and an off white vest – it was a sensible choice for although it was bitingly cold outside the body heat around the bar made it as hot as an inferno. I had finally managed to make my way to the near

226

end of the bar which was being served by a woman of around forty years of age with a deeply orange skin topped by dirty blonde dreadlocks and hooped earrings that were even larger than the young barmaid's. She too had a vest top on and it was straining to conceal the prominent bust underneath it whose décolletage rose majestically from it and was crowned with a selection of gold linked chains.

Although I had been forceful enough to push through the crowd and reach the bar itself I still expected to wait behind the other people at the counter many of whom were looking at their watches impatiently or waving tattered twenty pound notes in the air to gain her attention. Something about me seemed to catch her eye however, maybe it was just my strange face in a place normally occupied by locals and regulars, and she came to me ignoring the protestations and oaths of the people stood alongside me. I could feel their eyes burning into me.

"What can I do for you love" she asked in a deep, thick and strangely sensual voice. As I saw her close up it struck me that beneath all the layers of make up and fake tan she was still a very attractive woman and I could feel the energy bouncing off of her.

"Just a cider please – sweet if you have it." I could feel the eyes burn into me again as I asked for a drink that was considered womanly in these parts. I watched her pour the pint and she shuffled slowly from foot to foot as she did so as if dancing by herself on the floor.

She brought the pint back to me and asked with a conspiratorial smile if there was anything else that I wanted.

"Er, yes there is actually, I replied, "I'm looking for an old acquaintance – old friend I should say. Vicky Gallagher. I understand that I can find her here."

"Vicky? Yeah she's here all right – I didn't know that you were here for her just like everybody else is. She'll be here in just a minute okay. And if you get impatient and want a more mature service just let me know, love." She winked as she said this and I smiled back before she turned to the customers who were becomingly increasingly restive.

I drunk deeply from the pint glass that still bore the smudge of somebody's lipstick. I closed my eyes in momentary ecstasy as I did this and felt the soothing drink begin to ease away the stress that had been bearing down upon me. As I opened my eyes I saw the moustachioed man before me with a look of contempt in his eyes and a broad hairy finger pointing my way.

"Who do you think you are?" he opened.

"I don't know what you mean?" I responded.

227

"What? You don't know who you are? Well I know what you were doing – you were chatting my missus up."

"No, no – not at all. I was just getting a drink" I protested while waving my free hand furiously.

"Well, just watch it. Because I am going to be keeping my eye on you and if my bird comes to serve you again then you had better tell her that you don't want anything okay?"

I looked back at him silently wondering whether to protest my innocence or not when the music suddenly changed and to my relief the barman turned his back on me and walked to the other end of the bar.

The song 'Gangsta's Paradise' by Coolio had now begun to blast from the speakers at unbearable volume. The crowd around me cheered and moved forward almost universally. I could imagine how it would have been a popular choice among this throng but I was surprised at their reaction.

Sporadic cheering continued from time to time and then as the crowd moved as one to a side of the bar I saw the reason for their enthusiasm: a young woman was moving among them and she was the star turn that they had all, men and women alike, come to see.

She wore a green army style cap and combat fatigues that consisted of a camouflage vest top with a zip down the front of it and very short and tight hot pants in matching camouflage colours. She wore bright red stilettos with a heel four inches high and carried a plastic imitation machine gun that she ran roughly between the legs of the men around her causing a cheer to erupt every time that she did this.

She removed her cap now, to the accompaniment of another cheer, and a long cascade of hair, dyed bright red, fell across her face. Shaking the hair out of her face I saw her beautiful and thin face that was crowned by a large pair of lips that pouted as she danced. She looked every inch like a younger version of Lamara and as I watched Vicky Gallagher dance wildly before me it was as if they could have been twins rather than the cousins that they were. My eyes were fixed on to her now and she seemed to hypnotise me as she danced.

The toy gun was placed behind the bar and her zip was undone as her brightly painted fingernails ever so slowly removed the vest top from her thin body. She followed this up by shimmying out of the hot pants thrusting her ass at the people around her and slapping it provocatively as she did so.

She was down to her underwear now, small and red to match her shoes, and as she continued to writhe before the baying crowd the music changed again and now it was 'Bohemian Like You' by The Wannadies that was playing. The crowd were pressing against her now and groping her freely as she squeezed through them. She bent over and gestured for one of the men to undo her bra which he did with fingers that were shaking either through nerves, excitement, drink or a combination of all three. She returned the favour by slowly running her hand up and down the crotch of his jeans and briefly slipping her hand inside them before dancing away and waving her bra triumphantly in the air before throwing it to land behind the bar. The crowd were in a frenzy by this point and the air was full of shouts and shrill whistles. The mass of people blocked my view again but when I could see Vicky once more she was dancing completely naked amongst them with a beautiful smile on her face. She climbed up onto the bar now and danced energetically along it as the men looked up in awe at her and flicked beer from their glasses onto her legs in a strange show of appreciation.

The music stopped as suddenly as it had started and the previously silent man who had been standing next to me with his tongue poking from the corner of his mouth said:

"Don't worry, lad. That's tame that is – the second half is always a lot better."

As he said this a pint glass had already begun to circulate amongst the punters who were pushing five pound notes into it in a mixture of appreciation and expectation. I was wondering how to catch Vicky's attention – she didn't seem to have noticed me and she might not have recognised me if she had. All at once however I felt a tiny hand grasp mine and the still naked Vicky pulled me behind her as she made her way to her room backstage. From the oaths that followed behind us I could tell that I wasn't making many fans amongst the regulars that night.

She led me into a small and musty smelling room with a tiny cupboard and a table with two chairs at either side. She sat down at one chair, looking magnificently naked before me, and I sat down opposite her. A packet of cigarettes and a pink plastic lighter were on the table and she placed a cigarette between her inviting lips, that bore such a sibling familiarity, and I lit it for her. Vicky inhaled deeply and then blew a ring of smoke into my face. I looked at her closely now and she looked very thin and tired and her legs still held fading bruises. Her nails were chipped and eaten away but as my eyes strayed from her relaxing face to her small breasts that held a claret birthmark alongside them and then back to her full red lips it seemed that her fragile vulnerability somehow increased her beauty.

"What are you doing here, John? I haven't seen you in more than a year – since before our Lamara passed away. Me and her mum went to visit her grave at Christmas you know. For the anniversary. There was nothing from you I noticed. How could you do that after all those years? Auntie wanted to visit you but I said sod you, what do you care?"

"It's been hard for me Vicky, it's been really, really hard for me."

"It's been hard for us all, John – look what I've ended up doing. Here, help me with this."

She stood up now and threw a bottle of baby oil to me. She continued to smoke as she turned her back to me and I rubbed the oil deep into her shimmering skin as I fought back the passion that was growing within me.

"I came here to see you Vicky, you know. It's not a coincidence."

"Well I don't believe in coincidence anyway John. Why did you come then?"

"I can't sleep at night, Vic. Can't concentrate, can't do anything. I keep blaming myself. I need something to help me, Vicky. You were always my favourite among Lamara's friends, you must have known that?"

"Maybe. Yeah, I suppose so. But what do you want me to do for you, because if it's a bit of the other that you want you can forget it – she was my cousin after all."

She had turned to face me again as I continued to rub the oil into her skin. I looked at her now with pleading and pathetic eyes hoping that by concentrating on her face I could forget the alluring sight before me.

"You know what Lamara used, and I know that you use it too. Well get this, Vic, I used to use it too. I can't get hold of it now."

"You? You never used it in your life – too straight laced you are."

"Not really, I used it on the sly. Can't you see it in my eyes – I just need a little to help me through darling, just a bit. I can pay top dollar."

"So you came all this way to score some H? I'm disappointed in you, John Halle. Hold this."

She passed her burning cigarette to me which I placed between my lips as if imagining her lips next to mine. She opened the cupboard now, which housed her clothing as well as a shiny PVC outfit for the second act. It also held a small pink telephone that she now held to her ear and whispered into with one hand shielding the mouthpiece. After her negotiations were ended she flipped the lid of her phone closed and somehow, with eager help from me, squeezed and cajoled her way into the tight nurses uniform.

"Wait here, John", she said, "I'm sending the best man over for you. Blondie will get you a good deal alright." She placed a card into my hand now and announced: "if the smack doesn't kill you then look me up sometime." I placed the card into my pocket before I watched her head out to the baying crowd beyond the door.

I sat patiently in the room trying to wipe the baby oil that covered my hands onto the table's surface. I could hear the crowd outside and I could hear them getting louder and louder but I didn't have long to wait before a rear door, which I hadn't even noticed before, opened and the man known as Blondie stood before me.

He was a tall man of average build but an undeniable air of menace hung around him. He was dressed in designer jeans and a Gap t-shirt. His arms were covered in tattoos including one that announced his name 'Blondie to the world'. The peroxide hair on his head had been cropped short and I noticed that one eye seemed larger than the other until it struck me that it must have been made out of glass.

I held out my hand for him to shake and he took it briefly and firmly. I had hoped that he would swap the package of heroin over whilst we shook hands but it seemed that this wasn't the way that he conducted his business.

"Alright, John Halle, it seems that you're a good friend of Vicky's eh? Cracking lass that one isn't she? Well up for fun." His small talk was delivered in a grating Mancunian accent but I wanted to conclude the deal as quickly as possible.

"Yeah, yeah. Have you got the stuff mate. I will pay."

"Pay? Of course you're going to pay" he laughed, "but not here. Come with me."

He walked with a swagger out of the door and I followed behind him. A large black BMW was waiting outside of the door and I climbed into it alongside Blondie. The man in the driver's seat was shaven headed and bull necked but he didn't say a word as we drove through the streets. Blondie had gone quiet now which made me uneasy.

At last the car stopped in front of a warehouse building. The driver climbed out of the car first and then Blondie pushed me out of the car before him. Things were going wrong and now it was my turn to make the small talk.

"Are we here then Blondie? Have you got my stuff inside?"

"Inside – yeah that's right, John Halle, the stuff's inside so get in there

231

and we can get our business sorted out."

I looked around me to get my bearings but there were no lights here and everything was dark. The driver of the vehicle had his powerful hand in the small of my back now and he pushed me roughly forwards. As soon as we had entered the warehouse the driver twisted my arm behind my back making me cry out in pain and leading me along the disused building in agony we paused outside of a door that had a shuttered grill along the top of it.

"What do you want?" I groaned through gritted teeth.

"You will see, you will see" Blondie replied. He took a key from his pocket and opened the door before me. The strong arms of the driver, that I had been powerless to resist, threw me into the room where I fell with a thud onto the floor. The door was closed loudly behind me and I heard the key turn in the lock.

A light came on and shone harshly and unshielded above me so that I had to close my eyes until they adjusted. Looking across the room I saw that I was not alone. A large man, of even bigger build than the driver, was propped up in the far corner where ropes bound his legs and arms. His mouth was taped up and some of his hair had been crudely hacked away. Blood covered much of his face and had spread across his shirt. Despite the almost inhuman sight before me I soon recognised that this man, this wreck of a man, before me was Osbourne – the giant who had rescued me from the Hoyland cemetery on the previous night. I didn't want to consider what, or who, had reduced him to this mess.

It was then that I noticed the gun that lay on the floor between us.

Chapter Thirteen

I placed my hands flat on the cold stone floor and raised myself to my feet. A sudden agonising shock ran through my left arm, which had been twisted behind my back, when I put the pressure on it and I rubbed it vigorously in an attempt to alleviate the pain. I turned back to door and tried to pull it open but it remained firmly locked and the shuttered grill across the window allowed me no clue as to what was happening outside.

Had Vicky betrayed me? I had known her well when I had been living with Lamara, her cousin, and had always liked her more than Lamara's other acquaintances – she had a vibrancy around her, a beautiful smile and mischievous sense of humour that always seemed to brighten up any room that she entered into. Lamara and Vicky had been more like sisters than cousins, they were soul mates who would always turn to each other when they had problems; at times I would feel excluded and resentful at their closeness but I could never allow myself to be angry with her long. And yet it seemed that Vicky Gallagher had sent this man, Blondie, to meet me at The Nelson's Arms in the knowledge that she would be sending me to this fate that confronted me now. If this true then it could only mean that Vicky was somehow linked to the Barnsley mystery that I had become so terribly embroiled in since I had first seen Georgie, the girl on the bus, just three days previously. As I turned and looked around my cell I wondered how much longer I would have to think about such things and if my story had reached its final act?

Osbourne was wearing the same clothes that had been on him when I had met him at St Peter's cemetery on the previous evening but they were torn now and strewn with mud, dust and blood. The man who had tied and bound me, with the able assistance of his Sergeant, was now himself tied and gagged and was helpless and immobile before me. The room that we shared was cold and bare except for the unshaded light bulb that blazed overhead and the gun that lay provocatively on the floor between us.

I walked across to the gun now, cradling my left arm against my chest as I did so, and bent down to examine it more closely. I was no expert in firearms, and had never fired one in anger in my life, and was unsure if it was real or an imitation. I picked it up and it felt surprisingly light yet solid in my grip. It was around eight inches long and was jet black and sleekly beautiful, a weapon that had been designed as much for its aesthetics as its killing power. A badge was embossed on its handle and this announced that it was a Beretta 92 FS. Not knowing whether the safety catch was on or not, or even whether the gun was loaded, I placed it back onto the floor as carefully as I had picked it up.

As I deposited the gun back into the centre of the room I looked across at Osbourne and saw that his eyes had opened now and he was staring back at me. He was nodding his head at me as if to indicate something and so I crossed the room and knelt before him. He looked even more pitiful close up and his face which had seemed so gentle and feminine for such a huge man was now streaked with blood and grime. His nose had been broken and his eyes were blackened at either side of it. Thick tape had been placed across his mouth and ended at the back of his head. I reached around and pulled at the tape but it was tightly fastened. I pulled harder and at first it moved little by little away from his hair and then, as I gained more purchase on the tape, I ripped it off in one powerful and fluid movement. The tape that I now held in my hand was matted with hair and blood; I threw it to the floor with disgust and wiped my hands on my jacket in an attempt to clean them.

Osbourne had tried to stifle his scream but the pain had overcome his pride and he groaned deeply as the tape was pulled off. He pulled in air deeply now as if he was a drowning man who had just surfaced from the sea for the third time. He moved his head forward and was trying to speak to me but his mouth was dry and his lips cracked and all he could manage was a whisper. I moved closer to him now so that I could discern his words:

"My pocket, quickly my pocket. Inside. Take it, hide it. Quick, they will be coming for us soon."

The effort that he had put into gasping that handful of words seemed to have exhausted his last reserve of energy and he slumped back against the wall with his eyes closed. I squeezed my hand into the inner lining of the fleecy jacket which was pressed tightly against his body by the ropes. As I groped for the pocket I could feel his chest heaving in and out and his heart was beating quickly and heavily. At last I found the inside pocket and within it was a folded piece of paper which I managed, with some effort, to pull out. I saw now that it was not a folded piece of paper but an envelope that had been folded in half but before I could read who it was addressed to I heard the sound of footsteps behind the door and saw that the shutter which had been placed across the grille was now being opened. With one swift motion I placed the envelope into my sock and manoeuvred it underneath my foot. I was walking back to my corner of the room when the shutter was finally opened and I saw the mismatched eyes of Blondie staring in at us.

"What's going on here then eh, gentlemen? What's all this noise – wake the dead you would." He laughed as he said this but I remained silent. He continued:

"Now then, Mr Halle, what have you been doing to that big bloke over there? It took us a lot of effort to get that tape on and now you've gone and ripped it all off. I don't really approve of that. What were you planning to do, have a nice chat about the weather?"

Once again he laughed as he said this but I just wasn't in the mood for comedy.

"What do you want with us?" I shouted back at the face that was leering in at us through the grill.

234

"You're a very direct person aren't you, Halle? What's wrong – are you in a hurry to go somewhere?"

"Get on with it. Just because you think you're funny it doesn't mean that we all agree with you. I'm getting tired of your game."

"Oh this isn't a game. This is far from a game. Let me explain the situation that you find yourself in. You're in the wrong place at the wrong time – it seems that you make a habit of that? Well as you see, there is a man in this corner that has been rather too much trouble to us. A dishonest man: a man who would stab his friends and colleagues in the back if given the chance. What do you think about that?"

"I think that it takes one to know one."

"Well maybe that's because you don't understand the situation, Halle. Maybe you don't understand anything?"

"Well why don't you enlighten me then?"

"Enlighten you? Well let's get straight to the point then. This pathetic specimen of a man opposite you needs to be punished. People have to learn that if they cross us then there is a big price to pay."

"Us? Who is us?" I interrupted Blondie to ask but he carried on without acknowledging me, his voice becoming deeper and more threatening as he spoke as if his words were being spat out from between clenched teeth:

"A big, big price. Do you see that gun there? Of course you do. Well let me ask you a question, have you ever fired a gun before?"

It was my time to remain silent now but the sickening fear rising within my stomach made me forget the pain that had been gnawing at my arm. The silence continued for a few seconds until Blondie became impatient of waiting for me:

"I will take that as a 'no'. Well, that's no problem it's easy to pick up – just like the gun itself. Remember to hold it nice and steady and to squeeze the trigger, don't pull it. It's a beautiful gun, the best in the business – you should feel honoured at using a weapon like that, beginner that you are. Has it all sunk in yet, Halle? No answer again eh? You were happy to talk a few minutes ago. So here is what is going to happen: this man must die and you are going to be the one to kill him. There is one bullet in that Beretta and the safety catch is off. You are going to point that gun squarely at him and shoot. It's a pity that the gun will have your finger prints all over it, but I hear that you did have some sort of vendetta against him so I'm sure that it won't come as a surprise to anyone. I might even drop you down at the police station myself so that you can confess anything. Maybe you'd want to go on the run for a while though, eh? Enjoy your freedom while you can, Mr Halle, because they are sure to catch up with you soon."

"And what if I don't do it? What are you going to do – shoot me instead?"

"Shoot you – what do you take me for? It's you that's going to be the cold blooded murderer. No, we need you alive to enjoy the rest of your life behind bars where you belong."

"I'm not going to do it, you know?"

"Oh, on the contrary I know that you will. I will give you five minutes to shoot him. And if you stubbornly refuse then I'm going to send people after Vicky Gallagher, your old friend, and those people won't need five minutes to take care of her. And if you still refuse then guess what? I hear on the grape vine that you have another woman in tow as well? Down there in South Yorkshire. Don't think that we won't get to her. Two for the price of one. Think about it John, this man doesn't mean anything to you so go ahead, pick up the gun and do the right thing. And then, I promise, your two women will be safe. You can trust me. Five minutes, that is all you get."

The shutter was placed across the grille and it was a relief not to look at that one true eye staring manically at me and not to have to listen to that slow and grating voice. I sank down onto my knees in despair and then lay flat on my back with my arms across my eyes to shield them from the fierce light that was still blazing away overhead. I remained like that for a minute and at that point there was a sharp rap on the door and a voice cried out: "One minute down, four to go."

People often say that modern society is stressful and full of difficult decisions but for most people they normally consist of things such as where do I go on holiday or can I afford to pay for my gas bill or should I go for a drink with the new admin assistant at work and if so will the wife find out? It was at this point that I realised how difficult a decision really can be.

I raised myself up again and sat on the floor with my arms tucked around my knees. I looked across the room and saw Osbourne still slumped against the floor. His eyes remained closed but his chest was heaving in and out. He didn't say a word or open his mouth as if to utter one and it seemed that he was simply waiting for the end to come. Could I prolong his agony or would it be better, kinder even, to simply put him out of his misery?

As my eyes moved back towards the centre of the room and the Beretta handgun that lay there another rapping noise was made on the door and the same Manchester accented voice announced that two minutes of the allotted five had already passed.

I stood up now and walked back across the door. I tried to pull it open again as if hoping that some superhuman surge of strength would come to my aid but the door remained as immobile as it had when I had first tried to open it. I spent futile seconds feeling my way across the walls and over the floor to see if my eyes were deceiving me and whether a hidden exit was somewhere to be found. The walls and floor were cold and solid to the touch and as the third rapping announced that another minute had gone a cold sweat began to form on my forehead.

It was decision time and I had to reach it quickly. I had been close to Vicky for a number of years and although she had always had a propensity for getting into scrapes she had an inner warmth and kindness. It was hard for me to believe that she would have betrayed me or had any idea of the treatment that awaited me: the conclusion that I reached was that she simply knew Blondie as the local dealer who could supply the drugs that her old friend had requested. I had little doubt that if I chose not to shoot the man before me then Vicky Gallagher would be killed just over a year after the family lost another of their young women, Lamara. Although I couldn't physically see Lamara at this time, as I had previously, I knew that she was somewhere watching me and I believed that I knew what her decision would have been.

And then, of course, there was Rosa Galloway. I hadn't even known that she had existed before this week but now it seemed that she had quickly become the major force in my world – a friend and yet already more than a friend. It seemed clear to me that if required Rosa would risk her very life to help me and how could I then put her life at certain risk by my inaction? I pictured her sitting by the telephone, waiting for the call that would never come, while death would be closing in on her at every second.

So the final member of this trinity was Osbourne himself. What did I know about him? He was a police officer who had somehow got led astray or had followed orders to the extent where the line between right and wrong had been irreversibly crossed. It was true that he had provided me with a timely warning in the cemetery and had fought valiantly against the gang of assailants thus allowing me to escape. It was also true, however, that he had tied and beaten me previously and although I accepted that it wasn't at his bidding he had been one of the two rogue police officers who had left me to my own fate in the woods where one wrong move could have sent me plummeting into the waters below to drown. Another rap came on the door, more insistent and voluble this time, and the voice shouted at me that I had one minute left to do the right thing if I wanted to save my two women. My decision was made. I walked across the floor and although my steps were quick my heart was heavy. I raised the gun from the floor now and it seemed somehow heavier than when I had held it a few minutes before. While I had no experience of shooting a gun the memories of a hundred bad movies came back to me and instinct took over. I raised the handgun to shoulder height now with my right hand outstretched before me. The Beretta had sights positioned at the rear of the weapon and using these I lined up a spot just inside of Osbourne's left shoulder. I was aiming not to kill him but to shoot him in a place that would not prove to be critical: the problem, of course, with this plan was that my lack of practise meant that while I aimed to give nothing more than a flesh wound in reality my shot could have gone anywhere.

My hand was shaking as I held the handgun in front of me, both from the weight of the gun, which I calculated to be around two pounds, and the weight on my shoulders. I breathed deeply and slowly to steady my heart rate but my hand continued to shake and so I brought my left hand over to steady it and held the gun in both hands at arms length. Outside of the door I could hear a countdown beginning with ten. When the numbers reached seven I squeezed the trigger.

My eyes closed automatically seconds before I heard the click of the hammer and a rush of wind as the bullet left the barrel at phenomenal speed. A blast of hot air rushed out with it and the recoil of the gun shot through my painful left arm forcing me to drop the gun on the floor with a cry of pain.

Osbourne had not made a sound but as I looked up ruefully, as if in a nightmare, I saw that he was now flat on his back on the floor and immobile with eyes closed. The wall that he had been leaning against was covered with a splash of blood and broken fragments of cartilage. I dared not approach Osbourne's body but by careful manoeuvring of my head I could see that the left front of his fleece jacket was covered in a dark spreading mess.

I had no emotion within me to cry, it was as if I had nothing left to give at all; I was just a shell of a man who was barely alive. I sat down on the floor next to the dropped handgun and held my head in my hands.

The door opened with a creak but I was still in a state of shock and I had neither the will to leave nor the energy to do so. The driver, still mute and menacing, entered the room noisily and as he walked past me he gave me a vigorous slap on the back as if in congratulation: almost as if I had become one of them now. He walked across to the corner of the room and, wearing gloves whilst he did so, dragged Osbourne's body across the floor leaving a thin trail of blood streaking behind him. I looked up as they passed me and while Osbourne still made no sound I thought that I had seen a flicker from his eyelids and the faintest rise and fall from his chest.

The body was dragged out of the room and the door was once again closed behind me. I was alone now, alone with the enormity of what I had done and the growing fear in my mind that it would be my turn soon: that the next time the door was opened it would be Blondie entering the room with a gun in his hand and then it would be my guts that were spread across the wall. I wasn't ready to die yet and spent agonising moments trying to think how to escape from this situation. On the other hand I had already seen a vision of myself dying in a fire and Blondie had said that he would need me alive to take the rap for the slaying of Osbourne; while a life behind bars didn't appeal to me at least it could buy me some time.

The door opened again and looking up I saw the man known to me only as Blondie enter the room. I resolved to make myself appear to be as weak as possible but my survival instincts were taking over and I was steeling my energy to make decisive move should the chance come. His face was smiling now and he sat down cross legged on the floor near to me so that he could enjoy his moment of gloating. I rolled back onto the floor cradling my arm against my chest and breathing deeply and he sat there looking at me with a large and smug smile for two silent minutes before he finally spoke:

"Well done killer. Easy, wasn't it? What are you doing flat out there – it's no time to be resting on your laurels now is it?"

I rolled over and supporting myself with my right arm half sat up so that I was looking straight at the mocking Mancunian whilst appearing to be on the point of collapse.

"This is what we are going to do now, Halle. My driver, chauffeur I suppose I should call him as I am in the presence of a gentleman, has taken Osbourne to dispose of his body. When I say dispose of it I really mean leave it somewhere that it can easily be found. And then they are going to come looking for the killer. I am going to take this gun and leave it somewhere in the vicinity of Osbourne's body. I'm not going to touch it of course because I'm wearing gloves. What's that? You forgot to wear a pair? That was careless of you. I am going to keep you in here for a couple of days until the manhunt really gets under way. Don't worry I'm going to leave you some water and a packet of peanuts. I'm not inhuman you know? Anyway in a couple of days I will simply let you go. Fly where you will, Halle, it's only a matter of time before they catch you. And that's going to be a bad day for you – they really don't like cop killers you know."

"Why me?" I whispered in a strained voice so as to give the impression that I couldn't even speak.

"Why not?"

"What about the ring?"

"What ring?"

"Don't you know about the ring then? Your boss, the big man himself, has given me until midnight to bring a certain ring to him. He won't be happy when he finds out that you stopped it."

"I don't know what you are talking about, Halle. I'm the only big man around here."

His voice had changed now and I could sense the uncertainty grow within him.

"You're not the main man – you're nothing but a minor lieutenant with a woman's name and a glass eye. How did that happen, did he beat it out of you? Just imagine what he'll do to you this time."

"You ask too many questions for a man in your position. I wouldn't advise you to talk too much in prison or you could end up like my poor old chauffeur – he can't talk at all without his tongue. Maybe it would be safest to do that to you as well eh?"

I continued to whisper as if I was at death's door but the more threatening Blondie's words were becoming the more flustered he became. I could see that my gambit was having the desired effect.

"And maybe it would be safest for you to give him a call and tell him what's happening here. Maybe it's you that needs enlightening this time. Here is the picture as far as I see it: your boss, big cheese that he is, has put out word among all manner of low life to look out for John Halle. You have taken his instruction too literally because he doesn't want me killing, like he did with Osbourne, or incarcerated. I have something that he wants and tonight I was going to give it to him. I can't do that if I'm trapped in here."

"Oh yeah? Well why don't you just tell me, tell your friend Blondie, where this ring or whatever it is can be found and then I can take it to him myself."

At last Blondie had confirmed that my hunch had been correct. It was

240

time to play hard ball:

"I can't do that, Blondie. It's well hidden in a secret location. I could give you instructions but there is no way that you would find it. Why don't you drive me over there, back to Barnsley, and then you can keep your eye on me the whole time. After I've handed the ring over well then I guess that you can just go back to your original plan."

Blondie was caught in two minds now and he stood up and paced around nervously in front of me.

"Just give him a call and see what he says" I suggested and to my relief the small time drug dealer, who seemed to think that he was a major gangster, turned his back on me and produced a mobile telephone from his pocket. He began to punch numbers into the phone and then held it to his ear as if waiting for an answer. I had no time to waste now and the energy that had been circulating through me and had increased with the adrenalin that rushed through my system gave me the speed and power to act before Blondie knew what was happening. I grabbed the gun from the floor, holding it by the barrel, and leaping up I reached Blondie in one stride and brought the gun down with a sickening crack on the side of his skull. He fell to the floor and blood began to flow quickly from the gash on the side of his head. His good eye rolled in its socket and then closed as his head lolled unconsciously upon the bare stone floor.

I checked his pulse but it was still beating strongly and I had little doubt that he would soon regain consciousness; I didn't want to be around when that happened. His mobile telephone had dropped out of his hand when he fell and on impact with the floor it had shattered into many pieces. I scrabbled amongst the debris and found the sim card which I slipped into my back pocket. I rifled hastily through his pockets and found a roll of banknotes which I took in order to make things harder for him when he came round and a section of plastic debit and credit cards which I folded and then snapped in half. His inside pocket also held a bunch of keys which I took from him.

Using my shirt as a cloth I made an amateurish attempt to wipe my fingerprints off of the weapon and then, holding it in my shirt, I rubbed Blondie's hands across it before dropping it at the side of his prone body. Leaving the room hurriedly I walked further along the side of the empty warehouse until I came to another door situated next to a window that looked into a furnished office. I tried the door but it was locked and so removing the keys from my pocket I finally found the key that unlocked it and walked into the room heading straight for the wooden desk that occupied the centre of the room.

I sat in the leather chair that was placed behind the desk and it responded to my weight with a luxurious spring. I swivelled around in the chair, allowing myself a brief moment of relief at still being alive and free against all odds, and then began to search the drawers on the desk.

The first drawer contained nothing but an alarm clock and assorted stationary along with a dismantled set of scales and a selection of hypodermic syringes still encased in their disposable packaging.

I struck gold with the second drawer. Inside was a significantly large sealed bag that contained smaller envelopes filled with a richly brown powder. I tore open the bag and removed two of the envelopes full of their deadly golden cargo. Alongside the heroin were files and sheets of paper inside green cardboard folders. I flicked through the uppermost folder and removed it from the drawer with a vague feeling that it might contain information that could prove useful.

I opened the uppermost drawer again and besides a syringe which I secreted in my inner pocket next to the heroin I took an A4 pad of paper along with a pen and an envelope. My mental faculties were at their peak now and at last I began to think two steps ahead rather than simply reacting to the situation that I found myself in. I hurriedly created a letter as if it had been written by Osbourne and placed it into one of the envelopes that were also contained within the drawer. Lifting my foot up from the floor I took the letter that Osbourne had given me, which had surprised me when I saw that it was addressed to Superintendent Pearson at the South Yorkshire police headquarters, and then copied the address onto the blank envelope in front of me. I then placed my fake letter back underneath my sock and put the genuine letter from Osbourne into my inner pocket where it nestled alongside the drugs and needle.

I had struck Blondie with a heavy blow from the butt of the gun and he had been unconscious as soon as he hit the floor but he was a big strong man and I doubted whether it would take him long to wake from his enforced sleep. I rose from the desk and spotting a bottle of sparkling Evian water on the desk next to a packet of dry roasted peanuts I remembered his words and decided to return the favour that he had so graciously promised me.

With no time to waste and my heart beating rapidly within my chest I ran across to the room that had held me and found Blondie still stretched out on the floor. I dropped the water and peanuts alongside his still breathing body and after taking one last look at that pathetic dealer of death I left the cell, closing and locking the door behind me.

If the mute and mutilated driver returned now then my hopes would take a swift downturn and so I raced out of the building as quickly as I could. To my astonishment I saw that wherever the driver had taken Osbourne's body, shot but still alive for that moment at least, he had either done it on foot or, more probably, used an alternative vehicle for the grisly task because the large black BMW 730 that had brought me to this desolate warehouse was still parked nearby. I ran across to the car and flicked through Blondie's key fob until I found the one that I was looking for. It had been a long time since I had last driven, and I had hated it with a passion then, but it was late night and the roads were empty: I had no choice but to confront my fears and get back behind the wheel.

Out of habit I had climbed into the left hand side of the vehicle and almost laughed at my foolishness as I found myself sat in the passenger seat. I shuffled across to the driver' seat and gripped the steering wheel tightly in my hands hoping that the memory of how to drive would somehow come back to me.

I looked around and switched on the overhead light before allowing myself a few precious seconds to familiarise myself with the instruments and controls that lay in front of me. I fumbled for the levers on the chair before realising that everything was operated electronically on this luxurious car which was quite unlike anything that I had driven before. After a period of trial and error which had sent the windscreen washers swishing and the electronic sunroof opening and closing I eventually managed to position my seat so that I could press comfortably down on the pedals. I looked in my mirrors and checked the blind spot over my shoulder as if I was sitting my driving test all over again. At last I started the engine pressed the clutch down and brought the revs up before removing the handbrake and raising the clutch from its biting point causing the car to move forward, with staccato hops at first, into the night.

I tried to remember the direction that the car had taken when it had brought me here and I used that memory until I came to the first signposts that pointed the way back towards the town. It felt strange to be driving again and although it was a stolen car I felt that this paled into insignificance when I considered that in the last hour I had shot a man, locked another in a cell and was driving around with two substantial packets of a Class A drugs in my pocket. This wasn't a night where I wanted to be pulled over by the law.

I halted at a traffic light and reached into the pocket where I had placed the card that Vicky had given to me. It contained her address, telephone number and a message that read 'I hope that you get the chance to get in touch with me.' She hoped that I would get the chance? Maybe she knew more than I was giving her credit for and she remained the one person whose motives remained unclear to me. The address was in a nearby suburb of the town called Almondsbury and it was time that I got some answers from her.

The lights turned green and I stalled the car. I restarted the engine but nerves were beginning to affect my driving skills, or more accurately my lack of them, causing me to stall the engine again. I began to worry now, it surely wouldn't be long until the driver returned and found Blondie locked in the cell with the car gone. Once he had revived sufficiently then he would certainly come looking for me and I didn't rate my chances of escaping from him in a car chase to be very high. Thankfully the car started at the third attempt and I drove on through the quiet and sleeping streets, with one eye nervously on the rear view mirror, as I headed towards Almondsbury and Vicky Gallagher.

I skirted around the town centre in an effort to avoid police patrols and the abundance of traffic lights and soon reached the suburb of Almondsbury. It was famous in the district for providing Huddersfield's most distinctive landmark, the Almondsbury Tower. It stood atop Tower Hill and looked down on the nearby town centre, designed to look like a turret from a Middle Ages castle it was in fact a carefully designed folly from Victorian times and now provided tourists and students the chance to have their photograph taken against its elegantly pointless backdrop. It was not an area of the town that I was overly familiar with but as I drove slowly through its streets, the tyres slipping occasionally on the icy road beneath them, I turned my head from left to right and eventually found Thorn Street which housed her at number 48.

The street was lined with cars but none of them as extravagant as the BMW that I now brought to a halt in a space that was available three doors down from Vicky's house. I climbed out of the vehicle and looked around me as if expecting to see shadowy figures looming behind me but nobody was in sight. It was by now in the early hours of the morning but lights were shining from many of the houses and from number 48 I could hear thudding music that seemed to be seeping out from the pores between the bricks. At least I knew that I wouldn't be disturbing anybody.

I knocked loudly on the door to give myself a chance of being heard above the music. A window opened across the road and a large bellied man with a wispy strand of hair hanging from the middle of his bald head leaned out and shouted at me, in no uncertain terms, to stop banging. His breasts wobbled as he shouted and he slammed the window closed as I remained silently ignoring him.

The door was pulled open with a flourish and I was about to enter without waiting to be invited when I saw that it wasn't Vicky who had answered the door but another woman altogether. She was at least ten years older than Vicky with black skin and hair that had been tied back into a pony tail. She was wearing a pink dressing gown, faded in places, that she hastily pulled the cord across, just failing to hide all of her ample flesh from my gaze. She prodded me in the chest now and shouted at me in a dark and resonant voice that I felt certain would get the man across the street leaning out of his window again:

"Get away from here, you."

"I'm after Vicky."

"I know you are. You've been after her a long time haven't you – I thought that she had told you to leave her alone?"

"Are you sure that you've got the right person? I've never been here before – I just need to speak to Vicky that's all." I protested my innocence but it seemed to have little effect on the formidable woman that was stood before me and was still struggling gainfully to cover her modesty with the inadequate dressing gown.

"Never been here before?" she snorted with derision, "I have seen you hanging around. Now go away before I have to make you go away." Fortunately Vicky had heard the conversation and it seemed that she had recognised my voice for before she even came round the corner to join our altercation she was saying to her housemate:

"Adele, you've got the wrong person. He had long hair, don't you remember?"

Adele didn't like to admit being in the wrong, it seemed, for she continued to eye me with suspicion before saying:

"Well they all look the same to me. Let him in then, do what you want. It's only my house after all. I'll leave you love birds to it." She turned her back on me and pounded up the stairs with a heavy and deliberate stomping of her feet.

Vicky was stood before me now wearing a blue pair of slippers, in the style favoured by grandmothers everywhere with white woollen collars around the ankles, a skimpy pink thong and a cropped t-shirt that bore the legend 'Porn Star'. She looked at me with narrowed eyes at first but then she gave me her familiar sly smile and pulled me into the house closing the front door that had been letting in the chill night air. She led me by the hand into the living room that smelled strongly of sandalwood and stale cigarettes but was otherwise in a neat and tidy condition. Still leading me she took me to a large cream coloured sofa, with cushions in the shade of pink that seemed to be compulsory in this house, and putting her arms around my neck she placed her mouth upon mine and kissed me greedily. This took me by surprise and it was almost as if I was kissing Lamara again rather than the cousin who was like her in so many ways. I found myself responding automatically and before I had time to consider what I was doing we had fallen onto the sofa where we continued to kiss each other wildly. She was undoing the button and zip on my trousers now and my hand was reaching up inside of her t-shirt to her small and firm breasts that felt warm in my hand. Suddenly the nonsense of what we were doing when compared with the enormity of the situation facing me, and feelings of guilt towards Rosa, hit me simultaneously and I pushed Vicky from off of me before rolling from the sofa and refastening my clothing with one hand while I smoothed my hair with the other.

"What's up?" she asked me with a hurt look on her face.

"This isn't the time or the place Vicky. It really isn't. I'm sorry it's not you it's just that, well I wasn't expecting it. What got into you there?"

"Well I was just glad to see you again."

"Glad or surprised?"

"What do you mean?" Her hurt voice had now been replaced with one of suspicion.

"Nothing, nothing at all. Look, you really mean the world to me Vicky and I'm sorry that I've not been to see you since Lamara died. But it's been hard for me."

"So I can tell."

"No, look you don't understand but if you give me a chance I'll try and explain things. We need a good long chat."

"Come on then, Mr Talk." She stood with her hands on her hips now.

"Not here. Look I really need a big favour from you, alright. Can you drive?"

"Of course I can. You know me, John, I've been driving since I was fourteen."

"Well follow me then and you can do some driving for me. My cars parked outside."

She pulled on a pair of jeans that lay next to the sofa and in the hallway climbed into some dark blue Converse sneakers and a cream coloured leather jacket that hung on a coat stand. When we got outside she stood wide eyed and shaking her head as she saw the car that I had opened the

246

door for. Without saying a word but with a look of incredulity still on her face she sat down in the drivers seat and, taking the keys that I offered to her, started the car before speeding into the night at a pace that had me scrambling for my seatbelt.

"Slow down, Vic, just keep to the limit alright? I've got a special something here that I want to keep secret."

I patted the breast of my jacket as I said this and Vicky got the picture. She nodded again and then turning her head to the left and looking at me she said:

"Well you won't be keeping it secret from me John. I know whose car this is and I know that he wouldn't have lent it to you. So why don't you just give me the lowdown on what's happening here? If I'm going to be in trouble then I want to know what kind of trouble it is."

"How well do you know that Blondie guy?"

"Well enough."

"Is he a friend of yours?"

"An acquaintance more than a friend. A necessary evil I suppose you could say. Anyway, what's with all the questions? You're supposed to be answering mine."

"Right here goes. Blondie came to pick me up while you were doing your second act – how did that go by the way?"

"It went fine, made a lot of money. Stop changing the subject."

She gave me a fierce look now and I decided to tell her the story with one or two changes to it: I still wasn't entirely sure if I could trust her.

"Okay, sorry. I was just taking an interest that's all. Well, anyway Blondie meets me at The Nelson's and says that we can't do the deal there so I get into the car. This car."

"Who was driving it?"

"Some woman or other."

"A woman? What was she like?"

"Long blonde hair, curly. Quite young and sophisticated. Very glamorous."

I looked across and saw that Vicky had a perplexed look on her face and a frown on her forehead. I continued:

"We drove out to a house. I don't know where it was, I had other things on my mind, but it was in the suburbs somewhere. Very big it was. Double garage, manicured lawn with a waterfall feature. It might have been hers, I suppose, because she unlocked the door and ushered us in. Once we were in the house the atmosphere changed. Blondie forced me into a room and locked me in there. It had a big solid door that he locked behind me and then I saw that another man, a person that they called Osbourne, was locked in the room with me. Are you believing this so far, Vic?"

"Go on".

"Well this part is going to be harder to believe. In the room was a gun. Through the door Blondie shouted that I had to shoot him, this Osbourne guy, before he would let me out."

"And you did it?"

"Yes, I did it."

"And then what happened?"

"Blondie came into the room and it was obvious that I was going to be the next victim. Well, still having some semblance of wits about me, I took the gun and brought it down, crack upon his head. I rifled through his pockets, got the car keys and a packet of junk, and that more or less brings me up to where we are now."

"So let me get this straight, John. You have killed two people in the last hour, yeah?"

"No, no. I don't think that I've killed either of them. I'm as bad a shot as I am a driver and I think I only wounded Osbourne and Blondie was just unconscious, he's probably come round now."

"But why did that happen in the first place?"

"Well, Vicky that is a long, long story. Strange things have been happening to me lately. Some dangerous people seem to think that I've got something that they want."

"And have you got it?"

"Got what?"

I was waiting for her to say 'the ring' but she simply replied:

"Whatever this something is."

"I might have."

"So I guess that the word has gone out to people that John Halle must be found."

Did she guess that or did she know it? I answered:

"It seems so, Vic. It seems so."

"So here we are in a stolen car belonging to a drug dealer that is going to want to kill you when he remembers what happened, you have a packet of heroin in your pocket, most people this side of the Pennines are looking for you, and you may or may not have this thing that people seem to be looking for? Have I got that right?"

"Yes, that's a pretty good summary. I could have saved myself a few

248

minutes there couldn't I?" I was feeling in control of the situation now and my usual dry humour, if such it could be called, had returned.
"And you expect me to drive you around after all that?"
"Well, yes, what else do you have to do on a Thursday night?"
"Okay, you're on." She pressed her foot to the floor again and the car shot off into the night. I kept reminding her to keep to the speed limits but it was as if I was talking to myself, it seemed that she found it easier to drive at a hundred miles an hour rather than thirty.

I told her to head for Barnsley and we were soon heading through the broad country roads that joined the two towns. I knew that something wasn't right. Vicky had taken the story much too calmly: it was true that she had enjoyed a rather dissolute life up to this point and being on the wrong side of the law was nothing unusual to her but the only time that she had shown any sign of alarm was when I had mentioned the glamorous woman who had been with me and Blondie. I was glad that I had chosen to embellish that part of the story – if Vicky was, as I increasingly suspected, somehow linked with this Blondie and I had revealed that he was actually held in the warehouse then she might have driven straight there or at least sent word of his location. Now I had sown seeds of doubt in her mind.

Vicky continued to ask me questions and it could have been from understandable curiosity or she could have been trying to gain information that could have been of use to her later. I was as cagey as I could be without rousing her suspicions too much and fed her a mixture of truths, half-truths and downright lies.

Throughout the journey, which due to the lack of traffic on the roads and Vicky Gallagher's flagrant disregard for any speed limits was a surprisingly short one, I kept looking into the rear view mirror expecting at any moment to see a police car or Blondie and his henchman following me, not knowing which would have been least welcome to me. If Blondie had recovered by now then surely his first point of contact would have been Vicky, the woman who had put him in touch with me, and it wouldn't take long for her housemate or the angry neighbour to tell him what had happened.

Suddenly I remembered the threat that Blondie had made in the cell and I cursed myself that I had been so preoccupied with my own safety that I had momentarily forgotten about Rosa. I flicked through the directory on my mobile phone and dialled her but although I let the number ring and ring until it cut itself off, and repeated this on two further occasions, no answer came. I tried to fool myself that she had been under stress and

249

might have fallen into a deep and undisturbed sleep but really I knew that she would have been waiting by the telephone as I had instructed her. I tapped out a text message and sent it to her. It read simply 'Get out of the flat now. It's not safe. John x'

I slipped the telephone back into my pocket and when Vicky asked who I had been calling I told her that it was the dog sitter. I was in a troubled mood again now and when I looked up into the rear view mirror again I saw Lamara suddenly sitting there in the back seat, unseen by the cousin who was sat in front of her driving the vehicle.

I had grown accustomed to the idea that I could see people that were hidden to others, that I had a link to the other side of the divide that ran between life and death, but it still caused my heart to jump. She was serene and beautiful now; her eyes sparkled and she gave me a broad smile as she looked straight at me. I turned around to face her now and it was almost as I remembered seeing her in the first few happy months of our relationship. She gave me one last smile and then she turned her head to face the back of her cousin Vicky. Her face changed now and took on an angry countenance as her lips became thinner and her head bowed. She raised her left hand now and I saw once again that she was holding a card – it was the Five of Swords that she had picked out at Madame Irina's house. The medium's words came rushing back to me then: the Five of Swords represented dishonour or loss and betrayal by a friend. As I recalled these words the vision of Lamara turned to give me one last look again, and a smile that was almost of gratitude, and then vanished before my eyes. I turned around slowly to face the front again and I looked across at Vicky Gallagher with contempt as I realised with a sudden clarity, as if the sun had appeared from behind a bank of clouds, that it was she who had somehow betrayed the cousin who had been more like a sister to her. I could have told her to pull the car over then and there and placed my hands around her throat until she told me the truth but I knew that it would take a more subtle approach if I was finally to find the truth about how Lamara had died, and Georgie too who seemed to be linked to her although as yet I didn't know how they were linked. I was brooding silently as Vicky reached the outskirts of Barnsley and then, following my directions, on to the house of my friend Steven. I tried to keep a note of friendliness in my voice as I gave Vicky directions and answered, in a manner, the questions that she continued to throw at me but it was a hard act to master and Vicky seemed to be becoming more and more suspicious. At last, and not a moment too soon, we reached the side street cul-de-sac that held the house of Steven

Carter. At my instruction Vicky pulled the car up as close to the house as possible but we couldn't park on the driveway as that was now occupied by an ambulance that had its signal flashing on top of it sending blue shafts of light racing across the large bay windows of the neighbouring houses.

I hastily removed my seat belt and left the car door swinging on its hinge as I raced across to the scene. There was a commotion coming from within the house and Ed was standing by the opened doors at the rear of the ambulance.

"What's happened?" I asked Ed with a despairing voice.

"It's Dicky Clay isn't it? That doctor's just about gone and killed him."

Chapter Fourteen

So now it seemed that my new and not so fond acquaintance Robert Mitchell, commonly known as 'The Doctor', had succeeded in beating Richard Clay to within an inch of his life and the poor wreck of the man was now to be dependant upon doctors with a more traditional bedside manner. It didn't come as a surprise to me as I had noticed the barely concealed psychosis within Mitchell when I'd first caught his eye in the takeaway. Death and violence had become a regular occurrence in my life over the past few days and I am ashamed to admit that at that point I cared little whether Richard Clay, who had shared many school years with me, lived or died. My only concern was whether or not I could still get the information from him that had been promised to me. My quest to obtain the drugs that Clay had been craving had led me to a terrifying ordeal in Huddersfield but now that I had kept my part of the bargain, against all odds, I was desperate to hold Richard to his.

I turned to Ed again who was stood by the opened doors of the ambulance, eyes downcast as though he was ashamed to catch anyone's glance, and asked him:

"How bad is he, Ed?"

"Pretty bad, John. That doctor gave him a pretty bad going over, I tried to restrain him but there was just no stopping him. And do you know what, John? That stupid Little Dicky Clay didn't say a word. He just lay there whimpering. It was just like he used to be at school when he used to get bullied mercilessly. It was terrible, John, terrible. This isn't the life for us is it, John? We're not cut out for all of this violence."

251

I wished that I could have been living in Ed's safe and insular world where violence is a momentary intrusion and where tomorrow would see a return to quiet cups of tea in front of a gas fire, biscuits being dunked in time to the rhythm of the latest video showing on MTV. It seemed that violence had sought me out as his constant companion and I didn't even know if I would see tomorrow: the odds were fifty-fifty at best.

"Where is he?" I asked but before Ed could answer I saw two paramedics carrying the body of Richard Clay on a sturdy plastic stretcher that had large straps fastened across the frame to secure the body upon it. For one moment I thought that the sheet had been pulled across Clay's face as if he was already dead but as they drew closer I saw that it was merely the patient's emaciated state that made his head almost disappear under the sheet that was wrapped over him.

His thin face, which when I had last seen him had been reddened from the vicious slaps that the doctor had thrown at him, was now swollen and misshapen beyond recognition. The crimson patches had now been replaced by a bruised purple hue across the whole of his face and both eyes were closed except for tiny slits that peeped out from beneath his puffed up eyelids. I thought of Ed and Steven in the house with the doctor while this terrible beating had been going on and wondered how they had allowed it to escalate to this level. It would have been easy to judge them harshly but as I had shot a defenceless policeman earlier that night I wasn't in the best moral position myself and so I let it pass. Richard Clay's grotesque head remained motionless, as it seemed that he had while he was attacked. His two skinny arms hung over the top of the sheet and rested on top of the straps on the stretcher. The scabby fingers on his right hand closed and opened involuntarily as if counting time, one contraction every second, and this was the only sign of life from the pathetic man.

Two paramedics were carrying the stretcher. The man at the front of the stretcher, that is close to the feet of Richard Clay, was a tall thin man with red hair that had been subject to an attempt to dye it blonde which had left it a strange washed out shade of orange. He walked with slow deliberation and it was hard to imagine that even the most frantic of emergencies would have been able to motivate him to snap out of his sloth like torpor.

His companion at the rear of the stretcher, looking down upon the purple hued balloon that was Clay's head, was a small man with tired eyes and an angry look upon his face. He had a shaved head but a full beard which made me think that he had run out of razor blades half way through the operation. His green paramedics uniform failed to hide his substantial paunch and he puffed breathlessly as he carried the light weight of Clay upon his stretcher. The little man was a bundle of energy, however, and the effect of this is that he was wanting to walk at least twice as quickly as his younger companion and the stretcher banged into the knees of the taller man at every step. Coupled with the height difference which resulted in the stretcher being sloped at an angle as it was carried it seemed likely that it was only the tightness of the straps binding my old school friend in place that stopped him slipping onto the icy floor below. Looking beyond the stretcher now I saw Steven walking behind them with a concerned look upon his face that registered both anger and shame. As the stretcher, and its human cargo, passed by me I distinctly saw a look of recognition flash into the slits that doubled as Clay's eyes and I smiled back at him with a nod of my head as if to signal that I had not forgotten him.

The stretcher was loaded onto the ambulance with some difficulty and a series of complicated movements from the little and large paramedics that made it seem as if they were practising some badly choreographed ballroom routine. Clay was now securely in place within the ambulance and the taller man climbed slowly out of the back of the vehicle. He walked around the outside of the ambulance and climbed into the driver's seat with as much enthusiasm and vitality as if he had been looking at a particularly complicated jigsaw puzzle where the challenge is to place one pattern of baked beans next to another rather than performing such a vital role as ambulance driver. Placing my left foot onto the metal plate that rested below the still open doors I levered myself up into the back of the ambulance.

"What are you doing in here? Get out at once" the smaller paramedic, who had been left alone with the silent Clay, barked at me.

"I'm his brother. I just wanted a quick word with him and then I'll get out. Is that okay?" I asked but the tone in my voice suggested that this was a rhetorical question rather than a request. He said nothing but, although his fierce face grew redder, he turned away and inspected the dials of the machinery around him.

Looking out of the corner of my eyes I was confident that the ambulance man was not looking in my direction and so I reached into the inside pocket of my jacket and withdrew one of the two packets that I had placed into there. Holding it tightly within my fist I leaned over towards Clay and spoke volubly to him:

"My brother, my brother. What now? I will get whoever did this don't you worry. All that you have to concentrate on is getting better. Just make sure that you get better alright?"

As I said this I shook hands with Clay and passed the package surreptitiously from my hand to his. Without looking at the package, unable to raise his head from its prone position, he felt at it with his fingers and satisfied with this examination he clenched his fingers around it with a vice like grip where he would hold it until he could find somewhere safer to secrete it once he reached the hospital. His mouth moved now but as no audible noise was coming out I angled my head and leaned across the ambulance's makeshift bed so that I could hear his words. He whispered:

"Tommy. Old pavilion. Graveyard. Under the floor." I squeezed his hand genuinely this time: he had kept his side of the bargain, despite all he had been through, and his words at least suggested where my next port of call should be.

"Yes, don't worry about that. Of course I will visit you." I practically shouted this so that the paramedic turned to face us again and I brushed silently past him as I climbed out of the ambulance. As soon as I had stepped out the doors were closed behind me with a metallic clang. The flashing blue light revolved upon the top of the vehicle but it took another minute or so before the ambulance finally moved away at a moderate pace.

I looked around now and saw three people standing behind me: Vicky had left the car and joined Ed and Steven at the front of the house.

"Another one eh, John?" Steven asked with a fake bonhomie as if he was trying to forget what had happened in his house. "It seems that you're becoming as popular with the ladies as I am. Maybe you've been making a few notes after all?"

"This is Vicky Gallagher – Lamara's cousin. You've seen her before."

"Lamara's cousin? Oh, right." Steven had never attempted to hide his dislike of Lamara and in an instant he lost interest in Vicky too and his face resumed the same solemn look that it had worn when he had been walking behind the stretcher bearers.

"Can you wait in the car for me a minute please, Vicky? I need to have a quick word with Steven here."

Vicky smiled at me, and said goodbye sweetly to Steven and Ed, who watched as she climbed back behind the wheel of the large car that I had appropriated, but she had a distrusting look in her eyes and I wondered how long she had been stood behind me and how much she had seen of

254

what had happened in the ambulance. The handover of the drugs, from one palm to another, would have remained unseen by Steven and Ed but Vicky had too much experience of that side of life to remain oblivious to the transaction.

"We need to talk." I said to Steven in a low, calm voice as I looked him straight in the eye.

"Look, about Richard. I had no idea that that was going to happen. I only wanted to help him. It got out of hand. You know that I wanted to help Richard don't you?"

"Of course I know that" I reassured him in soothing tones, "but it's something else that I need to speak to you about."

Steven ushered me back into the house and we walked into the hallway. I took the opportunity to remove the documents that had been taken from Blondie's office, hidden under my jacket, and place them unseen underneath the copies of FHM Magazine and Golfing World that lay stacked on a table in the hallway. Ed followed behind us but whilst I walked into the luxuriant living room with Steven, I heard the footsteps of Ed run quickly up the stairway. The conversation that I had with Steven would be interrupted at regular intervals by the sound of retching followed by rapid flushes of the toilet: Ed was a strong man but he had a weak constitution.

Steven Carter had enjoyed a good and rewarding career as an Information Technology expert. His house was decorated in the height of modern good taste, which clashed dramatically with my idea of taste that seemed to have gone out of fashion around forty years beforehand. The room that I had been ushered into now, and in which Steven and I had spent many enjoyable and drunken evenings in before, contained all mod cons and was decorated in bright and vibrant colours. To my mind, however, it seemed to have lost an important element of humanity amongst the electronic heart that beat robotically within it.

Steven sat down upon one of the three sofas that were placed around the spacious room, each of the same design but with subtly different combinations of colours that were designed to complement each other. This would have to be a brief conversation, I was eager to use the information from Richard Clay to track down Poor Tommy, and so I remained standing with my arms now folded across my chest. Steven stayed sat upon his sofa and as I looked down upon him it was as if I was addressing a misbehaved child.

"I need your help Steven. I need a big favour, no questions asked. I'll tell you all about it later but right now I just need you to do something for me. Will you help me Steven?"

"Yeah, mate of course I will. Is tomorrow alright?"

"It's too late tomorrow. I mean right now."

"Now? It's the middle of the night."

"I know it is, and I wouldn't normally ask you. You know that you can rely on me, I'm Mr Boring, Mr Dependable. Well at the moment I've got in a fix and I need you to deliver a letter for me. That's all it is. But it's got to be done tonight – right now. Okay?"

Steven gave a big sigh and looked at the floor as if hoping that I would have vanished by the time that he looked up. It was a bad time to catch him I suppose, but we had always been there for each other throughout our lives and I was confident that, however much of a protest he might make, I could rely on him again. He looked up and I hadn't vanished.

"Okay, mate. I'll do it. Pass it to me and I'll get it over and done with. Maybe I can get some sleep then, eh?"

I nodded my head in a show of appreciation. I reached into my pocket again, ignoring the other wrap of heroin which was still secreted in there, and removed the genuine copy of the letter that Osbourne had written. It was still unopened and I passed it into the outstretched hand of my friend Steven Carter.

He looked at the address and then looked up at me in surprise:

"The police? A Superintendent? He isn't going to see me at this time of night is he man?"

"Be persuasive Steven. That letter is very, very important. It has to get into his hands tonight. Whatever happens, give that letter to nobody except Superintendent Pearson. All you need to know is that one of his officers, a guy called Osbourne, is in grave danger. You could be saving his life. Look, I've got to go. I promise I will explain it all to you later. Over a pint or two, on me." If I get the chance, I muttered under my breath.

"Okay, I'll go now. Ed can stay here until the police arrive."

"Police?"

"Yeah, the police. I had to call them along with the ambulance after Rob attacked Clay up there. I didn't know he was like that, John. I knew that he was a big powerful man, of course, but I swear that I didn't know that he would act like that."

"Where is he now?"

"Who knows? He ran off into the night. The police will catch him soon enough. I came clean with the cops on the phone, I told them everything."

"Everything?"

"Yeah, about the intervention I mean. They said that I'd got nothing to worry about but that they had to get hold of Rob. They kept asking who else was involved as well."

"Did you mention me?"

"No, not at all. You weren't here when it all happened after all. The strange thing was that the officer just didn't seem to believe me. He kept describing someone, someone who, well sounded a bit like you John. Is that what this letter is about?

"Don't ask. The less you know then the better it is for you. Just get it to Superintendent Pearson as quickly as you can. Oh, who were you talking to you in the police by the way?"

"Well it started off at some call centre, some telephone battery hen on the line. Then it got switched across to the local station and some Sergeant or other came on the line. He will be on his way over here in a bit."

I didn't need to know the name, I knew which Sergeant would be speeding towards the house as we spoke. I shook Steven's hand, as if it might be for the last time, and headed for the door. Steven shouted after me:

"I'll leave Ed here and set off with the letter now. You owe me one though! Hey, nice motor that Vicky's got there by the way. What does she do for a living?"

"She is a stripper" I called back.

"Really? She must be bloody good."

Despite everything I couldn't help a smile coming to my lips at this thought. Yes he could be a well intentioned fool, naïve to the cruel ways of the world, but I knew that when the chips were down I would always be able to rely unquestionably upon Steven Carter.

Vicky had already got the motor of the car running and as I climbed into the passenger seat the BMW was producing a powerful purr that was ready to increase to a mighty roar at the push of a pedal. She looked across at me and without saying a word she pulled out of the drive as I was pulling the seat belt across my chest and clumsily trying to clip the belt into its fastener.

"Where to?" she asked but as she was already speeding towards Hoyland it seemed that she had little need of prompting.

"Do you know where Shelby's Shack is?" I asked and was surprised at her answer.

"Shelby's Shack? Yes I know it. I went there once with Lamara."

"Well can you take me there please? I'm looking for something there."
Vicky continued to drive at her preferred speed, breakneck, and there
didn't seem a second's hesitation in her choices – she knew exactly
where she was going and which turnings to take. I had lived in the area
for the majority of my life and I didn't know where Shelby's Shack, the
name given to me by Festa when I had cornered him at the beginning of
this long and testing night, was. Vicky Gallagher had never lived in the
area, to my knowledge, but seemed sure of the location and claimed that
she remembered it from a visit with Lamara which must have been over
a year ago. The suspicions that I held about Vicky, loathe as I was to
hold them about a woman that I had once been fond of, had grown now
to the point where I knew that I could no longer trust her and wanted to
be away from her company as soon as possible.

We drove on through Hoyland and as we passed the town's police
station, small like the town itself, I saw a police car heading out of the
station car park. With relief I saw, in the mirror, that it was heading in a
different direction to us and towards Steven's house where the Sergeant
would find himself too late to catch the prey that he was really after.
We continued our journey through the freezing black darkness of a
January night, and soon we reached the outskirts of the neighbouring
village of Elsecar, tracing the same route as that fateful bus had taken
carrying me and Georgie together on Tuesday of that week.

We were nearing the railway station now and I wondered if the area that
had seen that woman so mercilessly crushed would still be marked out or
whether a makeshift shrine would have been placed at the roadside for
people to leave flowers and heartfelt poems for people they didn't know.
I didn't get the chance to find out because before we reached the railway
station Vicky turned the car right down a small alleyway that ran by the
side of a large building. There was barely enough room to squeeze the
car down the alley but Vicky managed it with considerable ease: If she
had ever decided to take her driving test then she would have passed it
without doubt but I knew that she had never liked to do things the easy
way. The alleyway now became a gravel path that we travelled noisily
down. Vicky had finally been forced to slow the car due to the prevailing
conditions but it still sent chips of gravel flying with a crack into the air
as it drove along.

The track widened out into a broad semi circle now and then came to an
abrupt stop as did the car that Vicky was driving for me.

"Is this it? Where's the shack then?" I asked her.

"It's over there", she replied pointing to a moderately sized building which seemed to be in a state of disrepair. There was no road or path leading to the shack, as it had become known, but as I squinted through the darkness I saw that it lay around a hundred metres away across a grass covered wasteland.

"Nice place. I can see why you came here with Lamara."

"She liked to show me the sights when I visited. What are we looking for?"

"We are looking for nothing, Vic: I'm afraid that this is something that I've got to do on my own. I do need you to do a big, big favour for me though Vicky."

The smile, which had been unusually absent throughout the journey, returned to her lips now and her eyes sparkled.

"What is it John?"

"I've got something that I need you to deliver for me. It's very, very important that you deliver it for me in person. A life could depend upon it. I've known you for years, Vic, and you're as good as family to me. I couldn't trust anybody else with this."

"Let's have it then."

I took off my shoe now and then my sock, finally removing the letter that I had hidden in there. Vicky laughed as she took the letter from me and I admit that it must have looked a comical sight.

"Yes, go ahead and laugh Vic" I said allowing myself a chuckle too, "but that's the only place that I could keep this thing safe. So please, please get this delivered for me. It's imperative that this goes right now. Is that okay?"

She looked down at the address but showed no surprise that it was addressed to Superintendent Pearson. Instead she simply looked up at me and in a steady and sincere voice she promised me:

"Don't worry John, I'll make sure that this gets delivered alright."

She leaned across and we kissed passionately again before I climbed out of the car and she performed a circular turn and then drove away with the letter that I had deliberately faked earlier that night. I'd like to pretend that I hadn't enjoyed the kiss but I am sure that you're perceptive enough not to believe that. It had certainly been a more pleasurable kiss than the one which Judas had bestowed, but was it just as treacherous?

I had an appointment at Shelby's Shack at the following midnight, which as I looked at my watch I saw was still over twenty hours away, and contrary to the story that I had given to Vicky I had no reason to be there now: I had pretended otherwise to avoid her finding out that I was really on my way to meet Poor Tommy O'Callaghan. I felt sure now that Vicky would take the letter not to the Superintendent but to Blondie or maybe even to the unknown Mr Big of the operation and when she talked to them I wanted her to give them as much misinformation as possible. The ruse had also given me the useful knowledge of where Shelby's Shack was located: I would be here again at midnight, alright, but I was strangely confident that by that time it would be John Halle who would be pulling the strings.

I resisted the temptation to walk down to the large looming building known as the shack: whatever was in there could wait. Turning around I walked back up the gravel pathway that led to the alleyway down which Vicky had driven. The track crunched underneath my feet but there was nobody around to hear it. I soon reached the alley which ran alongside a large building which seemed to shine creamy white in the dark night. Reaching the front of the building, just before turning left towards Hoyland, I realised that this building, now in disrepair from years of inactivity had once been that local cinema so beloved of children in the area and the place where little Rosa Galloway had sat eating popcorn and sucking on a straw protruding from a Kia-Ora carton, wide eyed and amazed as she watched the little alien who wanted to phone home. Phone home. I took my mobile telephone from my pocket and pressed the redial button to connect me to Rosa but again, although it rang and rang, there was no answer.

A fading sign still announced that this building had once been the Elektra Palace but nobody had queued to come here for a long time. Paint had been daubed or sprayed onto the wall and I didn't have to peer too closely into the gloom to know that it was another tag from Festa who liked to place his pathetic scrawl on as many places as possible. Maybe he was in hospital now? Even he couldn't scrawl his names unnoticed on the hospital beds: that thought comforted me as I retraced the route that Vicky and I had taken and walked through the still and bitter night towards the town centre and the unsuspecting Tommy O'Callaghan.

My old school friend Richard Clay had only been able to whisper a handful of words to me as I had bent over him, ears straining to capture every word, in the back of the ambulance but it hadn't taken me long to work out the location that he was referring to. By the time that I had finished speaking to Steven Carter I knew exactly where Poor Tommy was hiding and I just hoped that he was still there when I paid him an unexpected visit.

I wrapped my arms around myself and slapped myself harshly across the rips from time to time in an effort to beat off the freezing chill that was creeping through my clothing and had seeped into my aching bones. My body was fatigued but my mind felt sharper than ever and I knew that I had no time to rest. I saw no traffic on the streets, it seemed that even the joyriders were at home tonight rather than venturing onto the icy roads. In the distance I heard the melancholy wail of a siren and I turned around from one direction to another in an effort to work out where the sound was coming from but it faded upon the still air before I could guess whether it was a fire engine speeding towards a post pub chip pan fire or the Sergeant and his men looking for me. I pressed on regardless.

If I felt my spirit or legs flagging for a moment I called to mind Richard Clay's words: "Tommy. Old pavilion. Graveyard. Under the floor." I'd given him the package that he wanted, the heroin that his body craved even more after the beating that had been administered upon him in such cruel and cowardly fashion, and it would have been easy for him to have kept quiet but he used his last reserves of energy to give me the information that I had sought. He had kept his part of the bargain and I felt a sudden concern for him – earlier I hadn't cared whether he lived or died but now I realised that I wanted him to pull through after all.

The location that he had referred to was a place well known to myself, Richard, Steven and Ed from our schooldays. The graveyard that had been referred to was the cemetery of St Peters church where I had met Osbourne on Wednesday night. Adjacent to the cemetery was Kirk Balk School, the local comprehensive school that provided a depressingly adequate education for children from a large catchment area. Alongside Kirk Balk was a large playing field that ran from the sports centre at one side of the school across to the cemetery at the other side. These playing fields contained, amongst the empty crisp packets, discarded cigarette packets and assorted flotsam of teenage life, a rugby pitch, a football pitch and at the far end of the playing field was a rudimentary cricket pitch with white painted markings to signify the boundary. At the foot of the cricket pitch was a pavilion which had once been sparkling white and solidly beautiful: the pride of the local sports teams. The football, rugby and cricket players now preferred to get changed in the backs of cars or even out on the field rather than endure the dilapidated and dirty conditions of the pavilion which seemed as if it would collapse from moment to moment. This pavilion backed onto the cemetery itself and I knew that it was here, or in its environs, that I would find Tommy O'Callaghan if he was to be found at all.

I had reached the war memorial now that stood at the bottom of the broad road which led to the cemetery and the pavilion that was alongside it. It was here that Georgie Galloway had pointed to as she was carried past it on the bus, unseen to everyone but me, and it was nearby that Tommy O'Callaghan had discovered her lifeless body if the papers were to be believed. My eyes focussed on the poppy wreaths that still lined the foot of the memorial. Their icy coating gleamed under the starlight and I felt how although it was fitting that these brave men, lions led by donkeys, were remembered so fondly there were so many other people that had passed away unmourned and unnoticed down the years. I knew that Georgie was with me now although I couldn't see her this time. A breeze suddenly sprang up in the previously calm night and as it was whistled past my ears it seemed as if it was Georgie's voice itself that chanted 'You're doing well, you're doing well' as it hurried past me.

I skirted around the cemetery that had held such threat to me earlier in the week but although my eyes were drawn unavoidably into its dark interior nothing met them other than row upon row of stones bearing silent witness to the inevitability of death. Would there be a stone for me one day, one day soon perhaps, or would the fire that I had seen destined to consume me leave nothing to be buried?

I was walking at the quick pace that I had sustained since leaving Vicky's car, the car that I imagined she was keen to reunite with its rightful owner Blondie, and I soon reached the school's expansive playing field. In daylight it would offer a canopy of colours, browns, greens and greys that would turn to yellow blankets full of dandelions and buttercups in springtime, but at night time it was just a dark and soulless mass that glistened with white rime in places. I walked towards the pavilion with light steps and baited breath but it was impossible to stop the gentle crunch of the icy grass underneath my feet.

I had reached the periphery of the pavilion now. It was a rectangular shaped building, one story high and I estimated that its dimensions were around six metres by eight meters. The white paint had peeled away in many places revealing the rotting woodwork underneath. There had once been a wrought iron fence around the pavilion and a dark green gate had permitted access to and from the cricket pitch. This ironwork had long since gone but it was still possible to trace its impression on the floor around the building. Thin looking boards, full of splinters, were now in situ where once had been glass windows that had opened at strategic moments when warm hands would hand out cooling glasses of home made lemonade or wizened looking oranges that had been sliced into quarters. The only thing that was new about the building was the solid looking door, painted in a streaked blue, that had been placed upon it and which had a thick chain tied around its handle and secured with a large padlock.

I approached the door cautiously. The chains looked to be unmoveable and I wondered how I was going to gain access to the building and, just as pertinently, how Poor Tommy could have accessed it. Had Richard Clay been lying after all? I pulled at the chain forlornly with little hope of success and the answer was revealed. The door wobbled on the opposite side and I saw now, through the darkness, that whilst the side of the door that contained the handle had been securely fastened the screws had been removed from the hinges and as I pulled at that side of the door it opened enough to allow me to squeeze through into the building itself. As I climbed clumsily into the interior I expected to see a sickly pair of eyes staring back at me but all that greeted me was a black nothingness. The air was fetid and hung heavily around me. I held my breath and then heard a shrill cry as something seemed to grab onto my right foot. With my heightened reactions I lashed out with my free left foot and saw an unidentifiable black shape fly across the air and crash into the wall opposite. As it rushed past me now, with a squeal of pain, I saw that it was a rat that had made its home in this pavilion that otherwise seemed to be deserted.

My eyes had not yet grown accustomed to the darkness within the building and I walked with outstretched hands around the cricket pavilion. My touch reached nothing but a succession of rough walls that were wet and clammy to the touch and I had to wipe cobwebs from my face at regular intervals spitting them out as they draped themselves into my mouth. As my eyes began to adjust slowly to the lack of light it became apparent that there was nothing, and nobody in the room. I stood motionless in the centre of the room with my hands in my pockets as I wondered whether somebody else had reached Tommy before me and questioned what hope had I of finding him now? As I paused there, motionless and deep in silent thought, I heard a faint rustling and scraping noise as if more rats were in the vicinity and then I noticed faint sparkles of light that seemed to emanate from between the floorboards in a corner of the room. I realised now that I had ignored the word 'underground' from Richard's instructions and I lowered myself gently onto all fours, my knees becoming wet and dust covered in the process. As I crawled towards the faint rays of light I saw that a section of the floorboards had been cut into a square pattern as if it was a trapdoor. My mother had always told me to knock before entering anywhere and, although she was now sunning herself in the Algarve while her son risked his life in the freezing North of England, I followed the example that she had taught me. Rising back to my feet I stamped my feet three times upon the trapdoor and then stood back, smacking the dust from my knees, and waited for my host to arrive.

I didn't have long to wait and I could hear the noises from below growing nearer and louder. At last the door was raised from below and I saw the shaven head of Poor Tommy O'Callaghan rising 'de profundis' from out of the depths. He looked very much alive for a man that I had been accused of killing, but I had learned not to place too much trust on such appearances. As his eyes met mine, though, it looked as if he had seen a ghost and his head began to disappear downwards again and the door to close behind him. With one movement I jammed my foot into the door before it closed and kicked it fully open. Tommy grabbed my heel now and as he pulled at it I lost my balance and fell crashing down upon him. As my body impacted with his he fell too and we crashed ten or more feet together careering off a succession of wooden steps as we fell. I lay dazed and winded at the bottom and my ribs, that had barely recovered from the beating that they had suffered two days previously, suffered paroxysms of pain every time that I breathed in. I lay flat upon my back for a few seconds with tiny stars and flashes of light circling before my eyes. As the stars faded, and I felt a remnant of strength returning, I turned my head to its side and saw the thin and bedraggled figure of Tommy lying next to me, motionless except for his sunken chest which rose and fell dramatically.

We rose to our feet at the same time and looked warily at each other. Tommy spat upon the floor and then coughed up a dusty phlegm. A fire seemed to rise within his eyes now and he gritted his broken, uneven, teeth before lunging towards me.

"Stop there Tommy!" I shouted and he stopped in his tracks just a foot away from me. His body was still tense and ready to spring into action. "I've got to warn you, Tommy, that I've already shot somebody tonight. Don't make me do it again." I patted the pocket of my jacket as if to indicate that it might just hold a gun and Tommy, taking the hint, slunk away from me with a look of defeat on his face like a scalded dog.

"Why do you want to say that to me sir? Why do you want to come here, into Poor Tommy's humble abode and then be all about threatening him?"

He had walked away and sat down upon an upturned crate, covered with an embroidered England flag, that seemed to serve as armchair in Tommy's hovel. An air of resigned defeat had quickly settled upon him and it seemed now that any threat from him had disappeared. I looked around the cellar and was surprised to find that such a place would exist beneath the humble cricket pavilion. It was a large and roughly hewn room with lime green walls and seemed much larger than the building above it. Electricity provided the power for two light bulbs and a portable television set was stood upon another crate. Plastic carrier bags were scattered around the floor some of which seemed to contain clothing and some of which contained tins and collections of food. Empty beer cans, with their sides crushed in, were piled in one corner of the cellar and I saw used and discarded needles scattered across the floor. A small electric fire was plugged into a power point on the cellar wall but the mediocre heat that it generated did little to dissipate the cold air that caused our breath to issue forth in clouds before us as we spoke. It was a stinking, demeaning and wholly inadequate place to house a human being and it was almost as if the rats had received the better deal upstairs.

I walked across towards Tommy and pulled a crate over to act as my chair. I had expected the crate to be empty and light but it was evidently full of some unknown product and so with an effort I dragged it across towards him before perching on top of it and looking deep into his yellowy eyes:

"Why would I want to do something eh? I think you know who I am, Tommy, that's why you were so anxious to close your door upon me. Who were you expecting Tommy? Blondie?"

"I don't know any Blondie."

"No, maybe you don't. But I'm sure that you know his boss. What's his name?"

"I don't know what you mean, sir. All of these questions. Waking Poor Tommy up in the middle of the cold night to ask him question after question. Why should I answer any of them, eh? Now there is a question for you to answer."

I potted the pocket that held my imaginary gun again before answering: "On Wednesday morning I was visited by Her Majesty's police force. They asked me some questions as well. It turns out that they think that I have killed you. Now isn't that a funny idea to have?" I looked him in the eyes again and saw that he was giving me his full attention although he didn't seem to appreciate the humour in my words: "Now, of course, what I am wondering is that if I am going to be arrested, and let's face it incarcerated, for killing you - well then I may as well do it anyway, hadn't I?"

His eyes were wide open now and he held his hands before him in his familiar begging gesture. When he spoke his voice shook:

"Oh, sir. No, sir, you don't want to do that to Poor Tommy. Poor Tommy is your friend sir."

"Well then you had better start acting like a friend, hadn't you? Fast. And you can quit with that 'Poor Tommy' act too – you're not at your bail hostel tonight are you? I'm not interested in Poor Tommy. No – Thomas O'Callaghan is who I'm interested in."

"Thomas O'Callaghan" he repeated as if the name was only vaguely familiar to him, "that's a name that I haven't heard in a long time. Poor Tommy is all I ever hear these days."

"A long time, is it, Tommy? Well how about ten years ago. That's what you were called then isn't it? And, my friend, that is what I want to hear about now."

"Ten years ago? I can hardly remember ten days ago."

"No, well let's have a try shall we. I think that this is something that you will remember very well, something that will stick in your memory."

"Perhaps Poor Tommy, I mean Thomas, needs it jogging a bit sir?"

"Oh. I'll jog it all right. Let's get this straight. I won't shoot you unless I really have to but don't be stupid and think about trying any rough stuff again because we both know that there would only be one winner there. In fact I may have something for you if you answer a few simple questions for me." I let these words hang heavy in the silence before reaching into my inside pocket and pulling out the remaining packet of sticky brown heroin. I waved it tantalisingly in front of his face which produced a broad grin upon his features which disappeared as I placed the packet securely back into my pocket.

"I see that I've got your attention now Thomas, and so let's get to the crux of this matter, shall we? I'm sure you know what I want to know about, you're not as stupid as you pretend."

"I'm not stupid at all, sir."

"No I don't suppose that you are. And as you're not stupid please stop calling me 'sir' and call me by the name that you know I have."

"Okay, Halle. What do you want to know?"

"I want to know about Georgie Galloway, Tommy. I want you to tell me all about her."

"And then I get what I want?"

"In a manner of speaking."

"How can you be sure that I know anything about her?"

"Because I was looking through some old newspapers and I found a photograph of you in a report about her. You found her body, I know that much. And, Mr O'Callaghan, I'm psychic. Believe it or believe it not. But I can see Georgie, she comes to visit me. And guess what? She is here right now sitting behind you, her eyes are burning into your skull."

This was a lie, as was the impression that I was carrying a gun, but as before the pretence worked it's magic upon the nervous and gullible man that was sat before me. He jumped up in startled fashion and turned around, eyes wide and mouth open sucking in air, as if expecting to see her himself. He looked back at me and I pointed an outstretched finger at the area behind him and gave a nod of my head as if to indicate that she was still there. He sat down again but from time to time he shivered as he talked.

"I can't tell you everything, sir. I mean Mr Halle, sir."

"John."

"Poor Tommy can't tell you everything John. Do you want me to become a ghost too? It's more than my life is worth, sir. My poor, pathetic, baseless life. But it's the only one that I've got, ain't it?"

"Who said that you had to tell me everything? Just tell me what you can, as long as it's all true, and then I'll fill in the gaps myself."

He started his story now, and it was interrupted along the way by long pauses as if he was trying to remember or as if trying to calculate how much he could safely tell me and how much of the story he had to conceal. At one point he reached into his pocket and drew out a self rolled cigarette and a chrome plated lighter. His hands were shaking so much that he found it impossible to light the cigarette and so I held his hand that contained the lighter and moved it across to the cigarette for him. He flinched as I touched his hand but I carefully guided it until the cigarette was lit and fetid smoke filled the air as he spoke. I didn't interrupt him other than to make grunts of acknowledgement from time to time and I rolled my hands as if to encourage him to tell the story. As his tale went on he seemed to need less and less encouragement and there were less pauses as if he was finally unburdening himself of something that had oppressed him heartily for too many years. His tale went like this:

Thomas O' Callaghan had been born in Athlone, right in the centre of Ireland, in 1970. There was a depression that held the country in its grip at the time and so as soon as little Tommy was old enough to travel the family relocated to Sheffield in England where his father had been guaranteed employment in the steelworks. The inns around the steelworks stayed open throughout the night, in contravention to the laws of the time, so that the burnt and dehydrated furnacemen could drink their draughts of bitter at the end of their shifts that finished at two, three or four in the morning. Tommy's father began to drink heavily and all the young boy could remember were the screams and protestations when his father returned in the early hours.

Tommy had been but a baby when he left his native land and had never had a chance to acquire an Irish accent and yet every child at the schools that he attended knew his history. He didn't fit in. He was a Paddy. He was bullied relentlessly and tried to gain favours by performing petty thievery and running errands for the older and larger bullies. He was suspended and expelled frequently and so moved from one school to another where the sad sequence would inevitably begin over again.

He finally left school at fourteen, nobody cared that he no longer turned up for class – it was a relief to all concerned. By this time Tommy specialised in shop lifting and pick pocketing and it was only a matter of time before he became known to the police who would arrest him as a precaution every time that they saw him. Soon he found himself in a young offenders institute, a borstal as they were then, like Brendan Behan without the brains. He learnt quickly and soon graduated to prison itself, serving a variety of short sentences. It was in prison where he had learnt the lesson that still served him well up until that day – namely that well to do people hate to be confronted by the people that they consider to be beneath them, the very dregs of society, and will gladly pay them amounts of money to be rid of them as quickly as possible. The trick, of course, was to make them pretend that they were not acting out of fear or prejudice but rather that they were doing the poor man a favour: a wealthy man, and everyone was wealthy when compared to Thomas O'Callaghan, will pay good money to retain his pride.

The other life changing moment that happened to Tommy in prison was his introduction to drugs. He had smoked a bit of weed, and drunk heavily of course as he had since the age of eleven, on the outside but he really met the love of his life on the inside: heroin. He found that many inmates were glad to be locked up because heroin was so much easier to get inside than it was outside. It was smuggled in during visits and passed from mouth to mouth as inmates kissed their wives with gleeful passion, or it would be hidden within their bras or knickers which would be rifled by the thankful prisoner as he groped her openly across the small circular tables in the visiting room. At the more open prisons it was hidden inside tennis balls which had been stitched up to conceal their innards and then thrown over the razor topped fences. However it got into the prisons, it got into the prisons: and soon it got into Thomas O'Callaghan.

Tommy O'Callaghan emerged blinking into the sunlight on a February morning of 1990 having served six months of a one year sentence for theft. Christmas dinner had consisted of turkey sandwiches and mince pies that tasted of cardboard. No attempt had been made to educate or rehabilitate him and he found himself homeless, unemployed and unemployable. He slept on the streets, begging every day and living from hand to mouth, picking the pockets of those who stopped to throw a ten pence piece his way. Things changed when he was approached by a man called Freddy Chester. He could name him with impunity, he said, because Freddy was dead and, he added with a conspiratorial wink, many people were rather glad that it was that way.

Freddy had seen him on numerous occasions and recognised in him a man who had reached the bottom of the well, a flexible man with no morals who could be bent into doing whatever he was bid to do as long as it helped him to survive from day to day. Freddy dragged him from the streets and recruited him into his army of beggars that worked many and varied scams throughout South Yorkshire: they would rattle tins for fake charities; deliberately walk in front of reversing cars and scream that they had been run over until the drivers paid up to placate them; they would take photographs of middle aged men entering massage parlours and then menace them into giving them money in return for the negatives; they would steal goods from one shop and then return them, still tagged up, to another branch where they would obtain a refund. Tommy was involved in all of these little cons that, when added together, produced a not inconsiderable sum for Freddy Chester who directed them to their duties every morning as if commanding his own private army.

Tommy was off of the streets now and living in a basement flat, paid for by Freddy, with two other accomplices. In Tommy's mind Freddy was a benevolent man, a powerful man, a don in the making but he was to find out that the man he had thought was a general was merely a foot soldier. One summer morning Freddy came to the flat unannounced, as he often did, but this time he was accompanied by another man and the contrast between the two couldn't have been greater.

Freddy was a thick set man with a scar down one cheek that started just below his eye and ended near his thin mouth. His preferred mode of dress was a designer tracksuit festooned with gold chains and he wore a sovereign ring on each finger. The man with him was in his mid to late thirties possibly and immaculately dressed in a fine suit of navy blue and black shoes that sparkled when the light caught them. He was tall and slender but his broad shoulders hid an immense strength. He was deeply tanned and his black hair was sleeked back. The only jewellery that he wore was a golden tie pin upon which diamonds flashed.

Freddy had a look of resigned displeasure on his face and, in contrast to his normal mouthy persona, would only speak when the elegant man addressed him. Each person, Tommy included, was made to introduce themselves. The other men spoke about the work that they could do, the petty misdemeanours that they engaged in from day to day. Tommy spoke to the man about his childhood, feeling somehow that he could trust a man who stood before him more beautiful and imposing than anything he had seen before or since. The man took Freddy to a corner and they whispered before turning back to the three men standing patiently against a wall. Freddy instructed the other two men to go with him and I was to go with the stranger.

It was at this point that Thomas O'Callaghan made clear that he couldn't, under any circumstances, give me the name of this man. It was more than his life was worth he said, but as he spoke to me I knew that what little was left of his life was worth little indeed. As an alternative to calling him 'the man' or 'the stranger' throughout his story he ventured to call the man Dwyer. He assured me that this wasn't the man's real name but I memorised it just the same – I knew that Tommy was too unimaginative to have come up with a name that would be too far removed from the reality.

Dwyer announced that he had been impressed with Tommy's story: he came from Irish roots too and they had to look after each other. From that moment on Tommy became almost a servant to Dwyer – living in or near his houses and chauffeuring him from one appointment to the next. Dwyer had a lot of business appointments, and would move from town to town. He was a very wealthy man and everybody that met him was both courteous to him and fearful of him. It came as a surprise to Tommy when he heard that Freddy Chester and his two old flat mates had been found guilty of carrying out a series of jewellery raids across Yorkshire and given long and punitive prison sentences: the particular surprise to Tommy was that the main raid that they were convicted of, and had pleaded guilty to, had occurred in Leeds on April 28th 1990 – Tommy had been with the men in Sheffield throughout that day. Tommy knew when to keep quiet and never broached the subject; he had been the lucky one.

Dwyer was never troubled by the law, he had contacts everywhere who tipped him off, for a price, whenever there was a whisper of any trouble brewing. For example it soon reached his ears that Freddy Chester was becoming increasingly unhappy at his spell in prison and that he would start singing if he wasn't given the treatment that he believed he had been promised. He got the full treatment all right: by the time he had reached the bottom of the E-Wing stairs he was already dead.

Dwyer had no morality, no sense of right and wrong – the only distinction in his world was between people who had money and people who had no money. He didn't hide from Tommy his drug dealing businesses, his prostitution rackets hiding behind the façade of inner city saunas, the protection money that his many henchmen would demand and receive from new businesses. To launder the money, and out of his own perverse desire to attain respectability, he owned legitimate businesses too: property companies, leasing companies, he owned whole fleets of taxis that would ferry drugs from building to building when they weren't carrying passengers.

Dwyer was a man without ties, he moved around as business dictated. In the latter part of 1990 he was working from plush offices in Barnsley overseeing some legitimate business in the town including a nightclub that he had recently bought. He drank little, and shunned any form of drugs altogether, but soon Tommy noticed that he began to spend more and more time in the nightclub, hanging around at the bar as if he was Humphrey Bogart. And then the girl began to hang around with him. The girl that was, of course, Georgie Galloway.

Tommy had never seen Dwyer with a woman before: all that he'd seemed to care about was money but now it seemed that Georgie had caught his heart as it had never been caught before. She had been spectacularly beautiful, he conceded with a jealous grimace, and had spoken with Dwyer as if he was an old childhood friend, an equal. She brought youthfulness and vitality to Dwyer's life. She brought fun and sex.

Soon they were spending every waking moment together and Dwyer began leaving more and more of his business dealings to his older and more trusted lieutenants. On one particular morning, it was around bonfire night to his recollection, they entered the office, where Tommy was positioned by the door as usual like the lapdog that he was, as excited as children. Georgie rushed up to him and waved a huge ring in front of his face with a large green, flawless emerald upon it. Dwyer was nearly twice her age and she liked discotheques and fashion whereas he liked nothing but business of one kind or another. It was a ridiculous engagement.

Dwyer was anxious that Georgie keep their good news to herself for the moment, and especially anxious that she keep the ring to herself. He told her that he had had it made especially for her, to her own design and specification, and that he didn't want the world to see it until their wedding day. No date was ever given or asked for as far as Thomas O'Callaghan knew.

By the time that December arrived Georgie's manner had begun to change. She had been a flighty and frivolous woman, often drunk and full of mischief: Tommy had been very fond of her, as was every one who came into touch with her. Now, though, she hardly drank and she laughed less and less. She was withdrawn and spent many hours locked in rooms with Dwyer while the heavy sound of arguments could be heard from within.

On 28th January 1991, he will never forget the day he said, he remembers that Dwyer and Georgie were engaged in a particularly fierce argument. Voices were so raised that the whole street could have listened in and there was the sound of objects being smashed. The door opened now and Georgie rushed out in tears, blood issuing from her split lip. She ran out of the building and Tommy would have run after her if Dwyer hadn't signalled to him to let her go.

Throughout that day Dwyer had sat brooding in his large black leather chair, rocking backwards and forwards in silence. By that evening his mood had grown increasingly dark and he sent Tommy out, in his beautiful new Mercedes-Benz car, to look for her and to return her to him at all costs. He made it quite clear that if he couldn't return with her then he wasn't to return at all. There was an evil coolness within Dwyer's eyes but a vein bulged upon his forehead as it pulsed. Tommy was scared for Georgie but he was more scared for himself.

Taking Dwyer's car, safe in the knowledge that no policeman would attempt to stop it, he trawled the streets and eventually found Georgie talking to a thin, pale faced young man outside a town centre bar. He pulled the car up alongside of her and, before the man could make too much protest, he bundled her into the back of the vehicle and drove back to Dwyer's office.

Georgie had cried constantly throughout the journey and had pleaded with him to let her go free. She even promised Tommy that they could run away together, they could just keep driving until they reached another city many, many miles away where Dwyer couldn't reach them. It sounded like an attractive proposition for around ten seconds, which was the time that it had taken Tommy to realise that there weren't any cities where Dwyer couldn't reach them.

They had reached the offices now and Georgie kicked and lashed wildly at him as he tried to drag her from the back of the car. They struggled for what seemed like an eternity but eventually he managed to carry her into the building while she screamed and pleaded with increased vigour. Dwyer was waiting for them inside and he smiled at Tommy and told him to wait there. Georgie had suddenly become calm, as if frozen with terror, and at Tommy's beckoning she followed him up the stairs in resigned silence. Tommy waited for hour after hour watching the clock tick by and not daring to move. It was the early hours of the morning when Dwyer came back down the stairs cradling her in his arms.

He told Tommy that Georgie had become very tired and he gave him an address in Hoyland where he said that her parents could be found. Georgie was placed into the back of the car with a thin line of drool hanging from the corner of her mouth and her eyelids fluttering timidly over her closed eyes. Tommy was ordered to drive her to the parents address but as the journey progressed she became more and more unresponsive until, as he neared the destination she suddenly sat bolt upright with an agonised look upon her face and then fell backwards along the seat. Tommy pulled the car to an immediate halt and dragged her out of the door before laying her upon the pavement. He pushed at her chest and breathed into her mouth, just as he had seen in the movies. It was to no avail, she was already dead.

Thomas O'Callaghan spoke no more but burst into a high pitched wailing as if his soul was collapsing inside him. I knew that he had been living with that scene replaying over and over inside his head for the last ten relentless years. Removing the packet of heroin from inside my pocket I placed it on the crate next to him and as he grasped the packet his tears came to a snivelling stop.

"You've done well, Thomas O'Callaghan. It wasn't your fault that she died, don't you know that? That's what Georgie wants me to tell you. You are the one that's been suffering, living a self imposed sentence, but she wants you to help me to bring her real killer to justice. What's his real name Tommy?"

"I can't tell you, you know that."

"Well where can I find him then?"

"If you try to find him then you might as well be dead already."

"What happened to the ring?"

"I thought that you knew more about that than anyone, Halle?"

"Don't believe everything that you hear. Well let's try a different tack then: why were they arguing?"

"Why do you think that she had stopped drinking before Christmas? She thought that her whole future was with him, she wanted a family with him. Some men just aren't that keen on that idea."

As he said this a crashing noise came from upstairs and I could hear the trampling of four feet, possibly six. I motioned to Tommy to hide behind a crate:

"Wait here", I told him, "I'll speak to you again in a minute."

That was a lie as I was never to speak to him again. I climbed the stairs and lifted the door to be greeted by flashlights that were shone directly into my eyes. Momentarily blinded I was pulled through the doorway and pushed onto the floor of the pavilion itself. I blinked and as the vision returned I saw two police officers standing over me.

The nearest one looked at me with disgust as he said in a flat, lifeless tone:

"John Halle, you're under arrest."

"What for?"

"Where do you want me to start? You are under arrest for the false imprisonment of Mr Richard Clay, for the assault on the aforesaid Mr Clay causing grievous bodily harm and for the murder of Mr Thomas O'Callaghan."

Chapter Fifteen

For nearly thirty years I had led a simple life, keeping, as far as possible, to the straight and narrow. I had dabbled with drugs from time to time when I was younger, that is true, but those days had been left behind me and now I suffered with feelings of guilt if I found that I'd walked out of a supermarket without paying for a packet of wine gums that had rolled in between the pages of a newspaper I'd purchased.

Well when I say 'now' I suppose that I should really say 'recently'. I was only a few days into the year that I write of, the year 2001, but things were already very different. In those last few days I had passed heroin to an addict on his way to hospital; I had stolen a car; I had assaulted a graffiti artist, although I use the word artist in the loosest possible sense, and left him curled up and bleeding at my feet, and I had shot a defenceless police officer. Yes, it seemed that I had left my meek and boring life in the past but I consoled myself that I had been left with no option but to carry out the crimes that I have reeled off, I was working towards a greater good that meant that moral values and legal responsibilities would have to take a back seat for a while.

Things had reached a head now though. Two police constables stood before me. The one who had addressed me was tall and slim with a shaved head and tanned complexion, his blue eyes shone out from amongst his golden complexion but there was a vacancy about his features that made it impossible to read his emotions. The other officer was smaller with unruly black hair that reached over his ears and beyond his collar, his uniform was creased and his shoes were muddy which provided a total contrast to the immaculate appearance of his colleague. This man had remained silent but fidgeted as his colleague spoke and looked constantly from one corner of the pavilion to the other as if unable to stay still. I had just been informed that I was being arrested for the false imprisonment of, and assault upon, Richard Clay and the murder of Thomas O'Callaghan. In contrast to my earlier list of crimes, that had seemingly gone unnoticed and unpunished, I was completely innocent of these accusations that had been pronounced against me. I smiled at the irony of the situation, but it was a foolhardy smile of bravery for the reality was that I felt sick to the pit of my stomach.

I looked the shaven headed officer in the eye, his colleague made me nervous with his twitching and tics and so I avoided making eye contact with him, and it seemed that he was waiting for me to speak. I got the impression that he was waiting for me to say one wrong word so that he could use this as a pretext for punching me or kicking me to the floor. Well, if that was his intent then he would do it anyway sooner or later and so, with a heavy sigh, I addressed him:

"You don't even believe that yourself do you?"

"What do you mean? Believe what?"

"That I killed, murdered, Thomas O'Callaghan. He's still alive as you well know."

"Do you think that this is some sort of game, a joke?" he sneered back at me in his strangely asinine voice as his colleague stood behind him with right and left legs twitching in sequence one after the other, "you stand there with that stupid grin on your face – there is nothing for you to smile about. Murder is a serious business."

Business? Yes, for some people murder was indeed a business. There was to be no reasoning with this man, no way out, and so I held out my hands in front of me.

"Aren't you even going to read me my rights then? Or don't you bother with formalities around here?"

The shaven headed officer spoke again with a voice even flatter and more listless than before:

"You have the right to remain silent; but it may harm your defence if you do not mention, when questioned, something that you later rely on in court. Anything you do say may be given in evidence."

The nervy constable was still silent but he walked across to me and forced my hands, which were held together and proffered in front of me, behind my back. He fumbled with the handcuffs that he was fixing around my wrists so that it seemed that either the handcuffs or he, or both, would fall to the floor but eventually he managed to affix the cuffs onto me.

"Thomas O'Callaghan's not dead you know? Why continue this charade? You won't be able to convict me without a body you realise?" Neither officer spoke now but the blue eyes flashed back at me with a look of contempt. It was time to remain silent myself as the unkempt officer, who smelled vaguely of stale cigarettes and mouthwash, positioned himself behind me and began to push me forwards heading out of the pavilion and onto the sports field that surrounded it. The talkative constable walked in front of me so that we formed a chain of three and he walked in a stiff fashion as though his knees were incapable of bending and with his arms swinging rhythmically at his side in military fashion.

The night sky remained dark and unwelcoming as I was led out towards the police car that had been brought onto the field and whose blue light radiated from on top of it sending sweeps of azure rotating across the field. The long haired man behind me thrust my head downwards so that I had to continue my walk to the patrol car with a hand pressing firmly against my skull and my eyes able to see nothing other than my mud splattered shoes. In the moment before my vision had been so diminished I had thought that I'd caught a glimpse of another figure, smaller and stockier than the three that had now reached the police car, standing alongside the pavilion but it could have been a trick of the light caused by the blue beams bouncing across the frost covered grass and onto the dirty white structure of the dilapidated cricket pavilion.

The nervous and dishevelled man took his place behind the steering wheel and I climbed into the back seat of the car alongside the shaven headed man whose blue eyes burnt fiercely into me at every second as if there was nothing that he would like more than to bring his tanned fists down upon my pasty white face. Our driver fumbled with the key in the ignition and I hoped that he would prove to be surer behind the wheel than he had in his other actions. The car had just moved off when I heard a sound behind me that seemed to have come from the pavilion that we had left. I wanted to turn and look behind my shoulder but this time it was the other officers turn to grip the back of my head so as to prevent me from moving it. I flicked my eyes up to look in the rear view mirror but I could see nothing through it. The sound had been muffled and brief but to my mind it had sounded like a gun shot, perhaps one that had been carried out with the aid of a silencer. I guessed that finding the body of Thomas O'Callaghan wasn't going to prove a problem for them after all. We drove the short journey from the sports field to the small town's police station with me exercising my right to silence and the other two seemingly not in a communicative mood either. A sombre quiet filled the air as I sat there like a statue not knowing what was waiting for me next. Was this how it would all end for me: a life sentence, with a recommendation that I serve at least twenty years? Twenty years spent behind bars looking longingly at that little tent of blue called the sky. How often would my parents visit me? It was a long way to come from Portugal to England to visit a son who had let them down so shockingly and in such unexpected circumstances. Steven would come, and Ed too along with my other friends like Gail and Mick, Bethany and Bernadette; as the years went slowly by their visits would become less and less frequent until I became just an unsavoury incident that had occurred at some point in their past. Would Rosa come? Would she believe me, she who knew more about the situation that I found myself in than anyone? Maybe she would continue to fight for justice for me from her new base in London?

Where there is life there is hope, that phrase never seems to ring more true than when one really reaches the bottom of the well – it's the human spirit that keeps us fighting long after all hope of success seems to be gone. For Thomas O'Callaghan that last ultimate hope had gone along with the life that nourished it. Poor Tommy. He had been ripped from the land of his birth as a child only to be confronted by a life of humiliation and crime and an eventual friendless death when he finally became of no use to the man who had used him so over the years: the yet to be found

Dwyer who I was determined to bring to justice one way or another if his summary justice didn't crush me first.

Calmness had descended upon the long haired policeman as he drove through the streets. I had worried that a sudden twitch from him might send his steering wheel flashing to the left or right and the vehicle crashing into a lamppost or a wall under its guidance. My fears proved unfounded and the steely look on his face seemed to indicate that he was concentrating with such intensity upon his driving that he had forgotten the tics and twitches that afflicted him. We soon reached the modest, square shaped police station and manoeuvred down the side of the building to a compound hidden at the rear and enclosed by fences made of wire.

At the very moment that the car was brought to a halt, the handbrake engaged and the engine shut down the man's nervous reactions appeared again so that he had to fumble embarrassingly with his seat belt and car door before he could join me and the officer with the menacing blue eyes outside of the car. My arms were still handcuffed behind my back as I was led down the walkway and through the double doors at the front of the building. The dawn hadn't arrived yet and nobody was around in the streets to witness my moment of shame.

The double doors led into a public waiting area that had wooden panelling and a plethora of posters on the wall warning of everything from pick pockets to AIDS and global warming. It was like the reception at a doctor's surgery but without the six month old magazines. A balding, middle aged officer with spectacles was stood behind the plastic topped counter at the rear of this reception and as we entered he looked up from his paperwork, which as I passed him I noticed was actually a copy of the following days form from the Racing Post, and nodded at the two officers who had brought me in: 'Morning West' he said to the shaven headed officer with formal reverence, and 'how do you do, Phil' was the warmer greeting that he extended to the less salubrious policeman.

As we approached the counter the bespectacled officer pressed a button which was secreted underneath the panelling and the door that lay in front of us opened of its own accord. We passed through the door in single file, with me sandwiched between West and Phil, and carried on in this fashion down the corridor that we had now entered. A selection of rooms were contained on both sides of this corridor, some with glass fronts and some rooms that appeared to be holding cells with a grate across the door that could be opened and closed as required. These doors

278

made me think back to the warehouse room that I had been locked in so fatefully only a few hours previously. It was going to be harder to escape from this incarceration, and I didn't expect to find a loaded gun on the floor of any cell that I would be placed into in here.

At the end of the corridor we reached a wooden door, with a reinforced glass window occupying its upper portion, which West pushed open and I was prodded into the room by Phil who twitched along behind me. The central point of this room was occupied by a large desk which extended, counter like, to the floor and there was a table to the side, with orange plastic seating on either side. A sink unit was placed in the corner with a navy blue towel hanging from a wall mounted ring next to it.

Another police officer was stood behind this desk. He was a sergeant, judging by the stripes that he wore on his jacket, but a different sergeant altogether to the one who had visited my house in tandem with Osbourne two days previously. This man was middle aged and portly with a ruddy complexion to his face. The buttons on his jacket, which was fastened to guard against the chill in the room, seemed to bulge and threaten to pop at any moment. Everything that he did was done in deliberate and methodical fashion and this extended to his voice whose flat Yorkshire vowels were delivered in a comical attempt at an upper class pronunciation which resulted in an 'H' being added to the front of every word except those which should have had one. He was the sort of man who would have liked to write with a pencil so that he could lick the end from time to time as if he was a clerk from Victoria's days.

Sergeant Squires, which was the name by which he introduced himself, greeted me in surprisingly warm fashion in sharp contrast to the cold greeting that he gave to Constable West. The handcuffs were removed from me now, with as much fumbling from Phil as there had been when he had attached them, and I rubbed my wrists to bring the circulation flowing back to them. I was instructed to empty my pockets and I did so placing their contents into a white plastic tray that had been situated upon the top of the desk. Feeling relieved that I had already distributed the two packets of heroin that I had been carrying it took me a manner of seconds to empty my pockets but minutes more for Squires to document everything with his slow and florid handwriting. At one point it appeared that his biro had stopped working and he shook it furiously to start the ink flowing again as West sighed loudly with impatience behind me.

I then put my gold coloured watch into the tray which I placed carefully beside my mobile telephone and next I was commanded to remove my shoes and belt. I never wear a belt but I placed my shoes onto the tray and stood in my socks with the uncarpeted floor sending shivers of cold into my feet. I signed a form which gave the police station rights to hold my property and then a plastic seal was wrapped across the tray containing my worldly goods and tape marked 'South Yorkshire Police Authority' was then passed over it to seal the container.

The Sergeant read me my rights again and asked if I understood what I had been arrested for. I replied that I understood the words but didn't see how they related to me. He nodded thoughtfully at me and I felt that at least I had somebody who held onto the outdated idea that a person was presumed innocent until proven guilty. The corpulent Sergeant then left his position behind the desk and walked across to me with a gait full of exaggerated importance and his head held high in the air to disguise his surplus of chins. He directed me across to a set of scales where I was weighed and I was asked to stand against a section of the wall which was marked in meters and centimetres. Out of my inherent sense of mischief I stood with my shoulders straight and the balls of my feet arched to add a centimetre or to onto my height. Next I was instructed to sit at the table as Sergeant Squires took my photograph in three poses: one looking straight at the camera and one each of my right and left profiles. I was disappointed that I didn't get an opportunity to hold a board up beneath my grim countenance with my name and a number upon it.

With that formality completed Sergeant Squires stretched a pair of thin latex gloves over his hand, which caused me a moment of consternation until he then produced an ink pad and two sheets of paper on which to record my fingerprints. Each finger in turn was rolled from side to side upon the ink pad and then pressed firmly upon its allotted position on the sheet of paper. The final rite that I had to undergo was that a swab, like a cotton bud, was removed from a sealed packet and then rolled around the right side of my mouth to collect saliva: this DNA sample was then sealed within an airtight container which was marked with my name and the date and time that the sample was obtained.

Sergeant Squires thanked me for my cooperation as if I was there as a guest of their hospitality rather than a murder suspect. He returned to his desk, where he continued his slow progress at recording the information that he had taken, and I was directed to the sink where I could wash the ink from my fingers. The water was hot and although I scrubbed and scrubbed at my fingers, and coated them in the soap that lay next to the basin, the ink that was upon them was thick and deeply embedded so that after minutes of washing them as best I could a fainter layer of ink was still clearly visible upon them.

West and Phil had been stood by the counter, Phil leaning upon it for support from time to time, while the formalities of my arrest were being completed and recorded. They whispered to each other from time to time but it couldn't be said that they were great conversationalists. West had kept his eyes fixed steadily upon me throughout the process and showed his impatience with regular glances at the watch upon his left wrist. He couldn't wait to start his interrogation of me, preferably without the desk sergeant, who did everything by the book, alongside him.

Satisfied that I had finished washing and drying my hands Squires addressed me again in the style of the well meaning uncle that he seemed to have cultivated:

"Right, Mr Halle, we have finished here. Now Constable West here, along with Sergeant Perrin, who you haven't met yet, will soon be asking you an initial series of questions. This one won't be the final questioning you understand? For offences such as the ones that you are accused of we shall have some CID bigwig down here to get to the bottom of it. Still, I must advise you that it is your right to have a solicitor present at the initial interview. Do you have a solicitor, Mr Halle?"

"No, I don't" I replied. I hadn't had much need for a solicitor in the rather less exciting worlds of bingo halls and call centres that I had occupied before this week had changed my life around so completely.

"Well, not to worry. We can arrange for a duty solicitor to come and sit with you. Would you like me to do that, Mr Halle?"

I had the idea that the interview that West and Sergeant Perrin, obviously the man who had abducted me on that Wednesday morning, planned to subject me to was going to be rather different to the one that Squires expected to take place. It was an easy decision to make and I nodded my head in acquiescence.

Constable West looked at me with disgust:

"You don't need a solicitor for this, Halle, it's only a few simple questions. A formality that's all. Stop wasting our time."

"It is Mr Halle's right to have a solicitor present, Constable, and I have noted his request that one be arranged for him."

I was pleased that the portly Sergeant had slapped the young officer down so and I grinned at West who scowled at me in return.

"So be it", said West with a voice full of spite and frustration, "but I hope he knows that he is really putting me out here. And, Halle, duty solicitors can be a bit hard to find around here at this time in the morning. That means that you're going to have to spend a little time in our cells. Probably not the sort of luxury that you're used to I'm afraid."

Sergeant Squires produced a key from beneath the counter and turned to address Phil whose knuckles had turned white as he seemed to be clinging on to the desk for dear life:

"Are you okay, Constable Tennet? Escort young Mister Halle here to cell C. Would you like a drink or a bite to eat, Mr Halle?"

"Yes please, sir. I'd really appreciate that."

"I'll send a coffee across and a plate of sandwiches in a bit. Maybe you should try to get a bit of sleep too, you look done in."

"That's what comes from killing people, Sergeant", was the retort from Constable West, "it's tiring work is murder."

Phil Tennet took the key in his shaking hand and led me through the door and back down the corridor to the cell marked C. I could feel those blue eyes burning into my back as I walked.

The key was turned clumsily in the lock and the heavy door, with some effort, was pushed open. The room inside was sparsely furnished with just two benches, that passed for both chairs and beds, a pile of coarse woollen blankets, and a steel lavatory without a lid on it. A strip light burned fiercely overhead that reflected harshly back from the white walls and dazzled my eyes as I entered the cell.

A man was curled up on the bench but all I could see was his mop of greasy black hair that poked out from the blanket that he had wrapped himself in. Phil shouted at him to get up and when this request was ignored he kicked him squarely in the midriff forcing the man to roll off of the bench and hit the floor with a thud.

"You sober yet?" Phil asked the man but before he had a chance to reply, if he was even capable of replying, he added: "get out of here, we need this cell for a proper criminal now. Get to reception, collect your stuff and piss off."

The man didn't say a word but, with a look of inebriated confusion plastered across his face, he let the blanket slide off of his shoulders and it formed a bedraggled pile on the floor. He staggered to the door which was held open for him by Constable Tennet and for every three steps that he took forward he took at least one to either the right or left. He smelt like a walking brewery. Phil turned and for the first time looked me straight in the eyes, there didn't seem to be much behind his glassy vision and after giving a final twitch and jerk of his neck he left the room and pulled the door shut behind him with a solid sounding clang. I heard the sound of the key fumbling its way around the lock and then I began to make myself at home in room C of Hotel Hoyland, not yet granted a star by the AA or RAC.

I walked across the floor to the bench that had been unoccupied. The stench that filled the room was almost unendurable and I felt quite drunk from the fumes themselves. A cold, wet feeling penetrated my socks and looking down I saw that I had walked unwittingly through a patch of urine that had presumably been left by the previous occupant of the cell. I trod carefully as I walked across to the lavatory and had to cover my mouth with my hand as my approach drew nearer to it. My eyes soon confirmed what my nose had already discovered and I saw that the pan was full, almost to its brim, of a heady mixture of urine floating atop a mass of vomit and faeces. I reached gingerly for the handle and pulled down on it but the flush wasn't working. Just looking at the sight made me feel violently sick but although I retched a couple of times I managed to swallow down its contents. I turned and walked quickly back to the bench that had been untouched by the squalid drunken man, all the while trying desperately not to think of the sight that had greeted me or the awful smell that permeated the air and seemed to seep into my skin at every second that I spent in that room.

There was no heating of any kind in the cell and I soon began to shiver violently. I picked up the blanket that lay neatly folded into a square next to the bench and wrapped it tightly around me as if mummifying myself. The blanket was rough and wiry, scratching my skin as it came into irritable contact with it; I tried not to look too closely at the crusty residue that was gathered in a patch on the outside of the blanket. So this was the start of my life as a prisoner? I closed my eyes and tried to will myself to sleep.

My attempt was unsuccessful: the bench was hard and I was in danger of falling from it at every movement that I took; the lights burned into my eyes both from the strip itself and its reflections that came back at me from every surface that I looked at and worst of all was that smell which assaulted my nose until it was impossible to think of anything else.

There was no clock in the room, in practise there was nothing in the room, and so it was impossible to say how much time had passed but it didn't seem long until I heard a loud knock rap upon the outside of my door before the grille was drawn back and the voice of West cried out in a sarcastic manner:

"Dinner is served."

The door was opened partially and I sat up on my bench with the blanket still wrapped tightly around me. West crept around the door cautiously and then placed a thin plastic tray onto the floor which he propelled towards me with a swift kick from his foot.

"Don't worry about paying for it, Halle, we'll just take the payment out of the cash that you handed over to us. I might as well take a little tip as well, that old dodderer Squires won't notice. He probably counted it up all wrong anyhow, he can't add up much beyond ten. You won't need it where you're going anyway."

He turned to walk out of the door and I was going to shout across at him to send somebody to empty the lavatory but before I could utter a sound he had completed his exit and the heavy door was shut and locked behind him.

I held my blanket across my shoulders like a cloak as I walked over to the tray which I shuffled across the floor with my feet. There was a cup of coffee in a cardboard carton with a plastic lid on top of it which emitted steam through the holes. A sandwich, cut into four quarters, was also on the tray and as I picked up a corner of the bread I saw that it was tuna and sweetcorn: one of my favourite fillings, but not much consolation when all things were taken into consideration.

I sat upright on the cold hard bench as I ate the sandwiches that had been left for me. As I chewed on the bread it seemed to mask the stench that filled the room and so I ate the four quarters with gusto. The sandwiches had been seasoned more than I would have liked and an aftertaste of salt lingered at the back of my throat. To wash down the meal I removed the plastic lid from the coffee cup and took a large swig of the drink. It was dark and unsweetened and it was so hot that it was hard for me to swallow at first. I blew onto the surface of the liquid and rolled it gently from side to side in an attempt to cool it down. The cardboard container was so hot that I had to move it from hand to hand as I held it and patches of red were left behind on the palms of my hand. Eventually the steam that issued forth in profusion began to fade away and the cup burned my hands less and less. I took a large gulp of the coffee and swallowed it down before I had even savoured its taste. Within seconds I was retching again and the cramp that gripped my stomach forced me to drop to my knees on the floor. My vision turned from colour to black and white and then faded before my eyes until I passed out upon the floor. When I came round I felt fine, in fact I felt better than I had for a long time. All of the aches and pains that I had accumulated over the week that had left me bruised and battered seemed a distant memory and I walked briskly around my cell stretching my arms above my head with contentment.

"What do you think then?" came the voice from the far corner of the cell.
"What do I think of what?" I asked without turning around.

"Of the sequence of events that I outlined to you just then; are you happy with it? Does everything fit together nice and snug? Haven't you listened to a word I've said, John?"

I looked at her now and wasn't the least bit surprised to see Georgie Galloway looking back at me. She was dressed differently now, wearing a floaty dress, in a pale shade of pink that finished just above her knees. Her slim legs were as white as milk and as enchanting as diamonds and she wore strappy pink high heeled shoes in a darker rose colour. Her hair ran over her shoulders and from time to time she waved the fringe away from over her eye. Her right hand held a cigarette that she dragged on like a metronome and on her left hand was the dazzlingly conspicuous ring that so matched her peerless green eyes. She was more than the girl on the bus now, she was a picture of elegance, a beauty that transcended the time that had seen her life cut so cruelly short.

She spoke with a distinctive Barnsley accent which contrasted sharply with the southern inflections that had been picked up by her sister. I had never heard her speak before, but I didn't find this surprising either. I felt at ease with the world as if whatever it threw at me now I would take easily in my stride.

"Sorry, Georgie. I was distracted. What sequence of events?"

"You were there, old man, you should remember it. The thin, pale man on the street – who is that going to be, John? You know that Dwyer was my lover and had been for a matter of months that were so intense it seemed like years. But as I got to know him better I found out about his cruel and violent temper: destruction was a hobby to him. Destruction? Is that the right word John?"

"It sounds okay to me Georgie."

"Good, because you have got to have all of this down pat ready for when you confront Dwyer. I want to make sure that it all makes sense for you. Some people blame me, you see. Some people even think that I was little more than a street walker, turning tricks for people who had money to burn – older men in smart suits. Can you believe that John? I asked you a question – can you believe it?"

She pouted at me and narrowed her eyes and so I shook my head as if to acknowledge that I couldn't believe it and she smiled back at me.

"That means a lot to me, John. And I know that you will make things right for me. Okay, so I wasn't an angel, but I didn't deserve what happened to me. I could have straightened things out. I would have been a great mother. You know what it's like to miss out on being a parent, don't you John? No need to answer that one, my little avenging angel. It hurts like hell. Send him to hell, John, where he belongs. Because he will do it again you know. Killing is nothing to him."

"But who is he? Who is this Dwyer?"

"Dwyer is Dwyer. What can I say?"

"But where can I find him?"

"You should know that better than me, John dearest. How should I know, I've not been around much for the last ten years?"

She had wandered across the room now and peered into the lavatory before wrinkling her nose in disgust and pacing across the cell floor until she stood by my side.

"You know, you really should get that toilet fixed. I have seen some filthy things in my time, but that really takes the biscuit."

"People keep chasing that ring that you're wearing Georgie, how about giving it to me?"

She laughed and held it up before my face so that I could admire its flawless beauty that so complemented her.

"You can't have this John, silly. It's not really here is it? You will find it if you look hard enough though. Follow your conscience. Do what you should have done twelve months ago. They do say it's better late than never."

"But what about that woman who died under the car – who was she? How did she come to have it?"

"You are full of questions, but you're a smart man. I thought that you would have found some answers by now? Think about Dwyer – what makes him so angry? Why does he suffer from psychotic rages that he struggles to control from day to day? It's all down to his family. I didn't have a perfect family either, John. No matter what Rosa might say – she doesn't know everything you see, John. Every family has its dark little secret. Oh by the way, talking about Rosa – I know that you've got a little soft spot for her, and I can't blame you for that although she isn't a patch on me. But then I'm not an option for you am I? Anyway, why aren't you worrying about Rosa a little more? I know that you don't really believe that she is asleep and hasn't heard the telephone ringing."

"What do you know?" I asked her with obvious anxiety.

"I only know what you know, John. I've only said what you already know, haven't you worked that out yet. I'm going to give you a piece of advice now, a parting shot: you're life is in very serious danger now – you could have less than an hour left to live and you are going to be faced with two choices. For my sake and yours, do not take the right one."

Georgie blew cigarette smoke into my eyes and then faded away into nothingness. I coughed at the smoke and then I felt a sudden flush of water hit my face and I opened my eyes to find myself face down on the cell floor, still coughing, and Constable West standing before me with a bucket in his hands.

"Nodded off had we?" he asked with a hint of sarcasm almost perceptible in his normally unemotive voice.

I was drenched from the bucket of water that had been thrown over my head and I shivered as I spat the water from my mouth and wiped it from my eyes. I raised myself slowly to my feet and my legs wobbled as I placed weight upon them. I felt numb and it was as if my body belonged to somebody else and was only vaguely following the instructions that were sent to it from my brain. A shrill buzzing sound echoed inside my head. A dirty looking pair of shoes, in the slip on style with no laces, were thrown my way now and I bent down to pick them up, all the while feeling on the brink of losing my balance and collapsing upon the floor.

"Put the shoes on, Halle, your brief's here and you want to look your best. Follow me."

After an uncoordinated struggle I managed to slip my feet into the shoes. They were at least half a size too big for me and lolled around my feet as I took my cautious and jelly-legged steps. West strode ahead, arms swinging beside him in his favourite military style, and it was difficult for me to keep up but we soon reached one of the glass fronted rooms where West held the door open for me as I entered.

The door was closed firmly behind me and West made his way around the table to sit down next to the man that I had previously only known as Sergeant. At my side of the table were two chairs, in one of them was sat a sloppily dressed man who I took to be my assigned solicitor and it was indicated that I was to sit in the other chair.

I sat in the chair with a thud which made the room swim before my eyes for a second. My solicitor introduced himself as Mr Silver but he didn't take the hand that I held out for him. He was a dark skinned man with receding and greying hair that made him look older than his years and an ill fitting pair of spectacles that he kept having to push back up his nose with a stumpy thumb when they seemed to be on the verge of sliding from his face. Mr Silver wore a brown suit that looked like it could have come from a charity shop and his white shirt was crowned by a vivid pink tie that hung loosely around his neck. He fiddled nervously with the cuffs of his suit jacket when he spoke and at one point a button, which had been holding grimly onto its thread, fell pathetically to the floor. A

287

large digital clock in the room announced that it was now 05:28 but this didn't stop Silver from looking at his watch every minute or so as if desperate to be somewhere warmer.

When Silver wasn't looking at his watch he was looking at the floor or shuffling the papers, legal aid application forms, which he had removed from his plastic attaché case. West's eyes, those ridiculously blue eyes that looked out of place surrounded by his almost orange skin, burned into me throughout my strange sort of interview. My own eyes, in contrast, were fixed steadily upon the Sergeant, Sergeant Perrin, who sat opposite me with a brooding malevolence. The terrible look in his eyes and his twisted mouth seemed to scream out that he had killed a man that night and I wondered how it wasn't obvious to everybody present.

My solicitor spoke to me now in smooth, almost soporific, tones that seemed remarkably calm when contrasted with the impatient body language that he displayed:

"Mr John Halle, these are very serious charges against you here you know? Murder, assault, false imprisonment. What do you say to that?"

"Not guilty"

"No, no. You don't need to say anything like that at this point. Save that until we get to the court. We just need to establish the facts here. I would advise you to answer all of the questions that these two gentlemen will raise in an honest and succinct manner. Once you have answered their question, that's it – you don't need to add any more detail. Stick to the bare facts. And if you don't wish to answer their questions then just remain silent and they will move on. You are under no obligation at this point to incriminate yourself."

I wondered at what point I would be obliged to incriminate myself but I just smiled falsely at Silver. I felt sorry for him, he had been dragged out of his warm bed to act as a pawn in a game that he knew nothing of and the best that he could hope for would be a pitiful legal aid cheque at some distant point in the future.

Sergeant Perrin pressed the start button on the recording device that was contained in the centre of the table but whether it was recording us vocally or visually I wasn't aware. He read out the date and time and confirmed the names of the people present and then stood up and paced around the room as he began the serious business of the interrogation. From time to time he cracked the knuckles of his hands, one after the other, and he looked at me with disgust when I threw his questions back at him.

"Mr John Halle, you are accused of the murder of Thomas O'Callaghan, and the false imprisonment of, and assault upon, Mr Richard Clay. What do you say about that?"

I remained silent and so he continued to press me:

"Aren't you even going to say that you're sorry? Show a little contrition?"

"I'm sorry that Tommy is dead, that's a fact."

"So you're sorry that you killed him?"

"I didn't kill him, and you know that I didn't kill him."

"I know that you did kill him. And we have the evidence to prove it."

"What evidence?"

"We found his body last night, and near him was the murder weapon. A replica Glock pistol that had been modified to fire real ammunition. Your finger prints are all over it."

This was no surprise as it would have been easy for Perrin to have the pistol brought to me and my fingers wiped across it while I was unconscious on the cell floor. Proving it was going to be more difficult but I had always believed that attack was the best form of defence and so I spoke now:

"I don't doubt that my fingerprints are on that gun."

My solicitor waved his hands at me and whispered to me to advise me not to incriminate myself and that I had no need to comment on evidence that had yet to be produced. I ignored his well meaning advice and continued:

"Yes, Sergeant, I guess that my fingers will be on the gun because you, or your trained monkey West here, probably put them on there."

"What? That is a ridiculous accusation!" Perrin shrieked and the scar on his cheek began to twitch again. I remained calm, which seemed to wind him up even more.

"Ridiculous is it? It's the truth. I was drugged in here tonight, either the coffee or the sandwiches or both had been tampered with and while I was unconscious on the floor my hands were wiped over the offending weapon in an attempt to frame me."

My attack hit home and West stood up suddenly as if he was ready to strike me to the floor but Perrin, his face twitching more and more, placed a hand upon West's shoulder and pushed him back into his seat.

My solicitor, Mr Silver, had an open mouthed look of astonishment on his face and only his professional code was stopping him from running from the room.

"And why should we want to do that, Mr Halle?"

"To cover up the real killer. You killed O'Callaghan tonight. When West and Tennet pushed me into the car I clearly saw you in the rear view mirror and you were entering the pavilion with a gun in your hand. I heard the shot shortly afterwards when I was already on the way to the station. You killed him, Sergeant."

I had seen no such thing in the mirror of course but I knew that this was what had happened and so I felt confident in my little white lie.

"This is a pack of lies. You are the accused here, Mr Halle, and nobody else."

Silver found his voice at last and managed to stammer out:

"I must say, Mr Halle, it just does not do to throw around ridiculous accusations like that. It doesn't do at all."

"Ridiculous. And lies, all lies" Perrin spat out.

"Well let me bring some more clarity to things and then tell me if these are lies as well: where is Osbourne?"

"Who?"

"Osbourne is a Constable based at this station. He came to my house with you a couple of days ago and then you both abducted me, tied me up, beat me and left me as good as dead."

"Where do you get these ideas from? Don't think that you can start playing that insanity card."

"Is it insane? Mr Silver, please ask if there is a Constable Osbourne here and when you find that there is ask where he has been for the last forty eight hours? Disappeared without a trace is the answer because Perrin and the rest of his hired thugs have seen to that."

West spoke up, unable to control himself any longer, with venom in his voice:

"Osbourne has been off sick, he has phoned in as per the regulations and it has nothing whatsoever to do with you, Halle, and the crimes that you've committed."

"Well how would I know anything about it then? I've never been to this station before and never had a hint of any trouble with the law until you came knocking at my door, how would I know the name of Osbourne and that he had been absent? I'm sure that Mr Silver can look into that for me?"

I looked across at the duty solicitor now and wasn't at all sure that he could or would do that for me. He looked at his watch with increasing frequency as if his only desire was to fly from the room and the increasingly tense atmosphere within it.

Sergeant Perrin leaned across the table and pushed a button on the recording machine to bring the session to a premature close. His eyes seemed smaller and more hawk like than ever and his face had grown redder and redder as he strove to contain his anger. The scar on his cheek grew more noticeable against this scarlet background and a small purple vein was throbbing worm like above his left eyebrow.

"I don't know what game you think that you're playing, Halle, but it's about time that you stopped it now. I am the one who asks questions, and you are the one that is going to answer them right, with or without the recorder. Do I make myself clear?"

My threadbare solicitor jumped to his feet now as if about to make an objection in court:

"Excuse me, Sergeant, you can't just turn off the recorder like that. I do accept that my client's behaviour was out of order but –"

He was interrupted by Perrin who pointed a trembling finger at him and shouted:

"Shut it, four eyes! Do you want your money or not?"

The solicitor sat down sheepishly although he could still be heard mumbling faintly under his breath. I smiled broadly at this development and the more irate that Perrin and West became the calmer my demeanour was. This served to infuriate them wildly, as I had expected, and they thumped the table repetitively during their questioning, all the time wishing that it was my head that they were slamming their hands against.

They took a different tack now and threw quickfire questions at me one after another, questioning my whereabouts at certain times and my relationship to various people, most of whom I had never heard of. It was all a charade and I let them know that I was wise to what they were doing. In answer to their questions I would shoot back answers such as: "Well you should know more about that than me" or "It doesn't matter what you say, or how you manipulate and conceal the facts, I will never be the criminal that you say I am and that you are." I even took to giving them advice from time to time, in my friendliest manner and with a pleasant smile playing upon my face, such as: "you know that you won't get away with this so why don't you just hold up your hands now, make things easy on yourself." At other times I would try to turn one policeman against the other, telling West not to let his superior officer drag him down with him.

The atmosphere was charged now and expletives fell from the officer's mouths like raindrops from the sky outside. I had to shout to make myself heard but exercising great control I kept my voice calm and level. My solicitor sat dumbly in his chair as if turned to stone. It was the sort of argument that one would have expected to find in a playgroup full of unruly children, with three voices all shouting at once and no attention being paid to what any of the parties said.

Time passed quickly in the electrified atmosphere of the interview room and glancing across to the clock I could see that the large white figures on their black backgrounds displayed the time of 06:20. In a sudden instant Sergeant Perrin's resolution cracked completely. With a cry that seemed like a primal scream he kicked out wildly with his right foot but his boot didn't find me, its intended target, instead connecting with the chair of Mr Silver who had been sitting silently and unmoving beside me with his eyes screwed tightly shut. In a moment of comedy the chair leg smashed upon impact and the three legged chair now tipped its contents onto the floor where Mr Silver lay as if stunned before scrabbling for the spectacles that had shot from the end of his nose onto the tiled floor. He placed the glasses back onto his face but one of the lenses had fallen out of the frame and he placed this into his right jacket pocket.

If he hadn't been so shocked then I'm sure that he would have cried but standing up and mustering as much dignity as he could, which was nothing, he walked quietly out of the room slamming the door shut behind him. I had been hoping that he would say 'I've never been so insulted in my life' so that I could have added 'you should get out more' but his timidity had won through to the last. I was in a strangely light hearted, almost elated, mood now and wanted to laugh out loud but as I looked at the rabid faces of West and Perrin, now alone in the room with me, my mood darkened.

"What's going to happen now then, Sarge?" I asked in a loud voice designed to hide the fear that was coursing through me.

"Now? Well, now we are really going to get to the truth aren't we? And let's get this straight – it's the truth as I see it, as I want it that counts not any stupid notion of reality that you might have."

"We already know that he doesn't want to cooperate. Why waste your time on him, boss?" West spoke in a sinister whisper now.

"Don't worry, Constable, don't worry your orange little head. We are going to use some persuasion on him. Draw the blinds will you?"

The two men smiled at each other and as West pulled the little cord that first dropped the blind across the window from top to bottom and then closed its shutters, the psychotic Sergeant moved slowly and menacingly towards me.

292

The room was dark with the blinds closed and amidst the shadows I could see that the Sergeant was standing directly in front of me now and West was behind me blocking my route to the door. I was looking at a beating anyway and so I decided to seize the initiative and strike first. With a quick movement I aimed my hand for the Sergeant's ribcage aiming at a target just behind his short and stocky body. My hand failed to make contact with his fleshy body but instead crunched against something hard and metallic that forced me to pull my hand back with a sharp cry of pain and surprise. Perrin now threw his punch at me but I had automatically reeled away from the impact that my fist had made and so his punch flew wildly through the air and was delivered with such force that he almost threw himself over with the air making a whooshing sound as his arm flailed past.

Perrin and his assistant West were both facing me now and as they edged closer towards me I backed slowly away from them looking desperately, but in vain, for anything that could be used as a weapon. I continued to back away step by step until my back impacted heavily with the wall behind it. The two officers smiled at each other and the shaven headed West directed a globule of spit from his mouth that hit me below my right eye and crawled slowly down my cheek.

It was 06:25 now and the clock seemed to be counting down my last fateful and miserable seconds. Perrin opened his jacket up and his right hand reached into the left breast pocket. With a crash the door of the interview room was pushed open and rebounded against the wall next to the doorway. A shaft of light lit up the room and I felt like St Paul did when he suddenly found the gates of his prison cell miraculously thrown open. It wasn't a glimmering angel that entered the room on this occasion but the altogether more human figure of Sergeant Squires. It was none less welcome a sight for that.

He spoke with authority in his voice now and it seemed to tremble with a suppressed anger:

"Your time's up here, gentlemen. Please make your way outside."

"On whose orders?" asked Perrin with sweat gleaming on his forehead and his right arm caught in still motion mid-air.

"On the orders of Superintendent Pearson" intoned Squires with a mixture of pride and anger in his voice.

A silver haired man strode into the room after Sergeant Squires. He had bags under his eyes and lines on his forehead but his appearance was somehow the more distinguished for it. He was immaculately attired as if he wore a new suit every day and his epaulets bore a single red and golden crown on a field of black. His shoes were polished so severely that I saw the whole room inverted within their toecaps.

The Superintendent didn't have to speak to command the respect of the room and it was as if he had an aura of power about him. The two officers turned around with slow reluctance and I took deep breaths as my heartbeat retuned to normal. Constable West walked out of the room shamefaced with his head bowed and not daring to look Superintendent Pearson in the eyes. Two plain clothed officers were waiting outside of the door and they grabbed his arms and led him around the corner.

Perrin, in contrast, showed no shame or remorse but held his head high with a sneer shaped upon his lips. As he neared the door he looked first at Squires and then at the Superintendent, giving them a look that was pathetic in its self importance but which in his mind let both men know that they didn't deserve to be in the same room as him. Finally he turned his head back towards me and, imitating West earlier, he too tried to spit at me but his mouth was dry, in betrayal of his inner feelings, and a small stream of spit simply dribbled out of his mouth and hung in a string from the corner of his lips until he wiped it away with the back of his hand. He walked out of the room as if nothing had happened but when outside the door voices were raised and a crashing noise was heard amidst the general commotion. The Sergeant and Superintendent both left the room in haste and I followed them into the corridor. A plain clothed officer was lying on the floor and his colleague stood in a daze, seemingly confused by the pace of events that had happened. Perrin was running down the corridor towards the reception doors and I was the first to react and pursue him.

As he reached the wooden door leading to the entrance of the police station Perrin smashed the flat of his right hand against a large green button and the door swung open. My oversized shoes slowed me down and made my movements clumsy but using the reserves of my energy I still had the Sergeant in sight as I too made my way through the doors and then into the fiercely cold early morning air.

Perrin was stood still and I looked to where his gaze was pointed. To my surprise I saw Osbourne there; it seemed that he would survive being hit by a truck. Osbourne had been cleaned up since I had seen him hours earlier and his left arm was tied in a sling that ran around the back of his muscular, trunk-like neck. In his right hand he held a gun that was pointing directly at Perrin. Perrin likewise had his gun, the previously concealed weapon that my hand had struck against in the interview room, pointed at Osbourne. Neither man spoke and no movement was

294

made: I almost expected to hear the sound of a music box ticking mournfully away encouraging the men to shoot at each other when it stopped but fate had other plans.

Perrin wheeled around on hearing my footsteps crunch upon the frost covered gravel outside the station's forecourt. In his confusion he forgot Osbourne and pointed his gun straight towards me. I saw his finger twitch momentarily upon the trigger and as if in slow motion I knew that I had to dive out of the way, in one direction or the other, if I was to have any chance of survival. I heard Georgie's words in my head again: 'You're going to be faced with two choices, do not take the right one.' I threw my body to the left and in that split second I heard two loud cracks that seemed to send a scream through the still air. I felt a rush of heat come over me with amazing speed and a stabbing pain and then everything went black.

Chapter Sixteen

I opened my eyes cautiously and with effort as if the lids had been glued lightly together so that I had to prise them apart. A harsh light overhead beamed into my newly opened eyes and I had to blink them open and shut a number of times before they adjusted to the new brightness. My mouth was dry again and my tongue seemed to be sticking to the roof of my mouth in sympathy with my eyelids. My back ached and I had little idea how long I had been laid in this position, or where I was. I raised my right arm to shield my eyes from the fierce lighting and saw that my right hand was heavily bandaged and covered with what appeared to be some sort of protective plastic covering. I heard noises and the sounds of feet shuffling besides me and realised, as my senses gradually returned to me, that I was not alone in the room.

At first all I could hear was a buzzing sound as the noises within the room merged into one another and my vision was blurred and faded around the periphery. Things became clearer second by second and soon I could distinguish the noises and voices one from another and the things that I could see became discernible entities, became people and machines and objects, rather than a jumbled mess of vague colours and shapes.

It seemed that my mind too was waking from a long sleep: when I had first opened my unwilling eyes it was almost an animal reaction as if I was functioning without thought or reason. Memories began to come back to me, at first in a trickle which soon became a flood, and with them came a raft of questions that initially I was unable to answer. I lay frustrated upon the bed as I wondered who I was, where I was, and who were the people who seemed to be gathered inquisitively around me with smiles of encouragement upon their faces?

For a few minutes that I struggled with these questions but it seemed like an eternity as I lounged in helpless frustration upon the bed which supported my aching body. My body which I had relied upon with such confidence throughout my life had stood up to its treatment well. Those punishing sessions that I had put myself through every morning, the pushing and pulling of weights and the sit ups that made it feel as if my stomach was on fire, had given my body the resilience that had been necessary to survive the shocks that I had put it through that week: if indeed it was still the same week?

Whilst my body seemed to be functioning as well as I could have expected, although it ached and felt strangely alien as if I wasn't sure that it would do what I commanded it to do, I was more concerned about my thought and mind processes - the cerebral functions which we all take for granted until they begin to fail us. The simplest things seemed beyond me: how could I have no recollection who I was, or even what I was? I wanted to scream out for attention, to ask questions of the people that were around me but I didn't know how to order my sentences, how to put one word in front of another so that people could understand me? Who were these people anyway that seemed to be taking such an interest in me?

I closed my eyes again, hoping that this time they would glue themselves together fully and that I would fall into a long sound sleep that would remain unbroken until I could function like a normal human being again, until I could once more be the man that I was sure I had been.

A voice, seemingly familiar to me but one that I could not have given a name to, called out one word now and that word was 'John'.

I knew then that that was my name, that I was John. The memories came back to me as if a tap had suddenly been switched on or as if a fuse had been changed and the electricity had sparked into life. My own questions, which had seemed so mysterious and unsolvable seconds earlier, were now answered with ease.

I was John Halle, of Barnsley. I had been leading a relatively inconsequential life since my lover Lamara had died more than a year ago and had been happy to keep myself to myself as I moved from one dead end job to another. Things had changed, but how had they changed

– how had they changed? Yes, I had seen the girl on the bus. Georgie she was called (even names were no problem for me now), but I was the only one that could see her: she had died ten years ago. Died or was she killed? That was the crux of the matter; that was what had brought me to the situation which I found myself in at that moment. I was a channel for these people, now crossed from our mortal world into the next one that we know so little about, to obtain their justice in this world - revenge I suppose you could call it. And then the whole story came back to me and flashed before my still closed eyes in seconds: my abduction; my meeting with Rosa; the painter who had given me Georgie's picture and onwards and onwards through meeting Vicky in Huddersfield, shooting Osbourne and being the last person to see Poor Tommy O'Callaghan alive. And then onto the present, where I had been incarcerated in the local police station on a variety of trumped up charges designed to keep me behind bars for the rest of my life, a period not guaranteed to be a long one all things being considered. Finally I saw again the Sergeant, Perrin as I remembered he was called, and then I saw nothing but a bright glowing flash come from the muzzle of the pistol that had been pointing at me.

"John – John Halle, can you hear me?"

There was that voice again, a feigned cheeriness in it designed to hide any traces of concern. I opened my eyes once more, with relative ease this time although they still felt tender as if sand had been rubbed into them, and answered the voice:

"Yes, I can hear you Steven."

The voice that had addressed me belonged to Steven Carter, one of my oldest and my closest friend. I looked around and saw other faces that were familiar: Ed the usually reserved and emotionless friend who I last saw standing by the ambulance carrying Richard Clay away; Osbourne, the gigantic police constable whose life seemed to have become intrinsically linked with mine and who now bore the scars to prove it; Superintendent Pearson, the powerful and imposing police chief whose intervention had proved so timely at the police station. A doctor was stood by my bed, looking down upon me with an air of fatherly concern and a female nurse was stood away from the bedside with her hands behind her back; her gaze was concentrated upon the doctor rather than upon me as if waiting to be called into action.

I had been an irregular visitor to hospitals throughout my lifetime. I had broken my ankle as a child, the result of falling from a wall after losing a playground wrestling match, and had slipped a disc in my back in an embarrassing ice skating incident that had left me flat upon my back in the hospital bed for three days with my skates packed firmly away never to be looked upon again. On another occasion I had suffered an allergic reaction to nuts, which up until that point I had eaten with gusto and without any noticeable side effects, that had made my tongue swell up within my mouth; I had been rushed to the infirmary where I was given an anti-histamine injection that reduced the swelling but left me gasping for breath throughout the night so that it sounded like the very air was being filtered through a set of bellows as I breathed in and out.

On all of these occasions I had shared the NHS wards with other unfortunates and we would take it in turns to keep each other awake with our moaning and groaning and the steady stream of visitors who were denied any privacy to tell their loved ones how they really thought about them. A stay in the hospital had always seemed to be a dehumanising and humiliating experience, so that on the whole it seemed preferable to stay in good health. Now, for the first time, I found myself in a spacious room with just one bed and occupied by nobody except myself: I imagined that I had some new found celebrity that had caused the hospital administrators to upgrade me in this way.

I wanted to speak again but my dry mouth gagged when I opened it. The doctor seemed to guess what I wanted and using his left hand he made a come hither gesture to the nurse who now sprang into action like an over age ball girl at Wimbledon. She walked with brisk stiffness to a plastic cabinet, badly painted to look like wood, and removed a disposable cup which she filled with spring water poured from a one litre bottle that was opened with a firm wrist action. With her right hand she placed the plastic cup in front of my mouth and with her left she moved my head forward, sending a slight shiver of pain through my neck as my head was raised from the pillow, and into position so that I could sip the drink. The water was tepid and flavourless but as I swallowed it, tentatively at first and then in greedy gulps, the life seemed to flow back into me.

I studied her face as I drank the water that she continued to hold in front of me. She had dark hair cut into a modern style of bob and her hazel eyes studied me with a medical detachment. Her uniform of shapeless blue shirt and dark blue trousers was spectacularly unflattering and she kept her emotions hidden within the unflinching face that looked fierce until I noticed the sparkle playing within her eyes. I smiled at her now to indicate that I had finished drinking and she cleaned the area around my mouth with a sterile wipe. She returned my smile briefly before walking

298

stiffly away and resuming her former position but that momentary upturn of her mouth had revealed the beautiful kindness within her heart.

It was the doctor's turn to step forward now. He was a short man of Asian appearance and was bald except for a strip of black hair that ran across the back of his head and above his ears. As he bent over to me the light reflected harshly from the top of his head which seemed to have been polished as vigorously as his patent leather shoes. A strip attached to his white uniform announced his name as Dr Rajanathan, from which I estimated him to be of Sri Lankan origin, and a delicate pair of rimless spectacles attached to his face increased his studious appearance.

Placing his thumb and forefinger on my wrist Dr Rajanathan measured my pulse and gave a slight involuntary nod of his head which I took to mean that everything was as well as could be expected. A metal dish was placed upon the bed side table and from this he removed a syringe which he held suspended in the air before rolling up the left sleeve of my standard issue pyjamas, in thick blue and pink stripes to ensure their suitability for male and female patients, with his free hand.

"This is just a glucose solution, Mr Halle, nothing for you to worry about. It will give you a burst of energy. That's just what you need after all that you've been through."

He spoke in a beautifully calm voice with an accent that could have come straight from a BBC broadcast of the post war years. It was impossible to worry about anything after his soothing words which seemed to hypnotise me as they came from his mouth. I lay back in a state of complete relaxation as the needle punctured the skin of my arm and the solution was shot into my vein. The water had been welcome but this liquid served to kick start my body with a shock; an enervating burst of warmth and energy spread through me until I felt as if I could have climbed out of the bed and left the hospital there and then.

The doctor placed the used hypodermic back onto the dish with the slow and deliberate precision of a surgeon. I raised my head from the pillow and looked down onto the silver tray. My reflection stared back at me and I was shocked by what I saw: it was still visibly me, of course, but it was hard to equate this deathly white drawn-faced specimen with the visage that usually looked confidently back at me from the oval mirror. Dr Rajanathan stood by my bedside now as if waiting for me to ask him questions. I didn't want to disappoint the doctor by cheating him of his right to impress people with his medical knowledge and so, after glancing again at my packaged right hand draped upon the bed, I ventured:

"Thanks for everything, doctor. My hand? What happened?"

"Don't you remember what happened, Mr Halle?"

"Well yes, vaguely. What I really mean, I suppose, is will it be okay."

"Oh yes, I'm sure that it will be okay very soon."

That was reassuring news but decided to press the matter; the answer to my next question brought me crashing back down:

"And it will make a full recovery then, whatever is wrong with it?"

"Well, no, I'm afraid not. I mean, Mr Halle, that it won't be like it was before. Let me show you what we have had to do."

I expected him to remove the plastic covering from my right hand but instead he produced a diagram of the hand, of a hand in general rather than mine, with different parts labelled in Latin upon it.

"Mr Halle, I understand that you passed out when you were shot and so you may not remember any of this."

"I was shot then?"

"Yes you were shot, but you were lucky", it was Osbourne that spoke now in the voice that seemed so small and incongruous compared to his large frame, "if you hadn't dived to the left the shot would have hit you square on. We wouldn't be talking to you now."

I turned back to look at Dr Rajanathan who addressed me again and pointed to parts of the diagram as he spoke:

"You were shot in the right hand Mr Halle. As the police officer correctly says, you were very lucky that the bullet only grazed your hand."

A graze? That didn't sound too bad. I'd received plenty of grazes in my school days and they hadn't hampered me too much. The involuntary smile that had appeared on my face was wiped off by what the doctor said next:

"The bullet hit the fifth finger of your right hand, the little finger so to speak. The impact upon this finger, however, was strong and there was considerable damage to the cartilage and bones along with significant loss of blood and synovial fluid." He pointed helpfully to the diagram as he spoke but all that I was interested in was what had resulted from the injury. I soon found out:

"Mr Halle, you may not like what I am going to say but you must realise that you have been a very lucky man in the circumstances, and that things could have been much worse. I am afraid that we had no choice but to amputate your finger above the first phalange."

A shudder ran down my spine when I heard that word 'amputation' with all its horrible finality. I lifted my right hand from the bed but I could see nothing underneath the cast and its covering. The doctor continued to speak indicating how my hand had been pumped full of a local anaesthetic so that I wouldn't be able to feel anything in it for a while and that the skin and tiny finger muscles had been stretched over the little stump that remained and stitched together as a sealant.

If my friends Steven and Ed had not been so close by I would have succumbed to the tears that were welling up inside of me, but instead I remained outwardly calm and displayed a stoic bravery that contrasted sharply with the inner despair that coursed through me at that moment. The pragmatist within me soon won out, however, and I came to the obvious conclusion that it was better to get a bullet in the finger than a bullet in the heart – the fate which would have been mine if I had dived to the right rather than to the left. Five years on from that incident, to the day that I sit here writing down my memories of that time, I am rather glad that it happened. The finger isn't completely gone, but the top two thirds of it are missing: it lends me a bit of character, I feel, and it always gives me an opportunity to invoke the gallows humour that I so love. I like to tell people that I have the amputated portion floating in formaldehyde within a little glass container that sits on my table next to the salt and pepper pots: it's completely untrue of course but it stops people wanting me to host dinner parties. On other occasions I joke about the man who comes round from anaesthetic and tells the doctor in a panicked voice 'Doctor, I can't feel my legs!', 'I know', replies the doctor, 'we amputated your arms.'

This ability to laugh at the situation came some time down the line from the moment that I write of now, but it was necessity rather than fortitude that stopped me from wallowing in my misery within my hospital bed. The doctor now announced that they were going to keep me within the hospital for twenty four hours for observation and, assuming that no complications occurred, I would be free to leave tomorrow afternoon. Twenty four hours as a virtual prisoner within the small yellow walled room? I looked up at the clock to see that it was now half past twelve in the afternoon, approximately six hours since I had confronted Perrin outside Hoyland police station and less than twelve hours until I had to keep my rendezvous with persons unknown at Shelby's Shack.

As had been explained to me I felt no pain in my right hand at all as I waved the lightweight cast around before my eyes. The glucose solution had worked well and I felt fine, almost reluctant to believe that I had been shot earlier that morning. The bottom line was that I had to keep that appointment at Shelby's Shack and I had to bring closure to this mystery that had cost me a finger and could so easily have cost me my life. Above all I was determined to help Rosa, and a setback like this wasn't going to dent that resolve.

Rosa! What had happened to her during the hours since I had left her on the previous evening? So much had passed since our low key parting but now it seemed that she was all that mattered. I wished that she had been there to put her arms around me or whisper soothing words as she fed me grapes but looking around the room I saw, as I expected within my heavy heart, that she was nowhere to be seen.

The good Dr Rajanathan seemed to know what I was looking for, or at least to know that I needed to be left alone to speak to the police officers, and so he said his farewells and reported that he would be back at four o'clock to check on my progress. The nurse, still hiding her kindly heart behind her formal exterior, removed the plastic covering which had been put upon the lightweight cast to aid its setting. She too exited the room now, although I imagined that I saw her give me a brief half smile as she walked through the doors.

So then there were five of us left in the room and for a moment it remained eerily silent as we each stood looking from one to another, all of us waiting to see who would speak first. It was Superintendent Pearson who spoke to Steven and Ed:

"Excuse me gentlemen, I am quite sure that you are very happy to see the splendid recovery that your friend Mr Halle is making", they made noises of approbation at this, "but I would be grateful if you would leave me and Constable Osbourne alone with him for a moment. There are some questions that we need to go through: I'm sure that you can appreciate the formalities that must be adhered to in situations of this ilk. You can wait outside if you so wish"

I don't know whether Pearson had acquired it through years of training or whether it came natural to him, but his voice carried such resonance that it was impossible to resist his bidding, and his requests became commands. Ed and Steven left the room and promised to see me later; Steven was going to wait in the television room that was apparently situated further along the ward and Ed said that he was going to visit Richard Clay in another wing of the hospital; I couldn't imagine that his visit would prove very welcome in the circumstances. I waved at my departing friends with my one remaining good hand and beckoned to the police officers, at different ends of the spectrum when it came to rank but both demonstrating what is best about the British police force, to be seated in the plastic chairs which were situated close to my bedside.

"Thank you for saving my life today, both of you" I opened the three way conversation with heartfelt honesty.

"That's not a problem, Mr Halle, it's what we are here to do" replied the Superintendent as if he imagined that he was some John Wayne figure arriving with the cavalry in the nick of time. I turned my head, still resting upon the hard hospital-issue pillow, to face Osbourne now. His left arm remained tied within a sling around his neck.

"I'm sorry about last night. I mean that I'm sorry for shooting you. I know that we didn't get off to the best of starts, but I didn't want that to happen." As an apology it seemed somehow deficient but it was the best I could manage and the truth was that if I had been faced with the same situation again I would still have pulled the trigger.

"Don't worry about it. I know what the situation was, Halle. You had no choice. It was a good shot by the way. Nice and clean through the fleshy bit underneath my shoulder, no major damage done and the doctor's say that I'll make a full recovery."

"How do you know that it was a good shot? Maybe I was aiming for your heart?" I fixed him with a cold stare now and for a moment I could see the uncertainty in his face before his thin mouth cracked into a grin and I returned his smile with interest.

"So what's the score then, sir", I asked Superintendent Pearson who was an imposing and impressive presence in the seat next to my bed, "am I going to be charged with shooting your officer here? If so then I might as well make a clean breast of things: I'd also like you to take into consideration that I stole a car, from a drug dealer admittedly but it still wasn't mine to take, and that I provided drugs to Little Dicky Clay who I believe is also ensconced in this hospital somewhere. If you hurry you might be able to find the stuff on him - it's all my fault though, sir, don't go punishing him." The guilty conscience was eating into me over the packet of heroin that I had supplied to my old school friend, and at least now I had done my best to alleviate the situation.

When Superintendent Pearson replied he spoke as if he were addressing a room full of a hundred people rather than talking directly to me: I soon learned that he was incapable of talking without making it sound like a speech.

"I hear what you say, Mr Halle, but what about the other crimes: the murder of Thomas O'Callaghan? The assault upon Richard Clay and his wrongful imprisonment?"

"I didn't do any of those crimes, sir."

"No, I know that you didn't. And let me make clear that I am singularly uninterested in the list of crimes that you have admitted to, off the record of course. I agree with Constable Osbourne here that while I cannot of course condone your actions you did what you had to do. We have bigger fish to fry, Halle, and we need your help to catch them. After that all will be forgiven and forgotten."

"Well as it seems that we are both after the same guy, then maybe we should go fishing together. How can I help you, Superintendent?"

"Well, suppose you tell me your story from the start – let me know how you ended up here. You can miss out the boring bits."

There weren't any boring bits to miss out, but I gave him as brief a précis as I thought possible. I declined to tell him about my psychic powers, I didn't want to end up in a more secure part of the hospital wearing a snug and sleeveless jacket, and I also avoided giving him the name of Vicky Gallagher, out of a misplaced sense of loyalty possibly but I could deal with her later.

I missed out seeing the girl on the bus completely and started by telling the Superintendent how I had witnessed the woman being run over by the car outside of Elsecar railway station on the Tuesday morning. I then related how I had chased after the driver only to find myself knocked unconscious by an unknown assailant. From there I mentioned that I had found a green ring by the roadside and that from then on I had been receiving threats from people trying to get the ring back from me.

I explained how I had been kidnapped by Perrin and Osbourne, who had the civility to look sheepishly at the floor as I said this, but had been rescued by Rosa Galloway. The threats had now transferred to her and first her beloved dog was kidnapped and now I had fears about Rosa herself who seemed to be unreachable at the moment.

I explained that somehow the events that had overtaken me seemed to be linked to the death of Georgie Galloway, Rosa's sister of ten years before: I purposely let both officers believe that this was one of those acts of coincidence that occur so spectacularly from time to time; this was easier for them to believe than the truth which was that Georgie herself had deliberately brought these things to my attention so that I could finally bring the truth about her death to light.

I neared the end of my brief summary and relayed how I had determined to track Thomas O'Callaghan down as he was the last person to have seen Georgie alive. This quest had taken me first to Huddersfield, where I had found Blondie and Osbourne, and then back to the cricket pavilion at Hoyland and from there onto the police station and the hospital bed with one little finger shorter than the other.

Both Pearson and Osbourne had sat silently while I recounted my story and after I had finished Superintendent Pearson rubbed his jaw theatrically while appearing to consider carefully all of the information that I had given to him. At last he spoke:

"So, Mr Halle, what, or who, do you think is behind all of this?"

"Well, as far as I can tell there's some guy operating around Yorkshire, operating throughout the country and abroad for all I know, who thinks that he is above the law. Who is above the law to all intents and purposes. He seems to be operating various cartels involving drugs, prostitution, armed robberies, protection. If a major crime is being committed around South Yorkshire then I'd imagine that if you could unravel the strands far enough, the initial orders would have come from him. He has powerful people in his pocket; whole police departments probably, no offence to yourself Superintendent. No doubt he has pet lawyers and judges who will do his bidding for the brown envelopes that he pushes their way."

"And what's his name, then?" asked Superintendent Pearson. It seemed obvious that he already knew the answer and was merely trying to find out how much I knew but I trusted this police officer completely and so I answered his question plainly:

"I doubt if many people even know his name, to be honest. But one person who did know his name was Tommy O'Callaghan to whom the man had been a mentor of sorts. He told me that the man was called Dwyer. He also insisted that this wasn't the man's real name but frankly I doubt if Tommy had the imagination to make a name up so he just attempted to cover up his mistake afterwards. So yes, Dwyer is his name I would say."

"Michael Dwyer, born in Dublin in 1952. Came to England as a child, and as far as the public see has become a very successful businessman." Satisfied that I was not concealing information from him the Superintendent was laying his cards upon the table, "He is a real pillar of the community is Michael, contributor to charity – I even believe that he has set up his own charitable fund to support a special baby care unit in this very hospital. Friends with members of parliament, Lords even. He has a large building and property portfolio. You may have seen some of his work around the towns and cities of Northern England; he seems to be putting up buildings everywhere."

"Dwyer Building Services" I shouted out interrupting the Superintendent's flow. I suddenly remembered the logo of this construction firm that I had seen emblazoned across flags that flew from a superabundance of new building projects: the logo that seemed to match in part the scrap of paper that Osbourne had slipped into my pocket on the morning that he had trussed me up in Shortwood. "ICES – that was the word on the scrap of paper, but it came from the headed paper of Dwyer Building Services. His influence spreads so widely into the police department that they even write upon pads of paper that are supplied by his construction company."

"Quite so, it seems", replied the Superintendent, "and now I think that it's about time that I told you the story from my perspective."

I sat upright in the hospital bed now, plumping up the two pillows and placing them vertically behind my back and head in support. I reached towards the bedside cabinet and Osbourne, always willing to help, stood up and retrieved the cup and bottle of water from their compartment. With his one useful hand he poured me a drink of water and handed it to me. I drank from it deeply and then nodded towards Superintendent Pearson in signal that I was ready to hear his story.

The Superintendent cleared his throat briefly and removed the hat from his head before placing it onto the floor next to his chair. It had escaped my attention that he'd still been wearing his cap, unlike the bare headed Osbourne, so natural did it seem upon him. He ruffled and then smoothed his hair before speaking and to me it seemed like another trait that he had learnt through years of public speaking.

When he did talk, Pearson held my full attention effortlessly. He started by explaining how he had come to make his timely intervention at the police station: Osbourne had written the letter before meeting me at St Peter's cemetery on Wednesday evening, he knew the dangers that were facing him and saw the letter as an insurance against some of the perils that awaited him; he was right to do so of course because whilst I made my escape he had been overcome by the feral group of youths, all under the employ and bidding of Dwyer although it remained unknown to them, and taken to Sergeant Perrin who eventually passed him on to the drug dealer known as Blondie, another pawn in the Dwyer chain. The letter, which had been hastily delivered by my loyal and unquestioning friend Steven, contained detailed information about Dwyer's corruption of Perrin and through him his infiltration of the local police station until it seemed that Dwyer himself was in charge of local law and order and decided who was to be punished and who had carte blanche to do as they liked. It also stated that if this letter was delivered to the Superintendent it could only mean that Osbourne's life was in imminent peril.

The Superintendent was not an easy man to get hold of at such an early hour of the morning but the genuine concern and insistence of Steven Carter had won through and before long the letter had reached Pearson at his home. Being renowned as a man of action, and of unquestionable integrity as Osbourne knew, he had realised at once the significance of the letter and had responded immediately by rousing his best detectives and heading straight for the police station at Hoyland. It was there that he had found me facing a bleak future in the company of the rogue officers Perrin and West.

West had been arrested without a struggle and had already revealed as much as he knew, implicating two other officers, a detective and a solicitor in the process. These men had been arrested and were currently helping with the enquiries but it seemed that none of them were privy to the sort of information that could point directly to Michael Dwyer himself being at the heart of the criminal activities. Perrin had been shot by Osbourne simultaneously with the shot that he had planted in me but he had still managed to reach a police car and make his escape. It was impossible to say how badly he was injured but an all area alert had been placed for him and his vehicle and Superintendent Pearson was confident that his capture would be imminent.

The Superintendent had specialised for many years in investigating the devilish machinations of organised crime and Dwyer had come to his attention on several terrible occasions. He specialised in cruelty, often administered seemingly for the pure enjoyment that he gained from it, and it was said that no man who crossed him would live for more than a month. His operations were constructed with the silky precision of a web, with the dreadful crimes hidden away beneath layers of legitimate activity, so that it seemed impossible to reach the murderous spider spinning and scuttling at the centre of it.

It now seemed that the ambitions of Dwyer were growing, he had numerous politicians of one level or another under his influence and the intelligence that Pearson had on him suggested that Dwyer was planning on standing for public office himself in the near future.

It wouldn't take long for word to leak back to that unflinching, unfeeling master of crime that his cartel in that particular area of South Yorkshire had been broken and the only assumption that could be made about his reaction was that it would be violent and disproportionately cruel.

Superintendent Pearson left me in no doubt that it was imperative that Dwyer be brought to justice as soon as could be arranged, immediately if possible, and this was where they needed my assistance: Dwyer, it seemed, had taken a personal interest in me and in this ring that he believed that I was in possession of; he had already arranged to meet me, either in person or through one of his lieutenants, to get the ring back. Pearson's plan was that I should go along with this meeting and be wired up so that I could record whatever was said or done in the hope that Dwyer would be implicated in something that they could finally get to stick on him.

The Superintendent gave a sigh and then stopped speaking before picking his hat from the floor and replacing it onto his head. Both he and Osbourne were looking at me with wide eyed expectation and with a tense look on their faces that made little lines appear at the corners of their mouths. No question had been directly asked of me as if there were not two options that I could have taken: to agree to the Superintendent's plan or to count myself out of it altogether. When I considered these options, the two men still staring straight at me without speaking, there was only one sensible, if dangerous, choice: Dwyer was going to reach me whatever decision I made, and it seemed that he already held Rosa and her dog tramp; if I wanted to get them back safely then I would have to meet him, and it seemed better to do it with the backing of the Police Department than without it. My mind was made up but I decided to get further clarification from the Superintendent before I revealed my decision:

"And if I say yes, if I agree to be a mole, then what security do I get? You've just been telling me how dangerous the man is. I'm rather attached to the nine fingers that I have left and I want to remain that way."

"Your security will be of paramount importance Mr Halle, just as important as the capture and conviction of Michael Dwyer, and so rest assured that we will be keeping an eye on you at all times. Mr Dwyer isn't the only one who can have secret operatives hidden around the country – even if you don't know that we are there, we will be at hand."

I would rather he had said that my security was more important than instead of just as important as capturing Dwyer but it was the best deal that I was going to get and if he had captured Rosa then I wanted to nail him just as much as the police did.

"Okay, it's a deal, Superintendent. I'll do it."

"Splendid" cried the Superintendent and rising from his plastic chair, small and uncomfortable for any but the briefest of visits, he extended his right hand before me. Seeing the grimace on my face, he took one look at the cast that encased my right hand and placed his hand into his trouser pocket before turning away. The Superintendent then paced the room as he outlined his plans:

"At four o'clock this afternoon Dr Rajanathan will examine you to see how things are progressing. He wants to keep you in here for at least another twenty four hours but doctors don't always know what's best for you do they? You would be bored just lying in here all of the time."

A period of peaceful boredom would have been just the ticket actually and I thought how much safer it would be to stay secure within the company of doctors. I was soon to learn how mistaken I was in that viewpoint but it seemed that Pearson had no intention of letting me stay in the bed as he continued:

"I will be here to persuade Dr Rajanathan that we need to take you away for questioning and that we will return you unharmed tomorrow. From here you will be taken to a safe house where you will be fitted with the recording devices and fully briefed on what to do and say. You will then be driven in an unmarked car to the rendezvous and the best of luck to you from there onwards."

I nodded my approval and repositioned my pillows before lying back onto the hard bed that seemed to be based upon a mattress made of rock. I had resolved to take a more proactive approach but now it felt that I was a plaything for the police department, no more than a puppet that moved and talked at their bidding as they pulled the strings. Let them think that if they wanted but I knew that if the opportunity came to bring my own justice to Dwyer then I would take that option whatever the instructions from the police puppet masters may be.

"I'm going to do whatever you instruct me to do Superintendent, I bow to your superior ability in this field", I intoned from my prone position on the bed and looked up at the ceiling following the course of a crack that had been roughly plastered over, "but I want you to do something for me. I was supposed to contact Rosa Galloway, the woman who found me in the woods you'll remember, but I tried to phone her throughout the night and got no reply. I'm worried about her."

"Then why don't you try to give her a call now?" suggested Osbourne as he reached into a large plastic container at the side of my bed and handed my mobile telephone to me. Looking down at this I saw that all of my clothing and belongings, which had been handed over at the police station, were placed neatly within the container.

"I can't use my phone in here – it's a hospital" I answered with a naïve indignation that brought a smile to Osbourne's lips.

"Don't be stupid, Halle, nobody believes that anymore. Mobile phones don't really interfere with the equipment you know, they just say that so that they can make more money on the pay phones. Go ahead and try her number."

The telephone was switched on and then placed into my left hand. With some effort, and a noticeable lack of dexterity, I managed to navigate the controls with one hand and held the unit to my ear after dialling Rosa's number. There was no ringing noise at all this time and the line was dead. Dead – I didn't like to think of that word in conjunction with Rosa. "No answer" I informed my companions, "if I give you the address, Superintendent, can you send some of your people to check it out? If they find anything suspicious then please let me know."

Superintendent Pearson agreed to this and although opining that it may be just a case of the battery in her phone being uncharged, a conciliatory remark that none of us gave any credence to, he promised that if she wasn't there he would endorse a high priority search for her. I gave him the address of Rosa and her description, which came easily to me as if I had seen her every day for the last year rather than for the last few days, and he noted this down in shorthand upon a notebook that was drawn from inside of his jacket.

"Well, Mr Halle, I must say that I really appreciate all that you have agreed to do for us today – it won't be forgotten. I will be back here at four sharp to speak to that Rajanathan fellow but I will leave you in the capable company of Constable Osbourne here and don't forget that my men will be around you at all times".

He smiled at me, which was the first change of expression that I had seen upon his resolutely serious face, and shook the right hand of Osbourne before walking out of the door and down the corridor in the company of a detective who had remained posted outside of the room. Osbourne, as you know, was a hugely powerful and resilient man but it didn't give me much comfort to think that we had only two useful arms between us.

My new friend was sitting in the chair which held him ridiculously as if a grown man was squeezed into a dolls chair. Reaching into the cabinet again he produced a bag of grapes and began pulling them off one by one without offering any to me. I interrupted his chewing to ask how he had escaped from Blondie's henchman and he explained that he had feigned to be more badly injured than he was, even though the pain from the bullet that passed below his shoulder had been excruciating. The chauffeur had propped Osbourne alongside him in the front passenger seat so that he could close watch as he drove him to be dumped and left to die in some suitably remote location. The car had soon been brought to a halt and the driver had climbed out to walk around the front and drag Osbourne out of his seat. The silent chauffeur had left the engine running as he did this and seeing his opportunity Osbourne, suddenly revitalised from his pretend stupor, jumped across to the drivers' seat before hitting the accelerator and driving straight into the chauffeur, sending him crashing across the street.

Many a man would have reversed over his body, now stretched across the road, for good luck before slipping the car into first gear and making a swift getaway. I would have done, and however unpalatable it may seem that is the truth. Osbourne seemed to be made of sterner stuff morally as well as physically and had left the car to examine the body of the chauffeur. He was unconscious with his mouth open and his eyes staring upwards into nothingness; at least there was no danger of the man swallowing his tongue - the man didn't have a tongue.

At this point Osbourne's left arm was hanging lifeless by his side with only the insistent stabbing pain to remind him that it was still there; using his one remaining arm he frisked the still and broken body before finding a mobile telephone in the man's pocket. Dialling 999 Osbourne waited dutifully for the ambulance, and the accompanying police car to arrive. Osbourne had wanted to relate his story to the West Yorkshire police officers without delay but at the insistence of the paramedics he was first taken to hospital in Huddersfield where the doctors patched him up as best they could; by a stroke of luck the bullet had passed cleanly through a fleshy part of his body and now it was just a question of keeping infection and shock at bay while nature did his work.

At first the doctors had taken his insistent ramblings as an ominous sign of fever but, after satisfying themselves that their patient was in the best condition that could be expected in the circumstances, they began to listen to his story with interest. Detectives were brought in who, after clarifying the tale with Superintendent Pearson's department itself, realised the urgency of the situation. After smartening Osbourne up they removed him from the hospital, much to the chagrin of the medical staff who were present.

Osbourne was first driven to the Police Headquarters on the outskirts of Sheffield but after establishing that the Superintendent had left for the Hoyland station they followed suit. It was at Sheffield that Osbourne had surreptitiously taken the gun that he had brought to Hoyland and confronted Sergeant Perrin with.

Looking at him now, it was hard to reconcile this man with the terrifying monster who had visited my house on that morning just two days ago.

Here was a man who had recently put his life on the line to do the right and honourable thing and, even in his present state, would not hesitate for a moment to do the same thing again. And yet earlier in the week he had been the one who had tied and bound me and landed kicks upon my ribs that had left me breathless and coughing blood. It was as if the senseless violence that Perrin had urged him to commit had finally opened his eyes, had been an epiphany for him where he suddenly saw the way that he wanted his life to go, and how far he had been removed from it. Hamlet said that conscience makes cowards of us all but its dawning realisation had made a hero of Osbourne.

We clasped hands together, my left upon his right, as we consecrated the brotherhood of the one handed. Yes, he had gone astray in his life but I knew as well as anyone how easy it was to be coerced into doing things that went against ones nature just by the sheer force of another's personality. Just as Lamara had exerted her influence upon me so had Perrin imposed his will upon Osbourne – it was all forgotten and forgiven now; this life isn't about how many times we fall down, it's about how we get back up.

"I want you to do me a favour", I said to Osbourne as if conveniently forgetting the huge favours that he had already done me and the bullet that I had sent through him spraying his blood upon that bleak and dirty wall.

"What's that?" he replied and we separated our hands now, the brief moment of bonding was over and it was back down to business.

"In the cemetery you mentioned the 'accident' with the Mercedes-Benz AMG. Do you know what really happened there?"

"I know that officially it was an accident but it's not a risky supposition to imagine that it wasn't an accident. Beyond that I don't know too much. Everything was cleaned up, covered up, before I got to see the details."

"Right, well I know that the woman was brought here and that she passed away in this very hospital. She had the ring, I'm sure that she did, and that must mean that she is right at the centre of this whole mystery. If only we knew who she was, if only we knew what she was."

"I see what you mean" he countered encouragingly.

"Do you? Well, it's a strange thing Osbourne but I could have sworn that she was a young woman when I saw her under the car, but they say that it was an aging woman that died. Does that sound strange to you?"

"Yes", he replied with his customary honesty, before adding, "but then there are lots of strange things out there. What do you want me to do?"

"Ever fancied being a detective Osbourne? You're too smart to stay on the beat for ever. I want you to speak to the nurses, to the administrators, and find out the name of that woman and as much information about her as you can. They won't tell you at first so just flash your big toothed smile at them – that won't work either because you haven't got the looks that I have, to be frank, but flash your warrant card at them and that should open the doors."

He smiled at me now, and although his face was much more handsome than my pale and drawn specimen could ever manage, I was the one lying in bed with a finger missing and so it was the least that he could do to leave me in my delusion.

Osbourne nodded his agreement and rising from his ridiculously cramped chair he pounded towards the door with thudding footsteps that reminded me of a baby elephant. Just before closing the door behind him he said:

"I will try not to be too long, Halle. Don't worry about me being absent. Like the chief said, we've got people around the hospital watching you even if you don't realise it."

It was a mantra that they all seemed to repeat but it offered little comfort as the door swung to behind him. I just hoped that any people that they had assigned to look after me would have two arms each and preferably two legs as well.

So here I was in hospital, and the person that I most wanted to visit me, Rosa Galloway, was nowhere to be seen. I lay back on the pillow; a feeling of warm contentment flowed through me although it was impossible to say whether it came from the anaesthetic, the glucose injection or from the joy of still being alive. I found myself thinking of my future, and dreamt of a large house in the breathtaking Yorkshire countryside, that land of fens and valleys unmatched anywhere in the world. Rosa would be at my side and maybe a little green eyed child too. We would play football on our lawn or go for walks where I could teach my child the names of the birds that we encountered: those that I didn't know I would just make up so that the little one would think that I was wise beyond compare. It would be a wonderful, unbeatable life and for a moment it seemed that it was almost within reach. Yes it was all a dream but to a man unaccustomed to such dreams, whose every night for the last year had been interrupted by sweat soaked nightmares, it was a glimpse of heaven itself.

Let it pass; every dream has its nightmare, for every life there is a death and the hospital where I lay was built upon death and traded in tears of

313

sorrow as well as joy. That poor woman, who ever she was, had died alone and friendless in a crushed agony in this same hospital that now accommodated me. I made a silent pact that I would find out who she was and bring justice for her as well as for Georgie and Lamara or I too would breathe my last in the attempt.

I found myself drifting into sleep again and my head nodded forwards upon the pillow as my eyes closed themselves. Many minutes had passed before a thudding noise and a suppressed cry brought me back to consciousness with a start. It was a doctor who had walked into the door of the cabinet, carelessly left open by Osbourne, as he walked around the bed. But this was a different doctor altogether to Dr Rajanathan.

"Hello, Doctor" I said in a cheerily delivered greeting as I came slowly round from the deep sleep that I had easily fallen into, "couldn't the other one make it?"

"No, I'm afraid not. He sent me instead. It's time for another injection so just roll up your sleeve like a good patient will you?"

He was walking closer to me now with his syringe primed and pointed into the air. I looked up at the clock and saw that it was only just after three o'clock and nearly an hour before I had been expecting a visit from Dr Rajanathan. As my faculties returned from their docile slumber the man began to look more and more familiar: he was a short and stocky man and he walked towards me with a definite up and down limp that had little to do with his collision with the cabinet - as the memory of that poor woman came back to me again I knew that it had everything to do with a different collision.

"Still limping I see?" I asked him with scorn and anger in my voice causing him to freeze in his tracks with the syringe still pointing skywards, "that must have been some crash on Tuesday, eh?"

I looked around the room in panic but Osbourne was absent, still engaged upon the mission that I had sent him on. I later found out that Superintendent Pearson had been true to his word and had disguised one of his men as a porter whose job it was to walk up and down the corridor looking into my room. It was the return of my bad luck that meant that he had chosen that moment to take a cigarette break in the hospital lavatory, wafting his smoke through an opening at the top of the frosted window.

The man, now in a doctor's attire, who I had last seen fleeing from the crashed Mercedes-Benz was suddenly on top of me and his deceptive weight pressed down upon my chest forcing me back into the solid mattress. He held my only good arm down to my side with a strength that I tried to resist but was powerless to stop. A mad look gleamed in his eyes and his pupils were wide and dilated, droplets of spittle accumulated in a frothy residue at the right hand corner of his mouth. With his free arm he brought the syringe down upon me from its deadly height.

Chapter Seventeen

I struggled with all of my power and with the strength of a man staring death in the face but it was to no avail. My assailant was heavier than he appeared to be as if he was one short and solid mass of muscle, most of it concentrated between his ears. His weight was pushed down upon my abdomen so that it was hard for me to breath and impossible for me to throw him off. My left arm was pressed tightly down by my side and it was as much as I could do to raise it from the bed for two seconds at a time before it was pushed firmly back down again. I waved my right arm around with impotent fury but the cast on my four fingered hand prevented me from using it.

As my attacker had brought the syringe down upon my body I contracted my muscles as much as possible and with a great effort pulled my left arm, which was trapped as if held in a vice, back into the mattress. The effect of this was that the needle only grazed against my arm upon impact rather than penetrating the skin itself. My attacker groaned through his clenched teeth, which were clamped firmly together whilst he pushed his full strength down upon me, as his syringe failed to find its target.

His anger roused he pushed down even harder as if trying to sap the last vital ounce of energy from me in preparation for his second attack. His head was forward and his face was pressed towards mine. His nostrils were flared and the veins on his forehead were so pronounced that it seemed as though they might pop at any moment. I was pushing against him with all of the force that I had left but inevitably his strength began to win out over my depleted body. I could feel the energy, the last momentary reserves of strength, draining from my arms and legs and before long I would be lying there as helpless as a baby, unable to move and waiting for the needle to inject whatever deadly cocktail was encased within the clear syringe.

His head was almost touching mine and was bowed with his eyes shut as a result of the physical exertion. He was so close that I could see the carefully hidden bald patches between the fine and sculpted strands of dark hair. The man pulled his head back and his eyes opened to accompany the leer of victory that had formed upon his face. He gasped words at me which I guess would have been something as original as 'time to die' but it was impossible to say what the words actually were as he barely possessed the energy to deliver them through his gritted teeth, resulting in it coming out as a rattling and wheezing whisper.

I acted instinctively and as my body and limbs were in one way or another incapacitated I turned to the sole part of me that I yet had an element of control over. I drew my head back deep into the hard pillow and pushed it forwards with as much speed and power as I could muster. The impact of my head upon his seemed to rock the room to the accompaniment of a thud that sounded sickeningly hollow; it felt as if tiny bones in my neck were cracking with the force of the collision. Stars flew around my eyes and popped in mid air explosions and a high pitched buzzing noise reverberated like an alarm within my ears. I lay back upon the bed and with relief I found that the man who had been disguised as a doctor was nowhere to be seen. The buzzing noise faded gradually and the stars that had gathered in front of my eyes were blinked away. My left arm began to tingle as the circulation started to flow through it again.

When I tried to raise my arm from the bed it flopped down again upon the bed sheet as if it had fallen off and was no longer a part of my body. Unable to use my other arm to assist in the process I rubbed my left arm vigorously upon the bed to return the life into it; soon I was able to lift it from the bed and wiped it across my forehead. Positioning this hand in front of my eyes I could see that it had a sheen of blood across it but it soon became apparent that the blood didn't belong to me.

A new groaning sound made me roll over in the bed and looking to my left I saw that my assailant was now stretched out upon the floor with blood flowing in free abundance from a deep gash that had been chiselled across the bridge of his nose. With an effort he was rising from his prone position now and had lifted himself onto one knee. He stood up onto his unsteady legs and they wobbled beneath him as though they belonged to a newborn deer rather than a short squat man of immense power. The look in his eyes showed unconcealed hatred and he limped across to me one heavy and unsure step at a time, stopping en route to pick up the syringe that had flown out of his hand and across the room.

The calm look within my eyes seemed to enrage him even more and he suppressed a shout of fury which instead escaped from his mouth in a hissing noise as of steam shooting out of a broken pipe. I remained unconcerned and smiled sweetly back at him. I had seen what remained hidden to him – the detective who had been assigned to look after me, disguised as a porter, had finally been roused from his crafty cigarette by the loud crashing sound that had echoed from my room. He had entered the room unknown to my attacker and stood quietly behind him now after motioning me to remain silent and flashing his warrant card that named him as Detective Sergeant Radford.

Radford grabbed my attacker around the throat and in the battle of the fake doctor and the fake porter there was only going to be one winner. It would have been a simple matter for Radford to ease the doctor gently to the floor, or against a wall, where he could have frisked him or incapacitated him with a pair of handcuffs. Instead he pulled his arm forcefully against the doctor's neck and lifted his knee quickly into the small of the man's back which sent him crashing in agony to the floor making a fresh jet of blood squirt from his already broken nose. Nicely, nicely can get results but excessive force often proves more satisfying. After a brief look down at his opponent satisfied him that he provided no further menace he held out his card to me again and introduced himself:

"Detective Sergeant Radford, South Yorkshire Police."

"I know", I replied, "what kept you so long?"

"Cigarette break", was his reply but at least he was being honest and so I responded in kind:

"Well, detective, can you stay away from the king size ones next time please?"

Within a matter of moments the room was full again. Osbourne soon returned although he was seemingly oblivious to what had happened and looked from the floor to me and then to the floor again with concerned confusion. He was followed into the room by Steven Carter, who announced in a shocked voice:

"Would you believe it, John? I just went along to visit Richard Clay and it seems that the police have found some drugs concealed upon him. Even in here he can get hold of heroin! What is the health service coming to, mate? Can you believe that?"

"I find it hard to believe, Steven. I'm shocked, just shocked. It seems that you can't trust anybody these days."

It was only at this point that Steven seemed to notice the scene that he had entered: there was a man, presumably a doctor, lying immobile upon his back with blood still spreading from his nose onto the tiled surface of the floor. I had this man's blood spread across my forehead and smeared upon my left hand and my short hair was glistening with the sweat that had matted it to my head. A police officer with his arm in a sling and a burly hospital porter completed the picture.

Steven seemed to reel physically as he took this in and held onto the corner of the door to steady himself. The uncomprehending expression upon his face made me laugh out loud, more in hysterical relief at my rescue than any real humour that I found in the situation.

My new acquaintance, the formidably imposing Superintendent Pearson, came hot on the heels of my old friend and pushed open the door with the self importance of a man who never has to knock before entering a room. The force and speed with which he pushed the door nearly caught Steven out so that he had to remove his hand quickly from the gap of the door, which he had been gripping, before he found his fingers trapped against the hinges.

The Superintendent, too, had been oblivious to all that had occurred but it would have been impossible to guess this from his countenance which remained professionally dispassionate. He removed his cap again and rubbed the top of his head as if preparing to speak but Steven beat him to it:

"I have absolutely no idea what's going on here but", at this point he turned to the Superintendent and addressed him directly, "I'm guessing that it's time for me to step out of the room again?"

"If you would be so kind, sir" replied Pearson with a delicate mixture of obsequiousness and superiority in his voice which made it impossible to tell if it was a request or a command.

"Okay, John, I don't know what's going on but I guess that you are in the best hands here. I promise that I will come and visit you again tomorrow."

"I wouldn't bother, Steven – I'm not going to be here tomorrow."

"Not here tomorrow?" he repeated with wide eyed amazement. By this time tomorrow I could be at home or in a hole in the ground and it seemed fifty-fifty which it was going to be, but I wasn't going to be laid upon the hospital bed and so in lieu of clarification I simply added:

"No, but I will be in touch tomorrow. Take it easy."

"And please, sir, do be sure to keep all of this to yourself. Do I make myself clear?" asked the Superintendent and by way of reply Steven gave a peremptory nod as he walked in astonishment out of the room.

318

Pearson quickly took charge and the three men sat down upon the plastic chairs which seemed to buckle under their collective weights. In contrast I roused myself from my bed and climbing out from underneath the covers I began to walk around the room finding pleasure in feeling the floor underneath my feet again. Already I had become so accustomed to the lightweight cast covering my injured right hand that I hardly noticed it swinging against my body as I walked.

At his bidding I gave Superintendent Pearson my account of the incident that had occurred: at no point did he make an effort to write down, or otherwise record, what I was saying but there would be time to take a more formal statement from me if I managed to survive the evening ahead.

During the course of my story another plain clothes officer, summoned by the Superintendent, came and collected the man who had been lying upon the floor with an expanding pool of blood around him. He was first cleaned up with the aid of sterile wipes, applied by the detective who was wearing disposable gloves, and then the handcuffs were fastened onto him before he was led out of the room. He was in a semi-conscious daze and seemed unsure as to who he was or why he was being arrested. I continued to recount my tale and made clear that I was quite convinced that the bogus doctor was the same man that I had seen fleeing, with a pronounced limp, from the scene of the car crash that had snapped me from my dreams outside of Elsecar railway station earlier in the week. At first when I had heard talk of a mysterious Mr Big who lay behind my woes, whose name I found was Dwyer, I had imagined that Dwyer and the man who had ran from the mangled wreck of the Mercedes-Benz sports car were one and the same person. I knew now that this little theory of mine was incorrect: he wasn't the kind of man who would do the dirty work himself; I imagined him to be a different breed of person altogether – more imposing, more terrifying, more deadly.

Superintendent Pearson had known the identity of the man as soon as he had seen him and he informed me that the man was Lou Robertson, known as Rocky Robertson throughout the criminal fraternity. This nickname was given not as an indicator of Italian heritage or any special affiliation with boxing but rather because he was short, squat and dark haired like the actor who had played Rocky in the films.

Rocky had been a petty thief in his younger days but had maintained a clean criminal record for many years now: not because he had gone straight but because he had left petty crime behind and moved on to serious crime where he had fallen under the tutelage and protection of

Michael Dwyer himself. Wherever Rocky Robertson was to be found, Dwyer was certain to be nearby.

The hypodermic syringe, still full of its vile liquid, was left lying untouched where it had fallen. Presently a scene of crime officer would collect it and send it to the police laboratories; when the results came back it would become clear how close I had been to death but for the moment Pearson was more concerned with how Rocky had got into my room without being challenged. Detective Sergeant Radford, a strongly built man whose dark skin had been paid for by hourly sun bed sessions and whose hair was sleeked back with enough grease to run a takeaway, looked to the floor rather than at the Superintendent. Inspiration failed him and he blurted out that I had asked him to fetch me a drink of coffee from the vending machine and when he came back he had found Robertson in the room before overcoming him in a fierce struggle.

It was all lies of course, but the Sergeant looked at me with such a pleading look in his eyes that I backed up his story. Pearson reprimanded me for being so careless and I felt like a schoolboy who has been sent to the headmaster for forgetting his homework again.

To break the awkward silence that had descended, and which filled the room more completely than the loudest noise could, I addressed Osbourne and asked him if he had managed to find out any information about the woman who I had seen lying crushed underneath the car that had been driven by Robertson – the information that he gave me turned out to be pure gold in more ways than one.

He spoke with reluctance at first, which I took to be a sign of nerves when speaking in the company of such a senior officer as Pearson, but his confidence increased as he talked. The woman was named Roisin, he hadn't been able to get her surname, and she had been eighty years of age. Originally from a remote town in County Meath, Ireland she had been living in England for the majority of her life and had lately been resident in the Carhill Care Centre, which seemed to be a nursing home in Sheffield. It was unclear why she had been in Elsecar on that morning but the internal injuries that she had received were so severe that there was no way that she could have survived and she had been pronounced dead at 12.13 on the 2nd of January 2001.

The woman that I had seen had seemed young and yet here I had it confirmed that she had been in old age, just as the hospital receptionist had said when I had spoken to her on the same day. Before this week I would have found the news incredible but after all I had seen, and after all that I had learnt about my abilities from Madame Irina, I knew instinctively that it was the same woman: while others saw the dying old woman I had seen Roisin as she would have appeared in the flower of young womanhood, at a moment of crisis in her life, just as I had with the vision of Georgie.

"You have done a great job there, Osbourne my friend," I thanked him profusely, "how long have you been a policeman for now?"

"Oh, a few years. A good few years now." He spoke with tiredness in his voice and looked suddenly older than he had seemed before: I realised that he had been through as much, if not more, than I had over the last few days.

"A good few years? And you are still a police constable? You're cut out to be a detective at least, surely? The force needs more good men like Osbourne, doesn't it Superintendent?"

The Superintendent chose not to answer my question but instead smiled back as if humouring me. I looked back to Osbourne now and he gave a brief upturn of his tired lips in acknowledgement. He looked as if he could fall asleep in his chair at any moment and probably would have done if the tiny plastic frame hadn't been so uncomfortable for his mass that was wedged precariously into it.

"Who did you speak to then, Osbourne?" I asked as a way of keeping him awake more than anything.

"What do you mean?" he replied.

"Well, who did you speak to in the hospital to get the information out of them?"

"Oh, I see. It was a matron of some sort. Matron Dee, that's who it was." Matron Dee? It sounded like she should be directing people to tables in a restaurant rather than helping to run a hospital but I was grateful for the information that he had supplied and which I resolved to follow up at the first possible opportunity.

The minutes had ticked by noisily on the clock and as four o'clock loomed the room became full again with the entry of Dr Rajanathan and the nurse who had assisted him earlier. The Doctor seemed surprised to see me on my feet but after running a quick series of tests, monitoring my blood pressure, physical and mental reflexes and heart rate all of which were noted methodically and illegibly on the black backed clipboard that he carried, he professed himself to be very pleased with the progress I was making - even if my blood pressure was slightly higher than normal. We all looked from one to another but reached a silent pact not to worry the doctor with news of the attack that had been launched upon me by Rocky Robertson.

The nurse brought me a plastic tray that was a sickly yellow colour and contained four recesses in it. In one of the round recesses was a dark brown mush which, when I prodded it with the white disposable fork provided, I found to be two thin slices of processed chicken covered in a thick gravy which had congealed on the surface. Another recess held a portion of lumpy mashed potato that had been so coated in finely chopped parsley that it looked like it had been topped with a freshly mown layer of grass. The third recess held a mixture made up of carrots, garden peas and sweetcorn all chopped up into tiny pea sized pieces. The fourth recess was home to an unidentifiable pudding in a substance that looked like a vague imitation of custard. There were two tablets which I washed down with a glass of milk that had been placed upon the tray and which wobbled threateningly as the nurse placed it onto a panel that slid out of the side of my cabinet and which served as a makeshift dinner table.

The Superintendent spoke directly to Dr Rajanathan and explained how they needed to remove me from the hospital to be questioned further. The Doctor disagreed strongly with this suggestion and both men, while keeping their voices level and calm, appeared to be getting heated in their vehement defences of their respective positions. It had been a long time since either man had found his instructions questioned and it was an interesting battle of wills to see which man would win.

From time to time they both looked at me to support their argument but I remained a dispassionate spectator and shovelled forkfuls of the overcooked and undernourishing food into my mouth to avoid having to give an opinion on the matter.

At times when the Superintendent seemed to be flagging, or when Dr Rajanathan's sheer speed of argument appeared to be on the brink of winning the day, Detective Sergeant Radford joined in on the side of his superior officer and eventually, as I had expected to happen, their argument wore Dr Rajanathan down and the forces of law won over the dictates of medicine. Reluctantly he agreed that I could leave with the officers that afternoon provided that they returned me to the hospital on the following day, without fail, so that I could spend the required twenty four hours under the doctor's observation.

I was relieved to be leaving the hospital, although I didn't know where I was going to go or what I would have to do. The only thing that seemed certain to me was that I was about to enter a highly dangerous situation that would give me the opportunity to end the mystery once and for all, and finally confront Dwyer himself, but could also mean that I was entering upon the final few hours of my life: it was a chance that I was willing to take.

The plastic container, which had been brought from the police station and contained the goods that had been taken from me after I had been falsely arrested, was now placed upon the unremittingly hard hospital bed. My clothes were lifted out of the container for me and whilst I recognised my underwear, socks and shoes the rest of the apparel was unknown to me. Pearson saw the surprised look on my face and explained that as much of my external clothing had been ruined by the events leading up to and during the shooting the police department themselves had provided this new clothing for me. It appeared to be of better quality, and certainly newer, than my own clothing and so I didn't object to their generosity.

I had finished off the meal with greedy fervour. It had been a plastic and anodyne meal but its additive packed blend of bland sweetness had been strangely welcome and if I hadn't been in such exalted company I would have raised the emptied tray to my face and licked the receptacle that had held the bright yellow goo that had passed as custard.

The tray had been cleared away and the drawer had been pushed back into place within the bedside cabinet. I sat up on the bed alongside my new collection of clothes and fumbled one-handedly at the buttons on my pyjamas: it was like trying to strain tea with a hoop. The men sat around nervously as I tried in vain to push buttons through holes using just my left hand: I was determined not to look helpless in their company. By the time that I was lying horizontally upon my bed, still twisting with frantic frustration at the first button, the nurse had seen enough and took silent control of the situation.

Curtains were drawn around my bed with a click clicking noise as the rings traversed along the metal frame; they were a jade colour and heavy looking and, as always seems to be the case which leads me to think that they are designed this way, at least two of the curtain rings were missing so that the curtains sagged down in the middle and didn't quite reach the end of the frame thus allowing people to look in at the sides.

The nurse was a model of stiff efficiency and hardly said a word other than a few gentle ticks of encouragement as she helped me out of my clothing. Standing naked before her I tried not to think of how commandingly beautiful she looked with her aloofness adding to her allure. She shook her head sadly upon sight of my nakedness but I like to think that it was the sight of my battered and bruised body that caused this moment of sympathy. All too quickly she had me dressed, even pausing to tie my shoe laces for me, and the curtain screen was drawn noisily back to reveal me as a new man in a dark blue suit, with faint cyan pinstripe, and a sky blue shirt that scratched me with its newness. It was time to leave my room and although I had only been there for a few hours it was a relief to be leaving a place that always seemed to me to smell of disinfectant and death and where I imagined a new contagion creeping along the corridor towards me at every moment. The nurse and the doctor left the room, after once again eliciting a promise that I would be returned on the following day, allowing me to be debriefed by Superintendent Pearson who stood up with his head held high and shoulders drawn back as he outlined his plan.

Pearson explained that I would be driven back to my house by Detective Sergeant Radford where I would await the arrival of a technician who would fit me up with the bugging device. Constable Osbourne would stay with me at all times and the house would be under constant surveillance from his undercover operatives. Pearson himself would return to police headquarters where he would take personal charge of the investigation but I wasn't to worry as he would keep me informed of the progress at all times and once his men had completed the formality of finding Rosa Galloway she would be brought to me as well.

I was going home again! The two days that I had been away felt like years and I was wistfully looking forward to sinking back into the armchair that seemed to have moulded itself around me. The dream returned of setting up a new life in the house once all of this was over, once I had seen that Dwyer was finally brought to justice, with Rosa alongside me and with no more worries or violence in our lives; yet whilst I had listened with outward conviction to the Superintendent's promise that Rosa would be easily found I knew within my heart that there was more to her silence than a late night shopping trip. I was prepared to do all that the police department wanted me to do but first they had to let me finish my personal mission. I addressed the Superintendent:

"You know that I'll do whatever you command me to do, ask me to do I should say, but before your technician comes round to hide this listening device on me there's something else that I need to do."

"What's that?" he answered with a tentative note creeping into his voice.

"I need to go to that Carhill Care Centre that Osbourne mentioned. I simply have to talk to the head of the centre and find out more about Roisin."

"I'm afraid that that's impossible" was the answer from Pearson and

Osbourne echoed the word 'impossible, from the chair that he was wedged into.

"Why is it impossible?"

"We are working to severe time constraints here, Mr Halle. We can't afford to waste time chasing after some dead old woman."

"You can't afford not to waste the time, sir. This death is linked inextricably with Michael Dwyer. It was no accident - I believe that he ordered her death for one specific purpose."

"And what purpose was that?"

"I don't know yet, but that's what I aim to find out." He seemed to be wavering now, rubbing the top of his head as he considered my suggestion, and so I pressed home my advantage: "And if you do this to help me, then I have a couple of things that might help you."

I had grabbed the Superintendent's interest now and I beckoned him over so that I could whisper in his ear. With hushed confidentiality I told him about the faked letter that I had given to Vicky Gallagher, although again I was careful not to name her. In the faked letter, from Osbourne to Superintendent Pearson, I had intimated that Osbourne had proof about corruption in the police department that was linked to a drug ring operating throughout the North of England. The letter was asking the Superintendent to meet Osbourne near a certain lay-by on the M1 Motorway at ten o'clock that evening. I didn't need to tell the officer, who was listening with attention to my whispered words, that if he sent his men to watch that lay-by they would catch Blondie and maybe other members of Dwyer's gang as well.

I also told Pearson about the documents that I had hidden at Steven Carter's house and the sim card from Blondie's telephone that I had placed in the back pocket of my trousers. Those trousers were now in the possession of the police department but Pearson assured me that he would get his men to search the pockets to see if the telephone's card, hopefully containing a myriad of interesting contacts, was still present. He was pleased with the information that I had given to him and so I asked for one last favour. I remembered the story that Poor Tommy O'Callaghan had recounted to me shortly before he was shot dead by Perrin, and it nagged away within my head. I asked the Superintendent to look into the details surrounding the conviction of Freddy Chester, among others, for the Leeds jewellery raids in 1990; maybe it was nothing but the more information that I had the better.

The Superintendent shook my hand in agreement and our whispered conference was at an end. Turning back to his two men, who sat upright in their chairs as he addressed them, he explained that before taking me to my house Radford and Osbourne would be driving me to the Carhill Care Centre.

A look of panic came into Osbourne's eyes at this instruction and he rose from his chair, having levered himself with difficulty out of it, to protest that he hated those homes and didn't like to be around old people in such places as it reminded him of his own grandparents that he missed greatly. It sounded unusually sensitive for the big man but I didn't like care homes myself so I could appreciate his perspective. I suggested to the Superintendent that Osbourne could remain at my house, ensuring that everything was secure there, whilst Radford and I continued on to the care centre. This was readily agreed to and Osbourne gave me an involuntary smile of gratitude.

We walked out of the room together in two lines of two. On the way down the corridor I saw the nurse again and she returned the smile that I gave her. I stopped for one moment and said:

"Thanks for everything Nurse –"

"Nurse Peters, Heather." She replied.

"Thanks for everything, Heather. How do I get in touch with you if I want to ask you anything?"

"Just give me a call" she replied and paused to write down her number on a scrap of paper that she handed to me playfully.

"Thanks, I may well be in touch. Oh, and say thank you to Matron Dee for me will you?"

"Who?" She had a puzzled look upon her face and it seemed that she too thought that I was trying to book a table in a restaurant.

"It doesn't matter" I reassured her and continued down the corridor with my three compatriots and then out of the hospital into the early evening air.

I remained in the unmarked police car when we reached my house and I passed my door key to Osbourne without hesitation: I felt that a bond of trust had developed between us now. I had little doubt that my noisy, and newly communicative, neighbour would be taking note of this strange man entering my house and that he would be approaching me to discuss it at a later date but I was happy to postpone our reunion for a couple of hours or so.

Radford used his police issue radio to contact headquarters and obtain the directions to the care home; it was located in one of the more rural suburbs of Sheffield, away from the city centre itself and heading towards the ravaged beauty of the Peak District. I thought, upon hearing this, that it must make it inconvenient for people who want to visit the residents there but I was soon to learn that the residents of Carhill weren't the type that received visitors.

Radford drove with his window wound down and his right arm resting upon the sill of the door as if he was in a Seventies cop show, seemingly oblivious to the freezing air that was sweeping into the car and which caused me to cough as the chill hit my lungs. He spent a lot of the journey looking into the rear view mirror but this wasn't to see if we were being followed or even to keep his eye upon the road, it was merely to check that his hair was still in place and he touched and smoothed his hair automatically every few seconds. As I studied his face with more care I could have sworn that he had moisturiser glistening upon his face and I believe that he would have worn eye liner if he could have got away with it on duty.

We had left the city itself and the congregated clusters of the suburbs behind, sand coloured stone for the more salubrious districts and red bricked for the less so, and were heading into the rolling hills of the countryside. Heavy deposits of snow could still be seen on the peaks in the distance passed Carhill itself. As we neared the Centre Radford achieved the task, that I would have thought impossible, of spending even more time preening himself. He expressed his hopes that we would find some attractive young nurses at the homes who would be unable to resist his obvious charms. He stretched in his seat and pulled at the crotch of his trousers as he said this.

We reached a driveway where an arrow pointed the way ahead to 'Carhill Resource And Residential Centre' and drove slowly along the uneven driveway that ran through a large perimeter wall. There was a heavy gate at the wall which was guarded by a man in a grey security uniform topped by a navy blue peaked cap; he wore sunglasses in spite of the approaching darkness and he had to remove these to peer at the warrant card which Detective Sergeant Radford held out of the open window of his car. The gate was opened without further delay and we continued to drive along the path to a large building which was built on two levels and had ivy growing across the front of it. There was a signpost here but the directions upon it were nonsensical with one arrow pointing to 'London 5000 miles', another pointing to 'Moscow 457 miles', and a third of the multitude of arrows pointing to 'Venus 22341 miles'. A peacock passed across the front of the car strutting playfully as it walked. Upon seeing Radford it seemed to recognise a soul mate and let out a piercing squawk. Echoes of the sound, of men and women imitating the mournful noise, could be heard in the distance coming from the small closed windows of the centre.

"Bloody hell, Halle," opined Radford as he stopped the car and faced me with shocked surprise, "this isn't no care home for the elderly you know? This is a nut house."

I wasn't sure if he had found the current accepted terminology but his assessment was on the button. He moved the car forward again and parked it within a bay marked with a yellow wheelchair to show that it was only available for disabled users - this was 'policeman's privilege' he assured me.

The entrance door was black and windowless and a brass plaque that was fastened to it read 'no unauthorised personnel beyond this point.' I was prepared to leave the leg work to Radford until it was time for me to ask the questions and so he pushed the door open and led the way inside. The hallway was darker than I had expected as though the lighting was deliberately subdued. A reception desk stood directly in front of the doorway and a large staircase spiralled away to the right, guarded at the bottom by another man in a grey suit and peaked cap with a look of boredom upon his face which suggested that each day was a struggle to count down the seconds until the end of his shift. A slender framed woman stood behind the desk shuffling a pile of papers. She had a pair of blue framed glasses that seemed to be too big for her face and her black hair was tied back in an off-centre pony tail that swung to the right of her head. Her nose was pierced and her dark mascara gave her a morose expression. Radford approached the desk with a broad smile displaying his chemically whitened teeth and smoothed his hair again before addressing the woman who was looking at him with surprised concern.

"I am Detective Sergeant Radford and this is Detective Inspector Halle" was his introduction and he held out a hand to her which she took timidly before returning his smile. With his free hand he produced his warrant card and showed it first to the receptionist before flashing it in the direction of the security guard on the stairs. I patted the breast pocket of my jacket as if to indicate that my warrant card, bearing the lofty title of Inspector, was kept there.

"We are here to speak to the boss, the big cheese, numero uno" he said, somewhat over egging the pudding I thought but to give him his credit he did seem to know how to speak to women and the receptionist, who had formally seemed so lacking in light, now giggled timidly and fluttered her eyes as she spoke to him:

"You need Mrs Sutton. Is it about Mr Alderman? I thought that you would be round eventually."

"Who?" he asked puzzled before regaining his composure and adding "No, it's about –"

I helped him out here and finished the sentence for him:

"It's about Roisin – the patient who died earlier this week. We need to speak to Mrs Sutton about it, but don't worry it shouldn't take too long." She nodded at me formally but as she spoke to her manager on the telephone she gave flirtatious glances to Radford.

We waited for two minutes during which Radford and the girl played eye tennis with each other. Eventually a wooden panelled door opened and we were greeted by a middle aged woman who had done everything that she could to look older than she was. Her blonde hair had been shaped into a severe looking bun and the faintest smudge of make up did little to hide the pock marked effect on her cheeks. A tweed jacket and skirt were not complimented by a pink blouse which was tied in a bow around the neck and her flat brown shoes failed to match with anything else that she wore. We introduced ourselves, I of course adhering to the title that the quick thinking Radford had given me, and we were led out of the reception area.

Radford turned and winked at the receptionist as we walked past her. "Not bad for a young 'un" he whispered so as to avoid the ear of the stern Mrs Sutton, "I like some of these goth girls: dark side, low self esteem, they let you do anything that you want to them."

He was like a dog on heat, and I wondered how he found time to investigate any crimes in between servicing his rampant libido. Even Mrs Sutton, with her too tight clothing stoutly buttoned for protection, would have been a target for him if she had provided him with the faintest encouragement. Fortunately for us all she provided little encouragement to anything and answered all of my questions with the enthusiasm of somebody who counts amongst their hobbies grass cutting and paint watching.

Her office was positioned a short way up the corridor and a prominent plaque on the door announced her as 'Dr Margarita Sutton, BSc MSc PhD.' There was a suit of armour positioned outside of her door, for no apparent reason other than to confuse the already confused residents, although the axe had had its head removed so that it looked as if the knight was holding a metallic pole.

The room was in darkness as we entered and when she flicked the light switch the strip light overhead spluttered and flashed so that the room alternated between darkness and light. She gave an exasperated sigh at this before climbing onto a wooden backed chair and banging the strip sharply at one end which brought the light back to its senses and at last, as she climbed down from the wooden chair and made her way to a large burgundy leather chair behind her desk, the room lay illuminated to us. There were two other chairs around the desk which we sat in without waiting to be invited. I sat in a leather coated seat, more basic than the one occupied by Margarita and which squeaked every time that I moved a centimetre or shifted my weight, and Radford sat upon the wooden chair that had been used as a step ladder. Two pictures were on opposite sides of the room, one a copy of a Canaletto landscape showing the Grand Canal bathed in sunshine and the other a photograph of Venice at night with the gondolas casting sinister shadows upon the water. A bookcase held weighty tomes on the matters of psychology and law and a large computer was perched upon her thick oak desk behind which she sat looking at us with expectation. I started the questioning:

"We are here to ask a few simple questions about Roisin, formerly one of your patients I believe. I can appreciate that you are a busy person, and so are we, so if you could answer my questions as quickly as possible then I'm sure that we would all be grateful."

"Roisin Galloway, you mean?"

"I'm sorry?" I replied as her question had taken me by surprise.

"Are you referring to Roisin Galloway, the lady who was killed in the car accident this week?"

I don't know why the name should have surprised me as it was what I had been expecting to hear. I regained my composure and answered:

"Yes, that's right: Roisin Galloway. Tell me what you know about her."

"Well, she is a bit of a mystery really. I understand that she was born in a rural community in the middle of Ireland in the early twenties. She said that she had one son, although we never saw him and have never been able to track him down, but that she became a bit of a pariah in her home town and so she and her husband immigrated to England. Her husband signed up to be an air raid warden during the war and, one night during the blitz upon the Sheffield steel works, he was killed by an incendiary bomb.

From what we can make out she then had to bring up her son on her own and it can't have been easy for her. She suffered a number of psychotic incidents throughout her life after this point, often manifesting itself in pyromaniac tendencies. While still a relatively young woman her mental health deteriorated to the point where she found it impossible to interact with other people and she would just sit by herself all day staring at photographs of her dead husband. I understand that it was her son himself, shortly after his twenty first birthday, who had Mrs Galloway sectioned. That was back in the Nineteen Sixties though, long before I came to Carhill of course."

"Before you were born, surely, Mrs Sutton" interjected Radford but to little effect as she continued to sit in her chair waiting for me to ask the next question.

"Have you got any photographs of Mrs Galloway?" I asked and she opened a brown cardboard file that was placed upon her desk. She thumbed through the first section of densely typed pages before passing me a selection of photographs that had been enlarged to A4 size. The first pictures were colour photographs of a sad and slender old woman aged at various points between sixty and eighty. What caught my eye most though was a photograph at the bottom of the collection: it was a black and white photograph of grainy quality showing a thin faced man wearing a flat cap which seemed twice as large as his head and a woollen suit. His piercing eyes seemed to look out of the photograph directly at me and next to him was a young woman, full of smiles, in a plain thin dress that seemed to contrast with her starkly black hair: this was the woman that I had seen crushed underneath the sports car. I threw the pictures onto the desk before Mrs Sutton and swallowed deeply in an effort to control the emotion that was swelling within me.

"She used to look at that picture all of the time, it was all that she wanted to do. Besides starting fires of course."

"And how long had she been here, in Carhill, for" I asked once I had mastered my feelings again.

"As I said: since the early Nineteen Sixties. Nearly forty years in all; she never left here."

"Never?"

"Never. Well, of course, I mean until this week. And see what happened to her then? We do provide a wonderful level of care here you know, Inspector Halle, some people just don't understand that."

"How did she come to be in Elsecar on that fateful day then?"

"I don't know I'm afraid. I really can't say. The funny thing is that, following the necessary assessments and rulings, she had been free to leave, or to come and go as she pleased, for the last three years. But she had never shown any inclination to do so."

"She was better then?"

"Well of course that depends on what you mean by 'better'. Many people experience episodes of mental illness throughout their life, some more extreme than others. There had certainly been a noticeable improvement in her health over the last ten years or so."

"And had she had many visitors over that period?"

"One or two, yes."

"Can you give me their names?"

"Confidentiality is everything in this line of work, Inspector Halle."

I had a theory in mind, but it was going to take a different angle to get the truth out of the hard faced woman sitting opposite me.

"Are all of the patients here in here on a long term basis, like Mrs Galloway was?"

"No, not at all. Some are here for brief periods: months, weeks or even days at a time. They come here when they sense that they may be close to a relapse: we have all of the latest treatment programmes here to enable them to return to their regular lives outside."

"And some of these patients may have been in touch with Roisin?"

"It's certainly possible; she was allowed to mix, to have association, more or less freely."

"And perhaps someone who first met Mrs Galloway ten years ago, when she was first allowed to mix with other patients, has recently been in touch with her again. Is that possible Dr Sutton?"

"It could be possible. Where is this leading? She was killed in a car accident wasn't she?"

"Killed by a car, yes, but they don't drive themselves. Tell me now, was a gentleman named Michael Dwyer ever a patient in this centre?"

Her eyes expanded noticeably at mention of that name but she regained her calmness to answer:

"You know that I can't answer that Inspector."

I stood up and thumped the desk which sent the brown file jumping to the floor and caused Radford to stop straightening his hair and look across at me. I was enjoying playing the role of a hard nosed detective but it was time to see how far I could go:

"What do you mean 'can't answer'? You will answer!" I shouted at her, "because if not then I will be back tomorrow and this time I won't be asking nice little questions about Roisin Galloway I will be asking questions about Mr Alderman that you might find harder to answer. Am I making myself clear Dr Sutton?"

The receptionist had sounded worried and cautious when she had mentioned this man and I had guessed that the centre had something to hide regarding his treatment. The gamble paid off and Margarita

answered in a hushed voice:
"Quite clear, yes. Mr Michael Dwyer was a patient for a short while here ten years ago. He hasn't been back since."
"Not even for a short visit? Not to see Roisin Galloway?"
"He did associate with Mrs Galloway ten years ago, they were friends if that's what you are implying, but he has not been back to Carhill since 1990. That's the truth, so if you have no further questions I would be grateful if you would leave me to my work now."
"Thank you, you've been very helpful." I held out my healthy hand but Dr Sutton made no attempt to take it and so I turned and exited, followed by Radford. On the way out I placed my left hand upon the gauntlet of the suit of armour and shook it vigorously: the knight didn't have any objection to this.
I was pleased to leave the dark and shadow filled building where your footsteps echoed behind you and the shouts of the patients could be heard resonating in the background. Roisin had lost her husband, her mind, her everything and had spent forty years in the institution before meeting her death underneath a sports car's crushing weight: that was another life that I was going to hold Dwyer accountable for.
As we were driving out of the grounds the peacock sauntered across our path again and we missed it by a matter of inches; it seemed to have a death wish and living there I could understand it. I turned to Detective Sergeant Radford who once more had his arm resting upon the window and was whistling as if he hadn't a care in the world:
"What do you think of that?"
"I think that I should have got a number from that little goth girl. Don't think that I didn't notice you get that nurses digits over at Barnsley – what's the world coming to when a four fingered freak like you, no offence, can get lucky and I can't?"
"No, what did you think of what Dr Sutton had to say?"
"I don't know. I wasn't listening; she was too constrained for my taste. Was it useful?"
"Yes, I think so. Very useful." The Doctor's information had been both useful and frustrating to be truthful but Radford didn't seem interested and so I ran the thoughts through my head as we drove in silence back to my house. That woman lying under the car had been Rosa's grandmother: she would have been unaware of her existence; it seemed to be a nice little family secret that the beloved nana was in a mental institution. Dwyer, a slave to nothing but his psychosis, had also been an infrequent visitor to Carhill and it was here that he met and befriended

Roisin, it seemed to be a trait of his to look out for his fellow Irish men and women who were down on their luck. When he later met Georgie, and fell in love with her for all that I know, he recognised the family connection and told her all about Roisin. Georgie had started visiting her grandmother, keeping the secret from her family, and somehow after her untimely death the ring that she had so cherished came to be in the possession of Roisin Galloway. How had the ring reached her and how had Roisin come to be carrying it twenty miles away in Elsecar on that fateful morning? She had been on her way to meet someone it seemed, but it was impossible to say who or why and the question taunted me as it hung in the air.

I was still deep in thought as I reached home but I was getting no nearer to an answer. Radford asked me if I wanted him to come in with me but Osbourne would be inside and I felt safe in that knowledge so I waved him off as he returned to his station. He seemed relieved to be heading back to his familiar world of assaults, petty thefts and minor menaces and to be leaving my mad world behind.

I patted the old familiar gate as I walked through it and breathed in the air deeply: it was good to be back. My only key had been given to Osbourne but trying the door I found that he had left it unlocked. I walked into the hallway and then into the living room but the heavy sound of footsteps indicated that he was upstairs. I climbed up the familiarly steep stairway and following the noise found Osbourne on his knees in my bedroom sifting through the debris that had fallen out of my previously upturned wardrobe and drawers.

"Saying a prayer, Osbourne?"

He turned around startled but then a smile returned to his face as he said: "I don't really believe in prayer Halle – I rely on myself to make things happen in my life. No, I was just tidying your house up a bit. I felt guilty about smashing it up last time so I thought that I should try and smarten it up again."

"Thanks, carry on, you're doing a good job."

It seemed that he had been thorough in this duty and the house already looked habitable once more.

"I've got something to tell you, Halle. I had a call from the chief, from Superintendent Pearson." A serious note had entered his voice.

"Go on" I said fearing the worst.

"His men have been trying to find Rosa. Her flat was empty and all of the doors were open. They can't find her anywhere."

I sat down upon the bed in dejection and placed my head into my hands, fingers on one side and a cast on the other. I had been doing all of this for Rosa, going through everything for Rosa, and I had to get her back. I felt a heavy hand pressing upon my left shoulder and looking up I saw the large but delicate face of Osbourne staring down at me.

"Why don't you give the chief a ring? He might have some more news?"

"Thanks, I will." Osbourne sent the Superintendent's number from his phone to mine and I stumbled down the stairs. I walked out of the door, it was easier to get a signal outside and I didn't want this call to cut out on me, and breathed in the cold night air that served to wake me from the dark thoughts that filled my heart.

The telephone was poised by my ear but before I could call a faint melody reached me. The sound was coming from my neighbour's house two doors away. It was guitar playing but of a better quality than any that I'd heard from him before. It was a plaintive and beautiful tune that I recognised instantly as 'Back To The Old House' by The Smiths: my favourite group and Rosa's favourite group too.

Suddenly the tune stopped with a crashing and discordant noise as if the guitar had been snatched from the player's hands and smashed upon the ground. I looked at the house and saw a gap in the curtains which were hastily pulled closed. I had managed only a fleeting glimpse into the room but the thudding heart within me confirmed that I had seen my long haired neighbour standing in front of Rosa Galloway.

Chapter Eighteen

I had left Rosa at her flat in a select suburb of Sheffield with instructions to wait by her phone for a call from Matt: the name meant nothing but it was the best way that I could think of to ensure that she stayed inside, which to my mind inferred safety, until I returned; I didn't know how long I was going to be gone and I couldn't have guessed what I was going to be put through.

My journey had taken me to Huddersfield, Lamara's old stamping ground, where I had met her cousin Vicky who had betrayed me by passing me to a drug dealer working for Dwyer. I had found myself incarcerated in a cell in a disused warehouse but managed to escape only to find myself arrested for a murder that I had nothing to do with. Superintendent Pearson, as honest as they come for a police officer and on a mission to bring Michael Dwyer to account, had arrived at the police station in timely fashion but I had found myself standing in the middle of a modern day duel. Take my word for it - that's not the best place to find yourself standing.

For all of that time the thought of Rosa had been gnawing away at the back of my mind, a dim shadow that haunted my consciousness. I had known that something was wrong with Rosa. Even when I found that I had lost a finger in the shooting my thoughts had soon turned back to Rosa Galloway, that kind and beautiful woman who had threatened to bring my heart back to life after its year long hibernation. And now, after returning home, I had glimpsed her through a hastily closed pair of curtains: she was only two doors away from me but still I didn't know how or why she had come to be there.

My mobile telephone was already in my hand and the number for Superintendent Pearson was on the screen just waiting to be dialled: I hit the button. When the by now familiar voice answered, in its stern formality, I whispered to him as if scared that my neighbour might hear my voice:

"Superintendent Pearson, it's Halle here – John Halle."

"Yes, I know who you are Halle. Is it about Rosa?"

"Well it is actually, yes."

"I am sorry that we haven't been able to locate her as yet, Mr Halle, but my men will find her soon, rest assured."

"Don't worry about it, I've found her myself. She's just down the street here, two doors away. Can you send some of your men over, I think that we need to pay a visit to my neighbour. I'm not normally one for dinner parties but I'm sure that he won't mind me dropping in on him."

"I'm on my way over, Halle."

"You're in Sheffield. Haven't you got anybody nearer?"

"No, I mean that I am on the way over. I was en route anyway so I will be there in four minutes."

Most people would have said five minutes, but I guess that accuracy was everything to the Superintendent. I crept back into the house and walked slowly and quietly up the stairs towards Osbourne, still harbouring a stupid supposition that if I made any sort of noise it would alert my neighbour and he would be able to escape, with Rosa, before we could apprehend him.

"Osbourne" I said with as soft a voice as I could muster, "I've found Rosa. Keep quiet and follow me."

He looked puzzled but closed the drawers, which he was still in the process of tidying in a most thorough fashion, and followed me out of the house and onto the still and quiet street. I pointed to the window where I had seen the two figures momentarily.

"That's where she is. I saw her with my neighbour just before he closed a gap in the curtains."

"How do you know it was her, Halle? You've been through a lot recently; the mind can play funny tricks."

"Don't you start going on about the mind, I've had enough of that for one night." I was thinking of my visit to the Carhill mental institution where I had found out the truth about the woman who I had seen underneath the sports car at the start of my crazy week, but Osbourne looked away tight lipped before speaking:

"All right, Halle, I believe you. If you say that it was her then it was her. But what are we going to do about it? Let's get in there now."

"Do you know what to expect in there, Osbourne? No, neither do I. And we've only got one pair of arms between us, don't forget. Don't forget – how could we forget? Anyway I've spoken to your boss, to Pearson, and he's on his way over so for now we watch and wait."

The temperature was dropping noticeably at the beginning of another dark winter night. I wished that the police authority had supplied me with an overcoat as well as the dark blue suit which I hugged at irregular intervals to keep myself warm. My watch had been returned to me at the hospital and placed upon me by Nurse Heather, (this had sent a brief thrill up my arm as I felt her fingers on my wrist) and now I found myself looking at the dial every ten seconds. At times it seemed that the thin golden hand was ticking backwards or had frozen. At the moment when I thought that the four minutes would be up I saw a police car heading towards me, with its light and siren switched off, and then pull to a halt gently by the gate that myself and Osbourne were standing in front of.

The driver of the vehicle, in the uniform of a police sergeant, stepped out first followed by the two passengers who had been sat in the rear of the vehicle. One, I was to discover, was a Detective Sergeant named Jackson and the other man, a thin specimen with glasses and a suit that looked two sizes two big for him so that he had to keep pushing the sleeves of the jacket back up his arm and hoisting the trousers around his waist, was a police authority technician whose job it would be to fit me with the surreptitious listening device ahead of that night's suicidal mission.

The driver walked briskly around the rear of the vehicle before opening the front passenger door. He stood there stiffly with his chin pointed in the air as Superintendent Pearson, immaculately dressed as ever with razor sharp creases running down the front of his trouser legs, climbed out and nodded at me and Osbourne in greeting.

Not a word was said but I pointed, with a hand that was tinged with orange and blue patches from the cold, to my neighbour's house whereby another nod from Pearson sent the police and detective sergeants into position at either side of the front door. The technician stood back as far as possible, seemingly more at home with his microscope than his fists; a nervous look flitted across his face and he chewed at his lips in a style which reminded me of a rodent.

The Superintendent himself marched up to the front entrance and gave two loud raps upon the wooden door. Before my neighbour had even had time to answer the door, or to think about laving from the rear of the building, Pearson stepped back and Jackson took his position at the front. He took a deep breath now and his nostrils flared as the chill was sucked deep into his lungs. Drawing his right foot back he kicked with all his force against the obstacle in front of him and his heavy black boot cracked against the wood just underneath the brass handle causing wooden splinters to shoot from the side of the door. The noise had been loud enough to attract the attention of the whole street and I could see lights being switched on in the front rooms of houses along the length of the road.

The door had been old and in need of some repair, it was already sagging and breached around its middle. The police sergeant, a steely eyed man with no trace of emotion upon his ebony face, took his well rehearsed turn now and facing sideways he swayed to his right, feet firmly planted upon the ground, before crashing his full body weight against the door left shoulder first. The door gave way completely at this charge and crashed to the floor of the living room, now open for all to see, with the policeman landing solidly upon it. Jackson clambered over his colleague and in his eagerness to get into the house he almost tripped over the police Sergeant's head as he raised himself from the floor. Regaining his balance he shouted 'Stop, Police!' in a voice that could have sent birds plummeting from the sky in obedience.

My neighbour, name still unknown to me at that time, had been living in that house so close to mine for more than two months prior to that night and although we were approximately the same age and had smiled pleasantly at each other upon sight I had never been into his house before. Following behind Pearson and Osbourne, with the technician still lagging dispiritedly behind, I decided that it was time to invite myself around.

The door was by now hanging askew from one lower hinge like a drawbridge and I climbed over it before entering the large living room which opened out onto the street. The room was brightly lit but the thick curtains across the window, in tandem with the darkness drifting in from outside through the open doorway, created a gloomy atmosphere within the room. The sickly sweet smell of marijuana seemed to seep from the walls themselves and there was a general feeling of disarray within the room where the floor was covered in scattered pieces of newspaper and a collection of ashtrays were filled to overflowing.

I had entered the house just in time to see my neighbour, who I had previously though of as an inoffensive and quiet man, brandishing his guitar as a weapon towards Detective Jackson. The front of the guitar was already smashed from the impact that I had heard in the street and two of the strings were snapped from the fret and hung loosely over the main body of the instrument. The long haired man did his best to look threatening, narrowing his eyes and curling his lips into an attempted snarl, but it was spectacularly unconvincing and as he continued to hold the guitar aloft with two hands Jackson grinned back at him with contempt. The guitar was brought down towards the detective's head but he parried it with both forearms crossed above him and the guitar splintered upon impact, snapping into two sections where the ash coloured body met the neck. A surprised look crossed the face of my neighbour then as he was charged by Jackson, with his head down in the fashion of a front row rugby player in a scrum, and pushed back into the wall which he then slid down with a thud, gasping for breath as he crashed onto the floor.

Rosa had been cowering in a corner when the house's front door had been so unceremoniously opened. My gaze had been engaged fully upon the one sided tussle between my neighbour and the detective sergeant and so I had not seen her presence in the shadows until she saw me and rushed towards me with her arms wide open. My heart leapt as I saw her and she wrapped her arms tightly around me pulling my body into hers. We rocked slowly together as if comforting each other and although I could hear a gentle and suppressed sobbing even I didn't know if it was coming from Rosa or coming from me. I pushed my face into the side of her neck, her head against mine, and filled my senses with the beautifully familiar smell of her scent as I stroked her hair reassuringly. We both looked up at the same time before disengaging and surveying the crowded room before us.

My neighbour was still curled up on the floor, I guess that rugby wasn't his game, but the police sergeant had now took up a position alongside him and by placing his arms underneath the man's armpits he raised him onto his feet before placing his hands into cuffs behind his back. The long haired man moved his head from side to side glaring at everybody who met his gaze but he made no attempt to escape or to resist his arrest. Superintendent Pearson mirrored him by standing before him with his hands behind his back too, before he asked:

"What's your name young sir?"

"I don't know."

"You don't know? That's rather unusual isn't it? No matter how much of that stuff you've been smoking here over the last ten weeks. It is ten weeks isn't it?"

Again there was silence; I guess that he didn't know the answer to that question either.

"Well then let me give you some help. I believe that I can enlighten you. Your name is Phil Tattershall, known as 'Busker Phil'. Am I right? No answer, so I can only assume that I am right. Well, people see a happy smiling face on you as you sit there in the streets playing your dross on that battered old guitar of yours. Nothing wrong with that is there?"

"There's nothing wrong with that at all. And you owe me a new guitar." He had broken his silence at last.

"I am afraid that my officer's arms were rather too tough when you smashed the instrument over them. I doubt, though, whether we could be held liable for the damage? And, anyway, you won't need a guitar where you're going to be heading." Sarcasm was proving to the Superintendent's forte.

"I don't know what you mean." He had reverted to his usual mantra.

"Oh, come on Phil, do try harder. You see, your busking wasn't very friendly at all really was it? When honest men and women came to give you their money your hidden accomplices would deftly pick their purse as they placed it back into their pockets. I hear that you were even a little partial to a bit of drug running on the side and a little bit of receiving and moving on of stolen goods. 'Phil the Fence' might have been a better name, eh? You would do anything to keep the boss happy wouldn't you?"

Another silence reigned as I and Rosa looked on and I caressed her shoulder where we stood. Pearson continued his questioning in the

340

friendly and conspiratorial voice that he had adopted but with enough of an undercurrent of anger and authority to keep Phil on edge:

"Silence again? Well, Phil, it seems that you were loyal to the boss and he has been loyal to you. You were just over a year into a four year sentence. You could have been out in five months anyway with a nice shiny tag around your ankle but you couldn't wait that long could you? As soon as they had moved you to that nice soft open prison at Wealdstone you simply walked out and there was even a chauffeur driven vehicle waiting to collect you. What did Dwyer need you for, Phil?"

"Dwyer, who's Dwyer?" he asked with mock incredulity but his voice lacked conviction which I found rather strange for an escaped convict. The Superintendent gave an exasperated sigh and turned his back on Busker Phil as if to signify that he had lost patience with the man.

"You really need to start helping yourself, Phil, you really do. You will be back in prison tomorrow, be assured of that, but it's up to us how hard things are for you. Sergeant, take over here."

"I'm not going to say anything about Dwyer, you know? I'm not stupid." This time there was a scared honesty in Phil's voice but the Superintendent gave a dismissive wave of his hand that signalled for Sergeant Jackson to take his place. The detective was all too willing to help out and stood directly in front Phil with a mean look upon his face that was held a matter of inches away from my neighbours visage which was all sickly pallor and straggled hair with scared eyes cast down to the floor. It wasn't hard to tell that the detective was in the mood for some old fashioned policing, where a gloved fist is more useful than a ballpoint pen in obtaining a confession, but he wasn't reckless enough to act while the Superintendent remained in the house and so he stood rock like and impassive before the trembling neighbour who I had known so little about.

Either the Superintendent wasn't aware of the undercurrent of his detective's demeanour or he was giving his tacit approval to it because he solved the problem by approaching Rosa and I with a smile on his face.

"Now, I am sure that you two have a lot to talk about but I'm rather afraid that I need to speak to you both as well. I think that your house just us up the street there, Mr Halle, may be better suited to us, don't you? There seems to be rather a draft in here. We can leave the busker in our Sergeant's more than capable hands."

With a sweeping gesture of his arms the Superintendent ushered us both out of the house before him and following behind were Osbourne and at the back as always was the technician. Busker Phil was left behind to face an unenviable session of questioning from the police and detective Sergeants. A crowd had gathered along the streets and many of my neighbours had stepped outside, risking the cold night air that was rapidly drawing in, to get a glimpse of the motley procession that passed before them. People who I had thought of as strangers shouted my name across the road and asked if I was alright and to all of their questions I simply answered 'everything's fine.' If I survived until the morning this was going to take some explaining away the next time that I visited the local shops.

Superintendent Pearson led the way, out of habit, into my house and as I followed after him, Rosa holding onto my left hand, I wished that I lived in a more salubrious location. It somehow seemed unfitting to find a man such as Pearson walking around a small terraced house with a look of bewilderment on his face. I had never felt that way before in my life, having been perfectly happy amongst my rented home's little nooks and crannies and its traditional design, but spending more than a few minutes at a time in the Superintendent's company brought out the hidden snob within me.

We congregated initially within my living room, the five of us stood around in crowded silence like sardines in a parlour game. Instinctively I felt like racing to the kitchen and making cups of tea for everyone but that would have to been to undermine the gravitas of the situation and I didn't feel like subjecting the present company to the powdered milk that I had stored away in a corner of my cupboard.

Pearson took charge with a number of orders, disguised as requests in his silken tones, and Osbourne was sent into the kitchen with Rosa to question how she had found herself at the house of Busker Phil whilst I was to remain in the living room with the Superintendent and the police technician. Brief smiles of encouragement passed between us, contained more in the eyes than the mouths, as she left the room and I hid the sense of resentment that I felt within me at the thought that Osbourne would get to question her before I did – that it was to another man that she would be pouring her heart out. Conversely, I had seen her looking with concerned surprise at my right hand which was encased in the lightweight plaster cast, and I was longing to tell Rosa what had happened to me. I wanted nothing more than to bask in a moment's glory as I recounted my bravery; I just hoped that there would be time for that later after the events of the night to come were over.

"So, what happens now?" I asked the Superintendent as I sat back into my favourite armchair, carefully holding my right hand aloft as I sunk into the chair's welcoming embrace.

"Wait there a moment, Mr Halle. I've brought something for you to look at." With these words the Superintendent wheeled around and walked out of the door, a chill blast of air making an unwelcome entrance into the room as the door was opened and then closed behind him. I looked up at the technician now and he averted his eyes nervously before my gaze. I motioned him to sit down upon my sofa and he obliged with a nod of his head, afterwards occupying himself by pulling up his trouser legs and the sleeves of his jacket as he fiddled nervously in the chair.

He was a man of few words and to break the silence I introduced myself and held my left hand out to him. He took it within his weak grip and the palm of his hand was wet and clammy upon mine. He introduced himself as Tim, a technical support officer for the South Yorkshire Police Authority. This seemed to be the limit to his conversational skills and he spent the awkward moments until the return of Superintendent Pearson staring at my living room carpet as if searching for spills and stains that he could analyse.

Pearson soon returned, accompanied by the icy draft that heralded his appearance, with a large plastic fronted case in one hand, this was now handed to Tim who had seemingly left it behind upon the back seat of the police car, and a leather embossed portfolio folder in the other. Pearson sat down at the far end of my settee, adjacent to the armchair which held me, and leaning across the arm he handed the portfolio across. He spoke to me in a whisper as if worried that Tim might hear, but the technician still seemed too engrossed in the carpet to take any interest in the Superintendent's words:

"I think that this file will be of interest to you, Halle. Thank you for bringing it to our attention, based upon the information that you have supplied to us I think that it could be very useful indeed."

I opened the folder up and found that it consisted of a number of sheets of paper that were each encased within their own individual plastic cover and then stitched into the leather folder itself. Some pages were official documents from the police authority or the crown court, many of which were marked with a 'Classified Information' stamp, and towards the back of the folder were extracts from newspapers that had been blown up so that each extract filled its own sheet of foolscap paper.

A cursory flick through the documents, which took me no more than a minute, was enough to convince me that this information would be very useful indeed. I raised my head and gave a nod of gratitude towards the Superintendent.

"Don't mention it Halle", he responded, "Have a look through it. It will take our TSO, I mean our Technical Support Officer here, around half an hour to get everything ready so please have a good rifle through the file. We won't interrupt you."

I saw now that Tim was removing a variety of miniscule gadgets, wires and leads from his case and arranging them in neat fashion alongside him. The Superintendent watched Tim at work as if allowing me an element of privacy to browse through the information that had been collected for me. I opened the file again and read through the pages in more detail now; some of the information was passed over after a brief glance but some of it seemed to jump out of the page at me as if shouting 'Eureka!'

The file was relating to the conviction of Freddy Chester in 1990 for a string of jewellery raids. From the information that I had been given by Tommy O'Callaghan, Chester had been a relatively small time criminal, a Fagin like figure coordinating a gang of beggars and conmen throughout Sheffield: jewellery raids seemed to be out of his league somehow. Tommy had also confirmed that he had been with Freddy on the day of the major raid for which he was convicted and yet he had pleaded guilty to the charge. If Freddy Chester had been taking a fall for somebody then it didn't take a great leap of the imagination to work out who the real culprit was.

The people who had been gathered in Court Number One of Leeds Crown Court had heard how a number of raids had been carried out on jewellers throughout West Yorkshire over a two year period. The raids had been meticulously planned and despite the large quantities that had been taken no witness had ever been found to testify against the gang. This had changed on April 28th 1990 when they had raided their most audacious target of all, Solomon's Gem Emporium of Leeds. This was no ordinary jeweller's shop – in fact it wasn't open to the general public at all. Solomon's catered for the jewellery trade only, and worked on special commissions from their infinitely wealthy clients; they would source the finest jewels to a customer's specification and anything could be found for the right price.

The raiders seemed to have been well informed on this day for the emporium had recently received a large consignment of gems from around the globe including some special articles of rare value that had arrived only two days previously and were soon to be delivered to their purchaser, an oil billionaire for whom money meant nothing but to whom beauty still had a value.

Mr Isaac Solomon and his wife Sarah had been woken during the early hours of the morning by a masked gang standing before their marital bed, all of them holding guns in their hands. At gunpoint the Solomons were impelled to drive the men to their emporium, unmarked from the outside but for a small plaque above the steel door, and unlock the doors and security gates. The gems were removed by the men and Mr and Mrs Solomon were left tied together back to back. In an act of spiteful cruelty one of the men, who had appeared to be the ringleader issuing silent commands to the other men through the movements of his hands, took a knife and made a deep slash across the right cheek of Mrs Solomon, a woman in her early sixties, and watched as her blood flowed quickly to the floor. With cut throat gestures he indicated that if they didn't keep quiet about the raid then his men would be back to silence them for ever. Many hours passed before the husband and wife were rescued by which time the armed gang had made a full escape. Mrs Solomon had lost a large amount of blood and was taken to St James' Hospital in Leeds but she was never to recover from the injury, aggravated by the shock of the ordeal, and died in her hospital bed three weeks later.

One of the features of the gang's previous raids had been their meticulous disarming of any security systems before the actual robbery took place. On the occasion of the Solomon robbery, I read, their luck ran out. Maybe they had allowed themselves to be distracted by the huge haul on offer but they missed a bank of security cameras and for the first time the police had images of the gang at work. Coupled with the information that the grieving Solomon had supplied them with, the police were confident that the net was at last closing around the jewel thieves. It was only a matter of time before they were finally caught, it seemed, but eventually Freddy Chester spared them any more trouble by coming forward and confessing to being the man who had organised the crimes.

There was no trial before jury as all of the men pleaded guilty at the first time of asking but when they were committed to court to be sentenced there was a media frenzy surrounding the case. There were discrepancies in the men's stories and it seemed as though the police, and the crown prosecution service, had to twist their evidence so that it fitted into the story that Chester and his gang had given them. Chester, the newspapers trumpeted, had committed many crimes using a variety of different aliases but nothing on this scale before.

The murder, or manslaughter, of Sarah Solomon had been gently pushed aside in the eagerness to secure a conviction as it could not be proven who had delivered the slash across her face that had condemned her to a deathly spiral. The judge, after a summing up to the media that left nobody in any doubt that the day marked a major victory over organised crime in the North of England, handed sentences ranging from four to seven years for the accomplices and a twelve year sentence for Freddy Chester which meant that he could not be considered for release until six years had passed. His nicely organised accident on the prison stairs ensured that he would never trouble the parole board.

"What happened to Mr Solomon?" I asked the Superintendent who stopped observing the actions of the technician and turned back towards me.

"He couldn't live in this country anymore. Whether from fear or disgust who knows? He lives in a luxurious house in Tel Aviv now."

"Israel? I wanted to speak to him."

"Well, there is a two hour time difference between us and them; it will be late at night now." I looked at the clock that ticked upon the mantelpiece, realigned by Osbourne earlier in the day, and saw that it was approaching ten o'clock. "What did you want to speak to him about?"

"What do you think that I want to speak to him about? The raid of course." I had spoken harshly to the Superintendent and I regretted it instantly but I just wanted to hear the aging jeweller confirm the theory that had implanted itself in my mind.

"Mr Halle, do you think that I got where I am today through luck? Or maybe you think that it's all down to nepotism, and that my Uncle George had previously been a Deputy Chief Inspector? He had, but that is by the by. I got to where I am today because I am a damn good detective. I know what you wanted to ask Mr Solomon because I wanted to ask it too. And that's why I spoke to him on the telephone one hour ago and why I was on my way to see you when you rang me this evening. He had retired for the night when I called but when I explained to his staff what I was ringing for then he was only too keen to help. It seems that he never believed that a yobbish and unworldly man like Chester could have been behind the raid, and the only desire that he has left in his life is to find out who was really responsible for his wife's death."

346

For the last hour my right hand had begun to ache now that the anaesthetic was wearing off and it seemed that the whole of my hand was itching underneath the plaster pot that encased it. Strangely enough it felt as if it was my little finger, most of which I knew to be missing, that was itching the most and I longed to reach my finger nails underneath the cast and scratch away until the compulsion disappeared. The Superintendent's words had produced a similar effect to this and as I looked at him with raised eyebrows all thoughts of the pain and irritation in my hand vanished.

"Go on", I responded, "Tell me what he said."

"Well most of the jewellery was never recovered, small individual pieces of various gemstones that vanished into the system never to be returned: even though its' collective value amounted to more than a hundred thousand pounds."

"Big money."

"To me and you, yes. But there was a bigger target here: you may have noticed that the newspaper coverage referred to the theft of special articles which had a rare value. The exact nature of these specimens was kept hidden, with the media's cooperation, so that they could instantly be traced if they ever came onto the market. They never did."

"That doesn't surprise me. Dwyer, obviously the man behind these raids, doesn't seem to be the kind of fool who would go straight out and sell the stolen pieces."

"Well yes, I admit that he is a clever man, that's how he has eluded us for so many years to the point where he is now a legitimate and respected member of society – with his eyes on parliament itself so I hear. So then, Mr Halle, as you are also a clever man what do you think these rare items consisted of?"

"Well I can't say that I'm an expert in the world of fine jewellery, Superintendent: I'm more of an Elizabeth Duke Cubic Zirconia man myself. But I expect that there were several gemstones of unusual size or clarity worth tens of thousands of pounds each."

"Tens of thousands of pounds each, eh? That much?" It seemed as if he was taunting me now, or at least revelling in being more knowledgeable than I was, but it's easy to be smart when you have the answer in front of you.

"And one item in particular that would be of interest to me", I continued, "I expect that there would be a large green emerald, perfectly green and perfectly costly."

"An emerald? That's what I expected too, Mr Halle. Possibly a

Colombian emerald, I understand that they are particularly prized amongst lovers of that gemstone. But no, there were no emeralds in the collection."

I was surprised at this news and it struck a sudden note of disappointment within my heart that had been racing. I had felt that I was getting closer and closer to the truth of the ring and the question of why it held such significance for Michael Dwyer.

"No, Mr Halle, there wasn't an emerald" Pearson continued with mounting excitement in his voice that had now ceased to whisper and which even diverted Tim away from his work momentarily, "but there was a large green diamond."

"A green diamond?" I asked with an incredulous pitch to my voice. As I have freely admitted I knew nothing about jewellery at the time but I think that many jewellery lovers would have been as surprised by the Superintendent's clarification as I was.

"Yes, that's right: a green diamond. Mr Solomon, one of the world's experts on this matter, explained it all to me. Diamonds don't just come in a clear form you know: they can also be found in blue, pink, black and orange varieties; these are all unusual variations and carry a marked increase in their premium to reflect this. In the trade they are called, with marvellous understatement, fancy diamonds. A very rare variety is the red diamond and the rarest variety of all is the green diamond. Most of the leading jewellers in the world, who spend every day of their lives dealing with the super wealthy, will never see a green diamond. Mr Solomon had a green diamond, one of the very few certified in existence, in his collection for a short period only. It was under the tightest security that could never have been penetrated until he was forced to hand it over at gunpoint."

"A green diamond? How much would that be worth then: A hundred thousand?"

"You're way off the mark, Halle. This one would have been practically priceless. In April 1987, exactly three years before the event that we are discussing now, a Swiss diamond dealer, a personal friend of Mr Solomon, purchased a red diamond known as The Hancock Red Diamond weighing 0.95 carats, approximately the same weight as the green diamond that holds our interest, for just under a million US dollars. The green diamond was rarer still, and a perfect specimen, and would have been worth considerably more although Mr Solomon won't give an exact value. It cost him his wife, and that to him is worth more than the money that he lost."

So Dwyer himself had led the meticulously planned raid to steal this invaluably rare gem and then, with no hope of ever being able to sell it on, he had placed it within a gold ring with a snake like band running underneath it as a present for his girlfriend: that must be what they call love I supposed but it had never struck me in that way, and when love gripped Dwyer it seemed to be a destructive and deadly force.

I flicked through the folder again, just watching the pictures pass in a blur as my mind dwelt on different things, when the final newspaper cutting in the folder caught my eye. It related the story of Freddy Chester's death, found dead at the bottom of a stairwell in Armley Prison. Well he was no loss to anybody was my immediate thought before I remembered that everybody is somebody's son or somebody's father. The story dwelt on the human side of Freddy Chester, who had been born in Chester itself by a strange coincidence. He had left a wife and two sons behind. The photograph which accompanied the story was a black and white picture and was old at the time but it showed Freddy and his two sons standing side by side with their fists clenched in front of them in a classic boxing pose. His children, who although unnamed in the story would have been in their early teens at the time, were already as tall as their broad and muscular father and they looked like young fair haired gladiators in the making alongside him. I closed the folder with a thud and handed it back to the Superintendent. I had seen everything that I needed to see.

The bugging device was ready to be fitted now and Tim and the Superintendent helped to strip me from the waist upwards before taping the small appliance around my chest with the device itself aligned against my left ribcage sending a faint pulse running up and down the edge of my body from time to time. Once my shirt and jacket had been put on again the device was completely hidden and completely silent and I felt safe in the knowledge that its presence would not be detected.

Rosa and Osbourne came back into the living room and she took her place by my side seating herself atop of the chair's arm next to where I had positioned myself. Osbourne informed the Superintendent that he had finished his interview with Rosa and he would debrief him at the station. Perhaps he would need to speak to me too at a later time.

We all stood up then as if knowing that our work at the house was done. Superintendent Pearson gave brief instructions to me and Rosa: he had arranged for an unmarked car to be positioned further up the street. Rosa would drive this car, with me as the passenger, to the allotted meeting point of Shelby's Shack. When we got there, I was to play hard ball and demand to speak to the most senior person present; I was to tell them that I had the ring securely hidden and that I would only hand it over to Dwyer himself. If they were unwilling to cooperate I was to call it Solomon's ring and that should be enough to get Dwyer's personal interest. Once I met him I was to engage him in conversation until he admitted being behind the theft of the ring, and his role in the long list of crimes that he oversaw. The downsides to this of course were that I had no idea where the ring actually was at that moment and in Dwyer I was dealing with a psychotic and sadistic killer. Pearson assured me that he would be listening to every word that was said and that they would ensure that I was safe at all times, although he failed to give me any specific details as to how they would do this. I gave Rosa a squeeze of her hand and then I was ready to go: looking death in the face had become a regular night's entertainment to me.

The five of us left the house together: me, Rosa, Osbourne, Superintendent Pearson and the technical support officer. I locked the door behind me crossing myself uncharacteristically as I passed the threshold. I was unsure of whether I would ever cross that beautifully familiar doorway again; I rated my chances of survival at evens but it was too late to back out now and my steps carried me along the street as if independent of my mind like a man walking to the gallows.

My long haired neighbour, who had seemed dully enigmatic before but was now the exciting mystery known as Busker Phil, was being escorted out of his house and loaded into a police car. His lips were tightly sealed and this was the way that he planned to keep them throughout any interrogation; he already had a bruise appearing on his left temple which could have been caused when he banged his head against the wall on his way to the floor. It could have been caused by a lot of things.

I shook hands with Pearson and I could see him mouthing words of encouragement although I wasn't listening to these words which washed so ineffectually over me. To Osbourne I simply nodded my head which he acknowledged in like fashion as if we both knew that we would be seeing each other again.

The Superintendent had pointed out the car to Rosa and had handed her the keys. It was a Fiat Panda in a sludgy brown colour and was hers for strictly one night only – this went without saying because it was hard to imagine who would want such a car for more than twenty four hours. It was parked just a few house lengths away and we walked to the vehicle without saying a word, both of our minds focussed on the night ahead and on the events of the past day. Glancing at Rosa I saw the steely determination etched upon her face that mirrored my own desire to see this matter finished once and for all.

We waited until we were in the car before we spoke to each other and it was a surprise to me to realise that these were the first words that we had spoken to each other that evening, having passed our time in my house by passing silent communications between us through our eyes and our hands and the invisible connection that bound us.

We broke the nervy silence by discussing how pathetic a specimen of car had been provided for us, a bucket of rust that could go from nought to ten in sixty seconds. The car sounded a screech of protest every time that Rosa shifted gear as if in acknowledgement of its ineptitude.

With the ice broken it was time for Rosa to tell me the story that she had already passed on to Osbourne of how she had come to find herself at Phil's house:

After I had left her in Hoyland she had followed my instructions and returned home to Sheffield to await a call from a man called Matt Sinclair – it didn't seem like the right time to point out that I had made the name up and so I let her continue her story. Shortly after returning to the house, and waiting for the phone to ring at every moment, she had heard a knock upon the door. She had remembered my instruction to remain in the house at all costs but a voice reassured her that it was Phil, John's neighbour, and that I had sent him to fetch her.

Opening the door she had recognised the long haired man, gentle in speech and bearing, who had spoken to her before and had provided her with a key to my house. Phil explained to her that I, not being a driver myself, had sent his good friend and neighbour to return her to Barnsley as I had now managed to resolve everything. The story had seemed plausible to her, I admit myself that it was reasonably believable, and so she had climbed willingly into his car.

The journey back to my home village had been passed in cheery small talk where Phil discussed everything from his political beliefs, surprisingly to the right of centre, to his favourite vegetarian recipes. Rosa had found reassurance in the familiar route that they had taken but found it strange when Phil insisted that I was waiting at his house rather than my own which was positioned just two doors further down the street.

Her sense of apprehension grew when Phil locked his door behind her and she found that the house had been empty prior to their arrival. His mood changed at once as he had pushed Rosa roughly into a chair.

She quickly assured me that this was the only time that he had manhandled her although he had threatened her on many occasions when he had thought her to be uncooperative. Phil had asked her many questions about her relationship with me and about a ring that he insisted I had stolen from his boss. It had been hard to follow his exact words because every second one that he used was a four lettered oath but Rosa, using her subtle charms, had managed to get him to reveal more about himself than he would have liked. From the description that she had forced out of him she had become convinced that the ring was the one that had been designed by her sister so many years before, but yet she had steadfastly kept any knowledge of this ring secret from Phil. It had been his plan to hold Rosa hostage until I returned that ring to the unknown figure who had been issuing Phil with his commands. Rosa had then whiled away the time nervously plucking away at Phil's acoustic guitar before he had smashed it in irritation just before our unexpected arrival.

She removed her hand from the gearstick now and went to grasp mine in gratitude but pulled away upon remembrance that my right hand was now encased in plaster.

"I'm sorry, I've been ignorant – I should have asked before. Your hand, is it broken John?"

"Broken? No, I don't believe so – although it might be actually for all I know. It's my finger really, it's gone." Finding no brave words which would couch my loss in golden tones I had resorted to my usual level of comedic pathos as if to underplay the whole thing.

"Gone? How can it just be gone?"

"It was shot off. Yes, I know that sounds incredible but believe me it was a long, long night. Try not to worry about it Rosa, when I was a young lad my local butcher lost a finger and he was alright – the sales of his sausages never recovered though."

"Some things aren't funny John."

"No, you're right Rosa" I admitted with resignation, "some things are deadly serious. But maybe I just want to go to the grave laughing. Look, in truth it's all been a terrible ordeal and I do promise that I will give you a full explanation later God willing; but for now I can't allow myself to dwell on it too much, does that make any sense? If I really faced up to what had happened, and what may be about to happen, then there is no way that I'd be able to go through with this game tonight."

"But it's not a game."

"I know that it's not a game, I know. But can't we just pretend?"

"Okay, John, we'll pretend. And when this is all over there are going to be no more games for us, okay?" She had given up trying to grasp my hand and instead stroked the back of my neck lovingly. It was the sort of touch that made me want to carry on living, which made me prepared to fight. I had always loved poetry and counted Marvell, that master of Metaphysics, as one of my favourite writers but when I felt her fingers on my neck it was impossible for me not to recall his couplet with a shudder:

"The grave's a fine and pretty place, But none, I think, do there embrace."

"Stop here a moment! I need to get something." Rosa executed my command without question and brought her car to a halt, accompanied by a screech of the brakes, outside of the petrol station with its late night convenience store that had come in useful to me for packets of crisps and assorted snacks on many a late night walk home.

I walked into the store ignoring the gang of identikit youths who had gathered outside wearing matching baseball caps and jeans with the crotch swaying just above their knees; they were throwing stones at a ragged looking cat that was cowering in a nearby doorway. The convenience store was almost empty at the end of a long day and the only food that was left were two ploughman's sandwiches and various chocolate bars with an extortionate mark up. I looked around the store before I found what I was looking for: bunches of flowers that were gathered in a large black bucket filled with dingy looking water. I selected the two bunches which looked the least pitiful and whose foliage showed the fewest signs of fatigued discolouration. I handed my money over to a bored looking woman who displayed a mouthful of half masticated gum when she spoke and then I carried the flowers back to Rosa's car.

At this point I should admit that I know absolutely nothing about flowers: I like them but I know nothing about them. One flower looks pretty similar to another to me. The labels on the two bouquets stated that they were mixed chrysanthemums, one bundle being predominantly yellow and the other being a mixture of white and purple flowers. It was time to take a punt: having the opened the door I handed the yellow flowers to Rosa before settling the other bouquet upon my lap and shutting the door behind me.

"Those are for you" I said as I watched Rosa's eyes widen and a smile broaden across her face until the edges of her lips were lost within her reddening cheeks. It had helped her to forget, if only for a fleeting moment of normality, what had brought us here and what lay ahead; I chalked it up as three pounds ninety nine well spent.

"How did you know that I liked yellow chrysanthemums so much, John? Honestly, I tell you – they're my favourite flowers."

"How did I know? I'm a man, I know everything." And I have a good record when it comes to guessing on a one in two chance, but I let those words linger unspoken in the air.

"Who is the other bunch for then?" There was no hint of jealousy in her voice just an honest curiosity. This struck me as a disappointment and if my heart hadn't been so heavy at that moment I would have undoubtedly tried to foster some of the green eyed monster's trait.

"I've got one more call to make, Rosa. Just one more call and then it's all over: then I can do what I've got to do."

"We've not got much time" she answered without looking at her watch. I looked at mine out of habit although it would have made no difference if the dial had said five past eleven, which in truth it did, or five to twelve.

"Well then we'll have to make time. I've been putting off visiting somebody for a while, and it's long overdue now."

"How long overdue?"

"About a year."

Rosa seemed to understand then and without me needing to issue any more instructions she drove the car onwards towards the cemetery which rested alongside St Peter's church.

"Do you want me to come in with you?" she asked after pulling the four wheeled pile of rust to a halt outside of the main cemetery gates that I'd vaulted in desperation earlier that week.

"No but thanks for asking. This is something that I've got to do on my own. Keep your eyes open and if you see anything suspicious, anything at all, then keep pressing the horn."

"Will I see anything suspicious? Do you think that there'll be any trouble?"

"No, don't worry about it. It was just a contingency plan that's all. By now whoever wants me should be waiting for me down the road at Shelby's Shack - they aren't going to waste their time here."

I took the bouquet and shut the door behind me but had only walked a handful of yards before I had to turn back. Reaching Rosa's door I motioned with my head for her to wind the driver's window down which she did with the aid of the grey plastic handle that had lost the circular head that should have crowned it.

"I forgot to say something Rosa. I don't know how I forgot, but I did. I just wanted you to know how much you mean to me – how much it all means: everything that you've done for me. If I never get the chance to speak to you like this again I want you to know – I just want you to know -" My words choked into silence as I struggled to swallow the sobs that were rising through me with an unstoppable force. She silenced me by leaning through the window and placing her lips upon mine. As we kissed, the salty tears formed a stream down the ragged contours of my face and melted upon the red painted outline of her upturned mouth.

I pulled my lips from hers with a triumph of my will over my heart and the smile that I gave as I turned away failed to hide the tears that ran ceaselessly down my cheeks. I didn't dare to look back at the car again but instead strode out with long quick paces towards the centre ground of the cemetery, twisting and turning the bunch of flowers in my hand all of the while.

My mind regressed to the vision of Lamara that had so recently haunted me. Bring something for me, she had begged, why don't you ever bring me anything? In Judaism people leave little stones on the sides of graves so that the departed spirit can look down and see that somebody has remembered them. It had been over a year and what had I brought Lamara, the woman who had been the whole of my life for so many years? I had brought her nothing; it had been as much as I could do to show at her funeral. It struck me that by this time tomorrow they could be organising my funeral, it was time to sort everything out while I still could.

Walking on instinct with the sobs turning my vision into a half sighted blur I soon found myself at Lamara's graveside again. I looked around and this time there was nobody else to be seen, no hidden creatures lurking on the edge of the blackness. It was uncommonly peaceful as I wiped my eyes on the back of my uncovered hand and then used the sleeve of my suit to wipe away the snot that had formed beneath my nose. The flowers were beautiful but how could anything else in nature, with all her splendidly bountiful treasures, match the skin, the scent, the unmatchable perfection that I had seen in Lamara Gallagher when my eyes first saw her walk through those doors that I had hastily pulled open for her?

I placed the bouquet carefully onto the gravel at the front of her memorial. To my mind Lamara had killed herself with her lifestyle, her narcissistic and self destructive choices; I had never forgiven her. But the last few days had taught me about death – had taught me that things aren't always what they seem. It was the first time that I had considered that maybe, just maybe, the death of Lamara Gallagher hadn't been as straight forward as it had seemed.

I dropped to my knees and knelt forward so that my head fell upon the floor and my left ear rested upon the cold headstone. "I forgive you Lamara, God knows I forgive you." I spoke it aloud to the elements through the loud sobs that wracked my body and shook my back up and down in spasms of sorrow.

I felt a hand upon my face, just as I had at the house of Madame Irina, and it was as if fingers were pawing at my cheek like plasticine. With my eyes open wide I saw that there was nobody there but still I felt those gentle and caressing fingers moving my head and turning it forty five degrees to the left before holding it in place. My head was frozen then as if held tightly by an unseen hand; I let my gaze settle where it was being directed and a moonbeam falling through the clear and cold night sky seemed to hit something before reflecting back into my eye. As if unable to do anything else, spellbound and moonstruck, I crawled forward like an animal on my hands and knees oblivious to the frost covered mud beneath me. I crawled forward faster and faster as I neared the object that lay just beyond Lamara's grave. I was upon it now and my fingers tore greedily at the soil around it and which covered all but the brief fragment that had captured the moon's ray. The soil gathered in little mounds on either side as I pulled and pushed it away and then at last I grasped the object itself and brushed off the mud that had collected upon it.

It was still warm to the touch as I held it up to the moonlight and looked with awe upon that green diamond ring with the golden snake entwined below it.

Chapter Nineteen

I lay back on the cold grassy surface staring up at the round, almost full, moon that seemed to be leering down at me from the blackly clear heavens. My tears had finally stopped as I was overcome by another emotion, a jubilant relief, which could have sent me into uncontrollable peals of laughter if I had let it. I felt like shouting out at the top of my voice but there was nobody to hear me except the long silent gravestones and Rosa who sat with patient expectation in the battered old car beyond the gates to the cemetery.

I held the ring in front of my eyes moving it backwards and forwards in my left hand, smoothing away the last muddy residues as I did so, mesmerised as it caught the rays of the moonlight above. So this was it, this was the stuff that dreams were made of and the thing that had come to be a nightmare to so many. A large green diamond mounted atop a solid gold band, designed to look like a banded snake, which was positioned underneath the stone in the shape of an X representing a kiss and the bond that had been made between Dwyer and Georgie Galloway. It was more beautiful than ever now, ten years after the exquisitely rare diamond had been stolen and fashioned into its present form, and it captivated my eyes completely so that I could have spent happy hours just watching the moon beams' dim light reflecting off of the ring's flawless surface. The gold and green in tandem tantalised the eyes and captured the heart but then, as I continued to twirl the ring before me, it was as though it took on a completely reddened hue to show that it had been forged with blood.

I knew that the ring was worth at least a million pounds cash, and probably considerably more after the passing of the years, but I also knew the terrible price that the ring had cost in human life. The first to feel the rings deadly provenance was the wife of the jeweller Solomon: her death shortly after the carefully planned raid that had snatched the stone had sealed the rings fate forever – it was destined to lure people to death with its beauty. Georgie, for whom the ring had been shaped to fulfil her innocent childhood dream, had been killed and was now crying out to me for vengeance; Freddy Chester had taken the rap for the theft but then been killed within the prison walls when he had failed to keep his mouth shut; Poor Tommy O'Callaghan, once Dwyer's favourite aide, had been disposed of when he had outlived his usefulness and in a belated attempt to stop him passing information to me; Roisin Galloway, a harmless old woman who had been devastated by mental illness throughout most of her life, had been killed in a supposed road accident whilst clutching the ring within her wrinkled hands.

Who would be next to feel the poisonous bite of that banded snake: the kiss of death? As I twisted it rhythmically above my eyes I knew that it held one more victim deep within the dark green stone: either myself or Michael Dwyer would not live to gaze upon the ring again. Mental exhaustion gathered atop of the physical pain that had been welling up inside of me during the course of the week; I closed my eyes and tried not to think about the dead people that surrounded me as if willing me to join their massed ranks.

Sleep was to be denied me once more as I felt a slapping motion against my knees and shins. I opened my eyes with a sigh as if disappointed to be dragged back to reality and I saw a familiar pair of hands sweeping the mud away from the knees of my trousers that had become wet and soiled from my desperate crawl towards the ring. I smiled at her and her full lips smiled back before breaking into a grin that revealed that gap toothed smile which had cast its unbreakable spell on me so many years before.

"What am I ever going to do with you, John? I thought that you would have learnt to look after yourself by now?"

It was the usual playful chastisement that I had grown to know and love during the happier times that I had spent with Lamara. I wasn't surprised to see her here, or to feel the touch of her gloved hands upon me as physically real as they had been when she had placed her hand upon me at Madame Irina's house; I knew now that there are some bonds that the grave cannot destroy.

"Well, Lamara, my beautiful little darling Lamara, I've tried my hardest. But you know us boys – we love to play around in the mud."

She smiled again and clasped my good hand within both of hers before pulling me to my feet with a force that was as alive as you or I. She held it within one of her hands, encased within a brown suede glove, and we retraced my steps back to her graveside. Picking up my flowers she lifted them up to her face and closed her eyes as she inhaled deeply, smiling as the pollen tickled her nose. She looked as beautiful as she had ever looked and wore a long white coat trimmed with a white fur effect collar that cradled her neck and tight blue jeans were on top of black leather boots with a pronounced heel. I had paid for them all, remembered the individual shopping trips that had seen me buy them: I had paid for so many things in our years together but none had seemed to please her as much as the flowers that she held so lovingly on that day more than a year after I had found her lying dead in my front room.

"I hope that you like the flowers? It's all that I could get, it's a bit late you see?"

"A bit late? You could say that, John. Around a year too late in my opinion."

It hit home. "I'm sorry. I couldn't face it. I just couldn't." The tears surfaced once again and I stifled sobs as I struggled to get out words in a jumbled fashion, leaving this remnant of Lamara to put them back together again: "Couldn't talk. No pictures. Nothing. Never mentioned. Couldn't visit. Couldn't move." Each staccato statement was punctuated by a deep intake of breath and a wretched sob that had lain hidden at the depth of my cold heart.

She held me tight so that my chest pressed against her full pleasing breasts and with one arm she pressed my body next to hers whilst with the other she cradled my head and wiped away the sly tears that betrayed me.

"Shush, shh, shh. It's okay, John, it's okay. I understand, I understand it all. But you were wrong to judge me like you did; I always wanted to be with you."

"I know" I said through my subsiding sobs.

"Do you, John? Well do you know how I came to be at your house on that day? Do you know that? Of course you don't, but you are getting very close to the truth and I know that you will have found the answers soon – one way or another. And then I want you to bring me flowers regularly, John. Do you hear me?"

"I promise that I will, Lamara." She placed the flowers back onto the memorial and took one last smiling look at them before turning and leading me away from the graveside. "I promise that I will bring you flowers, the most beautiful that I can find, if I survive long enough to bring them to you."

"You have got to keep fighting, John. When you stop fighting, then you may as well be dead already. This is what you were put here to do, John. You have been given a talent, you can see what other people can't, talk to people that others can't hear, you can feel the touch of people, spirits like me, that to others in your world are merely a whisper heard in the middle of the night or a brush of thread across the face as they walk down the street. Don't give this up lightly, John – you have to do what you were sent here to do."

I didn't know what it was that I had been sent here to do, or who had sent me, but I did know that if I was going to go out, if I was going to be another victim of that ring, then I was going to put up one hell of a struggle in the process.

"It's all about this ring, it seems, Lamara – it's all about this ring. Have you seen it before?" I removed it from my pocket and held it up to Lamara's eyes.

"Of course I've seen it before: it was me that removed it from your house that night. It's still our house in my eyes, John. I could see what danger you were in and so I spirited it away. Didn't I tell you that I had something for you if you brought something for me?"

"But what was the connection between you and Georgie then? Was it the ring?"

"No, no. It wasn't the ring at all. I hadn't seen it until you had. But it was the connection between me and Georgie that brought it to my attention."

"So what was this connection then? The one between you and Georgie?"

"Well let's see if we can work it out shall we?"

My attention had been fully focussed upon Lamara's bewitchingly beautiful face as I let myself be led by the hand away from her grave. I looked around now and was surprised to see that we were no longer by the graveside; we were not even outside. We were in a large room, as in a nightclub, and streamers hung from a ceiling with garlands collected in loops across the air. The music, coming from a DJ booth, was loud but was almost drowned out by the incessant chatter from the happy looking crowd of people that floated around us.

"Where are we?" I asked Lamara and after all that I had been through it was this sudden relocation which was the hardest for me to accept.

"We are in The BP. The Blue Parrot to give it its full name: Barnsley's premier nightclub, which isn't saying much. It looks like we got here just in time, John my love, it's their Christmas Party for 1990."

The hall was crowded but not by the normal mixture of youthful party goers that I would have expected to see at a nightclub's Christmas party. There were some younger people there, a smattering of people in their late teens and twenties, but the majority of the revellers seemed to be smartly dressed people in their thirties, forties and older. Most of the younger people that were here seemed to be attractive young women, some stylishly coquettish and some who were vulgarly painted into the tightest and smallest outfits that could withstand the nights rigours, who were to be found on the arms of thickset men with pronounced foreheads, extravagant tans and noses that were more misshapen than mine. If it was a fancy dress event then the theme seemed to be 'gold' as the men were dripping in it even more than the women and ostentation was the order of the night so that I felt ridiculously underdressed in my police issue suit and mud smeared plaster cast.

"Well this is some Christmas Party – it seems to have attracted all of the bright young things."

"You'll never lose that sarcasm will you? It's not your most winning trait. This isn't a public Christmas Party: it's by special invitation only – for the staff and friends of the proprietor."

One of those friends, or possibly one of the staff members, nearly reversed into me with a cocktail glass in one hand, inside of which was a green liquid and a golden umbrella, and a tiny sausage skewered upon a stick in the other hand. He moved one leg to the left and then took a larger step to the right before shaking his hips from side to side: he was doing The Timewarp in accompaniment to the music that had a large number of people dancing rapturously around us. I moved out of the way just before he fell over my foot and my shoulder brushed against his so that I said sorry out of habit.

"No need to apologise to him, John. He can't see us. None of them can see us."

"They can't see us?" I repeated for clarification.

"Of course not, we were never here– we only seem to be here because this is what you are supposed to do. You are here for a purpose, don't you get that yet? Just watch and see."

"And what about that fellow I just bumped against?"

"What about him? He didn't notice anything and if it does what will he think of it? It will just be another of those occasions where we bump into someone, or something, and we turn around and to our surprise there's nothing there. Or like one of those times when we are sure that we have seen something, or placed it somewhere, and when we come back for it it's no longer there. When people can't find a rationale explanation for something they just ignore it or they pretend that it never happened."

I didn't feel comfortable being the source of people bumping into unknown objects and so I moved carefully across the dance floor and stood with my back against a wall that thudded and vibrated in time with the bass line of the familiar old party tunes that were being played by the disc jockey. He was a man who seemed to be in a timewarp of his own, even allowing for it being 1990, with his white shirt open to his navel and dark sunglasses across his eyes so that he had to hold every record an inch away from his face in order that he could read the label.

Looking around the room I took in the revellers who were in various stages of inebriation but seemed to be having a universally good time: how many sorrows would those people know, how many frustrations and tragedies would befall them between that happy day at the end of 1990 and that day in early 2001 when I had found the ring by the graveside of Lamara Gallagher?

Lamara, who had crossed to my side again now, saw me looking around the crowded floor.

"Who are you looking for, John?"

"Oh, nobody in particular. I like to people watch as you know."

"Nobody in particular, eh? Well there are a few people here who might

361

be quite familiar to you by now."

"Are there? I haven't seen anybody."

She pointed the people out to me one by one, all of them appearing vaguely familiar although the passage of years had been kinder to some than to others.

Two men were in conversation with each other: one a small and bulky man who was sweating underneath the lights and with a scar across his cheek and the other was a taller man with a head that was completely shaved except for a pig tail of hair that hung from the base of his head. It was easy to recognise Perrin, presumably in the days before he became a sergeant at Dwyer's behest, but it was harder to recognise my secretive neighbour Busker Phil without his long hair until Lamara moved me closer to the men and I inspected his face from close range, all the while feeling strangely uncomfortable although I knew that I remained invisible to his sight.

Perrin seemed to be keeping a close eye upon a younger group of people who congregated around him, Phil being one of them, and it seemed that he was a Fagin figure to this rag tag army which seemed incongruously out of place amongst the more elegant party goers. He would bark instructions at them telling them not to rummage through the buffet with their fingers or to put down items that they dangled dangerously in front of them. From these instructions, and marked by the solid looking gold chain which hung around his neck, it seemed that he had stepped into the shoes vacated earlier in that year by Freddy Chester.

There was a raised area that looked down upon the dance floor and was cordoned off by a mauve coloured rope to show that it was reserved for VIP guests only. Stationed at the side of this rope was a young looking Thomas O'Callaghan – his youthful looks matching the mugshot contained within the Star newspaper's report into the discovery of Georgie Galloway's body that was to occur just a few weeks after this party had taken place. His face looked familiar, although less worn and haggard than it had been when I had last seen him, but his clothing was completely different. He had been dressed for the occasion by Dwyer and wore an as new black evening suit with the wings of his collar turned up to reveal a black satin bow tie. A white triangle of cardboard jutted out of his breast pocket in imitation of a handkerchief. It was his job to scrutinise the passes that people showed to him before he would remove the rope and usher them into the guest area with a subservient smile and a half bow. He looked clean, respectable, contented, happy, almost handsome: all of the things that nobody would have associated with Poor

Tommy in 2001; he was cheerily oblivious to the fact that the crooked policeman who stood nearby with the heavy golden chain and the youthful gang that he had recently graduated from would one day, just over ten years in the future, shoot him dead in a squalid hidey hole. I was pleased that these things remained unknown to him, happy that this man who deep down had a good heart, or at least a human heart, had enjoyed some moments of happiness in his tragically pathetic life. For we all have a life stretching out ahead of us and how many of us if we could see one year, ten years, thirty years into our own future would still spend our days with happy smiles upon our faces?

Lamara held onto my hand as she stepped across the rope one leg at a time. I followed her lead and strode across the rope in front of Tommy O'Callaghan who stared blankly through me. It was a relief to step into the VIP area as it had a more relaxed atmosphere than the rampant enthusiasm of the main dancefloor. The music, which still consisted of a mixture of party favourites and Christmas anthems and was at that moment playing Wig Wam Bam, was more subdued and the gentle murmur of conversation could be heard as a pleasant backdrop. It was a soiree where the assembled guests were discussing how their business had fared in the last twelve months – the difference being that for most of these guests their business was death and misery in one form or another.

Some of these special guests were standing and swaying gently to the music while smiling sweetly at the dreadful jokes that they regaled one another with; others had positioned themselves upon purple leather sofas with golden supports and their bodies sunk into the soft leather as they luxuriated in their nouveau riche ease.

Lamara pointed at two more of the guests now, both insignificant looking men with bags under their eyes and ties that were too wide at the neck and too short at the front, but they remained unfamiliar to me until she explained to me that they were members of parliament who had gone on to be leading lights in their respective political parties and on whom Dwyer had exerted a growing influence upon over the years which were to follow.

Staff flowed through this crowd within a crowd each carrying golden trays with champagne flutes and whisky tumblers upon them. The women were served by bronzed young men in tight fitting uniforms and the male VIP's were served by young waitresses, with permanent smiles and the patience of saints, in short black outfits with sheer stockings that glistened as they caught the lights reflecting down from overhead.

Following the direction of Lamara's glance I looked to the very back of the nightclub's cordoned off upper level and saw a man, with a woman by his side, holding court to a group of fawning acolytes who were hanging on to his every word grimly determined to nod and smile and laugh at the correct places.

The woman was of course well known to me by now but she looked older and more elegant than on our brief meetings. It was Georgie Galloway, still vibrant and full of life although the clock was ticking away unknown above her head, and she was wearing a long flowing dress of interweaving shades of lemon and lime that came to a halt just above her ankles at the front and brushed the ground behind her: everybody was being extraordinarily careful not to step onto the little train that her dress left. The sleeveless dress emphasised the pale beauty of her arms and she exaggerated her porcelain magnificence by the gentle pastels of the make up that she wore. A gold choker was across her elegant throat and golden bangles were collected across both of her wrists. The ear rings that she wore sparkled with the fire of the large diamonds that adorned them but she wore no rings upon her fingers. She stopped walking around the table now, which was a relief to the men and women who cleared a path before her at every step, and returned to the most luxurious and highly decorated seat of all where she draped herself upon the knee of an older and colder looking man, her arms flung loosely around his shoulders.

The man looked to be approaching forty years of age but his slender frame seemed to hold a wiry power and his hands were large with pronounced knuckles. His deeply tanned skin accentuated the crow's feet that had gathered around his tired looking eyes and the darkened skin was topped by short jet black hair that was parted near the centre in schoolboy fashion. He wore a white suit, in deliberate contrast to the people gathered around him, and a shirt that seemed white at some moments and electric blue when the light caught it. His shoes were mainly white with a black quadrant upon them as if in homage to the spats favoured by Chicago gangsters. His shirt was open necked revealing an expanse of curly black hair stretching across the upper portion of his chest and unlike everybody else in the room, myself and Lamara excluded, he wore absolutely no jewellery. He seemed remarkable only in his normality but this was my first glimpse of Michael Dwyer.

I approached him with caution as if still unsure that he couldn't see me but he continued his conversation oblivious to the presence of two interlopers to his grandly designed party held in this rundown nightclub: one of the many legitimate businesses that he used to launder the money that he made from his more lucrative illegal operations.

It was obvious from a distance that Georgie and he were in love with each other and as she draped her arms around his muscular neck she played with his hair or ran her fingers across the upper reach of his spine. Occasionally she would lean over as if to whisper in his ear and then use this as an excuse to nuzzle his ear lobe. He would smooth his hand across her legs in tender caresses but as I got closer I saw that he winced occasionally when she would make too obvious a show of affection for him and he would hastily unlock his hand from hers when she attempted to entwine them together. It was as if he was scared of loving her, or as if he was scared to show his love in public for fear that it might be considered a sign of weakness in his otherwise steely make up.

When he spoke it was in a refined accent that he seemed to have cultivated to hide any trace of where he might have come from or what class or background he grew up in. It was a soft voice so that all of his listeners had to lean forward to hear him and they talked quietly themselves as they were unwilling to risk drowning out his words. In spite of his best efforts the occasional hint of his soft Irish brogue would sometimes break through.

He spoke of his business acquisitions throughout the year but discussed only his legitimate dealings; it soon became apparent however that he was masking his operations under assumed names and that their true meaning was all too clear to the fear stricken sycophants who were in attendance upon him. When Dwyer spoke of his jewellery operations in West Yorkshire the crowd smiled and laughed with quiet appreciation. At other times he told slightly blue jokes or one liners that seemed to have been recycled from the previous years crackers: if you had heard the reception that those gathered about gave him, rousing bursts of laughter and even slapping of sides and backs, then you might have thought that the spirit of some great comic had entered the room and begun a new routine never dreamt of before.

Everybody seemed to love Dwyer, outwardly at least, but it was easy to spot the frightened look within their eyes as they held onto another false grin until their jaws ached. As I looked at the man holding court with such ill-gotten self importance I wished that I could have taken one of the heavy ash trays which were collected across the room and bring it down forcefully upon his head. There was a cold calculation within his every action and it was hard not to hate him at first sight so I didn't make the effort.

A man in a black tuxedo with a purple cummerbund fastened too tightly across his bulging waistline made his way through the crowd and whispered in Dwyer's ear now. At once the expression on Dwyer's leathery face changed and everybody took two steps backwards. He pushed Georgie gently from his knee and she pouted back at him but said nothing. Rising to his full, imposing, height Dwyer followed his flunky across the VIP area and out of the cordoned section, with the rope removed by O'Callaghan with as much speed as his fumbling hands could manage. I followed behind them with Lamara, and we dodged around the side of the rope before Tommy fastened it back into place. Neither of the men said a word but they walked with quick and purposeful strides and were sure of their direction. People, less skilled than the bowers and scrapers of the VIP area, would shout 'Happy Christmas Mr Dwyer' as he passed but he neither answered nor looked at them and the people at the sides of the shouters would shush them with fingers raised to their lips.

The party of four, Dwyer, the thickset henchman, Lamara and I, soon reached an emergency exit near to the disc jockey's booth which was now blasting out 'It'll Be Lonely This Christmas' to a rapidly emptied dance floor. The metal bar upon the jade coloured exit was pushed down and the door slammed open before we exited into the night air which seemed unusually mild and inviting for December. The sight that greeted us didn't seem as inviting.

Two shaven headed men, wearing tuxedoes and purple cummerbunds like the more elderly man who had whispered to Dwyer, were holding to the floor a thin man, or should I say boy, who appeared to be no older than his late teens and looked pathetically small and insignificant when compared to the men who held him down. Without saying a word Dwyer made an upward motion with his right hand and the two men pulled the hapless youth to his feet. He wore a thin white shirt and tight black trousers where a wet patch spread across the front as he saw Dwyer's angry face looking down upon him.

"What's your name, boy?" asked Dwyer.

"Sir, John Goodhall. It's John Goodhall, Mister Dwyer sir."

"I don't like that name. Well Sir John what are you doing here tonight."

"Sir, I am working in the kitchens."

"Are you a chef then?"

"No sir."

"A waiter?"

"No sir."

"No, those jobs are all too good for somebody like you aren't they Sir John?"

"Yes, sir, they are sir."

"All that you are good for is putting drink in a glass and food upon a plate, like a parasite living off of somebody else's hard and honest work. That's all that you are good for isn't it?" His voice had risen in pitch and volume now and the dark tan on his face seemed to grow paler as he became more and more agitated. The youth didn't even answer him then but stared at the ground with his legs shaking as if he would faint.

"You will answer me when I speak boy: is that what you do?"

"Yes, sir."

"Is that all that you do?"

"Yes, sir."

"Yes, sir. That is all that you do is it? Well then you must be calling my good friend here a liar, because he has brought it to my attention that it is not all that you have been doing tonight. Is he lying? Do you want to see me beat him to the ground?"

"No, sir."

"Right. Perhaps you would like to do it yourself, perhaps I should just let you fight it out face to face? Or maybe he isn't lying?"

"I don't know Mr Dwyer, sir."

"Well let me explain what I have heard and then you might have a better idea of whether he is lying or whether he is telling the truth. It's been brought to my attention that you have been drinking the champagne yourself and substituting the guests' drinks for something altogether less sparkling. You've been helping yourself to the food as well. Is that right?"

"No, sir, it's not true" was the barely audible whimper that came from the young man but his eyes were cast down and he was unable to bring himself to look Dwyer in the eyes.

"Oh, it is true. It's true because I say that it's true and what I say goes. Do I make myself clear?"

"Yes, perfectly clear."

"Good, Sir John, now you are learning. But what to do with you, eh? That's the question. If I let you get away with this then what's to stop all of my staff acting like you; helping themselves to my goods and thinking that they are somehow above my guests? No, that won't do at all – I'm a respectable businessman, I can't let dishonesty go unpunished."

Dwyer was circling around the young man now like a vulture waiting for its prey to drop. He had one finger pressed to his lips in a mock show of being deep in thought whilst he considered his options. He turned back to the boy and although he spoke in as civil a tone as possible the snarl in his voice was never far below the surface:

"I like dogs, do you know that? Love them, I do. They are loyal creatures, trustworthy, unquestioning. Perhaps I should introduce you to my dogs so that you might learn how to behave from them? Is that a good idea, Sir John, tell me is that a good idea?"

The young man struggled to escape from his captors but they held his arms fast as he wriggled like a worm hooked on the line that only succeeds in digging the hook further into his flesh. He screamed for mercy now in a pitiful voice but this just hardened the stone features upon Dwyer's face. He adopted a conciliatory tone:

"Okay, I suppose that we don't have to do that. It's nearly Christmas after all, and a time of good will for all men – even those who would betray and steal from their master, a man who has been kind enough to give them a job and pay their wage. But I am feeling magnanimous today; it must be the Christmas magic in the air. I'll tell you what I am going to do: I'm going to let you have a drink and a bite to eat on me. You were taking it anyway so why not have some with my blessing?" He turned to his corpulent aide now and snapped his fingers at him which sent the man scurrying into the club again.

There was a dreadful silence, broken only by the sobbing of the pathetic youth struggling with the two guards who continued to keep their firm grip upon him. I stood unseen and mesmerised by the terrible scene that was playing out before me but Lamara was already looking away as if aware of what was to follow.

The man returned now holding a bottle of champagne which he handed to Michael Dwyer with a faint bow of his head. The cork was still fastened into the bottle as Dwyer approached John Goodhall but he took the unconventional approach to opening the champagne by smashing the neck of the bottle next to the young man's squirming feet. The finest liquid now began to escape from the bottle in a bubble laden jet and Dwyer held it above the man's mouth, which he held open in his left hand while with the right he poured the drink down his throat until he coughed it up and champagne began to pour down his nose. When he blinked drops fell from the corners of his eyes. At this point the remainder of the drink was poured across the helpless youth's head and he stood there retching, a pathetic, sodden and coughing beast.

"Did you enjoy the drink then? It was on me, don't worry about the cost. It doesn't seem to have worried you before. And now that you have had a beautiful drink, fit for only the most refined palette, I think it's about time that you had something to eat too, isn't it?"

Once again a click of Dwyer's carefully preserved fingers sent his partner in crime scurrying forward. The henchman removed a pair of black gloves from the pocket of his evening suit and pulled them onto his hands at a leisurely pace before accepting the bottle from Dwyer. The remainder of the bottle was then smashed upon the floor so that large shards of green coloured glass were gathered around the drink pourer's feet.

The gloved man now gathered up pieces of glass one at a time and pushed them into the boys mouth, cutting gouges in the lips that at first remained tightly closed in protest.

"Chew your food, young man, chew it. We don't want you getting indigestion now do we?" was the advice from Dwyer who watched the scene with his arms folded across his chest and with a gleeful look sparkling in his eyes. His accomplice forced the mans jaw up and down as he chewed upon the glass that made a horrible crunching sound as it was swallowed down with a great effort. There was no let up in the depraved scene as large piece of glass followed large piece and soon the boy's mouth was one mass of blood that flowed down and covered the whole of his upper body. It was impossible to say where his lips started and ended. His eyes rolled within his head as the bloody torture continued unabated but I could watch no more and although I turned my head away from the red man the dreadful crunching sound, accompanied by animalistic screams, sickened me completely. At last Dwyer went back into the nightclub, leaving instructions for his men to make sure that Goodhall completed his meal and thereby sentencing him to a dreadful death, and Lamara and I followed him inside with relief.

The music was louder inside the club now, in an effort to drown out the screams from outside, and Dwyer strode back to his VIP area with a cold countenance upon his face and flames dancing in his eyes. The guests that had fawned upon him seemed to sense the change in his mood and they moved swiftly away from the area that they had occupied in close proximity to him so that only he and Georgie remained upon the luxurious sofa with me and Lamara in close attendance.

Dwyer drained his glass of whisky and slammed the thick glass of the tumbler onto the table in front of him causing Georgie to give an involuntary and frightened jump.

"What's wrong with you, darling?" she asked.

"Wrong with me? Nothing's wrong with me."

"You've been knocking back that whisky tonight, Michael. You don't normally drink at all."

He rounded upon her then and snarled into her face:

"I will do what I want to do. I'm not a child anymore, nobody tells me what to do. And people do what I tell them to do, hear me? I am sick of people giving me no respect and carrying on as they choose. When are people going to learn, Georgie, when are they ever going to learn? Oh, it would be so much easier for them all if they just did as I ordered them."

He turned his back upon her now and rested his forehead on his outstretched left arm which was sprawled lazily upon the corner of the sofa.

"But I do what you tell me to do, Michael, don't I?" It was the wrong question for Georgie to ask for it snapped him out of his lethargy again and he moved to within an inch of her face.

"Do you, do you now? What about that ring? How much effort did I go to, to make that ring for you? And I gave you one simple instruction which was to keep it hidden, keep it safe, at all times and only to wear it when there was only me about."

"Well I do that."

"Under duress you do. How much nagging did I have to endure tonight? 'Can I wear it? Can I wear it?' You cannot fucking wear it so you had better stop asking me about it. Questions, questions – everybody has questions for me as if my word isn't enough."

They were both silent now and Georgie edged away to the corner of the seat. A minute passed before Dwyer's fury exploded again:

"And then, of course there's the other thing."

" 'Thing' is that all it is? A thing?" Georgie reacted with her own fury now but she refused to release the tears that welled in her eyes.

"That's all that it is to me. In fact, no, it's less than that: it's a nothing."

"How can you say that?"

"Very easily. Did I say that I wanted a child? You should have been more careful, people should always be careful around me. Why should I want to bring another child into this stinking world?"

"It could bring us closer together, Michael. It would be a part of us. It would help you feel better about yourself."

"What do you mean? I feel great about myself. But I don't need another child."

"What do you mean by 'another'?"

370

"What do you think I mean? You aren't the only one, you know?" he answered with cruelty and ill concealed resentment.

"You said that I was."

"Oh, right and you believed me for once did you? Well let me lay it on the line for you. Georgie, you're a very special woman to me and you always will be. I'd never hurt you. But there was something, an incident – nothing at all really, with another woman."

"Who is she?" Georgie answered in a low and lifeless voice as if seeing the chasm opening up before her.

"She's not from around here. She's just a slip of a girl really, nothing to me. Only you, Georgie, mean anything to me. It was a just a one off incident really, one night that's all. But the stupid bitch telephoned me yesterday and said that she is in the same condition as you are. Just another incident that's all."

"Incident! These are lives that you're playing with, man, real human lives." She battered her arms at Dwyer with machine like rapidity but the blows bounced off of him until he drew his arm back and struck her soundly across the face with a 'thwack' that seemed to echo across the room and which lifted Georgie off of her feet and onto the floor. Shaking her head from side to side she raised herself unsteadily to her feet and stood motionless with a tiny trickle of blood descending from the corner of her thin pale lips. Dwyer stood up and confronted her, placing his hand underneath her chin and grasping her face within his hard fingers.

"Just get rid of the thing, that's all you need to do. I'll give you into the New Year to get rid of that nothing and then we can get back to how we used to be, okay? Don't question me, just do it. Don't make me have to do it for you."

He stormed away with his eyes glazed over, comprehending nothing so that he bumped into people blindly as he made his way out of the club leaving Georgie collapsed upon the sofa, her beautiful dark hair cascading over its side, with only the rhythmic blinking of her eyes to show that she wasn't already dead.

The show was over and the disc jockey turned the volume up once more until people started dancing again in the time honoured drunken fashion that shows that we are truly in the season of goodwill to all men. In Dwyer's world there was always no room at the inn.

I was walking with Lamara again, following her lead as I had done throughout the years, her hand pressed against mine and my fingers wrapped around hers. I was oblivious to the people around us and the music seemed to fade gradually away.

"Do you see much of Skye?" she asked me and I was ashamed at having to shake my head.

"Why not?"

"I just couldn't bring myself to see her. She reminds me of you."

"Not even on her birthday?"

"I couldn't do it, Lamara, I just locked myself in my house for the whole day. It was the only way to get through it."

"She adored you, you know John? She still would. You were the only father that she has ever had, the only real father. I want you in her life John, promise me that?"

We had stopped talking now and she looked deeply into my eyes. She looked clean and beautiful, the way that she always had when I first knew her and when me, Lamara and Skye had been a wonderful happy family together. Lamara was right, of course, I had been the only father that Skye had ever known and knowing what I now knew within my heart I was glad that that was the situation.

"I promise that I'll keep an eye out for her. And I'll always remember her birthday, if she wants me to."

"I know that she wants you to."

As our smiles engaged each other she pulled her fingers from mine and stepped back a pace from me so that I felt the cold night air blowing across my skin. We were back by her graveside again, and the sudden realisation sent a knife plunging into my heart.

"When will I see you again, Lamara?"

"Oh, one day. Sooner or later, John. Sooner or later, my love."

"I don't want you to go again."

"Everybody goes in the end, John. And now I give you this to do – find out why I had to go. I think that you know it all now if you look within your heart. Bring justice for me, John, that's what you are here to do. Look, here comes your other woman."

"What other woman?"

"The one that you got the other bunch of flowers for, of course." She laughed as she said this and I longed for her to stay so that I could hear her familiar ringing laughter until I could melt into the grave with her.

"Don't you worry, John, I'm not jealous. And anyway, I know that you gave the best bouquet to me. Don't keep her waiting, lover boy."

I turned around momentarily to see that Rosa Galloway was indeed striding across the cemetery towards me with her hands deep within her pockets to shield them against the increasingly bitter air which had begun to blow in whistling gusts around me. I turned back towards Lamara again but she had gone and all that remained was the hard stone that bore her name and marked the passing of twenty five years.

I'm not ashamed to admit that I had cried earlier in the evening when I had felt the cold touch of death approaching me, when I had thought of all the people that I'd never speak to again: people that would never hear me say how much I appreciated them, or how much I despised them or how much I loved them. Now that I had encountered death once more, had passed beyond its mortal boundary, I felt at ease and all sense of fear had left me. The grave was here, and its carved stone was before me, but I knew now that Lamara wasn't here: if she was anywhere then she was inside of me and inside Skye and she was with everybody else who still thought of her and remembered her from time to time.

Rosa's hand was placed gently upon my shoulder now and caressed it tenderly as I took what could be one final look at the memorial before me. I gave one last sigh out of habit more than emotion and when I turned to look Rosa in the face I knew that I was ready for whatever this dark and unforgiving night had waiting for me.

"I thought that you were staying in the car, Rosa?" I asked, but with no hint of anger or disappointment in my voice.

"I was worried about you, John. You've been gone a long time and it's already ten to twelve. We've got to get moving if you're going to keep the appointment."

I smiled at her with acquiescence and followed her past the cold and unvisited stones to the old car that was parked on the road outside. Ah yes, the appointment: it wouldn't do to be late. She made it sound like a job interview, but I suppose that like a job interview it was fair to say that the course of the rest of my life depended upon it. It had all started on the morning of the previous day when we had found her pet dog gone and a note left behind in his place; now I knew that I wasn't just going to collect the dog I was going to confront the source of all of this misery and death that had cried out down the years. I was to become the vengeance that these very stones were calling for and, coward at heart though I am, at that moment I was quite prepared to succeed or die in the effort.

"It looked like you were talking to somebody, John – is there something that you want to tell me." We had walked through the heavy iron gates now, closing them with a resounding clang behind us, and had reached the brown and unremarkable car that was ours for the night, courtesy of the police authority.

"Yes, Rosa, I might as well tell you", I started, "you lost Georgie all those years ago, and you wanted to know how she really died. Well, I know what happened, and I know why it happened."

I had her full attention now. "What happened?" was her question.

"Did you know your sister well in her last few months? What I really mean is did you see much of her – know where she was going and who she was with?"

"Well I saw her yes, in the house. She was out a lot though. She was always out a lot, she had lots of friends."

"Any friends in particular?"

"Do you mean this boyfriend that the story mentioned – the older man? I don't know. She never mentioned him; I don't believe that she could have kept a secret like that from me."

It's amazing what secrets people can keep, even from those that are closest to them, when they put their minds to it. And now it was my turn to keep a secret. Rosa was an innocently caring woman, always seeing the good in people and always believing that things will turn out for the best: I suppose that was why it hit her that hard when her sister died so suddenly. In the ten years that had passed by since Georgie's death the little sister's only wish had been to know the truth about the incident. The truth was that Georgie had, like so many other teenagers, become rebellious – drinking too much, staying out late, taking soft drugs. Reading between the lines it seemed that Georgie had become a good time girl, I'm reluctant to use the more common and vulgar term, who had sought out the company of older and wealthy men who could treat her to a lifestyle that had always seemed to be tantalisingly beyond her reach. It was this dangerous occupation that had brought her to the attention of Michael Dwyer, that most dangerous of men who lay behind a network of crimes that were hidden behind his legitimate façade. He had been attracted by her pale beauty and especially by her character, her feisty determination to stand up to him, but it was precisely this trait that had led to her death on that cold January morning nearly ten years before the date that I write of now.

I looked at Rosa's wide and trusting eyes and I knew that I couldn't tell her this; sometimes ignorance can be bliss. It was time to lie:

"There are a lot of questions that remain to be answered Rosa, I suppose that there always are when it comes to matters of life and death. What I do know is that one man in particular is responsible for her death, blameless and innocent though she was, for her murder." I turned away now as if to let this news sink in to Rosa's heart but really it was a deliberate action to discourage her from asking questions that I might not find easy to answer. When I turned back to her again I changed the subject away from Georgie:

"I lost someone too, Rosa – somebody who was very close to me. She was called Lamara and I suppose that for many years she was the love of my life. She died twelve months ago, on Boxing Day. I brought her some flowers tonight. And the strange thing is that it seems that the deaths of your Georgie and my Lamara are inextricably tied together, despite the years that passed between them."

"Do you still love this Lamara?" she asked with a hint of jealousy lurking ridiculously beneath the surface.

"I don't know, Rosa, I just don't know. It's all in the past: how can you love a wooden box and a handful of dust? But what I do know is that I'm just about to keep an appointment with the very man that's responsible for our losses."

"And what are you going to do then?"

"What am I going to do? I haven't got a clue, Rosa. But I'm sure that it will be interesting." The genuine smile that grew upon my face now seemed to disconcert her and we climbed into the car without any more questions being asked.

The car creaked and groaned at every gear change and at times it seemed that we would never make the short journey to Shelby's Shack but following my directions we eventually reached the narrow turning at the side of the old Elektra Palace cinema that led to the meeting place. There was a host of cars already parked along the rough gravel track: cars made by Mercedes-Benz, BMW, Jaguar, Audi, TVR; all of which made our vehicle seem pathetic and inept in comparison which is indeed how I must have looked to the people who were at the gathering.

There was a buzz in the air as if the very atmosphere was charged with excitement. I heard noises of people cheering that mixed with the shrill whining and barking of dogs and which grew progressively louder as we walked nearer. At one point Rosa stumbled upon the gravel that skipped out from beneath her feet so that I had to help her up and she felt like a rag doll within my grasp. Her face was as white as mine now and her lips were drawn tightly together.

I strode out in front of her as if impatient to reach my destiny. A sense of euphoria filled me to bursting point and a broad grin played upon my face. My heart beat with a bold quickness as I walked on willingly towards my death.

Chapter Twenty

Rosa was struggling to keep up with my pace as I strode out purposefully before her. She called out to me to slow down and I acquiesced for a handful of seconds before the adrenaline took over again and sent me walking off in front of her. We soon reached the broad gravel turning circle and could see Shelby's Shack in the near distance beyond the patchy grassland. Whatever awaited me there I was determined to meet it head on.

It seemed as though Rosa and I were the last people to arrive; there was a profusion of cars parked along the gravel and on the rough slippery grassland that followed on from it but we were the only two people outside. I had slowed down again to let Rosa catch up and she had grasped my left hand within hers so that this time there was no getting away from her. The noise from the building that we approached was getting louder and louder and I would feel my hand being squeezed from time to time when a particularly loud cacophony reached our ears. I squeezed her hand back as if to reassure her that everything was going to be alright but although my inner focus had given me a steely determination for the night ahead even my knees began to tremble a little. I convinced myself that this resulted from the harsh wind that whistled around us.

The 'shack' as it seemed to be called loomed large and cold before us. From a distance it had seemed to be a mediocre and insignificant building but now I saw that its dimensions were much larger than I had expected. The outside of the building was made of sheets of corrugated steel and there were no signs of any description to say what the building was or what it was used for. Large sections of the panelling were now covered in rust and rivets had come away or been sheared off leaving some of the panels gaping open through which the wind raced sending an eerie low pitched moaning echoing around the shack. The sound of men's shouting and dogs barking continued to grow stronger now that we had reached the periphery of the building although the wind, which was increasing in strength as the night progressed, competed with it in drowning each other out.

"Well, this is it, Rosa. The end of the road."

"So what's going to happen now then John? Do we just go in, find this man who wanted the ring, hand the ring over to him, collect Tramp and then go home?"

"Something like that, Rosa. Something like that."

Even Rosa didn't believe that things would turn out as easily as she had predicted, but I squeezed her hand and let her wallow in her innocent ignorance. If we had known what was waiting for us that night then I don't think that she would have let me walk through the heavy set unmarked metal door that stood before us.

I pushed at the door expecting to find it locked but it slowly gave way to my pressure, Rosa helping me to push it open so that we used three arms between us. We found ourselves standing in a dark and unwelcoming lobby with bare earth underneath our feet and the freezing fog of the night swirling around us, propelled by the howling wind which rattled through the gaps in the steel panelling. The room, if such it could be called, was wide but it only measured a short distance before there was another wall made of thick metal plating and which shone like a mirror so that we found ourselves staring at our somewhat distorted reflections, all long necks and short fat bodies, and it looked like there were six people present rather than three. Rosa and I were the first two and the third occupant of this lobby was a man who stood sternly guarding the door which was centrally located in the metal wall before us.

He was a tall and broad man with a shaved head that glinted in the dim light as if it was a beacon in a lighthouse resonating through the blackness. He moved not an inch upon our entry although his eyes seemed glued to me. He wore a large black overcoat with his gloved hands folded across his puffed up chest. I smiled at him by way of introduction but I got no sign of encouragement in return.

I walked steadily towards the door, not wishing to disturb the guard who looked like he could have snapped me in two like a biscuit about to be dunked into a cup of tea, but as I got to within ten feet of it the man finally stirred from his trance and moved in front of me to block my path.

"I haven't seen you before have I?" he asked with a thick Yorkshire brogue in a voice so deep that the gravel beneath my feet seemed to vibrate when he spoke.

"I don't know: you'd be in a better position to answer that one really wouldn't you?"

"What are you doing here then? Clear off."

"Is that the way that you speak to everyone?"

"Clear off, I tell you, and take your bit of skirt with you as well. This place isn't for the likes of you."

"Isn't it? How do you think that I found this place then? I didn't stumble across it by accident you know."

I seemed to have puzzled him now and I could hear the cogs turning arthritically within his lumbering brain; he wasn't sure whether I should be here or not and so I decided to press home my advantage:

"What's your name anyway?"

"Eh?"

"I asked you what your name was? I was told that I'd be able to come straight in."

"Were you now? Well perhaps I shall tell you my name when I've heard yours?"

"It's Halle, John Halle. I suppose that you've heard of me?"

"Can't say I'm over familiar with it no. I think it's about time you got out of here before I set the dogs on you."

"If you don't do what I say then I'll have the dogs set on you – they'd like that, someone as out of condition as you should keep them in meat and fat for weeks."

"Out of condition?", he spluttered now as I hit a raw nerve, "It's all muscle I'll have you know. And you don't want me to test it on you; I can tell you that for nothing."

"The only muscle you've got is that great lump between your ears. Now run along and find someone with half a brain – tell them my name and then come and let me in. Believe me, the main man is going to want to see me."

"The main man?"

"Mister Dwyer himself has requested the pleasure of my company. I don't want to keep him waiting because of somebody like you."

"Wait there" he requested but the tone of his voice had changed completely now and he couldn't get through the door quickly enough, almost colliding with its metallic side in his panic stricken haste.

"Who was he?" asked Rosa.

"Oh, I don't know. Just some jobsworth, you get them everywhere don't you? The type that says your name's not on the list so you're not coming in."

This could be the first time that my name actually has been on a list.

I passed the time by walking in circles and blowing into the air watching my breath form little icy clouds in front of me. Yes, my name would be on this list but it wasn't a prestigious roll to be included upon. I half expected the door to open to another half a dozen men like the man who had just left us but the reception that greeted us was to be very different. The door opened again and the shiny headed man resumed his former non-speaking role, the one to which he was ideally suited, although he had a sheepish look upon his face and seemed disheartened that he wouldn't have the opportunity to grind my bones and turn them into bread after all. Behind him came an elegant woman in an all red trouser suit and a white toothed smile pasted onto her face.

"Mister Halle, it is such a pleasure to meet you" she lied as she held out a well manicured and dark orange hand before me. I shook it loosely, worried that some of her tan might rub off onto my carefully cultivated paleness.

"And this is?" she asked looking at Rosa with the same obsequious falseness in her expression.

"This is my friend, Rosa. Rosa Harte." I wanted Dwyer and his cohorts to know as little about Rosa as possible, and the very mention of the surname Galloway might have been enough to rouse his suspicion if he had seen those same piercingly green eyes that she shared with her sister Georgie. I had thought on my feet and given her the surname of my favourite footballer of that time. Rosa, in her normal quick thinking manner, seemed to understand instantly why I had changed her name and she simply smiled back at the red suited lady and held her hand out to be shaken vigorously.

"A friend? How very quaint." The woman acted as if she had been to an expensive finishing school, and every word that she said and action that she took was delivered in the most calculated fashion. Not a single thing that she did seemed to ring true. Maybe she never finished the finishing school? She introduced herself as Carolina Fitzhern, a personal assistant to Mr Michael Dwyer.

"Really? How frightfully splendid that must be for you. What a wonderfully fulfilling job." I offered in imitation of her style but the smile that she gave to me was even falser than mine. She made a movement to grasp my right hand but stopped when she finally noticed the cast upon that hand.

"Oh, I am so sorry. I didn't see that you had an incapacitation to your hand."

"Yes, these incapacitations can be frightfully annoying can't they? I'm not surprised that you missed it – it's been designed to coordinate with my suit."

"Nothing serious I hope?"

"No, not too bad: just an amputation. Caught a bullet you see – I must remember not to catch them."

"A bullet? How dreadful." Everything was small talk to Carolina.

"Yes, perfectly dreadful. All in a day's work for such as us, eh? The last one I took was in the brain – I think that it's still trying to work its way out. Have you ever had that problem Carolina?"

She lost, possibly for the first time ever, her professional inscrutability at this question and faced me with a furrowed brow and a puzzled expression on her face as the doorman stood glowering at me from the sidelines. At last, she burst into shrilly false laughter:

"Oh, Mr Halle. You are one for the jokes aren't you? I will have to let Mr Dwyer know what a charming comedian you are. A bullet indeed! Come along now please, and you Rosie"

"It's Rosa" I corrected her but she seemed to have stopped listening as she took my left hand and bustled me through the heavy door that the unhappy guard held open for us.

The room that we entered into was a completely different world to the cold and desolate lobby that we had been waiting in and it would have been impossible to believe that opulence like this could be found inside such an outwardly dilapidated building. A thick golden carpet lay upon the floor so that your feet sank into it at every step producing an effect which was like walking upon sand until the legs became accustomed to it. Chandeliers hung from metal beams that stretched across the ceiling and burgundy leather chairs were organised around circular glass topped tables. A cream coloured piano had been placed towards a corner of the room although nobody was playing upon it. Three metal doors were situated around the room and at each of these were placed a bald headed doorman not dissimilar in appearance or temperament to the man that we had just left.

We were directed to a leather covered sofa and we sank guiltily into it forcing my feet off of the floor as the impact sucked us into the yielding luxury of the soft fabric. Carolina left us alone for a moment and I took the opportunity to examine my surroundings and the people who were collected around the room.

For such a large room it was sparsely populated. People were gathered in little clusters three or four strong as if one group didn't know another. The women were dressed extravagantly with long dresses and heels that must have been carried in their hands on their way across the winter-dead scrubland that led to the shack. They sported jewellery in pale colours designed to emphasise the deep tans that they all bore and which were shown off vividly through the dresses which were worn off the shoulder or slashed daringly to the navel and held in situ with carefully placed pieces of tape. They held cocktail glasses or champagne flutes in one hand and cigarettes dripped ash from the other sending grey plumes of smoke into the air from their stylishly thin fingers. If I hadn't known better I might have imagined that I was present at a plastic surgeons convention because all of the women wore the same high cheekboned perma-grinned look and seemed to have been botoxed to within an inch of their lives. The only thing that distinguished one from another was the colour of their dresses and their hair.

The women outnumbered the men greatly as if Edwardian rules applied here where gentlemen are in one room and ladies in another. The men that were here were in mixed apparel: some wore tweed jackets on top of cream coloured trousers which were splashed with flecks of mud around the ankles; some even wore evening suit although the bow ties had been removed and pushed into bulging pockets; others had opted for the casual look and wore designer branded jeans topped with thick polo-necked jumpers. They all looked uncomfortable as if the ones wearing suits should have been wearing jeans and the ones in jeans should have been dressed formally. There was much running of fingers around neck lines and the suits that were buttoned up looked ready to pop at any moment. Cigars were the order of the day for the men and they chomped on them mournfully as they stood in glum silence next to a chattering, smattering of women and wished that they could be elsewhere.

The 'elsewhere' that they wished to be in was self evidently located behind the central of the three doors that led out of the large under populated room as cries and cheers could be heard coming through the door; somehow the noise seemed quieter and more muffled than it had when approaching the building from outside.

Rosa was casting a critical eye upon the room. As a professional designer herself this building didn't seem to catch her approval at all and she shook her head slowly as she spotted more overbearing opulence that was mere chintz in her eyes. The designer of this interior, which I took to be Michael Dwyer himself as he wasn't a man to listen to the suggestions of others, had yet to master the art of understatement. Rosa was unusually silent and I could tell that while she may be pretending to concentrate on her favourite subjects of décor and design she was really preoccupied with thoughts of her dog that we had come to collect in exchange for the ring. Maybe there was even a thought for me somewhere within her head, behind Tramp but above the carpeting? Nobody approached us while we were sunk into our chair behind an empty glass table and indeed when people did catch our eyes they quickly looked away and moved further into the centre of the room. It seemed that mingling was strictly forbidden and that these people only talked to people that they already knew. After a few minutes of people watching, my nerves beginning to grow within me as each second passed, I saw Carolina sashaying back to us with her hips swinging from left to right at every step. From a distance she looked like a vision of beauty, a matinee idol in a red dress, but as she got closer the very falseness of her appearance, from her orange tan to her fake lashes and bleached smile, obliterated any residual beauty that may still have remained. She was a middle aged director's wet dream but however much she swayed her hips before me I wasn't going to find her much of a temptation. She held two champagne flutes in her hand and she offered them to myself and to Rosa with that smile which had already become irritatingly familiar.

"Champagne pour tu" she said as if she had slipped into some bizarre fantasy where we were all friends together in a French chateau rather than the guests of a homicidal maniac in a ramshackle old factory unit that threatened to blow away if the wind increased.

"Oh, thank you very much Caroline."

"It's Carolina" she corrected me in her best headmistress voice.

"Of course it is and this" I said pointing to my beloved friend beside me, "is Rosa, not Rosie."

An awkward moment of silence followed which wasn't helped when Rosa tried to push her glass back into the hand that had proffered it.

"I can't drink this I'm afraid, I'm driving."

"Driving? We can arrange a lift home for you both if you like? I take it that you are living together? I understand that that's what friends do these days."

"I'd rather drive myself if that's okay?" Rosa replied with little attempt to hide her dislike of the tottering woman before her.

"Attached to your car, are you? I can understand that – what make is it? Audi? BMW? I simply adore German cars."

"Yes, it's something like that. Anyway, I don't drink and drive so I will have to pass on this one."

"But my dear, one little glass isn't drinking and driving and believe me you don't have to worry about the police here."

Mention of that word almost brought a bead of sweat to my forehead as I suddenly remembered the wires that had been taped around my chest leading to the hidden listening device. I took a large swig of the champagne to disguise my fear. It tasted like the most exquisite honey as it slid down my throat with the greatest of ease. I was tempted to ask if I could take a bottle or two home with me.

"This is absolutely wonderful" I stated with the first honest statement that I had made since entering Shelby's Shack. This seemed to be good enough for Rosa as she took a sip too.

"Okay then, I will have just this one glass. But that's it, you understand, because after this it's strictly water for me."

"Aqua for Rosa" responded Carolina as if making a mental note.

"I'd prefer water, thanks."

I stood up from the sofa with some effort as my legs sunk back into it and my right arm was not able to support my weight or help my attempt in any way. Eventually Rosa managed to push me forwards and I stood facing the personal assistant with a sheepish countenance on my face.

"You're not going already are you, Mr Halle? There is a person coming to see you very shortly, I absolutely promise that he won't be long."

"Oh no, it's not that at all. You see, I just need to er, what's the polite term these days? Powder my nose?"

"Ah, you would like to use the loo. I see. Well here, let me show you the way and we can leave Rosa here to finish her drink in peace."

She placed her long fingers onto my right elbow and guided me across to one of the side walls. It was only when we got closer to the panelling that I could see that a door has been hidden within it and that a thin sign saying 'Gentlemen' had been fastened upon it.

She pushed the door open without looking in and I entered into the room that had been painted yellow and which smelled like an English country garden. There was only one cubicle and opposite it was a large marbled sink below a huge mirror. Next to the mirror was a man in a dark blue suit with gold brocade on his shoulders and a peaked cap upon his head. He held a plush towel folded over his arms and a selection of bottles of scent was gathered on the marble surface next to him. He nodded at me as I entered and I nodded back before making my way into the cubicle, trying to forget about his brooding presence outside of the door.

I bolted the door securely shut behind me and this was the trigger for gentle music to start ringing from the speaker which was situated directly above my head. It was opera music played at a barely audible volume and was another attempt to add a touch of civility in such a barbaric place. As soon as I had convinced myself that the door was firmly closed I untucked my shirt from my trousers and lifted its tails up to allow access to the transmitting device which had been strapped across me by the Superintendent's technician. It had been explained to me that the transmitter had only a limited broadcasting span of not much more than an hour and so it was my responsibility to activate it at the most opportune moment. Reaching underneath the small round box containing the main core of the device I pressed the tiny switch and felt the signal pulse softly against my ribcage. I tucked my shirt in again and next I sat upon the seat of the toilet and removed my shoes and socks as quietly as possible, carefully trying to avoid banging my feet into the fastened wooden door in front of me. I removed the ring from my pocket, allowing myself one last lingering look at the green diamond that sparkled upon it, and wrapped it in thick toilet tissue before placing it between the second and third toes of my right foot. I clenched these toes together to hold the ring in place as I pulled my socks and shoes back on and after giving the toilet a flush which brought the music to a halt I was ready to return to the main concourse of the building.

I slid the bolt back and opened the door cautiously expecting to see the unblinking stone like face of the attendant looking at me with suspicion. In fact I found that he had been dismissed and Carolina herself was standing before me with her hips pressed against the marble sink and her hands palms down and flat upon its surface with her breasts pushed forward and fighting against the red fabric of her dress.

"Aftershave, Mr Halle?" she asked as if it was completely natural for me to find her in the gent's toilet.

"Oh, er, yes thanks."

"Which scent would you prefer?" she indicated the collection of bottles with a sweep of her hand but without taking her eyes off of me for a second.

"Oh, I don't know really – whichever you recommend."

"Try this one" she said holding a clear bottle in front of me which was shaped like the torso of a body, "it's very masculine."

She sprayed two shots, on either side of my ears, and then rubbed them gently into my neck with her finger nails scratching along the top of my spine as she did so.

"Would you like a hand with anything? It must be hard for you in your present condition" she asked in a voice that seemed to purr. Before I could answer she had placed her lips to my neck at the point above the

384

aftershave's residue and her left hand was directed straight to the crotch of my trousers where she started to lower the zip.

I was startled and pulled myself away from her. She made an attempt to grab me again and as we struggled either my body or hers pressed against the taps on the unit and sent a cold spray of water shooting across us leaving large wet patches across the front of my suit and her dress. Her ardour seemed dampened somewhat and I fastened my zip again before making a hasty exit through the door.

I made my way back to Rosa's table where I saw her looking at the floor with impatience and tracing a pattern upon the carpet with an outstretched foot. I sat myself next to her and sunk into the sofa with a sigh of relief.

"Are you okay John?", she asked, "You were gone for quite a while there."

"I'm fine, Rosa, just fine." I saw her look with suspicion at the dampened front of my trousers but she was too well mannered to say anything. A handful of minutes later Carolina came back to our table and I avoided her stare as if she was Medusa. Rosa's eyes focussed upon the large dark patch across the front of Carolina's previously immaculate dress and her eyes widened as a sulky pout came onto her face.

"The gentleman wishes to see you now, Mister Halle, if you will be kind enough to follow me."

We both stood up to follow the rhythmically swaying Carolina out of the room but she motioned at Rosa to resume her place upon the sofa:

"I am afraid that the room where I am taking him is for gentlemen only, my dear. I will arrange for somebody to bring you a nice glass of water here, if you like?"

"I don't care if the room's for aliens only – I'm coming with him okay?"

Carolina shrugged her shoulders and rubbed her palms as if washing her hands of the matter:

"Okay, come along. You two are pretty inseparable for a couple of friends aren't you?"

We crossed the room following behind the mesmerising sight of Carolina's posterior, clad tightly within the confines of that red dress, wiggling from side to side one buttock at a time. The handfuls of people scattered across the floor moved out of our path as we approached them and I could see the questioning and suspicious looks that they gave us as we passed by.

By the time that we had reached the metallic door located in the centre of the rear wall the noise had become a shuddering bass like orchestra of shouts and groans and the barking of dogs. The bald headed man who guarded this door was the largest of the three door men and it was as if he had no neck but that his head was moulded straight onto his vast barrel of a chest. A swallow was tattooed onto his left and right temples and his small and baggy eyes stared emotionless into me as he stepped aside to allow us access into the room that he was so ably guarding. Carolina held the door open and I followed after her; the scene that greeted my eyes was so horrific that I was nearly sick on the spot but I composed myself enough to turn on my heels and block Rosa's passage into the chamber.

"You can't come in here, Rosa, wait out here for me will you?"

"What do you mean I can't come in? I thought that we were sticking together?"

"We are, Rosa, we are. Just not here, alright? Look, I will explain later but I just don't think that you would want to be in this room. If you wait out here then I promise that I will come and find you soon. You'll be perfectly safe out here."

"And you will be safe in there?"

"I'll be as safe in there as I will be anywhere else."

"And what about Tramp?"

"Tramp? Oh yeah, I'll bring him out for you once I've sorted everything out. Don't worry about a thing Rosa. What could go wrong?"

Everything could go wrong, and if they found the bugging device concealed upon me then I would have been better off dead. Perhaps the incident in the toilet with Carolina had been her attempt to see if I was concealing anything? These were the thoughts that ran through my head as I watched Rosa Galloway walk reluctantly, and with a sad and hurt expression on her beautiful face, back to the leather chair that we had occupied. I pushed the door open again and found Carolina waiting for me on the other side with a twisted smile on her face and all signs of pretence gone.

It was noisy and crowded in the room to which I had been granted access. Cries filled the air, shouts of encouragement mingled with oaths and angry threats. A smoky haze fogged the chamber causing my eyes to sting and my throat to close. The acrid smell of blood and urine, an air of death, offended my nostrils and above all else was the pathetic whining of the dogs straining at their leashes.

The room had been turned into a miniature arena centred around an oval space which was enclosed by sheets of iron four feet in height with rolls of barbed wire twisted around the inside perimeter and layered upon the top of the sheeting. Benches were raised around the arena at four different heights so that there were around fifty or sixty people sat there. At the far end of the oval arena were two men in brightly coloured shirts, watched over by another bald headed man in the guards' attire of long dark overcoat and black gloves, who were acting as bookmakers. Carolina had been wrong to say that it was gentlemen only for a collection of young women, barely out of their teens, mingled amongst the men bringing them drinks or pushing lighted cigarettes into their mouths. They were all attired in various states of undress so that it seemed that they were wearing more make up than clothing.

Only a few days earlier, when I had been walking through the snow bound streets of Sheffield, I had seen the animal rights activists handing out leaflets in protest against dog fighting and I had hurried past them scarcely believing that such spectacles could be found in modern day England: now I found myself in the very middle of such an event and I wished that the activists had been more successful in their attempts to have the bouts ended.

There were three tables sat close to the oval arena but away from the main grandstand formed by the benches: these tables were reserved for special guests only and it was to one of these tables that I was directed by Carolina. I sunk into the chair despondently as she swung herself away from me to fetch the man who wished to speak to me.

At either end of the steel sheeted oval were two dogs, both of them bull terriers and bearing the scars of previous fights in livid welts that were etched into their fur. They had been starved and taunted in the days leading up to the fight and they were straining at the leashes held by their handlers, two bare chested men covered in tattoos and with the veins bulging in their forearms as they struggled to hold their charges back. As the dogs grew more and more frenetic in their straining and their barking and whelping grew keener the air of excitement around the arena increased. Bets were shouted across to the bookmakers who took a mental note of the gamble within their heads without ever asking for the money first: they were keeping a running tally of each man's account in their heads and it was a matter of honour to these men, otherwise without honour, to settle in full at the end of the night.

At last the dogs were released from their leashes and the two handlers exited quickly through steel gates that were bolted shut behind them. They positioned themselves alongside the arena with sharpened switches in their hands that they would beat their dogs with from time to time to drive them into greater frenzies.

It was a sickening spectacle as the two beasts launched themselves upon each other, sinking their razor like teeth into one another at every opportunity which would produce a pitiful whimper and gouges of blood which mingled with the sawdust scattered onto the floor. One of the dogs soon gained the upper hand leaving its victim with the right side of its face gaping open from a huge wound that had been opened in it and it crashed into the walls and to the floor blinded by the blood that flowed from its eye.

The sight was too much for me to bear but the men on the benches were up on their feet roaring their approval and inhaling deeply to take in their beloved smell of warm blood. I sunk deeper into my chair and by doing so lowered my eye line to below the tops of the steel sheeting giving me merciful relief from the horrific show that continued to unfold so one-sidedly in the ring. From time to time sprays of blood and sawdust would rise from the arena and scatter itself across the most bloodthirsty portion of the crowd who were gathered on the front row.

I closed my eyes and tried to think of more pleasant things: holidays that I had spent on the west coast with Lamara and Skye or the one night that I had spent with Rosa with her warm body pressing against mine, but the smell and sounds of the arena made this act futile.

Feeling an arm pressing upon mine I opened my eyes but rather than finding an emissary sent by Dwyer I looked up to see the eagerly smiling face of a young woman who had perched herself on the chair next to me and pushed her firm young body into mine.

"What's your name?" I asked, hoping that conversation, any conversation, might somehow block out the hellish scenes around me that were oppressing my senses.

"My name is Tallulah."

I laughed somewhat cruelly at this. "What's your real name, sweetheart?"

"It's Tracy."

"Stick to Tallulah."

Tracy Tallulah was a small young woman, around five feet in height, and with naturally dark skin and eyes that were so dark they looked like black holes. She wore a ridiculously tiny bikini in a vivid pink colour that made a glorious contrast with her dark pigmentation: it would have been looked upon as obscene if she had dared to wear it on a beach. Glitter shone from the corners of her eyes and her dark hair fell in ringlets around her unspoilt face. She was undoubtedly beautiful, stunning to look at in a way that can knock the breath out of a man like a punch into the guts, but it was a depressing sight to see her draping herself over me like that at the whim of a debauched gangster.

"I'm John by the way, pleased to meet you as you can tell. How old are you Tallulah?"

"I'm twenty two." She didn't look a day over eighteen.

"And what are you doing here next to me?"

"I've come to see if you want any fun?"

"No offence, Lulah, but I don't really think this is the place to come if you want any fun."

She extended her lower lip and fluttered her painted eyelids and if I couldn't hear the wretched dog's death rattle then I might have found her faux innocence to be alluring.

"Well, how about a drink then John?"

"Now that's a good suggestion, run along and fetch me whatever their best tipple is and get one for yourself while your at it. It's on me." The champagne was way out of my budget of course but I couldn't foresee a scenario where they would be asking me to settle my bar bill at the end of the night. I watched her skinny legs carry her away and my lust was tempered by a sad vision of the wreck that her beautiful body would become before another ten years were through.

She came back with two glasses of champagne and sat on my lap as we drank them; she deliberately let a trickle of champagne drip from the corner of her mouth and I wiped the wine away with the back of my hand as her eyes had willed me to do. I was so enthralled by the young enchantress in the bikini that almost covered everything that it was supposed to that I failed to notice the hulking large stomached man who lumbered towards us. He smacked her on the back of her shoulders leaving a large red hand mark upon her delicious skin and she left the chair immediately with a haunted look within her eyes.

The man was wearing an evening suit but the jacket would never have had a chance of fastening across his burgeoning stomach. He was bald but not through choice and short grey stubble covered the area above his ears; upon one of his many chins there was a grey goatee beard. His face was scarred and worry lines furrowed his forehead. The years had not been kind to him but I thought I could still make out a remembrance of the man in the cummerbund who had spoken to Dwyer at that Christmas Party over ten years ago.

"Mr Halle" he said and although he had said it as a statement rather than a question I still found myself affirming that he was right. He held out a large thick hand that seemed to dwarf mine as I took it and the pressure that he exerted seemed to squeeze the life out of my fingers without any malice aforethought from him.

"You don't need to know my name, Halle, all that you need to know is that I've been sent by Mr Michael Dwyer."

"That's good enough for me."

"Good; it seems that you are a straight talking man, like us Northerners should be, and I like that. Carolina over there likes to put on all these airs and graces, but what's the point of that? At the end of the day she can call herself a personal assistant or whatever and put on a show of respectability but we all know that she is nothing more than a jumped up painted whore. Wouldn't you agree, Halle?"

"Yes, I suppose that I would when you put it like that."

"I'm glad to hear it. Carry on like this and we should be able to conclude our business with the minimum of unpleasantness."

A complete lack of unpleasantness would have been my preferred scenario but I suppose that was too much to ask for.

"So let us get straight down to business then, we both know why we are here. Have you got the ring?"

"Yes I've got it."

"That's the right answer, Halle – that's the answer that gives you the chance of walking out of here alive and going back to an uneventful life with your bird. As you can probably guess, Mr Dwyer is rather perturbed at the effort that he has had to go to to get his hands on the ring. And if he looked into it further then he may well find that you personally have been rather obstructive: that's not a good thing for you to do. But maybe he's mellowing in his old age and as long as you hand this ring over now, and as long as you whisper a word of this to nobody for as long as you live, then I am assured that he will bear you no grudges. That's a good offer isn't it? A most generous offer for somebody like you: somebody that he could simply crush."

He clenched his fist threateningly to emphasise the crushing but I knew that the truth was that he would already have crushed me if he had known where the ring was.

"That sounds like a fair offer, I suppose."

I had become lost in our conversation and it was only now that I realised that the crowd had become silent again. The ripped and torn carcass of one of the dogs was dragged from the pit with its innards protruding from its stomach and dragging red slime along the floor behind it. The victorious dog followed behind, held on a tight rein by a bare chested attendant, with fresh scars of victory gouged into its flank and the blood of the opponent dripping from its satiated mouth.

Dwyer's accomplice noticed that my attention was momentarily diverted and he waited for me to turn my gaze back to him before he continued, with his palm outstretched:

"Well let's have it then, Mr Halle. No time like the present is there?"

"Let's have what?" I asked in a pathetic attempt to stall for time and to gain a few more seconds to add on to my life.

"Don't mess with me Halle. Now isn't the time to stop with the plain talking."

"I don't have it on me, I'm afraid."

"You don't have it on you?" His voice remained calm but a red hue began to appear on his face and he flexed his knuckles in an unwelcome fashion. "You said that you have it."

"I do have it, just not on me at the moment."

"Then why did you come all the way here tonight without the ring?"

"Because I want to give it to Mr Dwyer personally. No offence intended to you, my friend, but I want to speak to the top man himself."

The man rose dramatically to his feet and his expansive gut rubbed against the rim of the table. Aging though he was, he was still an intimidating sight: a man could punch away at that stomach for hours on end and get nowhere. I had angered him but it was a chance that I had to take.

"The top man?", he yelled so that the assorted lowlifes gathered in the less than grandstand stopped their mumbled conversations and their privately struck wagers and turned to look at our table, "I am the top man as far as you're concerned."

"Calm down", I taunted him recklessly as the adrenalin flowed through me reaching my mouth before it climbed up to my brain, "you want to look after your blood pressure in your condition."

"You want to start worrying about your own condition, my son."

"Do you know, and it only struck me earlier tonight, but I couldn't really care less about my condition? Now, I don't mean to offend you, but I am only willing to talk to Mr Dwyer himself. I can give him what he's looking for, don't you worry about that."

He sat down again, crashing heavily onto the leather armchair that faced mine so that he bounced up again a second later before making a final landing within its yielding cushions. His hands were shaking with rage and I guessed that he would have flattened me already if he hadn't been under strict instructions from Dwyer not to do so.

"Mr Halle", he said in a shaking voice to match his hands, "if you survive tonight then we may well meet again one day, so it really is best for you to keep me onside, nice and friendly like. Now I have been sent here to do a job for Mr Dwyer, and I will follow his instructions: that's what everybody has to do. I can't just go back to him and tell him that some little piece of shit like you, a wet leaf of lettuce that can hardly stand on his own legs, has ordered him down here."

"Well then, he isn't going to get his diamond is he? He isn't going to lay his hands on Solomon's diamond. And believe me, I'm more than willing to hand it over to him."

"What did you call it?"

"You heard me. You see, old man, I may have difficulty standing on my legs but I can still use my brain. You just run along and tell the boss that I want to see him and that he will want to see me."

He was wavering in his actions now and it was as if half of him wanted to go and speak to Dwyer and the other half, ruled by his machismo pride, was glued firmly into his chair.

"He isn't here, Halle. So you'll have to deal with me won't you?"

"Well I think that he is here. Somewhere."

"And I think that you do have the ring on you. Somewhere. So what should I do about that?"

"Oh I don't know – why don't you push a bottle of bubbly down my throat like you did to that glass carrier at the nightclub all those years ago."

"You what? I don't know what you mean but I'd shut that big mouth of yours if I was you, Halle." For such a big man he looked mightily scared at this point.

"I thought that you liked straight talking?"

He had had enough but rather than lay into me, which would have been a ridiculously uneven fight even if I'd had the use of both arms, he clicked his fingers in the air and shouted an instruction to the handlers who were stood bare chested and unmoving to 'bring it on.'

He sat grinning at me as two new dogs were brought into the ring. One was the familiar and expected breed of bull mastiff, growling as it toyed with the chain that tied it so cruelly and which was pulled around it's neck to the point where it nearly throttled it with every movement. The other dog was more unexpected: it was a golden coloured Spaniel that lumbered towards the ring with a wide eyed stare as if drugged. The crowd hooted with laughter as Tramp was brought into the ring with cries of derision and mocking chants drowning out his pitiful whelps.

"I wonder who is going to win this one, Halle? Would you like to make a bet?"

I remained silent as I weighed up my options.

"The strong always win, Halle. That mastiff is a killer, trained to kill all it's life long."

"Well it's not the only one here is it?"

"Carry on being smart, Halle. But how do you think that bird's going to take it when she finds out that you let her pathetic little toy get ripped to shreds in the ring? I'll give you ten seconds to think about it. Hand over the ring and it can go free with your woman tonight. That's your only way out of here. Ten seconds start now."

He held up his digits to the crowd who chanted the numbers with growing excitement as he lowered one finger after another. The mastiff, of irregularly large size and with huge muscles rippling underneath its tattered coat, was already feeling the lash from its pink eyed handler and was being driven into a frenzy so that it jumped up and down on the spot with saliva falling in great globules of spit from its fangs.

The ten seconds seemed to pass slowly and every one felt like a blow being landed directly into my heart. I knew how much the dog meant to Rosa who would be sitting glumly in the nearby room putting all of her faith, against the odds, in my ability to return her beloved pet to her. Tramp was more than a pet to her, he was her best friend and constant companion – he had ably replaced her family after all of her family had died. And yet if I rescued the dog, by simply handing the diamond over, then I was letting the man who had caused the death of her family to escape. For the undeniable truth was that Dwyer had been responsible for the death of everyone in Rosa's family: he had personally caused the death of Georgie when she had disobeyed his orders once too often, this had led to the suicide of Rosa and Georgie's parents who were overcome with grief and the knowledge that they had also hidden away Georgie's grandmother in a secure mental hospital never to be seen by the family again; finally the orders of Dwyer had killed Roisin Galloway herself, carefully contrived with the connivance of his friendly police officers to look like a car accident. My will was the only thing that could bring Dwyer to some sort of justice: he now stood on the brink of more power than ever, with his eyes on political as well as financial muscle, but if I could somehow talk to him, confront him in person, then maybe I could garner the evidence that Superintendent Pearson had sought for so long. Either the dog or Dwyer was going to be freed: I was the only one with the power to choose.

The countdown was progressing as expected and the crowd noise grew louder but through it all my keen hearing heard another faint voice crackling nearby. It was saying 'make him stop it, make him stop it.' Barely audible though it was I recognised it instantly as the voice of Dwyer himself and it was coming from the person of the hulk before me. It seemed that I wasn't the only man who was wired up on that night and that Dwyer had been listening in to our conversation and relaying instructions to his cohort through a hidden earpiece. He must have been shouting at some volume for me to pick up his words above the baying crowd but I knew then that I had the upper hand: that Dwyer would do anything to get his hands on the ring that had eluded him for ten years and which now lay so close to hand.

The countdown had reached three know and I could see the handlers releasing the catches that held the chains to their dogs. Tramp stood with a frightened look upon his normally elegant features and his tail curled between his legs. I stood up purposefully, putting on the best act of my life in an attempt to make others feel that I was confident and uncaring, and shouted at the fat man opposite me in a voice that Dwyer couldn't have failed to pick up over the earpiece:

"Fine, set the dog on it, kill it. I don't care. But I'm walking away from here with the secret of the million pound diamond and if I have to take it to my grave then I will do. If that dog dies then he will never see the ring again."

The man, whose grin seemed permanently etched upon his face but was then a smile of fear rather than mockery, had stopped counting at one but the crowd had finished it for him and with a click of the catches on the metal leads the dogs were released. Tramp stood cowering in the corner as if almost dead with fright before the first savage bite landed upon him. The mastiff ran towards him bouncing and jumping as it ran in a manner that seemed comical to the audience who laughed in merry anticipation of the spectacle that they were about to witness.

The mastiff jumped into the air in a death leap but at the same instant the crowd seemed distracted and their heads suddenly turned to look up into the air at the fair corner of the room. There was the noise of a violent commotion and a murmur from the crowd that merged with the snarl of the killer dog. A crack rang out and the dog fell dead to the floor banging its skull against the lowered head of Tramp as it fell. I looked up and saw that on a balcony far above us, that I had not even noticed prior to the incident, was Michael Dwyer himself shivering with rage and holding a smoking gun within his hand.

The murmuring stopped now and a deathly hush descended upon the crowd as Dwyer disappeared from view only to reappear seconds later from a door at the rear of this chamber with the gun still in his grasp. His hand which had shook so violently when I had seen him on the balcony, but which had still delivered a lethally accurate bullet into his fighting dog, was now still again and he seemed to have regained his calm as he approached my table. I knew from the vision I had seen of him at the party ten years ago that this was when he was at his most dangerous.

"Mr John Halle. I didn't expect to have to make your acquaintance." He didn't hold out his hand and I didn't offer mine.

"Well life's full of surprises."

"And now, all thanks to you, I have had to kill that dog that I loved so much. How are you going to repay that?"

"I can think of a million ways."

"Well you wanted to talk to me and so here I am." He held his arms out wide now causing people to duck as they came into the line of fire of the pistol that he clutched so casually.

"Well let's do a deal, Dwyer."

"I don't do deals."

"Then it's about time that you started. I've got the location for the ring and trust me you won't find it without my instructions. But first of all I want you to keep to your side of the bargain and let the dog go free."

"I don't do deals, Mr Halle" he reiterated before striking a more conciliatory tone, "but I suppose that I had already promised that and I am a man of my word."

"The ring is nearby, it's in Hoyland buried under the soil somewhere" I lied thinking of the location that I had found it in, "I want to see Rosa drive away safely with Tramp and then I will take you to the ring."

He thought for a moment: "Okay, Halle, but how do you know that after I get the ring I won't get rid of you?"

"Well that's a chance that I'm going to take."

"And you're doing all this for a woman? I've loved women too you know, but I won't make that mistake again."

On his instructions Tramp was lifted out of the ring, its shaking legs barely able to hold it upright and it was carried by one of his bald headed henchmen into the next room, with Dwyer and me following side by side. Rosa leaped up from her seat when she saw Tramp and ran towards us with a mixture of joy and concern. She took the dog, who now showed the first signs of recognition and began to thump its tail, in her arms and smoothed its hair while planting kisses upon its head. She turned to look at me now and I answered her unasked question with a steady voice:

"Rosa, I want you to do exactly as I say. Just take Tramp and get in your car. Don't say a word, do you understand me?" she nodded her assent, "Myself and Mr Dwyer here will see you off and we will wait outside for five minutes until you've gone just to make sure that nobody follows you."

"Why would you do that, Halle?" he asked in an offended voice, "I've already given you my word that they can go."

"Well then you won't mind waiting five minutes will you?"

It went exactly as I had planned it. The whole building grew silent as we walked through it. On the way towards the main entrance we came once again to the bald headed doorman who had first greeted us in his inimitable fashion. I spoke to Dwyer as if he had become a friend:

"You know, Mr Dwyer, this man was really quite unpleasant to me on my way in. I think that he needs a bit more training."

Dwyer took the welcome opportunity to unleash some of the frustrated violence that had been welling up within him and without saying a word he punched the man in the rib cage causing him to double up in agony and then launched kick after kick into the mans head until he lay unconscious on the floor. Throughout his silent beating the man hadn't dared to raise a fist or a word in his defence.

Rosa had looked away throughout this short and sharp assault, cradling her dog within her arms. We continued our walk to the car park, Dwyer rubbing his fist as he followed, and we watched as Rosa climbed solemnly into her car with the dog placed carefully into the back seat. She followed my instructions to stay silent and even Tramp didn't make a noise. It was deathly quiet as we watched the brown wreck of a car drive out of sight with Rosa casting one last sad look over her shoulder. I fully expected that to be the last sighting of her that I would ever have.

Five minutes passed in tense silence and as the final second of this time went by Dwyer pointed his gun at me and spoke in a threateningly calm voice:

"So you see that I have kept my word and now it's time for you to keep yours. Where is the ring?"

"Follow me" I said and started walking away from the shack. Dwyer followed behind me and I was pleased to see that he walked alone, his acquaintances from the building seemingly too scared to be near him in his present state of mine. The flaws in my plan became apparent now as I realised that I had no idea where to tell Dwyer that the ring was hidden. I tried to talk to him as we walked but he was uncommunicative.

"Where did you get the ring from then, Dwyer? Solomon and his wife?"

"That's got nothing to do with you, Halle, just tell me when we get there."

I reached a patch of rough ground at the head of the track near to where it met the Elektra Palace. This place was as good as any and as my survival instincts began to return I knew that I had to make one last attempt to escape.

"I think that this is the spot."

"Here? Right here? This close to the shack? I thought that you said it was hidden in Hoyland."

"I lied. If you knew how close in proximity it was then you would have found it yourself. I hid it under that bush on my way here tonight."

I pointed at a sparse wintry bush that we had just passed. Dwyer ran towards the shrub in ecstasy and as soon as he turned his back on me I took my final opportunity and ran from him as quickly as my legs would carry me.

As I reached the corner of the disused film theatre I looked over my shoulder to see Michael Dwyer, that man with the deadly aim, pointing his gun straight at me with his finger squeezing the trigger.

Chapter Twenty-One

The night air was cold and was brought crashing against my body by the strong wind that howled around me, but the blood that ran through me at that moment was even colder. I had already seen with my own eyes how deadly accurate Michael Dwyer was with a gun when he had delivered a lethal shot to his bull mastiff dog as it was springing through the air. I knew then, as I saw the trigger reach its biting point, that there was no way that he could miss.

It takes a split second for a finger to exert enough pressure upon the trigger of a handgun to send the bullet speeding out of its chamber and towards its target but it was as if the world had frozen and that fraction of a second seemed to last for an eternity. I had time to face the certainty of my death, just as I was facing the bullet head on. It had been a good life, all in all, and I had managed to cram a more than reasonable amount of experiences into the relatively short time that I had been allotted. I can't say that my whole life flashed before my eyes but I felt a huge rush of emotion surge through me that seemed to contain the whole totality of my feelings down the years: I remembered the unconditional love that I had been given from my parents and the all too conditional love that I had received and given in equal portion to a handful of women who had meant more to me than a darkened fumble with the lights switched off; I thought of the life changing sense of pride, happiness and fulfilment that I had experienced briefly when I was part of the happy family of myself, Lamara and Skye; I thought of the hatred, that all consuming anger that had engulfed me after the death of Lamara and that had forced me into a reclusive shell under which I had sheltered for more than a year; more than this anger was the hatred that I bore for Michael Dwyer, that unfeeling stone hearted man who I had sworn to bring to vengeance but who had now defeated me as he had so many other people – I was to be consigned to the long list of people whose lives he had destroyed. All of these feelings and many, many more, memories both happy and sad, flowed through me in that split second and filled me so completely that the effect in its totality was a crazed euphoria that made me feel like I was floating through space, as if I was no longer tied to this earth and I felt as if time was nothing but a collection of memories that all existed simultaneously with one another. Yes, it had been a good life when I considered everything in its measure and the miseries and sorrows that I had experienced just like everybody else were eclipsed by the huge portions of happiness that had filled my life. The split second was over as I heard the click of the trigger which would precede the roar that would end my life. I was ready to go.

The wind continued to gain strength around me sending the dead winter leaves flying into the air in scattered spirals. The corrugated panelling that made up the exterior of the large building, confusingly known as a shack, that we had just left was rattling in the distance sounding as if great hammers were being brought down upon the keys of an oversized xylophone and the wind moaned in low tones as it squeezed between the panels. It took me a few seconds to realise that the one sound that I hadn't heard was the air shattering bang that I had expected to come from Dwyer's pistol.

The euphoria that I had experienced while awaiting death was rapidly disappearing to be replaced by a nausea that crawled up from my stomach and lodged itself in my throat so that I had to struggle to stop myself being sick. I opened my eyes again, which had closed of their own volition at the moment that I had been expecting the end to come, and saw Dwyer standing with a puzzled look upon his grey face which was followed by a stare of disgust that was directed at the gun which was held in his right hand and which he now shook violently in the air.

It seemed as if God himself had smiled down upon me, or at least Georgie and Lamara had been acting as my guardian angels, for at the very moment that Dwyer had chosen to shoot me dead the pistol had chosen to misfire, or rather not to fire at all – its shooting mechanism had become locked in a freak incident that had put the pistol temporarily out of action. I didn't want to put the protective powers of God to the test again and now that I felt that my feet were once more planted firmly upon the floor I resolved to take advantage of Dwyer's confusion and run.

I set off at a sprint as if I was blasting out of the blocks in an Olympic final and I was already well into the distance before Dwyer realised that I had fled. I allowed myself a brief glance back over my shoulder to see that he had placed his gun into a holster that was concealed under his jacket and had now commenced his pursuit of me. The wind buffeted me from side to side and when it changed direction it almost blew me fatally from my feet. After the energy of my initial sprint start had burnt itself out I was finding it hard to run at all into the elements and my legs seemed to grow heavier and heavier at every step.

I was considerably younger than the cruel and desperate man who pursued me and had been in a passably fit condition but over the week I had suffered a succession of injuries and had eaten little and slept even less. I could feel the overpowering tiredness take me in its tightening grip until I was running only on memory, as a result of mental exertion rather than physical exertion. I could hear the footsteps growing louder and nearer behind me as I continued to run in a straight line with little idea of where I was going or how I would escape. Dwyer had only kept me alive so far because he felt that I was the only man who knew where the green diamond was hidden. The fact that he had attempted to shoot me dead showed that he had finally reached the correct conclusion that, despite my protests, I had the ring hidden upon me. As soon as Dwyer caught up with me this time then he would not hesitate to kill me and search my body until he found the ring which was hidden within my sock.

I had reached, despite the best efforts of the pounding wind that tried to batter me back towards the shack, the end of the gravel path, not noticing the procession of expensive cars that lined either side and had passed in a blur, and found the alleyway that ran between the high walled sides of the large buildings that flanked it. Rather than sheltering me from the elements it seemed to act as a wind tunnel and the cold wintry air knocked at me twice as hard now, sucking the last remnants of breath out of my lungs so that I walked at crawling pace accompanied by a wheezing rattle that gargled from my mouth. Turning the corner onto the main road, King Street, I was offered three possible directions to run into. With my left arm outstretched to its full extent I propped myself against the building, body doubled up, and knew that I couldn't run another metre.

I had taken Dwyer by surprise, his concentration being directed totally upon his non-firing gun, when I had first sprinted away from him and had managed to gain a good head start but I knew that he was closing upon me with every second that I spent leaning against the cold stone wall. My only hope, slim as it was, was that some of Superintendent Pearson's men had been watching me from a distance or that Rosa had driven straight to them and that they would even now be coming to pluck me away from the danger. I raised my head and looked in all directions down the streets – there was no sign of any car or any knight on a white steed coming to rescue me. The first faint trickle of air began to fill my lungs again so that I managed to straighten myself up once more. I was standing outside of the disused cinema that had once been the glorious Elektra Palace so beloved of the children of the area. The doors and windows were boarded up but the ground floor window to my right had a flimsy looking piece of chipboard across it that had already started to pull away from its moorings at its top left corner. Grasping this corner with my only remaining useful arm, my right arm being placed out of action by the cast that had been put over it, I pulled with all my might. My legs still felt like jelly from the sprint but my arm had enough strength in it to pull the board away from the window, slowly at first followed by a ripping noise as the old and weather beaten board splintered way from the rusty nails that served to hold it in place. With half of the board being ripped away it was then easy to bend and pull the remaining covering aside so that I had created a hole large enough to squeeze my thin frame through and I soon crashed through the window into the musty smelling darkness that lay inside the Elektra Palace. There was a longer drop inside than I had expected from the positioning of the window on the outside of the building and I hit the floor with a thud that sent a short jolt shooting through my spine, luckily managing to avoid smashing my injured hand against the floor. The building was completely dark in a way that only buildings that have been unused and unoccupied for years can be. I raised myself to my feet and at every step that I took I could hear a crunching noise from beneath my shoes. The fetid smell that hit my nose was like a hundred takeaways that had been left to rot for the past ten years and as I walked blindly through the building I had to brush cobwebs away that stuck themselves to my face and found their way into my mouth where I spat them onto the floor with disgust.

My eyes adjusted slowly to the total blackness of the building and I could make out the faint shapes that marked out the furniture and fittings of the erstwhile cinema. I could discern posters that hung on the walls, peeling around the edges, and flyers and magazines that were thrown in slovenly fashion onto chairs that sent plumes of white dust dancing into the air as I brushed past them. It was as if I had stumbled into a cinematic Titanic that had been abandoned at a minute's notice and had lain undiscovered and undisturbed for years.

I was looking for somewhere to hide from Dwyer although of more use would have been something that I could use as a weapon against him. When he reached the end of the alleyway and found me gone it wouldn't take him long to notice the gaping window with the board ripped away and then he would be climbing in to follow me. He was still a powerfully built man and in a fair fight I wouldn't stand a chance; the Corinthian spirit didn't interest me, I was prepared to fight as dirtily as I could if it would give me a chance of surviving the night.

I had reached a large desk that had served as the reception, ticket office and sweet shop all rolled into one. It was impossible to keep away the happy memories of times spent in this exact same spot as a child, sucking noisily upon round apple flavoured lollipops as I queued in excitement to watch the latest 'Herbie' film. Lollipops were going to be of no help to me this time. I frisked my hands across the dusty surface of the desk and the compartments that formed nooks and crannies beneath it but all that I found were leaflets, scraps of paper and large rolls of tickets still waiting to be ripped off and handed over to children and their parents. Many of the compartments were home to spiders and other creatures, naked to my eye, which scuttled away as I fiddled around them. The papers of the lower compartments were covered in slime left by rats that had trailed across them or used them as bedding.

I had reached a stairway now that I knew from experience led to the two cinema screens themselves. I could see the shadowy outline of a railing running alongside the staircase but as soon as I exerted pressure upon it the frail banister crumbled away in my hand. I climbed slowly up the stairs, leaning against the damp wall for support, straining my ears to listen for the sound of other footsteps creeping through the building but the only sound that I heard was the powerful motor of a car in the distance.

Reaching the upper floor of the building I found a large corridor which ran between two sets of double doors at either end and where a rope was still stretched across the middle although its function of separating one shouting queue of snivelling schoolchildren from another had long since been made redundant. My heart was still pounding within me from the desperate run that I had embarked upon after fleeing from the gunman and I was losing my battle to calm it down so that I could listen for any noises other than the thudding of blood.

I knew that I wouldn't have time to search both cinemas and so I headed towards the left of the two screens, left having proved an auspicious choice on the previous night. The doors had become stiffened by inactivity through the years of neglect that had fallen upon this once beautiful building but I loosened the bonds by landing heavy kicks upon the wooden doors which soon began to give way allowing me to push them slowly open.

The doors led onto a wide aisle that proceeded down a series of steep steps towards the screen itself and I almost lost my footing as I slipped upon the uppermost step sending my heart into my mouth before I managed to regain my balance two steps further down. It was all futile I realised, my flight had been in vain and I may as well have saved time by giving myself up to be shot on the gravel path that led from here down to Shelby's Shack: what possible weapon could I find in an abandoned cinema with which to take on a cold blooded killer like Michael Dwyer? All that was to hand were ripped up leaflets, threadbare and chewed away cushions and empty cartons that had once held toffee coated popcorn.

Out of habit, and with nothing better to do, I continued to walk down the stairs at a steady pace until I reached the middle row where I edged myself along the row of wooden seats, stepping cautiously as if still expecting to hear the objections of people whose view was being obstructed, until I found a seat that seemed to me to be central to this room known as Screen Number Two. I dropped into the hard and unyielding chair and held my head in my hands as an unbearable weariness descended upon me. I straightened my hair, which short though it was had been blown out of all shape by the powerful storm outside, and then rubbed the sides of my face which felt thin and strange to my touch. All thoughts had emptied from my mind and I remained seated with my head in my hand, resembling nothing more than a badly designed shop dummy.

"Luke! It's a trap!" I looked up to see a grainy image flicker into life on the screen in front of me. Princess Leia was being bundled into an elevator by white armoured storm troopers, kicking and struggling as she went. Stars flickered in and out around the screen reflecting the dust that had become ingrained on the tape. I ducked down instantly and then squeezed myself between the seats and the floor as 'The Empire Strikes Back' continued to play upon the big screen, a reminder of the film that had been showing there before the Elektra Palace closed its doors for the very last time.

I could hear the flickering sound of the cinema projector spluttering and whirring back into life after an enforced twenty year absence. The lights too returned to life now, flashing on and off in strobe like fashion for the first few moments until they remembered how they were supposed to work. I crawled along the floor between the two rows of hard seats, covering my new suit in dust, filth and discarded shards of chewing gum, now as hard as marble, as I slithered along like a snake with one arm. At every moment I expected to look up and see the stony face of Dwyer looking down at me behind the barrel of a gun but I could hear no other sounds in the room.

I reached the end of the row and poked my head around the corner of the last seats, ready to pull it back if I could sense a size eleven boot flying towards it. My movements were restricted by the seating that hemmed me tightly in and I had to look first left and then right with all peripheral vision cut off. With the lights now blazing down upon me I could see how filthy the cinema really was and the roaches were scuttling around in a corner doing their own little dance of death. What I couldn't see was any evidence that another human was present. I pulled myself to my feet with understandable caution before looking around the cinema with amazement as the film continued to play itself out before me.

A knocking noise came from above but I stood rooted to the spot, unable to move through a heady combination of fear and animal stupidity brought on by the complete exhaustion racking my body.

"John, come up here." The female voice that cried out was even more familiar to me than that of Princess Leia, who had now been carried out of sight on the silver screen, and had a Yorkshire warmth to it that would have seemed out of place in that land far, far away. It was enough to snap me back to reality and with an external groan which reflected the weariness that the voice had produced in my soul, I raised my tired head to see Vicky Gallagher waving down at me.

I felt helpless to resist her words; despite my earlier promise to myself it seemed that once again I was becoming a puppet to be toyed with and to follow people's instructions as they pulled my strings. I walked with enforced slowness towards the rear of the cinema finding it a huge effort to raise one foot in front of the other as I climbed the steps one at a time. I didn't even have the energy left to question why Vicky was there or how she had found me, I knew somehow that all would become clear if only I could make it up to the projection room where she had positioned herself.

I had pushed myself through the double doors again and almost fell across the rope that ran centrally down the corridor. My none too nimble attempts to avoid this separator sent me stumbling against the walls and it was only then that I realised that, at the very end of my energy levels, I was shuffling along as if drunk swaying from side to side as I walked. In the middle of the corridor was a metallic door, with most of its blue paint peeled away to reveal the rusting tin underneath, upon which could still be read a faint sign saying 'Staff Only – No Entry'. I felt strangely guilty as I pushed at the door but before I could apply any real pressure it opened quickly before me and I fell through the doorway face first. The thin arms that caught me buckled initially with the downward momentum of my weight but then strengthened and pulled me to my feet before I hit the stairway that had opened out in front of me.

"You're in a bad way, John. You look a complete mess."

I stood staring almost uncomprehending at Vicky as she held me in her arms. She in her turn looked splendid, immaculately made up with a little black dress which shimmered under the lights, with black knee length boots and with long earrings that sparkled with diamonds and emphasised the childlike beauty of that face which had not yet sunk into terminal decline. I was too tired, or too disheartened, to speak and so she led me up the stairs with one deceptively strong arm around my shoulder and the other hand placed firmly upon my hip to guide me.

I allowed myself to be directed and as we entered the projection room she led me across to a green covered chair that I was gently lowered into and which seemed to me to be so comfortable that I could easily have fallen asleep on the spot. It would have been a sleep that there was no waking from.

"Well isn't this very nice, John? Our first night out at the cinema, the flicks, after all these years of knowing each other. Nobody ever took me to the cinema, you know? Little Vicky Gallagher was only good for one thing, that's what everybody thought – why waste money taking her places and treating her like a human being when you're going to get what you want anyway? That's just how people thought. It's really cruel. Too cruel." Her words faded away and maybe I imagined that I saw a tear come into her expressive eyes as she cast her head down and let her scarlet-dyed hair fall around her face which stared at her boots, lost in the past while I remained lost in the present. She raised her head again, pursing her lips, as she gave little nods more to herself than to me. Vicky had perched herself upon the ledge next to the projector with the tips of her pointed feet barely reaching the floor. A long, thin window behind her looked down upon the massed ranks of seats in the cinema and directly out towards the old cinema screen. It was a large room and there were other seats, similar to mine, further into the interior as well as a large bank of antique looking electrical equipment. A large bookcase, containing a handful of manuals that had been left behind when the cinema closed, was stationed towards the end of the room and beams hung underneath the roof carrying lighting equipment. The bare wooden floorboards had reels of film piled upon them next to ledger books and newspapers that had turned yellow with age. There were gaps in the floorboards that still creaked although nobody walked upon them. Vicky remained lost in thought seated upon her ledge on a space where she had carefully removed the dust before seating herself. She opened a packet of cigarettes, which were removed from a dainty looking black and silver handbag that was positioned on the floor, and tapped her selected cigarette upon the back of the box before lighting it and sucking on it pensively.

"Did you like the film then John, it's Star Wars? It wouldn't have been my choice but then that's all that is showing it seems. It's a nice touch though isn't it? You see, I'm not just a pretty face."

I remained seated in my chair, finally feeling another reserve of energy helping me to win my battle against sleep, but I said nothing. Vicky had become silent too now, although she looked at me quizzically with narrow eyes as her cigarette was completed in rapid fashion. The wind was becoming increasingly strong outside and its howls, audible where we sat inside the upper extremity of the Elektra Palace, drowned out the spinning reels of the projector.

"Say something, John!" She shouted with her nervous anger finally getting the better of her, "Aren't you going to say anything?"

"It's the Empire Strikes Back, not Star Wars." I wasn't even a fan of the films and felt embarrassed at having said even this much: if they were to be my last words, I reasoned, they wouldn't sound particularly impressive upon my headstone.

Vicky shrugged, having resumed her calm control again, before lighting another cigarette. Time ticked by as the film played to its most unappreciative audience. Maybe it was time to talk after all?

"How long do we have to wait, Vicky?"

"Wait? What for?"

"For Dwyer to arrive of course."

"Who is Dwyer? I don't know what you mean John." An unavoidable grin crept onto my face at this barefaced lie and Vicky grudgingly dropped her pretence with a sigh: "I don't know, John. I suppose that he'll be here soon enough."

"Well you seem to know what you're doing Vicky, or at least you think that you are. But let me warn you that things don't always turn out how you'd expect them to."

"Oh, I think that that they will work out fine. You see, I'm tired of living in everybody's shadows – it's finally going to be my time. Aren't you going to ask me how I got here, John?"

"If you want to talk, talk. Maybe it will calm your nerves like those cigarettes that you're chain smoking? Maybe it will even convince you that things will work out fine this time? Go ahead, darling; I don't care one way or the other."

She took drag after drag upon her cigarette and then pouted at me with a look that was eerily reminiscent of her cousin Lamara. I could sense that she wanted to talk, wanted to unburden herself, but after so long spent lying it was hard for her to admit the truth even to herself. I decided to speak for her:

"Listen, Vicky, why don't I do the talking here, and you can correct me if I go wrong?" It was her turn to shrug now and so I continued, occasionally straining my ears that caught the faint shuffle of feet treading on the floor below us:

"After you left me last night you drove straight to Blondie's house but didn't find him there. I'd tried to plant the image in your head that he was seeing another woman but even you're not dumb enough to fall for that one. In fact you're just not dumb at all are you? You hide your calculating mind behind a playfully vacant exterior. From Blondie's house you went to his normal hang outs and eventually found him lying on the floor of the disused warehouse where I had left him.

406

He was real mad and that was when you opened the letter that I had passed you to deliver from Osbourne to the police superintendent. That letter arranged a rendezvous between the two where Osbourne would blow the lid on the whole Dwyer operation and his network which extends to Blondie and therefore extends to you as well, I guess? I suppose that you know by now that I wrote that letter?"

"I didn't think that you had it in you, John? I always had you down as a sap."

"Did you? Well, I'm a quick learner. So Blondie, along with assorted low grade henchmen turned up at the allotted time and at the allotted place hoping to get rid of Osbourne, the Superintendent and anyone else who may turn up. The trouble was, of course, that the police were lying in wait in large numbers and heavily armed. A no-brainer like Blondie never stood a chance. I don't know how many years inside he can expect to get but I'd be surprised if he could count up to it without taking his shoes and socks off first. But you, Vicky – you are a completely different kettle of fish."

She remained silent, stretching and contracting her legs that barely reached the floor as if to ward off cramp, but she smiled at the back handed compliment that I had paid her.

"How did you escape? I don't really need to ask that do I? You stayed in the car while Blondie and his gang hopped off to do the man's work. When you saw that things were going wrong you shuffled across to the driver's seat and put the hammer down – I've seen how you are more than capable of driving like a maniac.

And then you were on your way over here to meet up with Dwyer and give him the bad news but when you saw, in the distance, my old familiar figure breaking into this ruin of a cinema you put two and two together and followed me into here to make sure that I stayed put until Dwyer himself arrives. Is that about right?"

"I guess so", she admitted, "that's about right. Maybe you underplayed my role a little but then I'm only a woman so I guess that you would. You got from A to B."

"I'd put that gun down if I was you, Mr Dwyer, we both know that it isn't working. Whatever you want you can have. I'm tired of running." The wind had died down long enough, before changing direction and gathering in its gusting ferocity, for me to hear the footsteps below. I had looked between the cracks in the floorboards and seen a tall figure moving around. He had crept up behind me with surprising stealth but I had been studiously watching his reflection in an old film can where the dust had refused to settle or had been blown away by the opening and closing of the door. When he had finally raised his gun again, Vicky Gallagher's eyes growing wider all the time, I had disarmed him with my calm statement. He holstered his gun again before speaking to me: "Just because it didn't work last time, don't be so sure that it won't work this time Mr Halle."

"Well even if it doesn't work then I suppose that you'll just batter me over the head with it. The end result's going to be the same isn't it?"

"Undoubtedly. Get up out of your chair Halle and sit over there." He motioned to a chair that was seated at the far corner of the room near to the half empty bookcase. I rose from my seat without protest and sat in the chair that I had been directed to. Dwyer lowered himself into the seat that I had warmed for him and as both he and Vicky turned their cold eyes upon me I saw that my path to the exit was sealed off by their presence.

"Good evening, Vicky, thank you for directing me here. It was a most helpful phone call."

"I'm glad to help you, Michael. You know me, always willing to accommodate."

I realised then that Vicky had been right and that I had underestimated her role in the matter: if she had Michael Dwyer's personal telephone number to hand then she must be much more than the girlfriend of one of his pet drug dealers. The truth began to hit me and it hurt.

"Vicky, how could you do it?" I asked.

"Do what? Betray you? That's easy enough, John, more than easy. It's nothing personal – I always saw you as a nice enough guy in a harmless sort of way. Not too bad looking either when the lights are off. But you were never right for Lamara you know? She was a free spirit; she wasn't there to tie down. No it was easy to betray you John, for the right sort of money. That's the only thing that's worth having in life. Isn't that right, Michael?"

"I suppose so. I've had it for so long now that I can't remember what it was like to be without it." The soft Irish lilt had returned to his voice now that he didn't have to hide it from his peers.

"But what about Skye, she looked up to you? Don't you think that her child tied Lamara down before I came along?"

"I couldn't care less about kids, John. One is pretty much the same as another to me. They just take up your time and money."

"You know, Vicky, you have finally surprised me. I would have thought that you doted on that child."

408

"Well, I guess that I'm a good actress. I learnt it by dancing naked in front of pot bellied men every night and pretending to be in ecstasy."

"You two", I said pointing to Vicky and Dwyer in turn with an accusatory finger, "are like two peas in a pod: I'm not surprised that you've managed to gravitate towards each other. But just for your record I wasn't talking about your betrayal of me when I asked how you could do it."

"I don't know what you mean" she spat out but she climbed down from the ledge now, wiping the residue of dust from the seat of her dress, before turning her back on me and lighting another in her chain of cigarettes.

"Oh, you know what I mean okay: I'm talking about your betrayal of Lamara, the cousin who was like a sister to you. And I know that you loved her, nobody is that good an actress. But I see how it all happened now: how your desperation overcame all of your emotions, all of your instincts, until only greed remained. Go ahead, darling, carry on smoking that cigarette as if you don't care but I know that you can hear me."

"Are you going to let him talk to me like this?" she asked Michael after a brief turn of her head brought him into her line of vision.

"Let him talk, why not? He is a clever man, I like to hear clever men talk. I could have used someone like him if he wasn't so pathetically un-self-centred. Let him talk, what harm can it do? We're going to shut him up soon enough."

"You see I've finally worked out Lamara's secret. She was only young when she became pregnant, a mere slip of a girl. Isn't that how you would describe her Dwyer?" His raised eyebrows and slight nod was the signal for me to continue. "I can't blame her for falling for an older man with lots of money and a shady reputation. I guess that it added to the attraction for her. So she had Skye, your own daughter Michael, and you abandoned her. Or rather you tried to threaten and cajole her into getting rid of the baby. But she persisted, despite all of your threats, even though she had to hide herself and the child away from you. You didn't look too hard, angry as you were you were happy so long as you never had to confront them again, so that you could go on pretending that there were no lives that you were responsible for."

"Did I ever ask for a child?" Dwyer was staring straight into me now and I felt the burning gaze that had signalled the end for so many people before me.

"Well, in this life you don't always get what you ask for. Like Mrs Solomon for example." It was his turn to look away but I didn't find any evidence that it was through a sense of shame or regret. Once more I addressed Vicky who had her back to me again.

"So things had been going smoothly for a number of years. Lamara turned her attention to nice, simple guys – to me and the stable, unchallenging life that I could give to her and to Skye. That wasn't enough for you was it Vicky? You were jealous of the happy and quiet life that your cousin, the one that you felt somehow inferior to despite the love that you held for one another, had created and you dragged her back to her Huddersfield haunts where you reminded her of the lure of drugs and dangerous nights.

You were making a living hand to mouth, working as a dancer, a stripper, and a drug courier. It was through the local dealer Blondie that you were introduced to Dwyer here who was always on the lookout for pretty young women to dance at and liven up his parties. He took a particular shine to you with your Irish heritage - that seems to be his thing. Unfortunately for her, Lamara must have gone along with you one day when you went to do your entertaining. She knew who Dwyer was straight away and scared though she was she confronted him. She never could hold her tongue and as Dwyer has never been a man to take any criticism then I guess that this made him very angry. Are you listening yet Vicky?"

She had turned to face me again now with angry indignation replacing the seductive smiles that she normally favoured.

"Lamara was scared, and she was right to be scared. She was coming back to my house on that Boxing Day because she was afraid for her life and I was the only man that she had ever felt safe with. It was you, Vicky Gallagher, that telephoned Michael Dwyer and told him where she was heading. He came to my house while I was out and forcibly injected a lethal overdose into her arm to make it look as if she had killed herself. What a nice Christmas present that was for me to return home to. You might as well have killed her yourself, Vicky. You killed your own cousin, as close as a sister, for a handful of money. You've reached rock bottom now, you really have gone as low as you can go."

"Yeah well we can't all be perfect can we?" she answered with her voice quivering and a blinking of her eyelids that showed how she was battling to keep from crying. She threw her cigarette to the floor and paced up and down before me; the very sight of her made me sick as I thought of that young and promising life that she had destroyed and the beautiful little girl that had been left motherless.

Dwyer remained calmly seated within his chair but he clapped sarcastically at the end of my story:

"Bravo, Mr Halle. You have a very logical mind. Or maybe it takes an illogical mind to unravel our machinations as well as you have done? It's a shame that we have both had to deal with the same woman, this Lamara, because when they mess with me Halle, they die: they just die. And now it's your turn, if you would be so kind as to give me the ring."

"The diamond ring? The one that's worth a million pounds or more? What's money to you, Dwyer?"

"You know why I want it, so why don't you just hand it over?"

"Maybe I don't have it on me any longer?"

"Don't try that trick on me again, Halle. If I have to hack you into pieces and sift through your bones I will find it."

"I know where it will be, Michael." Vicky had piped up again, eager to add more treachery to her growing list.

"Go on then, Victoria. Enlighten me."

"He always hides things in his socks, Lamara told me about that years ago and it was there that he hid the letter that betrayed Blondie tonight. Do you want me to search him?"

"Please do. Go ahead."

She approached me with a glint in her eye and a grin that disfigured the face that had once looked so appealing to me. I didn't struggle as she removed the shoes from my feet and then the socks, right first, followed by left. She shook the shoes initially and then ran her hands up and down the socks before turning them inside out and shaking them above the floor. Nothing came out.

"Nothing. Absolutely nothing" she shouted and threw the socks back at me. I placed them calmly back onto my feet, my left hand being surprisingly still and calm while my heart raced within me, and watched as Dwyer rose from his chair in an explosion of rage. He reached my chair in a few quick strikes and landed a punch across my face that bust my upper lip upon impact and sent blood spraying across my left cheek. "I haven't got it I tell you." I was still calm and the adrenalin coursing through me had anaesthetised me to any pain. My composure seemed to distract Dwyer but as he appeared about to strike me again Vicky grabbed hold of his arm.

"I think I know where it must be. I saw him scrabbling around between the seats in the cinema down there and I thought that I'd seen him fumble with a popcorn carton. That's where he will have hidden it before he came up here to see me. Just wait here and keep your eye on him and

411

I'll go and fetch it."

"Go on then, but don't be too long. If you can't find it in five minutes make sure that you come back up here to watch me rip his head off."

She left us quickly, seemingly eager to follow her master's instructions, and Dwyer returned to his seat, arms twitching involuntarily upon the limbs of the chair as he kept his eyes fixedly upon me. The door was closed behind us and Dwyer seemed to be counting the passing minutes in his head.

"That ring means so much to you, doesn't it?" I asked with a ridiculous casualness. He grunted in reply.

"It's not the money is it? You need to get that ring back for two reasons. One is the pure sentiment that you created it for the only woman that you ever loved in your life, Georgie, the pale faced green eyed beauty who calmed you down when your anger threatened to drive you back to madness. And yet she too was killed by you, because she dared to want a child by you. Isn't that right?"

"And what's this got to do with you?"

"It's got everything to do with me; it's the reason why I've ended up here
: to fight for Georgie when nobody else can; to ensure that you never get your filthy blood reddened hands on that green diamond ring that was hers. You must have had a dreadful childhood – it scarred you so much that the only thing that terrifies you is the thought of bringing a child into the world that would have to endure the horrors and torments that you went through. Maybe you were scared that it would turn into a monster just like you?"

"I'm not scared of anything. Nothing can hurt me now, I'm Michael Dwyer."

"You can hurt yourself though can't you? Drive yourself into madness never to return. And it was that pathological madness that drove you to kill Georgie, the woman that you loved, ten years ago when she disobeyed you once too often: when she said that she was going to have your child and there was nothing that you could do to stop her. Oh, you showed her how you could stop her alright. In a forerunner of what you would do with my Lamara, you pumped her full of drugs and sent her off in a car with Tommy O'Callaghan to die."

He was crying now as he rocked backwards and forwards in his chair.

"That's one reason of course. But the other one is even more important to you, because that ring is the only thing that links you to the Solomon robbery. You were unusually careless on that one weren't you? It will be

412

easy for tests to prove that you owned the ring and you've used the same banded logo for your business designs as you did for the ring itself. That green diamond is incredibly rare as you know and it would only take Mr Solomon, now safe in Israel, a second to identify it. How easily it would then be to place you yourself at the scene of the crime that left Mrs Solomon dead. You would be brought to justice at last, and how pleased that would make certain people. You need that ring to make sure that it doesn't fall into the wrong hands, what a pity that you'll never have it again."

"Why don't you think that I will get it, Halle?" he had stopped snivelling and his voice had regained its customary coldness.

"It's been a long five minutes hasn't it?" I gave by way of reply. His nerves were on edge again and we both climbed out of our chairs, looking edgily at one another.

"You see, Mr Dwyer, it seems that I didn't know Vicky Gallagher at all but she certainly knew me well. I guess that I am a man of regular habits and I do always keep things hidden in my sock as she had said. The green diamond ring was safely hidden within my right sock tonight but it wasn't there when she had finished searching it. She did seem in a hurry to get out of here didn't she? You know, even above this wind, I thought that I could hear the click of a key in a lock as she closed the door behind herself."

For the first time since he had sat down in the chair that I had recently occupied he turned his attention away from me and rushed towards the door bull-like. He pulled at the rusting iron handle with all the strength that he could muster but the door moved no more than a fraction of an inch. Undeterred he continued to pull at the door until, despite the cold air that filled the room like mist above a grave, vivid beads of sweat gathered on his forehead and dripped from his salt and pepper eyebrows. Reddening patches appeared on his impeccably tanned face through the exertion that was getting him precisely nowhere.

Vicky Gallagher concealed a devious mind beneath her harmlessly dizzy exterior; one that she had been honing throughout the years spent hiding her frustrations and envies. She would have entered the building closely behind me, unbeknownst to me, but whilst I had been crawling slowly through cobwebs she had used her time more productively. It was Vicky who had decided to test whether the electricity supply was still working after all of these years of neglect and it was Vicky who had found a forgotten set of keys to the building that she had now used to devastating effect. She had not known about the green diamond ring but had soon picked up on the words of Michael Dwyer and when a fleeting opportunity had presented itself she had grasped it and flown before we could know what she had done.

I sensed that I had the upper hand over Dwyer at last as he pulled at the door like a broken man. I wanted to taunt him, to heap mockery upon his murderous head. I had thrown my dust covered jacket to the floor and now untucked the shirt from my trousers.

"It's no use Dwyer, she will have jammed it from the other side as well as locking it. Why don't you face it – she has taken advantage of your inability to believe that anyone would dare to take advantage of you? That's the complacency that comes with old age I guess? And why don't you look what I've been doing?"

He turned around slowly, the veins bulging in thick worm like strands upon his right temple, and saw that I had lifted my shirt from over my chest revealing the listening device, pulsing away as it sent its silent signal, and the wires that were taped across me.

"You don't control the whole police authority you know, Dwyer? Some of the good ones are listening into us right now. Some of the others have been busy rounding up a collection of your worst men all evening. I wonder how many of them will talk? Like everybody else, they will be glad to get rid of you."

"Well what do you want to hear: I killed Solomon's wife? I killed Georgie Galloway? I killed Lamara Gallagher? I had Tommy O'Callaghan killed? Is that what you want to hear?"

"That's a start isn't it? But you're killing days are over now, Dwyer. It's all over for you."

"Maybe there's time for one more? I can always make time for a smart boy like you."

He leapt towards me but I had felt my strength and energy returning as I was sat in the chair facing him and it seemed as though I had the strength of all of his victims flowing through me. He was quickly upon me with his pistol raised in the air as a bludgeoning weapon and his free hand was wrapped around my throat. I raised both of my knees to my chest and kicked him away with an ease that surprised me and left him rising to his feet with a puzzled look upon his face.

It was my turn to run towards him now and in the absence of any other available weapon I had picked up one of the tins containing film reels that lay liberally scattered across the room. It was a flimsy weapon and he parried my blow with ease before spinning me around and throwing

414

me across the room so that I landed with a thud upon the ledge overlooking the cinema below.

As I stumbled around I had crashed into, and then rebounded off of, the projector so that it wobbled and then fell to the floor bringing to a sudden end the night's screening. It was then that I noticed, that we both noticed with wide eyed surprise, that the cigarette which Vicky had so casually discarded had been smouldering within the bone dry and dusty heap of papers which had been clumped at the back of the projector. The smouldering had given way to smoke which had turned into flames that had already begun to take hold. As if signalled by our eyes alighting upon it the conflagration suddenly developed in ferocity and with a huge amount of old waste to consume, much of it covered in dubious liquids that had sloshed upon them during the haphazard clearance of the building, it spread rapidly across the centre of the room leaving me in one half and Dwyer in the other with a growing wall of flame between us.

I remained rooted to the spot in frightened shock but Dwyer made one final half-hearted attempt at wrestling the door open before finding it just as immovable as before. The madness that had lurked beneath the surface for all of his adult life was the only thing that remained to him and he sank to the knees letting out a horrific howl as he tore at his clothes. A moment of clarity gripped him and looking up he saw my figure cowering in the opposite half of the room: I was the man who had brought him to this, the little nondescript man, an imperceptible nothing, who was bringing everything crashing down upon him.

Things were indeed beginning to crash around us as fittings and lights that were flimsily attached to the roof flaked away under the increasing heat. A look of hatred beyond all that I imagined came upon Dwyer's face and covering his head with his crossed arms that were held before him he crashed through the wall of fire towards me. He seemed oblivious to the sleeves blazing upon his arms as he swung fiery sweeps in my direction. Woken from my daze I backed away from the inhuman killer before me but he brushed everything aside that came between us. With one swipe he threw a lighting rig to the side which I then saw, as if in slow motion, crashing towards me. I jumped out of the way landing upon the floor as the metal of the rig crashed and clanged beside me. In its turn the rig had been supporting a timber beam that ran across the roof and this now fell with unavoidable speed landing upon my midriff and knocking all strength out of me so that I lay pinioned beneath it with its end blazing away.

Dwyer seemed finally to have realised that the sleeves of his jacket were ablaze and although he whirled madly, thrashing them upon the walls and floors, it was hard for him to find any surface that was not already aflame. My stomach felt crushed so that it was hard to breathe and the heat was so ferocious that whilst I had so far avoided the flames I felt as if I was in the centre of an oven and being roasted alive whilst the thick black smoke that circled above my head made me retch as it drew nearer. The impact of the beam had dazed me with its unexpectedness rather than its weight and remembering the techniques and muscles that I used in my daily weight lifting exercises I strained and then pushed and finally managed to guide the beam away from my body. I crawled upon the floor with every step painful and with the fire closing in around and above me. My death was coming to me just as Madame Irina had shown. I lay back against the ledge as glass and burning plaster rained down around me. It was a cruel way to go. It was then that I saw the girl on the bus, Georgie, for the last time. The heat was so intense that I could feel my lips blistering upon my face and although I tried to look back upon my life and make some kind of peace with the world it was impossible to think of anything but the red, red heat. Some people will say that it was a hallucination but after all that I had already been through I know that what happened was the truth: Georgie stood before me again, in the same sandy jacket and blue and white striped shirt that had so caught my attention when I first saw her. The small crucifix shone below her neck. Her pale, washed out features were in contrast to the reddening skin of myself and Michael Dwyer who, with his own flames finally extinguished, stood staring at me with eyes that registered nothing. She placed her hands upon my face and it felt as if it was ice itself that was caressing my skin.

"It's not your time yet, John Halle, it's not your time" she whispered into my ear and then planted a cold and soothing kiss upon my cheek. It seemed to me that she took my hands and raised me to my feet with no need for exertion from myself. Georgie led me to the bookcase that stood in the corner of the room and which was the last remaining thing that had not yet been touched by the flames that raged around it. Her glance beckoned upwards now, to the summit of the bookcase, just as I had seen Georgie gaze out towards the sight of her death when I had seen her on that bus less than a week previously. I knew what was meant by her signal and with renewed confidence I placed my foot upon the lower shelf and levered myself up with my left hand, using my right elbow and forearm in support in lieu of my cast-bound hand. The bookcase was sturdy and easily took my weight; gripping with my left arm for all that I was worth whilst using my right arm for leverage I soon made the perilous steps, with the choking smoke gathering around me, to the top of the bookcase. I knelt on top of it with just inches to spare between my head and the ceiling and the hellish fire burning below me with Dwyer as the devil incarnate surrounded helplessly by the inferno.

With amazement I saw then what was hidden from below: there was a skylight in the ceiling painted to resemble the rest of the roof. Pushing at it with childlike glee it opened out easily before me and I felt the relieving wind howling in from outside carrying the flames to the far end of the room with its gust. I climbed out of the opening with as much haste as I could safely manage. The roof that I now sat upon was so hot that I could barely touch it but it ran steeply down to a ledge, five feet below me. Directly beneath that ledge was the edge of the roof itself which preceded a drop of some four stories to the street below.

I looked down upon the scene stretched out across the street: police cars and ambulances were assembled around me and I could make out Vicky Gallagher being loaded, cuffed, into a squad car. Just as her arrival had been timely to catch me the arrival of the police, alerted by the signals from my transmitter, had been timely enough to catch her. I saw Rosa too by the side of the brown car: she had driven, as I had hoped, straight to Superintendent Pearson who was directing the operations below with Osbourne, his arm still tied in a sling, a huge presence besides him.

If I had thought that all that remained was to wait for the arrival of the fire brigade to rescue me then I should have known that things wouldn't work out that simply.

I was holding onto the tip of the roof grimly trying to ignore the heat that was still rising around me when I saw a barely familiar figure climbing through the skylight to join me. His face was red and raw looking and was covered with black patches from the soot and smoke in the room below. The cold blast of air that had suddenly entered into the projection room had wakened Dwyer from his stupor and seeing my escape route he had followed me out. The wild look remained in his eyes and he bared his teeth at me as he hissed. I edged away from him but my footing skidded upon the ice bitten roof and I felt my hand give way as I slipped down the roof. There was a gasp, audible even at this distance, from the crowd gathered below but suddenly and remarkably I felt a firm hand grab hold of me and pull me slowly back up until my feet rested upon the ledge and my hand once again gripped the pinnacle of the roof.

"You saved my life" I said to Dwyer, unable to believe it.

"Oh, you aren't going to kill yourself Halle" he gasped, in a croaking voice which was accompanied by a retching cough, "that would be much too easy. I want you to look into my eyes as I kill you. You are going to watch and see how easy it is for me to kill an insect like you - none of your friends down there can help you now."

He had removed his gun from the holster again and raised it above his head before crashing it down towards me. With no time to think about my perilous balance upon the roof I turned aside catching Dwyer's leg with mine as I inched away. It was Dwyer's turn to slip now and his gun fell out of his hand and thudded off of the roof before making the long descent to the hard floor below.

Dwyer was a hugely strong man and having caught the ledge with both hands he had a firm grip upon it.

"Help me, man, help me like I helped you" he shouted at me in his smoke hoarsened voice. He was swinging his legs trying to wrap them over the top of the ledge and it seemed that in a matter of time he would have levered himself up again to relative safety.

"Oh, I will help you" I shouted back at him with a coldness in my voice that I didn't recognise and my eyes wide and unblinking, "I'm going to help you just like you helped so many other people. This is for Solomon" I stamped hard upon his fingers as I said this, all the while keeping my hand firmly gripped upon the roof.

"This is for Poor Tommy" I shouted again, my words lost to all but myself and Dwyer by the swirling wind, as I brought my feet down hard upon his reddened fingers.

"This is for Georgie" was my next shout and I could see that his fingers were beginning to release themselves from the ledge. His legs swung wild and free and his eyes bulged as he stared at me open mouthed unable to articulate the words that were tapped in his throat.

"And this, you lousy, evil, killing bastard – this is for Lamara Gallagher, the woman I loved."

I smashed my foot down upon his fingers with every ounce of strength that I had in my body and at the moment of impact I could feel the bones of his fingers crunch beneath me. I raised my foot and saw his hold finally give way as he plummeted towards the ground.

"Rot in hell, Dwyer," I screamed, "rot in hell."

His body fell for what was only a second and yet it seemed an eternity before an ear splitting crack announced that his body had hit the floor. It lay there lifeless and unmoving with his face smashed into the icy floor.

It was some moments before I realised that I could hear other sirens now and raising my head I saw fire engines heading towards me. I was hanging instinctively onto the roof with tears streaming unstoppably down my face and blurring my view of the people below.

A turntable ladder was soon on its way up to me and a fireman guided me gently into the cradle which lowered me to the ground. A silver blanket was placed around my shoulder and I was handed a salty liquid to drink.

The Superintendent was the first to march towards me and I found it strange that he saluted as he stood before me: I eventually realised that it was because he didn't want to touch my heat damaged hands.

"Well done, Mr Halle – John, well done on surviving. I will come and visit you in hospital, but don't worry – you've got nothing to worry about."

Rosa approached me next and, whilst careful not to touch my skin, she gave me a polite hug.

"Was that -?" she asked unable to finish her question.

"Yes, Rosa. That was the man who killed your sister: the murderer."

"And was she -?" Again she couldn't bring herself to complete her words but I knew what her question was and I was still man enough to lie to her:

"No, Rosa, she had nothing to do with any of it. She was a good young woman, just in the wrong place at the wrong time. Now she can rest in peace."

"They're going to take you back to the hospital you know, John, but you don't seem too bad. I'm sure that you'll recover fully in a few days. I'll pop by and visit you tomorrow."

"And what's going to happen in a few days, Rosa."

She had the grace to look embarrassed as she mumbled her answer:

"I won't be able to see you then, I'm afraid, John. I appreciate everything that you've done for me and for Georgie, and I know that I'll never understand most of what's happened, but I just can't hang around here after all of this. It's time for me to make a new start, I'm moving back down to London – the flat's nearly ready."

I nodded dumbly at her, in case my cracked voice should betray my emotion if I spoke.

"I will pop by and see you tomorrow though, John. Oh, and Tramp sends his love."

She gave me a wan smile as she turned away but I saw that she too had tears in her eyes. She was going to 'pop by'. Her dog sent me love! That was all that I had to show for the dreams that I had invested in her over those last few days. I couldn't blame her, of course – dreams have to be a two way thing if they are ever to work. She had devoted all of her energies and emotions of the last ten years to her sister – and now she could finally say goodbye to her she suddenly felt unbearably alone. I wasn't going to be the man to fill that void.

The last person who greeted me was Osbourne, looking larger than ever and with a smile lighting up his face as he welcomed me.

"What happens to me now then, Osbourne?" I asked.

"All that happens to you is that you recover in that hospital, while we round up the rest of Dwyer's connections, and then you collect a nice little pay day as the reward on that ring. There's nothing at all for you to be concerned about, my friend."

"But you saw me stamp on Dwyer's fingers. You saw me kill him."

"I saw nothing like that. I saw him slip, that's all, and that's what all the records will say."

"So we both turn a blind eye then?"

"What do you mean?" I didn't mean to dampen his enthusiasm but I wanted to let him know that I had slotted the last piece of the jigsaw into place:

"I was looking through the old newspaper clippings about the Solomon robbery and I found some old pictures of Freddy Chester. That wasn't his real name of course – it was just an alias that was given to him because he came from Chester. The newspaper gave some other aliases that he used as well. One of them was Ozzy Chester – we both know why that was don't we? It was because his real name was Freddy Osbourne and he had been born in Chester. I saw the photo of him with his teenage sons, great hulking brutes they were. I recognised you straight away.

So I guess that you went to visit him when he took the rap, willingly at first, for the jewellery spree. But when his promised rewards failed to materialise he grew angry and told you how this man, this big fraud called Dwyer, had tricked him. The trouble was that he told other people too and when word reached Dwyer it was easy for him to have Freddy disposed of. And you've spent the next ten years brooding over this and vowing revenge against the man who had your father killed. You joined the police force, they were unaware of your connections to Freddy, specifically to track this man down and you spent every spare minute investigating Dwyer.

The investigations eventually led you to the green diamond ring that you ultimately discovered Georgie had given to her grandmother Roisin at the special unit. It was you that had been visiting Roisin and you that had arranged to meet Roisin to collect the ring as evidence to convict Dwyer. Of course, Dwyer has spies everywhere and he made sure that it was his man who was there to meet that frail old woman rather than you. The woman was dead but the ring eluded you both - until today. I don't suppose that you're too interested in it now: he's dead and that's all that you ever wanted."

"Yes, Halle, that's exactly how it was. So what happens to me now?"

"To you? Like I said – let's just keep our little secrets. It seems that secrets have been doing far too much harm around here – let's bury ours without the need to bury any more people. Nothing for us to be concerned about."

We exchanged broad smiles before the waiting paramedic led me into the back of his ambulance and drove me back towards the hospital. I watched the faces recede away from me until they became indistinguishable blurs of light. With a strange realisation I found that I was happy once more – it had been an unknown feeling for so long. I had been dead for over a year, dead inside, but it had taken all of this to finally wake me from my cold hearted slumber. Dying wasn't the end, I had found, but it was overrated: I was ready to start living again. Through the slit like windows at the back of the ambulance I watched fresh flakes of snow float down from the sky and jig and reel as they got caught on the wind. The smile extended across my face as I watched them dancing just for me: it was as beautiful as life itself.

Lightning Source UK Ltd.
Milton Keynes UK
22 September 2009